the way I loved you

FIONA LUCAS

ONE PLACE. MANY STORIES

HQ
An imprint of HarperCollins*Publishers* Ltd
1 London Bridge Street
London SE1 9GF

www.harpercollins.co.uk

HarperCollins*Publishers*
Macken House, 39/40 Mayor Street Upper
Dublin 1, D01 C9W8, Ireland
This edition 2026

1

First published in Great Britain by HQ,
an imprint of HarperCollins*Publishers* Ltd 2026

Copyright © Fiona Lucas 2026

Fiona Lucas asserts the moral right to be identified as the author of this work.
A catalogue record for this book is available from the British Library.

ISBN: 9780008629083

Set in Bembo Std by HarperCollins*Publishers* India

This novel is entirely a work of fiction. The names, characters and incidents portrayed in it are the work of the author's imagination. Any resemblance to actual persons, living or dead, events or localities is entirely coincidental.

All rights reserved. No part of this publication may be reproduced, stored in a retrieval system, or transmitted, in any form or by any means, electronic, mechanical, photocopying, recording or otherwise, without the prior written permission of the publishers.

Without limiting the exclusive rights of any author, contributor or the publisher of this publication, any unauthorised use of this publication to train generative artificial intelligence (AI) technologies is expressly prohibited. HarperCollins also exercise their rights under Article 4(3) of the Digital Single Market Directive 2019/790 and expressly reserve this publication from the text and data mining exception.

Printed and bound in the UK using 100% Renewable
Electricity at CPI Group (UK) Ltd

Praise for Fiona Lucas

'Heart-wrenching and compelling'
Sarah Morgan

'Romantic and gorgeous'
Milly Johnson

'Poignant and emotional'
Judy Finnigan

'Unique and moving. A heartfelt read'
Woman's Own

'An emotional novel about the power of hope'
Holly Miller

'Made my heart ache'
Liz Fenwick

'A beautifully written story of love, loss and hope. I adored it'
Emma Cooper

'An epic story of love and emotion. Wow!'
Jane Linfoot

'A beautiful story'
Bella

'Poignant and uplifting'
Sophie Cousens

'Beautifully told and full of hope,
this love story will touch your heart'
Helen Rolfe

'Wonderfully escapist'
People's Friend

Fiona Lucas is an award-winning author of contemporary women's fiction. She has written heart-warming love stories and feel-good women's fiction as Fiona Harper for more than a decade. During her career, she's won numerous awards, including a Romantic Novel Award in 2018, and chalked up a number-one Kindle bestseller. Fiona lives in London with her husband and two daughters.

Writing as Fiona Lucas:
The Last Goodbye
Never Forget You
The Memory Collector
Always and Only You

Writing as Fiona Harper:
The Other Us
The Summer We Danced
The Doris Day Vintage Film Club
The Little Shop of Hopes and Dreams
Make My Wish Come True
Kiss Me Under the Mistletoe

For Andy, my best friend.
If I could go back thirty-six years and do it all again, I'd still say, 'I do.'

AUTHOR'S NOTE

While this book covers the years 2020–2022, in order to keep the focus on Luke and Jess's relationship, we have chosen to imagine the events of this story happened in a world where the Covid-19 pandemic did not take place.

TIN

A malleable silvery-white metal soft enough to be buckled by hand and cut with minimal force. When a tin bar is bent or broken, the arrangement of the molecules produces a unique cracking noise, known as a 'tin cry'.

CHAPTER ONE

JESS

I flinch as my husband's phone buzzes in his pocket. He ignores it and continues to stare straight ahead through the windscreen of the taxi. It's been doing that all evening, although, most times, he's swiftly left the room to check it. Occasionally, I heard his voice, low and rumbling, somewhere else in the house.

My arms are braced on the back seat, keeping me sitting ramrod straight. Much to my surprise, after he puts his phone away, he also puts his hand on the seat between us, close but not touching. I want to reach my little finger over and stroke his, but those few millimetres are a gulf that's too hard to cross.

We argued before we left the house. It was stupid, actually. We're sitting here, choking in this thick, awkward silence because of toilet paper. Yes, I'm not kidding. Toilet paper.

We have a house rule – if you take the last roll from the wicker container near the loo, you're supposed to refill said container with more rolls from the big cupboard on the other side of the room. Only, I always seem to find half a sheet left on the roll, so I reach for a replacement, only to find the basket empty. It drives me nuts.

And this evening, there I was, in my floor-length velvet dress and heels, only to have to waddle across the room with my knickers round my knees to get another roll. Luke sauntered into the bathroom just as I was washing my hands and I couldn't help it, even though tonight of all nights wasn't the time for one of our spats.

I *may* have been snarky, said something passive-aggressive about the loo roll fairy obviously having a day off today. He looked as if it was complete news to him that toilet rolls didn't walk themselves across the bathroom and deposit themselves within easy reach, even though we've had this conversation a million times before.

And so that's how we started arguing about toilet roll. Except . . . we weren't actually arguing about toilet roll at all, were we? It was just a safe outlet for all the unspoken disappointments that have been piling up, like skeleton bones in our closet, but it's getting harder and harder to shut the door and pretend they're not there.

I don't know how to describe it. Nothing that's happening is a dealbreaker; it's just not what I thought marriage would be after all this time. I thought Luke and I would have the fairy tale, even if others didn't.

'I'm sorry if I went off about the loo roll,' I say, sneaking a glance at him. 'I was just in a bit of a rush and . . . you know. Even if I was annoyed, I could have brought it up in a nicer way.'

'Yes, you could,' he replies, staring straight ahead.

I feel the air molecules between us vibrate with tension. So much for being the bigger person. 'Listen, Luke, I'm trying to—'

'I don't care about the stupid loo roll, Jess, even if you were snippy at me for something so insignificant.'

I have to close my eyes and count to ten. Insignificant to *him*, maybe! I turn my head so I can see his face properly. 'Then why have you been giving me the silent treatment ever since?'

He presses his lips together and the shake of his head is almost imperceptible. 'I haven't been giving you the silent treatment. I've spoken to you.'

I don't count monosyllables and grunts as full and free communication. 'Well, if you're not upset about the toilet roll, what are you upset about?'

Luke blinks slowly. This is not a good sign. That one tiny gesture usually means he's about to go into full shutdown mode, portcullis down, drawbridge up. I'm ready to scream. We're going to be there in less than five minutes. We don't have time for this.

'Luke . . . ?' I say, my tone both warning and pleading at the same time.

Eventually, he huffs out a breath and turns his head – not all the way to look at me, but more than he had been. 'You didn't seem overly impressed with the present I got you.'

My stomach hits the floor of the cab. 'No . . . It was . . . It was very . . . thoughtful.'

My husband snorts softly. 'You're a horrible liar, Jess.'

I swallow, unable to deny my reaction to his gift. But I also can't pretend it was anything close to what I would have chosen, given the chance.

'You didn't even take time to look at it properly,' he says, and the angry tone is mixed with something else. Hurt. Disappointment. It makes me feel like a total bitch, even though I'm disappointed too. But I can't tell him that, can I?

'We were running late,' I say, keeping my voice low and calm, trying to sound much more reasonable than I feel. 'And I needed to finish getting ready.' And I was already pissed off after the whole knickers-round-the-knees thing, which didn't help. I didn't realize that a) he noticed I wasn't thrilled or b) he's been stewing on it all this time.

'Fine,' he says, turning to look out of the window as we pull into the driveway of the Bickley Court Hotel, a converted manor house that was probably once deep in the countryside but now sits next to a golf course on the outskirts of London. 'Never mind.'

How could I have done anything else but pretended that I loved it? If I'd said how I felt out loud, he'd be even more upset than he is now. Besides, it wasn't that what he got me was horrible. Someone else might have loved it.

And that's my point, I suppose. I want to feel as if my husband knows me inside and out, that he *loves* me inside and out. And he can't, can he? Not if he doesn't even see what's really there?

The cab slows as we near the grand pillared entrance to the hotel. Just before it comes to a halt, I look down at our hands, then I brush my little finger softly over the top of his. But he moves away, ostensibly to open the door, so he can come around the car and get mine for me, but I know rejection when I sense it.

I want to grab for the handle and get myself out, but I know it'll only make things worse, so when he opens it for me, I take the hand he offers. Our eyes meet briefly as I plant my feet on the gravel driveway and stand up. Not exactly a truce, but an agreement that we'll paper over the cracks because, right now, it's showtime.

We walk up the wide sandstone steps and into the marble-tiled reception lobby and glue on our best smiles as we walk towards the function room. Around the open double doors is a display of silver and white balloons, and over the entrance, spelled in large shiny letters, is: 'Happy 10th Anniversary, Luke & Jess!'

A cheer goes up as we enter the hotel's largest function room. Shouts of 'Happy Anniversary!' and 'Congratulations!' are almost drowned out by the setting off of what seems like a thousand party poppers. A slow-falling trail of colourful tissue paper lands on my head. I brush it away, my smile wide and bright and artificial.

Luke's mum rushes over. 'Congratulations, darlings!' She kisses Luke on the cheek and envelops me in a warm hug. 'If you can get through the first ten years, you can get through the next twenty,' she tells us brightly as Luke's dad comes to stand beside her.

I nod and smile, of course. I can't tell her the truth, partly because I don't want to upset her – I love Diane to bits – but also because I'm not certain what the truth is. Sure, Luke and I are standing here at our tenth anniversary party but, toilet paper fights and anniversary presents aside, do we really have a solid foundation for the next couple of decades?

Up until a few weeks ago, I would have said of course we had, but as our anniversary approached, I started looking at our life together more carefully. We've both been so busy in our jobs – him at his family's building firm, me as a physiotherapist – that I didn't notice the distance between us. I think we've been drifting apart so slowly it would have been impossible to spot in the moment.

But now we're noticing. Which is possibly why we're getting snippy at each other about stupid things we probably would have just laughed about when we were first married. I think we need to talk. Really talk.

My father and stepmother appear before us, along with my twin half-sisters. More kisses and hugs. Someone thrusts a glass of Prosecco into my hand. Luke and I kiss them warmly, especially Adelola, who is known by her friends and family simply as 'Lola'. I know it's down to her that they've arrived on time. My father can be notoriously unreliable about times and dates and places, even though he's extremely detail-orientated in every other area of his life.

Dad met Lola a couple of years after his messy split from my mum. A mid-life crisis, possibly? All I knew was that one moment I was a normal seven-year-old, living in a three-bed semi with my parents and two cats, and the next there was shouting and fighting and Dad disappearing in the middle of the night to go and live with someone who wasn't my mum. She was devastated to discover he'd been having an affair with someone from work.

It didn't last. They broke up just over a year later. Dad went through what I call his 'teenage phase' and then he met Lola, who is all common sense and good manners, and he regained his sanity.

My dad's a strange sort. I keep in touch, visiting only once a month, even though they live fairly close by, and calling roughly once a week, but I never seem to feel that sense of togetherness — of family — that we had when he was living at home and I was Daddy's little girl. It's as if something broke and neither of us know how to repair it. I'm not resentful of Lola or the girls, though. I appreciate the woman who whipped some sense into my dad with her no-nonsense ways and soft laughter.

'Can we have a glass of Prosecco?' one of the twins asks, their eyes lighting up as a waiter goes past with a tray.

'No,' Lola says firmly, as my father opens his mouth but then sees his wife's expression and shuts it again. Lola is very particular about bad language and alcohol where her two daughters are concerned.

'We've got some mocktails on offer?' Luke says, pointing to a table set up in the corner, and sets off to fetch one each for them.

Charity, the older of the two by five minutes, rolls her eyes. 'We're almost eighteen, you know,' she says to her mum.

Constance jabs her sister in the ribs, warning her to tread carefully.

'Do you think I do not have eyes in my head?' Lola replies, unperturbed. 'Or that I do not remember birthing you?' The twins share a horrified look at the mention of the word 'birth' but their mother carries on. '*Almost* is the correct word. You are not eighteen yet. And if we were in Nigeria, I would have sent you to a serious boarding school by now that would train you well. Don't try me . . .'

Both girls look at the floor, but they are saved from what is promising to be one of her poetic rants because she spots Luke's parents across the room and, after warning the twins that the angels around them are shaking their heads, she drags Dad off with her to greet them.

Charity watches her mum go. 'She is *so* annoying.'

'Facts,' Connie says. 'She wouldn't even let us wear real lipstick this evening. It took all I had to convince her my tinted lip balm was okay.'

I give them both a sympathetic smile. 'It's not so bad to have a mum who looks out for you. I know it's annoying, but it's done out of love. All she wants is to keep you safe and for you to be happy.'

I would have put up with all the curfews and make-up bans in the world to have a mother like that.

'You probably don't remember what it was like being a teenager,' Charity says, trying to hide a cheeky smirk. 'Like, you're *old*.'

Luke arrives just in time to catch the comment and laughs as he hands each of the twins a Virgin Mojito.

'Monstrous child,' I mutter as I place my hands on her shoulders, turn her around and steer her in the direction of a huddle of people on the other side of the room. Some of Luke's younger cousins have arrived. 'Go and bother some people your own age while I hunt for my Zimmer frame.'

The large group of friends and family near the doorway begins to splinter as we greet more people. Some groups drift to the bar on the far side of the room, others nab tables set up around the edge of the dance floor.

It's then I spot Hannah a short distance away and my face lights up. She rushes over and kisses both Luke and I on the cheek. 'Congratulations on ten years!'

I pull her into a hug. 'I don't know what I would have done without you. You've been amazing helping me plan this thing.'

She squeezes me back. 'That's what best friends are for, aren't they?'

Luke waves to some of his old school friends who have just arrived and heads off to greet them. When he's out of earshot, Hannah turns to me. 'What did you think about the present? Did you like it?'

How much do I say? I don't want to be disloyal, but this is

Hannah – she's my best friend and one of the people I trust most in the world. I try not to grimace. 'Um . . .'

She narrows her eyes and studies me. 'You didn't like it? Oh, wow. I'm so surprised.'

'You knew about it?'

She nods. 'He asked me for some input.'

I'm stunned. How do I take this? My best friend doesn't know me very well either? Or am I just being selfish? It's just I had my heart set on something different, and I thought I'd hinted heavily enough for Luke to get the message but obviously not. In the moment, I'd been disappointed, of course I had been, but Han's reaction is making me second-guess myself.

She giggles nervously. 'I thought for sure you were going to catch on, because we've been texting back and forth setting it all up.'

For a split second, everything inside me goes still. It's *Han* he's been messaging constantly? Of course! I exhale softly and my shoulders unknot themselves further. It all makes sense now.

'It's not that I didn't like it so much, more that I was hoping for something else. I know there are these Victorian traditions about certain materials signifying different wedding anniversaries – paper, wood, wool, copper – but I was hoping, ten years in, that Luke might have gone with jewellery or something. I mean, I got it in the early days, when we didn't have much money, but now . . . Well, we're not rolling in it but we're doing okay.'

I think of the nice watch Luke is wearing on his wrist, my gift to him. Is it wrong to want something similar for myself? Something that says, *I value you. You're worth it.*

'Maybe it's not what you were expecting, but I honestly thought it was kind of sweet,' Hannah says.

'It's made of *tin*, Han . . .'

'Luke said it was pewter.'

'Which contains tin.' Luke filled me in on the nerdy stuff when he unveiled it, but I was so shocked I didn't absorb all of the details. All I could see was a large, grey metal wall sculpture in the space on our dining room wall that we've never known how to fill. I suppose it was artistic, but I'd wanted something more personal, something that said he was paying attention, that he knows me and what I like.

I look over to where Luke is chatting to Elena, an interior designer he worked with occasionally when he first joined his dad's building firm. We socialized with her and her husband quite a bit a few years back.

Hannah slings an arm around my shoulder and steers me in the direction of the bar. Both our Prosecco glasses are empty. 'If it makes you feel any better, when I was married to Connor, all I ever got – if I was lucky – was a bunch of last-minute petrol-station flowers.'

I stop walking and give her a hug. As well as her under-the-radar help with Luke's present, she helped me too, and I know it can't have been easy helping plan someone else's anniversary party when her own divorce has just become final. Although it's almost two years since Connor cheated on her and moved out, I know she wasn't prepared for the extra little stab in her heart when the papers arrived.

I talked Luke into us kind of 'adopting' Hannah in the aftermath. She couldn't face going back to the flat she'd rented with Connor, so she stayed in our spare room for two months, until she found somewhere new. Even after that she was constantly at our house, for dinner or brunch or just to hang out. Luke sometimes finds Han a bit full-on, but they've developed this big brother, little sister kind of relationship now that's so wholesome. I think it was good for Hannah to be reminded that not all men are selfish pricks.

I look over to where Luke, Elena and a few of his brothers, are all laughing and talking in a group, and the tension from our earlier tiff begins to fade. Maybe it's good for me to remember that too, no matter how strained the cab ride over here was.

Hannah follows my gaze, and she sounds almost wistful as she says. 'You're so lucky to have such a wonderful man; you know that, right?

That's what I've always thought.

More than one of my friends has expressed similar sentiments. A few have been properly jealous, and I can understand why. Luke is a catch – decent, hardworking, dependable. And it doesn't hurt that he's beautiful to look at. Probably more so now he's closer to forty than thirty and he's more roughened up and worn around the edges. I know I should be grateful for what I've got.

CHAPTER TWO

JESS

The party is a roaring success. The DJ plays 'Murder on the Dance Floor' and Hannah comes streaking over from the other side of the room and grabs my hand. 'Come on,' she yells over the music, 'it's our song!'

I laugh, remembering all our late-night dancing sessions in the flat we shared after a night out, singing into wooden spoons and spatulas, and let her drag me away. We dance for at least an hour without stopping to hits from our formative years and only stop terrorizing everyone with our moves when it becomes apparent my bladder doesn't have as much stamina as the rest of me anymore and I have to abandon shouting along to the Spice Girls for the ladies.

When I return to the ballroom, I can't see Hannah anywhere and the pace of the music has slowed. A thudding noise booms through the PA system as someone taps on a microphone, and I spin around to see her at the DJ's desk, grinning.

She finds me in the crowd and shoots me one of her 'don't hate me' smiles. 'I know you said no speeches, Jess, but we couldn't let the evening go by without a toast to you and Luke.'

A cheer goes up and I'm pushed towards the bright lights and noise. Luke too, it seems, as we end up standing a few feet away from Hannah, everyone circled around us. It looks as if we're going to have to endure this, like it or not.

A host of waiters are weave through the crowd, offering guests flutes full of fizz. Luke takes two and hands one to me.

'I'm going to keep this short and sweet,' Hannah says, garnering another cheer from our gathered friends and family. 'But we just want to raise a glass to you both on your tenth anniversary. It's no mean feat to have made it this far. And we love you both so much that I suppose we'll have to forgive you for being so sickeningly good together.' She pauses while a murmur of laughter rumbles round the room.

I try not to blush uncomfortably. But it gives me hope. Maybe if that's what people see from the outside, I'm overthinking everything. I mean, no marriage is *perfect*. There are always niggles. After ten years, maybe that's what it's supposed to be like. I was always one for unrealistic expectations.

'To Luke and Jess . . . May the next decade be just as spectacular as the first!' She raises her glass as everyone else does the same and drinks. 'And now we can carry on with the party. We thought it might be nice if—'

'Wait!' I shout and step up to the podium. Hannah looks surprised but hands the mic over to me as I come to stand beside her. I'm not known as someone who enjoys public speaking, but I feel I can't let this moment pass without saying something.

'Thank you, from both of us . . . ' I glance at Luke, and he nods at me to carry on, the hint of a smile telling me he's proud of me for being brave and getting up here. 'Well, we'd like to say how much we appreciate you all coming and celebrating with us this evening.' I glance round at all the smiling faces, each one truly happy for us, and a lump rises in my throat. 'I can't imagine a better way of marking this occasion than to share it with the people we love most in the world – that's you lot. And don't you forget it!'

There are a couple of whistles and cheers. A couple of my old uni friends blow kisses.

'That's what it's all about, isn't it? I'm starting to realize this as I get older and wiser . . . '

'Whippersnapper!' Great-Uncle Patrick yells and everyone laughs. But he's ninety-two, so he's probably got a point.

I carry on. 'It's about this . . . About family. About friends. Feeling connected with the people we care about. So, thank you again. And I promise I'm going to shut up now and let the DJ play some ABBA!' I hand the microphone back to Hannah and step down off the podium.

'No ABBA just yet,' she says. 'We thought that first you and Luke might enjoy having a dance to this old favourite . . . ' and the strains of Ed Sheeran's 'Thinking Out Loud' begin to play. It was in the charts not long after we got together and kind of unofficially became our song. Hannah had been pressing me for a playlist of songs over the years of our relationship to give to the DJ and now I understand why.

Luke holds out a hand. There's still a wariness in his eyes, but he's not looking as stony-faced as he was when we got out of the cab. 'Mrs Harris . . . Shall we dance?'

'I don't think we've got much choice,' I mutter as I step into his arms. Dancing was my favourite hobby as a teenager but Luke is a bit more challenged in that department, so we just hold on to each other and sway. It doesn't take long before other couples join us on the dance floor.

As the song ends and another one starts to play, Luke says, 'I'm sorry. I didn't mean to give you the silent treatment. I was just a bit . . . I don't know . . .'

It's okay. I understand what he means. While Luke can spout all day when he's feeling enthusiastic and happy, he struggles to find the words for more difficult emotions. I'm not sure he even gets to the stage of labelling them inside his own head before he whitewashes over them and pretends they're not there.

'I'm sorry too.'

All the anger and frustration leaches away and I lay my head on Luke's shoulder. He kisses me tenderly on my temple and I close my eyes.

Say something, I silently will him. *Say something that lets me know you're swept away by what you feel for me, that you'd die if you couldn't be with me. Give me hope for the next ten years.*

He draws a breath, getting ready to speak, and my heart leaps softly, just before he whispers into my ear. 'You know what, Jess?'

'What?' I whisper breathlessly.

'You're my best friend.'

Oh.

That's all?

Tears form behind my lids and I blink them away, glad he can't see them and that I'm hidden by the shadows so no one else can either.

When the song stops, Luke and I peel ourselves apart. 'I think it's time to give you your final surprise of the day,' he says.

My jaw drops gently. 'There's another one?' I suddenly start thinking about the eternity ring I pointed out to him a couple of months ago. He paid attention after all?

He nods, barely able to contain a smile, and takes me by the hand. While the rest of our guests close in on the dance floor, drawn there by 'Mamma Mia', he leads me outside, onto the terrace overlooking parkland.

As we move further into the darkness, and my eyes adjust to the light, I realize I was wrong about the terrace being empty. At the far end, a lone figure is standing, hands on the stone balustrade, staring out into the darkness. When she hears us approaching, she turns.

My heart stops. 'Mum?'

Her smile is nervous and she's squeezing her hands together in front of her ribs. 'Hello, sweetheart.'

I turn to Luke. 'What's going on?'

'I sent her an invite.'

'You did *what*?'

For the first time, his self-assured expression starts to falter. 'It's a family celebration, and she's family . . . Don't you think it's time?'

I take a last look at my mother, twin emotions plunging into my heart like daggers, and then I back away. A few more steps and I turn and stride back towards the function room. Luke hurries after me.

'I can't believe you!' I say to him in a hoarse and not particularly quiet whisper. 'You *know* how I feel about her! And you want her to come and celebrate our marriage? After everything she's done? Even after that stunt she pulled at our wedding? Unbelievable!'

Luke looks perplexed, which only makes me more annoyed. I've been very clear about going no-contact with my mother.

'It's been years, Jess . . . And she's sober now.'

I let out a harsh, dark laugh as my fingers close around a hefty brass handle on the outside of the doors leading back inside. 'She's always sober . . . until she isn't!'

'Jess . . .'

I shake my head. 'She has no right to be here. And you had no right to invite her!'

I haul the heavy door open, march straight across the dance floor, not caring how many people I bump into, through the hotel reception, and straight out the front door.

CHAPTER THREE

JESS

I summon an Uber with shaking fingers when I reach the end of the hotel drive, and stand shivering, holding on to myself, as I wait the four minutes for it to arrive. It's chilly for mid-May and, thanks to my dramatic exit, my wrap is still in the hotel cloakroom. Thank goodness I snatched my clutch from the table in the ballroom on my way through. It'd be a long walk home otherwise.

I'm so angry. So, so angry.

How *dare* Luke contact my mother without my knowledge? He knows how I feel about her. He also knows *why* I feel that way. He's the only person I've opened up to in the slightest about my toxic childhood. I just don't get it. Why, in all that is good and holy, did he think this would be okay?

Just thinking about how blindsided I felt, how the shock rippled through me like a volcanic tremor, makes my internal temperature rise, and I don't do anything to curb it, because it's much easier to be angry than it is to feel the other emotion that's scratching and clawing its way to the surface.

I don't want to feel any of these things. I want to lock myself in a grey box, with grey walls, a grey floor and a grey ceiling and to not feel any of it anymore. I want to be comfortably numb, as the song says.

The Uber arrives and I climb in the back. The driver probably thinks I'm an unfriendly bitch, because I just stare, stony-faced, straight ahead, as we drive home, ignoring his attempts at friendly chatter. I just can't. My jaw is spasming, and it's all I can do to clench my teeth together to stop them from chattering.

A black hole is opening up deep inside of me.

It's small now, only a pinprick, but if I'm not careful, it'll grow and grow and grow. And then I will fall into it, and then I won't know who I am anymore. That can't happen.

Luke is supposed to be my person, the one human being on this planet who will always have my back, but tonight has knocked all of that on its head. What if he isn't? What if my husband isn't who I think he is? The thought makes my insides swirl in cold fear.

I exit the cab swiftly, tapping on my phone to give the driver the maximum tip, and open my front door. Once inside, I ignore the light switches and head for the back of the house. I feel as if I want to hide, but property prices are high in South East London, and our house isn't large. Our starter house. We've been saving for the last few years to upgrade to something with more living space downstairs and an extra bedroom. I walk through to our kitchen, which is twice the size now than it was when we bought the house.

Large French doors lead onto our courtyard garden, and I sit at the small table that overlooks the pots outside. I zone out, and I have no idea how long I've been sitting there when the front door bangs and I startle. My heart begins to race. If only I could close my eyes and turn invisible, just as I did when I was a child.

A shout comes from the hallway. 'Jess?'

I don't answer. I'm too angry with him to give him even that. It's childish, I know.

I hear him opening doors, turning on lights. It isn't long before he's silhouetted against the kitchen doorway, peering into the darkness. He almost turns around again and heads upstairs but then he stops. A second later, a soft glow fills the other end of the room as he turns on the under-cabinet lighting. He walks halfway across the space but stops by the peninsula where the breakfast bar is situated.

The silence curdles around us, but eventually Luke cracks. 'I know you're upset . . . '

I let out a sharp laugh. 'You think?'

He tips his head slightly. 'Yes. I think. But I didn't think you'd be this upset. In fact, I didn't think you'd be upset at all. Surprised, maybe. But I hoped that, underneath it all, you might be pleased.'

His tone is calm and reasonable. It makes me want to punch something. 'You thought I'd be pleased?' I echo, trying to keep my voice steady and even. 'Why, Luke? Please tell me what was going on in your head so I can make some sense of this!'

He sighs. 'Over the last few years, you've said some things that made me think you were softening to the idea.'

My head snaps round. 'Like what?'

'Like . . . Like you've said something about family being important a few times, about how you wish you had one like mine. Like tonight! When you did your speech, and you said that it was all about family . . . '

I make a face. 'I didn't mean *her*. I meant us. Our family. The one we're in the process of building.' We've talked about trying for a baby for the last few years but haven't quite got around to doing anything about it.

'She is part of our family, Jess. You can't just erase her.'

I turn to face him fully. 'Can't I?'

He looks so confused. I know he doesn't get it. But why would he, with his perfect un-divorced parents and happy, successful siblings? Thinking about his family makes the tears fall. I hate crying in front of him. I cover my face with my hands, trying to hide the evidence, then I sniff loudly and look up at him. 'You betrayed me. What I said earlier is true: you had no right to invite her. Not after I'd been so clear how I felt.'

He opens his mouth.

'And even if you'd been right, and I was softening towards the idea of having her back in my life, you should have talked to me about it first. Not sprung it on me like some stupid *Long Lost Family* episode!'

'But I did try talking to you about it!'

'When?' I can't remember any conversations in the last few weeks when Luke has brought my mother up.

'Loads of times.'

'Give me an example?'

Luke shakes his head. 'I . . . I don't remember exactly . . . I tried maybe two months ago, and over the years, plenty of times, but every time I start to talk about your mum, you shut me down.'

'Isn't that my prerogative? She's *my* mother. And don't you dare try and turn this on me! I'm not the one in the wrong here.'

'I'm not turning it around on you!' He runs his hand through his hair and turns around on the spot. 'God, Jess . . . Why do you always have to assume I have the worst intentions? I was trying to do something good, something nice for you. Can't you see that?'

'Why can't you see that maybe *I* know what's good for me, and you don't always have to swoop in and try to fix things?'

He shakes his head. 'It's not like that and you know it.'

It is like that. But he's never going to admit it. 'And you haven't answered my question, not really. Why did you think this would be a good idea? I need to understand.'

'Like I said . . . family is family. And I see how much not having what I have hurts you. I see how much you want those strong family ties.'

His words are a stab to my heart. 'There's a reason I don't have what you have — not all families are as happy and healthy as yours, and no amount of trying will make them that way.'

Luke comes around the counter and comes to sit opposite me, waits for me to meet his eyes. 'You honestly don't ever want to see her again?'

'That's what I've always said, isn't it?'

'You can't give her another chance?'

'No.'

'But she's sober now . . . She got remarried. You've got two stepbrothers you don't even know about.'

I freeze momentarily. This is way too much information. Information Luke knows and I don't . . . I stand up. 'How do you know that?'

He splutters a bit. 'I . . . Well . . . '

'Have you been stalking her Facebook page?'

'No.'

Luke's just as bad as lying as I am, so I know he's telling the truth. So how did he . . . ?

'Oh, my God! You've met up with her!'

His face says it all.

'Behind my back?' I get up because, suddenly, I have to move, I have to . . . I run my hands through my hair, not even caring a hair grip or two go flying. 'I can't believe you!' I pace some more. Luke watches me nervously and I turn to him and laugh. 'She sucked you right in, don't you see? She's got you feeling sorry for her, but it's all part of the game. A game I refuse to play anymore!'

'Jess, I don't think so. I truly think she—'

I hold up a hand and he falls silent. 'You want to know why I can't give her another chance? Because she used them all up. She used them up falling down the stairs naked when I was fourteen and I had to drag her onto the living room sofa and cover her up with a blanket. When she missed my university graduation because she found some drinking buddies on the train down. When she went to rehab, because she was *really* going to do it this time, and then four months later I found her secret stash of tequila hidden in the laundry hamper. Each time I have given her "one more chance", she stomped all over it!'

Luke's eyes are wide. I've talked a bit about what my childhood and teenage years were like, but I don't think I've ever let the 'naked falling down the stairs' thing slip before.

'It was like living with someone who'd pulled the pin out of a grenade and was just walking around with it. You're just waiting for the moment it slips from their fingers – and it always does slip, or get dropped, when they're too wasted to care anymore. I couldn't live like that any longer. That's why I had to go no-contact. I thought you understood!'

I stare at my husband, my rock – or so I thought – silently begging him to come up with a reasonable answer.

'You're still angry with her.'

'You think?' Uh-oh. Sarcastic Jess is coming out to play. This is never a good sign. I try and form a more sensible reply. 'Yes, I'm angry, but that's just the top layer. Underneath I was disappointed with her. And not just the "Oh, well . . . better luck next time" kind of disappointed. I was crushed, Luke.'

Saying those words pops the bubble of my current anger, and it begins to drain away, threatening to no longer do its job of holding back the tidal surge of sadness. He's braced against the kitchen counter, solid and still, but I need to move again, so I walk back towards the French doors.

'I expect it from her,' I say quietly, and I can hear the threat of gluey tears that are currently stuck in my throat. 'The one person I didn't expect to let me down was you.' I turn and look at him. 'But you have, Luke. You really have.'

CHAPTER FOUR

JESS

Luke's face falls and he takes a step back. I know my words must sting, but it's the truth — he has let me down — and I don't know how else to make him understand that he's just set a bomb off inside our marriage.

I give him a couple of moments to process, hoping a light bulb might switch on inside his head, that he might even apologize, but he looks away, frowning. A short while later, I see the muscles around his jaw twitch and flex. Far from seeing the error of his ways, he's pissed off.

Well, so am I.

But I know one of us has to make an effort to de-escalate things, so I zip my mouth shut, go to the fridge, grab a bottle of Pinot Grigio and pour us both a glass, before heading for the living room. Luke follows. I flick on a couple of lamps and plonk myself down in an armchair, while he takes one end of the deep-red sofa I bought at a boot fair and had re-covered.

I breathe in through my nose, out through my mouth and reject the stream of caustic words I really want to spit out at him. When I feel I'm calm enough to carry on, I say, 'It wasn't your place to invite her to the party. At the very least you should have discussed it with me first.'

Luke gives a grudging nod then lets out a sigh. 'I wish I had now.'

Not exactly an apology, or a signal that he understands the gravity of what he did, but at least he's admitting there might be another way rather than Luke's way. That's a start.

'I wasn't a hundred per cent sure about getting in contact with her. I just . . . ' He trails off and looks into the cast-iron fireplace with Art Nouveau tiles that we spent months searching for in reclamation yards.

'You just thought you knew better,' I finish for him. It's the truth, and he doesn't deny it. 'But why think of doing it in the first place? I don't understand why it's so important to you that I reconcile with my mother.' If he knew it had the potential to go sideways, why did he take that risk? There has to be more to this.

It takes a full five minutes of Luke staring into his wine and frowning before he answers again. I don't break the silence. I'm not going to make this easy for him. Luke always wants to be the fixer, putting things right for everyone? Then he needs to fix *this*.

Finally, he looks up. 'You want to know why I invited your mum?'

I nod.

'I see how your broken family relationships hurt you, how they've scarred you, and I wanted something different for you. I suppose . . . I suppose I got desperate.'

'*Desperate?* About what?' Even when we were still in contact with my mother, Luke always found her challenging. I don't think he's been missing her charming personality and thoughtful gestures.

'I want the woman I married back.'

I look at him, sure my eyebrows are halfway up to my hairline. 'What are you on about? I'm sitting right here!'

He stares steadily back at me. 'Are you?'

'Am I what?'

'Are you right here . . . with me?'

I have no idea what he's trying to say. What is he talking about? 'Yes,' I whisper. 'What do you mean?'

He closes his eyes for a moment, exhales, then opens them again. 'It's just that when we met, you were different.'

The muscles between my ribs grow tighter, making it harder to breathe. 'Different how?'

'I think you were happier. You laughed more. You would do things on a whim.'

'Of course we're not going to be the same people after twelve years together. It probably wouldn't be a good sign if we were.'

'It's more than that.' He leans forwards, braces his hands on his thighs. 'We used to be . . . I don't know . . . It felt as if we were the perfect fit. I got you and you got me, and it was easy. And, yes, before you say anything, I know that relationships can't be like they are in the early days all the time. That wouldn't be realistic. But I thought we'd grow closer together over the years, not further apart.'

Oh. He's noticed it too. So much for secretly hoping it was just me overthinking. My stomach sinks and it makes me jittery. 'What has that got to do with inviting my mother to our anniversary party?'

'I know you have a painful history with your mother—'

I let out a sharp, gruff laugh. 'That's one way of putting it.'

'But ever since you cut her out of your life, I feel you're cutting yourself out of mine too. More and more . . . I just thought, if there was a way to bring some healing, some closure, it might help. Maybe we could salvage things.'

Salvage things? We're just in a rut, aren't we? But then I didn't know he's spent years watching me, judging me, and has quietly decided I'm not living up to his expectations anymore.

'I had to do something, Jess. I had to try.'

'To fix me? Because I'm broken?'

'No! To fix the situation.'

'Same thing!'

'No—'

Cold air stings the back of my nose and throat. 'I thought you loved me for me.' I want to shout the words but all I can manage is a hoarse whisper.

'I do!'

I shake my head, tears plopping onto my cheeks. 'No you don't. You want some other Jess – a perfect Jess. But I am who I am, Luke, with all my baggage. I'm not . . . I'm not even sure you know me anymore. And if anything proves that, it's what you did tonight!' And that stupid pewter wall sculpture he gave me as an anniversary present, but it's probably not a good idea to bring that up now.

'Jess, please . . .'

I shake my head and look past him to the living room door. 'I'm going to bed.'

'We need to talk. You can't just walk away.'

'I can't deal with it right now. We'll talk about it . . . later.' I take a few steps across the rug towards the softly lit hallway.

'No.'

I pause in the doorway, turning to look at him over my shoulder. 'No?'

'If you walk away now, nothing will get resolved. We'll just do what we usually do – promise ourselves we'll stuff all our feelings away for a night and get them out again tomorrow. But tomorrow never comes, Jess. It never comes.'

I stare at him and say nothing. He's already overridden me once tonight, ploughed through my boundaries with a bulldozer. I'm not allowing him to do it again, not even in this small way.

'You're not going to say anything?' he says.

'I told you – I don't want to talk right now.'

'Why do we always have to do things on your timing?'

'Because I'm not the one who betrayed your trust so spectacularly this evening. On a night to celebrate our relationship, you blew the foundations out right from underneath us. Is that what you want to hear?'

Instead of looking penitent, his expression pinches further. 'I did *not* betray you.'

'The fact you can't see that is the whole issue here.'

'What issue?' He stands up and glares at me.

'I can't trust you anymore.'

For a split second, he looks as if I've punched him in the chest, but then he meets my anger with his own. 'Maybe if you opened up to me a bit more, if you *would* talk about the difficult stuff, rather than just walking away or going to the gym or burying yourself in work, then I would have realized just what a huge mistake I was making. We could have avoided all of this!'

'And we're back to making it Jess's fault. Oh, goody!'

As well as being in charge of the people in his life, Luke is nearly always in charge of himself too. He rarely loses his temper, but when it goes, it goes. He lets out a growl of frustration so unexpected that I take a step back. 'We're going round in circles! I don't even know how you can say that. I tried to help you.

But you'd much rather paint yourself as the victim and me as the bad guy.' He's the one to break eye contact now, turning to pace towards the fireplace. He places one hand on the mantel then twists to look at me. 'Whatever I do, it's never enough, is it? You always find me wanting. If we had to receive a report card on our anniversary every year, mine would always say "could try harder". And you know what? I do try, Jess. Every day. And you just don't see it. You're oblivious!'

'You're the one calling *me* oblivious? That's rich!'

'If there's someone who's checked out of this marriage, who's not paying attention, it's not me.'

'You're the one who's always half-buried in his phone, tapping away text messages to goodness-knows-who at all times of the day and night!'

He drops his head and looks at the rug, arm braced against the fireplace. When he looks up again, he says, 'Well, it seems we're at a stalemate because I don't think you see me either.' He pulls his hand away from the fireplace and straightens, as if he's just made a decision of some kind, then he walks over to where his suit jacket is slung over the edge of the sofa and pulls a small gift bag out of the pocket and hands it to me.

'What is this?'

'One last surprise.'

Oh, no . . . He doesn't get to deflect this way. He doesn't get to be the hero, the good guy, after everything he's done. I shake my head and put the bag down on the side table next to the armchair without bothering to open it. It's not important at the moment. 'Like I said . . . I'm going to bed.'

He stares at me as if I've done something terrible. 'So you're not going to even try?'

'I will talk to you when I'm ready. It's just not right now.'

He stares at the box and his features harden. 'We both know that's a lie.'

I don't say anything. It doesn't *feel* like a lie in this moment, but I also don't want to admit to myself that I'm not always good on the follow-through when we have this type of discussion.

He turns and looks at the sofa. 'What if I were to beg you to stay and talk this through? Because I don't think I can ride this merry-go-round one more time, Jess. Yes, I possibly messed up tonight, but I wasn't doing it from a bad place. And I want the same things you want for our marriage! I want you to listen to what I think and how I feel, but when I try . . .' He gestures with his hand to me, my body rigid with tension and halfway out the door. 'I get *this*.'

It's no good. In this moment, I can't give him what he's asking. I recognize the strange sensations going on inside me, something that's happened whenever I get into a heated discussion ever since I was a child. I can't stop it. Everything inside me is slamming closed and shutting down. My heart is beating hard, my mind swimming.

He stares back at me and a look of disgust flickers across his features. 'Then I'm out, Jess. I've tried everything I can think of and I've got nothing left.' He strides past me into the hallway and grabs his coat from the hooks near the door.

'Luke, what are you—?'

He turns as he releases the lock and opens the door. 'I told you. I'm out. Done.' And then he steps into the night and shuts it softly behind him.

CHAPTER FIVE

JESS

I'm so stunned that I just stare at the back of the front door. What does 'I'm out' mean? My mouth moves but I'm unable to produce any words in response.

He just walked out on me! After *he* was in the wrong.

I rip the door open and march down the short path to the wrought-iron gate, which is swinging gently, but once I'm past the box hedge that surrounds our paved front garden and onto the street, everything is quiet. There is no noise, apart from a neighbour's dog barking, and the far-off city wallpaper of traffic punctuated by the odd siren. There is no movement, save for a scruffy-looking fox trotting along the other side of the road. It spots me, stares for a moment, then picks up its pace.

There is absolutely no sign of my husband.

I stare left, which leads to a rabbit warren of residential roads filled with red-brick Victorian terraced houses like ours and, ultimately, the park, and then I look right, which leads to the main road into Beckenham town centre.

Luke is much more likely to walk in open spaces to clear his head, so I turn left. I'm still wearing my heels and while my long velvet dress keeps my legs warm, my arms are freezing. I'm tempted to go back and grab a coat, but Luke has much longer legs than mine and he's already had a head start. If I turn back now, I might never catch up with him.

I make it as far as the road with the alleyway to the park and come to a halt. It's chilly and I almost expect my breath to come out as tiny white puffs even though it's May. There is no cloud cover, and the stars twinkle mercilessly above me. I shiver, not just on the outside but deep down in my core, and try to work out what to do.

While we live in a fairly safe neighbourhood, there is no way I'm going down an alleyway into a dark park alone, dressed like this.

After a few seconds, I huff and turn around, my pace much slower this time. There's no point in hurrying now. If Luke went the other way, I've lost all hope of catching up with him.

When I return home, I'm shocked to find the front door wide open, light spilling onto the street from our hallway. Did I leave it like that? I honestly don't remember. And how long have I been gone? Could someone have crept into the house? I hear a noise, but I can't tell if it's coming from inside or not. Are we being burgled right now?

I pause on the porch. 'Hello?'

No one replies. I step inside and grab a bunch of keys from the bowl on the shelf above the radiator and hold them in my fist, just in case. 'Luke?'

I close the front door behind me and the silence thickens. Creeping carefully along the tiled hallway, I peek in first the living room, then the kitchen diner. Empty.

I stand at the bottom of the stairs and listen. There are no creaks or groans suggesting someone else is here with me. The first floor is in darkness, so I flip on the landing light at the bottom of the stairs and do a circuit of our bedroom, the guest room, and the bathroom. We're hoping to add a loft extension at some point, but for now that's all my tiny house has to offer. And it's empty.

I walk back to our bedroom at the front of the house and sit down heavily on my side of the bed, dropping my keys on the duvet. He's actually gone. What do I do now? And when is he coming back?

I sit there in stunned silence for at least ten minutes. I'm trying to process current events, but it seems my brain is unable to do anything but receive information from my five senses – the wall is off-white, my shoes dig into the carpet beneath my feet, there's a vague smell of the perfume I spritzed while I was getting ready. Reasoning and understanding are beyond me at this moment.

And then I remember my phone.

I race downstairs into the kitchen and pull open my clutch, which is sitting on the counter where I left it. With shaking hands, I wake it up. There's a red badge on my messages app. Six messages! But when I open it up, it's all friends and family saying how much they enjoyed the party. Nothing from my husband.

However, there is one from Hannah: I saw Luke leaving the hotel but didn't see you with him. Are you okay? Call me x

My thumbs hover above the keyboard, ready to reply, but how do I even begin to explain what's happened in the last hour or so? I put my phone away. I'll get back to Han later.

I go to put my phone down and get back to worrying when I realize what an idiot I'm being. Quickly, I exit the messages app and dial Luke's number. I wait a torturously long time while it rings and then, of course, it goes to voicemail. I'm tempted to throw my handset across the room. When the beep comes, I realize I have no idea what to say so I hang up. The next three minutes are spent composing a calm, reasonable message but of course that's not what comes out of my mouth when I dial again. Instead, I garble something about not understanding and please can we talk but then it's like I leave my body slightly. I can hear my voice, but it doesn't sound like me. It sounds like my mother. Unhinged. Pathetic. Desperate.

Written word might be better. I open the messages app back up.

Luke?

Where are you?

I wait thirty seconds and then add, **Please come home. We need to talk.**

But there's nothing. No response. He doesn't even read them. *Where is he?*

I wander from the kitchen to the living room, staring at my phone screen, willing a notification box to slide in from the top and calm my galloping heartbeat. I know that Luke has a hot temper, but it takes a lot for him to lose it. When he does, he usually flares up, lets it all out, then calms down again quickly. It's often all over and done within half an hour and then he's ready to talk.

I check the time. It's been forty-five minutes since he walked through the front door now. Why isn't he answering? Did he mean it? Did he really, really mean it? He's out? Does that mean the same as 'over', or does he just need some time to cool off?

I clutch my phone to my breastbone, not sure if I want it to buzz or not. I'm angry with Luke for making the dramatic exit. Maybe I even wish I'd thought of it first. After all, I'm the one with the reason to be upset tonight. What did *I* do that was so awful? It's not wrong to be upset he crossed a firm boundary I'd set down. I'm so confused.

That's when I spot the gift bag on the side table. I slide into the chair, put my phone on the cushion beside me, pick up the bag, and carefully rummage inside.

There's a small box, the kind jewellery — possibly even diamonds — comes in. It's old, made of good quality navy blue leather with a tiny brass button for a clasp. Faded gold lettering is stamped on top, possibly the name of the jeweller, but too much is rubbed off for it to be legible.

Feeling sick in the pit of my stomach, I ease the lid open. Inside is an Art Deco eternity ring, a circle of delicate foliage. Each white-gold leaf is filled with two diamonds and in between sit tiny, deep-green emeralds.

I close the lid and stare at the wall. This ring doesn't belong to me, but I've seen it before.

It's Luke's great-great-grandmother's legendary engagement ring. Great-great-grandpa Joseph bought the ring in Paris then served as a soldier in the trenches, miraculously surviving the Battle of the Somme — all the while with the ring stitched into his pocket — to come home and present it to his sweetheart, Millicent, and they were married within a month. She always said the ring was her lucky charm, because it brought Joe home from the trenches to her safe and sound.

It was a true love match by all accounts, cut tragically short when, not much older than I am now, she died during an air raid in the Blitz. And the ring got passed down to her oldest son and then his oldest daughter after him, and everyone who wore the ring seemed to have an idyllic marriage, leading it to become part of family folklore. The only reason Luke's mum isn't wearing it is because his gran was still alive when she tied the knot with Ed. Since Luke is the oldest child, I could have been next in line to wear it, but I chose not to.

The tiny diamonds and emeralds glint in the light of the table lamp beside me. Luke was going to give this to me? Tonight? A cold swirling starts up deep in my stomach. Have I got this all wrong? Have I just made a horrible, horrible mistake?

As much as I've sensed a distance between us recently, it doesn't mean I don't love Luke. I love him with my whole heart and soul, more than I've ever allowed myself to love anyone else. And that's because I told myself this would never happen. With good reason! Luke always said he'd never give up on me and, stupidly, I believed him.

What do I do now? The thing I've feared most has happened to me. I don't know how to react, how to feel. I don't even know how to *breathe*. I ease the ring from its velvet cushion and slide it onto my left ring finger. I might not deserve its luck, but maybe I can borrow some, just for tonight.

Please don't let this be true, I whisper silently to any deity that might be listening. *Please give me a second chance. I'll do anything.*

And then I haul myself upstairs, fall into bed fully clothed, and cry myself to sleep.

CHAPTER SIX

LUKE

The park gates are closed. Crap. He stares at the vast metal railings for a few seconds. What the heck? He shoves his foot on the crossbar for leverage and vaults over, nearly catching his jacket on one of the spikes on top but just getting away with it.

He just needs some space, some fresh air, to help him think. All these houses squashed together make him feel claustrophobic. He knows Kelsey Park well. It's a common route on his runs. He prefers wild hills and rocky cliffs if he really needs to think and this is all manicured lawns, carefully tended flower beds and play areas, but in the bustle of South East London, it's the best he can manage within walking distance of home.

He makes his way down a tarmac path flanked by towering rhododendrons and then crosses a small bridge over a man-made stream. Once across, he turns left, joining the main path that weaves through the length of the park.

He passes a waterfall made with concrete blocks doing their best to mimic natural rocks. There must have been a natural stream running through this valley once, but sometime in the last century it was dammed and diverted to create a large pond, and then released again via the waterfall to continue its journey to the Thames, maybe seven or eight miles north.

He keeps walking along the path that traces the edge of the pond and onto a wide paved area with railings. During the daylight hours, small children stand at the edges, throwing handfuls of bird food into the water for ducks and geese with abandon. He always wondered if he'd be one of those dads, holding a plastic tub for a toddler wrapped up in a puffy coat, bobble hat and mittens, but it hasn't happened yet. Another thing Jess has had iron-clad control over. It took her so many years to be ready to talk about starting a family, that now he wonders if they left it too late.

Near the railings is a trio of benches. He picks the farthest one, sits down and closes his eyes, listening to the gentle slap of the water against its artificial banks, the rustle of wind in the mature horse chestnuts.

How does he go back to that house? How does he go home and pretend something inside him hasn't changed? He doesn't know what, and he isn't exactly sure how or why, but he felt it shift, like tectonic plates releasing tension after years of seismic build-up.

For more than twenty minutes, he sits in the darkness, playing the events of the night over and over in his head. Jess is being totally unreasonable but she's so stubborn and blinkered that she won't let herself see it. Her life would be better if she could find some peace with her mum; he's sure of it.

His phone buzzes in his pocket. He knows she's calling him, but he doesn't pick up. The next few minutes are punctuated by shorter beeps. He pulls his phone out and turns it onto silent, ignoring the handful of messages from his wife. He'll read them later.

But just as he's about to put it away again, another message arrives. He almost ignores it, presuming it's Jess again, but his lock screen says otherwise. He presses on the notification to open up the message.

Hey. Everything okay?

He hesitates. No. No, it's not.

A few moments later, a second message arrives: **I saw Jess leave the party and I couldn't see you anywhere either. Has something happened?**

He'd like to reply, but he knows he probably shouldn't, not in the mood he's in. He's about to lock his phone when another one lands. **Do you need to talk?**

He lets out a loud sigh. He really does. But should he? Jess is very sensitive about them discussing their relationship with outsiders. It would be the worst thing in the world if anyone thought that their marriage was anything less than perfect, apparently, because then *she* would be less than perfect, and that's just not an option in Jess's eyes.

But he's over it. Over all the pretending. Maybe he needs to think about his own needs, be a bit selfish, rather than always trying to do what's best for Jess? She doesn't seem to have any trouble putting herself first.

His thumbs move swiftly across the keypad. **Actually, I could do with a listening ear.**

It's a minute or two before the reply comes.

Where are you?

VELVET

A fabric made by weaving two different thicknesses of the material at the same time. One might think that the results would be uneven, but the technique gives rise to a dense, even pile with a distinctive soft feel that's almost impossible to resist touching.

CHAPTER SEVEN

JESS

I wake up but I'm so exhausted I can't even open my eyelids. Even so, I have a strange sense that something is off . . . wrong, somehow. I roll over and groan, and then my stomach rolls. It all comes flooding back: the argument, seeing Luke close the door behind him, running through the streets trying to find him.

I have no idea how late it was when I managed to slough off consciousness. I went to sleep clutching the eternity ring I found last night tightly to my other hand, half-hoping it would work its magic and I'd wake up to find Luke beside me, an arm draped over my hip. I run my fingers over my left hand to check if it's still there, but discover that not only am I not wearing Luke's great-great-grandmother's ring, I'm not wearing any rings at all. Did I take them off in the night? Did I have a moment of despair in the small hours of the morning and rip them off my fingers?

I'm so groggy that everything is a bit blurry when I crack my eyelids open, and I run my hand under the duvet to see if I can find them but find nothing but cool, smooth cotton. I reach out to see if I dumped them onto the bedside table, but there is nothing but varnished wood. I reach a bit further and . . . *crash!* Oh, God. I've just knocked the lamp onto the floor.

My eyelids snap wide open, and I sit up in bed. And then an icy bolt of lightning shoots through me.

This isn't my bedroom.

This isn't the bed I share with Luke.

Where am I?

My brain frantically tries to make sense of the information coming its way. Instead of the deep forest greens and neutrals of my bedroom, the walls are white and covered in prints I recognize from IKEA in times gone by. I even used to have a few of those myself when I was younger.

I turn my attention more fully on the fallen lamp. Thankfully, the bulb is intact, so I reach down, pick it up and place it back on the bedside table, but then I realize that piece of furniture also looks familiar. I had a similar one in my bedroom when I was growing up, something that had once been in my grandmother's house, and I'd eventually pestered my mum to allow me to paint it bone-white and distress it, aiming for that shabby chic vibe, and I'd changed the boring wooden knobs out for . . .

My fingers trace the delicate brass ring pulls, just like . . . Oh, my God! Just like this one. It can't be a coincidence. It can't.

I look around the room again, this time forcing myself to join the dots and come to what I realize is an impossible conclusion. I'm . . . I'm back in my childhood bedroom. But *how*? Why?

I leap out of bed and discover I'm wearing a pair of pastel checked pyjamas that were my absolute favourite in my early twenties. I didn't even know I had them any longer.

I cover my face with my hands, not wanting to see more. This is too much! On top of everything from last night, I can't deal with this right now. I want the world to make sense. Please, please, please, I beg God, or whoever else is up there, please make this stop. Because the only explanation is that I am in my mother's house, the very *last* place in this universe that I would choose to be.

It's not only my rings I can't find. I also can't lay my hands on my velvet dress or my clutch. Where have they gone? I suppose I could have left them in a heap somewhere, possibly in the bathroom, because I must have been rip-roaring drunk last night to not remember taking my clothes off, let alone recalling I'd travelled from Beckenham to my mother's house in Orpington, almost eight miles away. How did I get here? Did I get a cab? And *why*?

I sit down on the bed, my head in my hands. I feel sick, and not because I must have a hangover, because I don't seem to have one at all. Other than the churning in my intestines, my head feels fine, my mouth isn't dry. It doesn't hurt to look at the light streaming through the flimsy curtains. I feel sick because I've done what I said I'd never do. I resorted to alcohol to deal with my emotions. It makes me exactly like her.

I don't even know how I ended up going down that road. I'm not a big drinker. I might have a glass, occasionally two, when we're out socially, but I'm very, very careful about my intake.

It just goes to show how traumatic last night was for me that I resorted to this, and I'm slightly worried that after two decades of trying never to overconsume, I apparently found it so easy to slide down this path.

What am I going to do?

I blow out a breath and sit up straight. Well, I'm here now, but Mum is definitely *not* an early bird, so I might be able to slip out unnoticed. It's possible, if she was in a haze last night, that she might not even know, or remember, I'm here.

I start hunting for my dress, looking under the bed, behind the door, but it's nowhere to be found. I need a wee quite badly. So, although I'd rather not risk creeping to the bathroom, I don't have much choice, but at least I can retrieve my dress if it's there, before anyone who lives here starts to wonder where it came from.

Only, after inching my way down the landing, the dress is nowhere to be found. *Please,* don't say it's in the hallway, or worse, the front garden, and I skipped up the stairs and crawled into bed in my underwear last night!

I do what I need to do and glance in the mirror while I'm washing my hands. Thankfully, it's completely free of gloopy mascara and clogged pores. In fact, my skin is looking pretty darn . . .

I look up at the ceiling. Did Mum get rid of the horrible fluorescent tube? Because this lighting is seriously flattering. I'm having an honest-to-God Mirror, Mirror moment. If I didn't know any better, I'd think I was twenty-five again.

But then I notice something – the scar beside my left eyebrow is missing, something I acquired the year after I married, thanks to a trip down a flight of stairs in an Underground station. I lean in closer to the mirror and stretch the skin with my fingers, examining it closely. No. Absolutely nothing. It's as if it never happened.

But I don't have time to ponder that now. I have to get out of here before anyone gets up and discovers me. While Luke and I have both booked a day off for after our party, the residents of this house probably have jobs to go to this morning, and it's just after six already.

I creep back to my room and, once inside, lean against the

closed door, holding my breath for a few seconds as I listen for evidence of anyone else stirring, then letting out a relieved sigh when all I can hear is a rushing in my ears that thumps in time with my heartbeat. I need to find something else to wear, and I need to do it quickly.

The weird thing is that the more time I spend in this room, the more I realize it looks *exactly* the way it did when I lived here last, during that brief interlude when I was in between rental houses and had to come home for two months. There's a terracotta rug, bright floral cushions, all with a hint of earthy orange, and as much charity shop quirkiness as I could pack into it. Hasn't Mum wanted to update at all? And where do these supposed stepsons sleep? Surely they're not sharing this room. Or are they both squeezed into the box room? That hardly seems fair when there's a much larger room going spare.

I rummage in the chest of drawers, hoping there might be something I can slink home in. It's worse than I thought. There's a selection of old clothes still in here, which I must have left behind when I moved out, but folded just the way I like them folded. It's almost as if she's kept it as a shrine.

But I don't want to think about how much I might have broken my mother's heart by cutting off contact, so I pull out a pair of nondescript black trousers and a top. I also can't find my heels from last night, so I pull a pair of loafers from the bottom of the wardrobe, then help myself to some of the possibly ancient deodorant standing on the dressing table. I even find an old purse with some seriously out-of-date bank cards and some cash in it. I take it. It's mine, after all, so I'm not stealing, and since I can't find my clutch, I'm going to need those banknotes for the train or bus fare home.

I feel anxiety rising inside of my chest like a physical thing, pulling my ribs tight and making my breathing shallow. Before it develops into a full-blown, and probably noisy, panic attack, I swipe my phone, which is lying on the bedside table, and make my exit.

Home. Where I may have to face Luke.

Or maybe I won't.

I'm not sure which option is worse.

CHAPTER EIGHT

JESS

I tip-toe down the hallway of my mother's house and pull the front door shut as quietly as I can, before creeping down the garden path. Once I'm out of the gate, I start sprinting, and I don't stop until I'm well around the corner of the next road. My heart is thudding, and not just from the unexpected exercise.

What on earth is happening to me? Yesterday, I was thinking my life was a little mundane, that I wanted 'more', but the last twenty-four hours have been more than I can possibly handle. What do I do now? Where do I go?

Before I can make a plan, my phone dings in my back pocket. I pull it out, and it's only then that I take a good look at it, and that's when I realize it's not my phone at all, although I used to have one just like this years ago. I turn and look in the direction I've just come from. Did I pick up someone else's and, if so, where's mine, and why was this one charging in my old bedroom?

But then I spot the slight crack in the screen in the right bottom corner. My old phone was damaged in exactly the same place. In fact, it had an identical clear case too, although I see these everywhere, so that doesn't mean anything. On instinct, I press my thumb to the button at the bottom and my fingerprint wakes it up.

It *is* my phone. Just not my current one.

Why would Mum be charging up one of my old phones? I suppose it's possible she's lost or smashed hers – again – and desperately needed a replacement, even if only as a stopgap.

I really ought to go back to her house and post it through the front door or something, but it's making me feel itchy just thinking about walking in that direction. And, technically, it is my phone . . . but if Mum needs it she can have it. I'll just put it in a padded envelope and send it back to her via Royal Mail.

The notification at the top of the phone screen says I've got a message from Priya, one of my work friends from when I used to do a boring admin job before I retrained as a physiotherapist. I haven't heard from her in ages. However, it now occurs to me that maybe it's because she's messaging me on my old number and I forgot to give her the new one when I switched.

I open the message, intending to apologize and send her my current contact details, but what I read makes no sense: **Where are you? Janine is on the warpath this morning but hasn't noticed you're not here yet. If you're sick, you'd better call in quick!**

I frown. What is she talking about? I left Dobson's over a decade ago. Why does boss-from-hell Janine care where I am?

I text back: **Great to hear from you. We must meet up for coffee sometime. It's been too long.**

A few seconds later, I get a reply – a crying with laughter emoji followed by: **Very funny. Just get your butt in here asap. I'll try to cover for you.**

I have no idea how to respond to that, so I decide I'll wait until I'm sitting on the train to save her number and put it into my actual phone . . .

Only, I can't, can I? A thorough search of the bedroom at Mum's didn't even throw up my clothes from last night, let alone my clutch with my phone and keys in it.

My stomach sinks. Well, I suppose that makes my mind up about what I do next. I don't want to go home, but I don't think I've got much choice. There's only about £40 in this old purse of mine, and the debit cards expired over a decade ago. I'm hoping my bag is still in the house and that I somehow got to Mum's without it. I've got to find my phone. I need it for work, if for nothing else.

And Luke might have left you a message . . .

I want to shut the lid on that thought, push it to the back of my brain and not think about it. Even just picturing his face brings back the crushing, soul-devouring feeling of loss when I heard the words 'I'm out' last night and watched him walk out the door without looking back.

No, I think, as I mentally map out the route to Orpington station in my head. *I can't fall apart now. I just need to get home . . . I just need to . . .*

I don't know what I need. But I'm too tired and emotionally exhausted to process anything at this moment, so I focus on the practicalities: the ten-minute walk to the station, fiddling around with notes and coins at the self-service ticket machine – something I haven't done in a long time – and then finally plopping myself down on an empty seat in a commuter train heading towards London in eight minutes' time. Orpington is the start of this route, otherwise I'd have been standing, and the rest of the seats fill quickly. It feels like hours before the packed train finally pulls away. Thankfully, It's only a handful of stops to Beckenham Junction and I should be there in under twenty minutes.

As the train rumbles out of the station, I stare blankly ahead. My brain is stalled and I have no idea how to jump-start it again. I'm vaguely aware of train doors opening and closing, of people getting on and off. Somebody trying to edge their way down the aisle whacks me in the side of the head with their massive tote bag but all I do is blink slowly, then keep staring.

Eventually, my gaze is snagged by the front page of the newspaper the man opposite me is reading. **FERRY SINKS OFF COAST OF SOUTH KOREA**, the type at the top announces. There's a picture of stormy seas and rescue boats. My gaze drifts to another picture down to one side – the Princess of Wales greeting crowds and accepting a bouquet from a child, but the headline causes me to do a double take. The mistake I spot is only amusing enough to warrant a gentle huff but I burst out laughing, and then I find I can't stop. A couple of people narrow their eyes at me, but the woman sitting next to the guy with the newspaper smiles back. 'What's so funny?' she asks.

I shake my head, knowing I should clamp my lips together and try to keep it in, but it's as if the absurdity of my life has finally caught up with me. 'It's stupid, really . . . but you'd think *The Times* would get it right, wouldn't you?'

The guy with the paper realizes we're discussing his reading material and gives me a quizzical look as he closes the paper and inspects the front page. 'What did they get wrong?' he asks me, and I get the impression he's about to be offended if his daily paper has let him down. I almost don't want to mention it.

'The Royal tour in Australia – they've called William the Duke of Cambridge.'

Both of my travelling companions frown. 'What else are they supposed to call him?' the woman says.

'The Prince of Wales, of course.'

Newspaper Guy looks at me from over the top of his reading glasses. 'But that's Charles's title.'

Now it's my turn to frown. 'Not anymore.'

'Oh, my God. Has old Queenie given her son the boot and said Wills is going to take over next instead?' she says excitedly. 'I always said she should do that! Those poor boys . . . especially losing their mother in that way.'

Newspaper Guy rolls his eyes at both of us and opens up the paper again, clearly done with any form of commuter chit-chat.

I'm about to open my mouth and point out the obvious, but then I spot the date under the name of the newspaper. He's reading a newspaper from *2014*?

Well, I suppose it makes sense of what I thought was a factual error. The woman next to him starts talking with the older lady across from her about how she went up to Kensington Palace with flowers when Diana died. I tune her out and study the man sitting across from me instead. He looks like a normal City type, no hint that there's anything unusual going on there. But what does he do? Read the same old newspaper every day on the train into work? You'd have thought, after twelve years, he might have been in the mood for some fresh material. But then I think again about how I've been turning the doom and gloom on the breakfast news off recently, and I realize he might be on to something.

A pregnant woman gets on at Shortlands, so I offer her my seat and squeeze myself into the mass of bodies in the area near the doors. It's one more stop until I reach my destination, so I'll only be stuck in the crush for a couple more minutes.

Another newspaper is sticking out of the narrow bin next to the door. It's one of the tabloids but I notice that it, too, is sporting the wrong date. Even weirder, it's exactly the same date as *The Times* Newspaper Guy was reading.

I snatch it up to check my weary eyes aren't playing tricks on me. No, I was right the first time: 14 May 2014. Perhaps I judged the guy sitting opposite me too harshly. Has this become a thing since I last commuted into London more than eight years ago? If it has, I have no idea why. I look around the carriage in confusion, feeling that something is off. I can't quite put my finger on what – people are listening to their headphones or staring out the windows, just as they would do on any ordinary morning commute.

But then I catch sight of someone's phone over their shoulder. The calendar app on the home screen is also showing a number fourteen as today's date.

What is going on? Surely it should be fifteen? The fourteenth was yesterday.

Another message alert sounds on my phone and I realize I still haven't replied to Priya and it sounds as if she's getting a little desperate.

R U on ur way? Not sure how much longer I can make up excuses for ur empty chair!

What *is* she talking about? On my way where?

I'm about to reply, asking her what she means, when I get

the instinct to check something first. I pause, scroll out of my messages and return to my home screen.

What the . . . ?

My calendar icon also says 'Wed 14'.

And *Wednesday*? The anniversary party was on Thursday. Today is Friday.

Isn't it?

I'm still puzzling what this all means when the doors beside me open. It's my stop. People inside the carriage start jostling, getting ready to squeeze through the bodies and get off. More are waiting to cram themselves into the already stuffed and humid carriage. I angle my shoulder, allowing myself to squeeze between two people, and step down onto the platform.

I weave in and out of the crowd until I'm standing at the barriers. After pulling my ticket from my pocket, I pause before feeding it into the machine and look around, catching the eye of the railway employee on duty. 'What day is it today?' I ask.

'Wednesday,' the woman says.

'And the date?'

'Did you bring an old ticket?' she says, scowling. 'Because you'll need to buy a new one if you can't prove you've paid your fare.'

I shake my head. 'Just . . . ' I clear my throat ' . . . need to check something.'

She looks at me as if I'm an idiot, but says, 'May the fourteenth.'

My stomach drops to the soles of my feet. 'And the year?'

She gives her colleague standing a short distance away a 'we've got a right one here' kind of look and then adds, '2014.'

It's as if a warm and violent wind rushes not just past me but right through me as I register her words. I'm shaking as the barrier eats my ticket and then spits it out again. I'm carried through the ticket hall by the steady stream of people, all heading off somewhere with determination and purpose. Eventually I stop walking and they just tut and flow around me.

The only thing I can do is stare at my phone. My phone but not my phone.

And the stories in the newspapers are all from years gone by.

And Priya is texting me from a job I left close to a decade ago.

I pull up the camera on my phone, flip it to selfie mode and take a really hard look at what I see. The face staring back is me but, like my phone, it is also not me. At least, not who I am now. I look very much like I did twelve years ago, which means I was wrong about my skin looking as if I was still twenty-five.

If this really is 2014, I'm actually twenty-three.

CHAPTER NINE

JESS

This can't be real. It can't be! I'm just . . . I don't know . . . feeling delusional, or dissociated, or . . . something! At a loss for anything else to do, I let my feet follow the well-worn route from the station to our house. Once I get inside, I'll feel better. I can go to bed, maybe, have some decent sleep and, hopefully, wake up later today feeling ready to deal with the fallout of last night.

I do a good job of convincing myself that I'm just having a really bad 'morning after' experience as I walk down streets filled with row upon row of red-brick Victorian houses of various sizes and shapes, but when I reach our front gate, my stomach drops.

This is not how my house looked when I left it yesterday. The usually glossy black front door is red, the paint faded in places from years of afternoon sun. The tiled path Luke and I had put in last year is gone, replaced by crazy paving punctuated by weeds that have pushed through the cracks.

Not too different from how it was six years ago when we took down the 'For Sale' sign and entered our new home for the first time. However, it doesn't stop me walking up to the front door and rapping loudly on the knocker, hoping Luke will open it.

Even if he scowls at me, gives me the silent treatment, I won't care, because at least it will contradict what my five senses are telling me and I can remain safe in my bubble of denial.

No one answers. I take a couple of steps off the path so I can peer in the bay window. A pair of dingy curtains hang where there should be gleaming white shutters and I can see a sagging corduroy sofa. The sight of an ugly carpet full of orange and brown swirls is all it takes for my panic to reach the surface. I spin around, unable to look at what should be my front room, as my ribcage squeezes my lungs and my pulse gallops. I stumble out of the garden and back onto the street, but have to sit down the low garden wall because my vision begins to spin. How can this be happening? How?

I spend the next five minutes concentrating on my breathing, trying to coax my body out of a full-blown panic attack. A man with a dog walks past and stares at me, but he doesn't stop to ask if I need help.

Eventually, the adrenaline in my system diminishes. As soon as I am able, I get up and walk. I don't decide on a direction; I just move. Anywhere, as long as I don't have to stand in front of 24 Nightingale Road and know that it isn't mine. Not yet, anyway.

Am I dreaming?

No. It seems unlikely. The world is behaving itself, following the laws of physics and logic. I haven't teleported to anywhere different or walked down the street naked. Apart from the fact that I'm here, *now*, everything else seems to make sense.

A hallucination, then?

Possibly. Maybe, after losing my grip on the one relationship in my life where I felt safe, I've lost my grip on reality.

I suppose I could just sit down on a bench somewhere and

hope that I'll come to my senses, but there's a kind of nervous energy building inside me, a feeling that something important is about to happen, that I need to pay attention, and I'm too hard-wired to do the responsible thing to ignore it.

In lieu of any other sensible ideas, I go with the flow and follow the path already laid out for me. If Priya says I need to be at work, maybe I need to be at work. Perhaps being in the right place at the right time, rather than a puzzle piece jammed into the wrong part of the jigsaw, will help me make sense of what is happening around me.

I make my way back to the station, get on a train into London, and walk the old familiar route I did for four years when I worked at Dobson's as an administrator, then sneak into the office just after ten and pretend I've been there all along.

Priya sends me a thumbs up from her cubicle and I smile weakly back. I want to rush over to her and hug her tight, so glad to see a friendly face in the midst of all this madness, but Janine, the manager from hell, is prowling and I can't afford getting us both in trouble. I try to get stuck in to what I should be doing, but it's really hard to concentrate and act as if everything is normal.

It can't *really* be 2014, can it? But when I stop what I'm doing, and look around the office, I see all my old colleagues, looking exactly as they did twelve years ago. I have phone calls and meetings about things I vaguely remember but wouldn't have been able to recall the details if you'd asked me in 2026.

What on earth is happening to me? And why now? Why today?

I put the pencil I'm holding down and stare blankly at my computer screen.

Well, that is the one thing that does make sense. The fourteenth of May is probably the most important date in my calendar. Not only is it the date I got married and the date of every wedding anniversary afterwards, but it's also the day I met Luke. He always joked it was his lucky day, said we better keep doing important things in line with that just so we didn't jinx it.

And twelve years later, look where that got us. Maybe you *can* have too much of a good thing.

I always thought the work at this small firm of probate genealogists was easy, but after an eight-year break, I discover I have no memory of how to use Dobson's rather antiquated, custom-built family tree software, which results in me sending reports to the wrong people, accidentally deleting birth certificates linked to a pending case and then, just before lunch, Janine comes striding over to me.

'You have just embarrassed me hugely!' she says at an uncomfortable volume as I hunker down in my cubicle and try to look penitent. 'I asked for the details for the De Mornay estate and you sent me the wrong file! I just told a completely different potential heir their estranged brother had died and he was possibly the sole beneficiary of his rather large estate!'

I swallow. 'Um . . . sorry?'

Janine is not placated. 'I just spent the last twenty minutes apologizing profusely.'

'I . . . I . . . don't know how it could have happened,' I stammer. 'Was he really, really upset?'

Janine puts her hands on her hips. 'How would you feel if you thought for a few brief moments you were going to have a windfall of half a million pounds and then discovered it was someone else's inheritance? I had to quickly pull up the right family tree and recheck all the details.'

I frown. 'He wasn't upset about his brother?'

Janine lets out a frustrated huff. 'He seemed more upset he was still alive,' she mutters but then regains herself. 'But this is completely unacceptable, Jessica. You're going to have to rethink your future at this company if you continue to make these kinds of mistakes!'

Priya's head pops up from behind her cubicle partition and she makes a face, then mouths the words, 'he seemed more upset he was still alive' along with a rather passable impression of our boss's facial expressions and mannerisms, only to have to duck down again when Janine, who's almost at the door to her office, spins around to see what's going on. I clamp my hand over my mouth and screw my face up to stop myself laughing, only daring to move when I hear Janine's door slam shut behind her.

Slowly, I lift myself from my chair and look in Priya's direction. Her eyes appear above her partition, full of mischief, and then the rest of her face. 'Time for lunch?' she mouths, and I nod back enthusiastically. We laugh all the way to the café around the corner where we always used to escape and grab a sandwich.

'Excited about tonight?' she says, once we find somewhere to sit.

I release my chicken Caesar wrap from its cardboard and cellophane packaging and bite into it. I can't think of anything worse. How can I face Luke again – even the twenty-four-year-old version of him – when I know the thirty-six-year-old version of him has just shattered my heart into a million pieces?

Priya knows me too well, because after looking at me for a few seconds she asks, 'What's up?'

I swallow my mouthful and turn to her. 'I'm not sure I want to go.'

Her face falls. She's been so excited to play the role of matchmaker with me and one of her brother's friends. 'Don't say that! Listen, I know you didn't like the idea of a blind date, but I promise you – you're perfect for each other.'

I look down at my disposable coffee cup. Once upon a time, I thought that too. But it turns out what I think doesn't count. In 2026, Luke walked out on me. If that isn't a clear signal how far from a perfect wife I am for him, I don't know what is. I tried so hard, too. I honestly don't know what I could have done differently.

Priya must see the hesitation in my eyes, because she reaches for my arm and holds it gently. 'Will you do it? For me?'

I sigh and take another bite of my wrap.

★

I arrive at *Rive Gauche*, a bougie little restaurant just outside Borough Market a few minutes before seven o'clock. It feels as if I'm walking to my own execution. Either I'm having the weirdest dream of my life, or an extended hallucination, or I'm dead, this is the afterlife, and I'm being punished for my sins, which clearly revolve around my disaster of a marriage. A marriage I thought was 'not great but okay' until less than twenty-four hours ago. Or twelve years in the future, whichever way you want to calibrate the timeline.

This is all so confusing. If I start to try and work it all out, I just feel sick and dizzy, so I do what I do best: concentrate on the 'now' and push all the other stuff away to deal with another day. It's easier to follow the script that Luke and I set out for ourselves the first day we met. I know how it goes – we'll have dinner. We'll laugh and talk and get on like a house on fire. He'll walk me to the station, and I'll go home alone.

I'm not floating above my body as I enter the restaurant, but I do feel as if I'm detached from everything that is going on around me. A message arriving causes my phone to vibrate. I don't bother to check it. I know what it says. It's from Luke, saying he's running late because of signalling problems on the Underground.

The first time around, I thought he was making excuses, that possibly he was going to leave me high and dry, but now I know he was telling the truth, because he arrived at the restaurant breathless, twenty minutes late, and a relieved smile spread all over his features when he looked through the glazed front door and saw me sitting in a crimson dress at the bar. Priya and her brother had refused to show us photos of each other, so we'd both agreed to wear something red – me the dress and him a scarf.

Priya's reason at the time was that the 'effect' of Luke was better had first time in person. Later, she'd admitted it was also partly because she knew I'd say I was punching above my weight in the looks department and make excuses to get out of it. She was right, though. I almost *had* bolted when he'd turned that smile on me, sure he was going to be polite and charming but would then dash my hopes by never calling me ever again.

Priya also told me I needed to work on my self-esteem. She was one hundred per cent right. But that was then and this is now; I've tried to work on my confidence issues, so maybe I can bring an extra twelve years of experience to this night now I'm doing it second time around.

It doesn't stop my stomach churning as I perch on the bar stool, sipping a large glass of Pinot Noir, waiting for my future husband to arrive. Every ten seconds, I'm tempted to lurch off my stool and run for the door.

At about ten past seven, the door opens, and the sounds of the bustling market outside momentarily invade the restaurant. I look up to see a well-groomed man in a suit, overcoat and burgundy cashmere scarf walk in.

I remember wondering if he was Luke the first time I lived this day, even though his scarf was the wrong colour, and then being completely intimidated by how well he was put together, how expensive his clothes looked. However, thirty-five-year-old Jess has a few private physio clients who have a penny or two to spend, and isn't as intimidated as twenty-three-year-old Jess was, so when he sits on the stool next to mine I don't bury my head in my phone to avoid interaction.

He also orders the Pinot Noir and as he's waiting for the bar staff to fetch it for him, he turns to me, his eyes appraising. 'Are you meeting someone here?'

'Yes.'

He nods, as if this means something to him.

I take a sip of my wine. 'Blind date?'

One corner of his mouth curls up. It makes him look a bit rakish, a nice offset to the mannered appearance. 'Something like that.'

I give him a polite smile, more because I don't know how to respond than because I think what he's saying is amusing.

He turns to face me fully. 'I think I may be the one you're waiting for.'

I open my mouth to explain that he's got it wrong, but then an idea crashes into my brain on a flash of white-hot lightning. My smile grows warmer. 'I think you might be right.'

CHAPTER TEN

JESS

When Luke comes dashing through the restaurant door at twenty past seven, the stools by the bar are empty. He looks around and the hopeful smile slides from his face. Even though I know he doesn't know what I look like, I shift back in my chair, taking advantage of a potted palm.

The guy with the cashmere scarf is called Brandon, and he's something big in commercial real estate, apparently. I *may* have hijacked his blind date by letting him think I'm the person he's supposed to be meeting, but seeing as another woman hasn't turned up looking for him, I'm not feeling too guilty on her behalf. Brandon is being classy and charming, and he thinks I'm the bee's knees. Why *wouldn't* I want to have dinner with him rather than the man who just stormed out of my life, basically implying I'm not good enough for him?

Luke stands near the restaurant entrance with his hands on his hips, scanning the room for a full minute, the lumpy red, homemade scarf hanging round his neck, even though it's May and he must be sweltering. His nan always knits him something for Christmas. It is always hideous. How a woman who's been knitting for more than four decades can create such monstrosities I'll never know. It was one of the things I loved about Luke that he always wore what she made him, no matter how ghastly it was.

I almost feel sorry for him. I almost stand up and try to attract his attention.

But then I think about how this can't possibly be real, how I've already lived this day once and it happened the way it happened. Maybe I slipped and fell when I was chasing after Luke after our big party. Maybe I'm in a coma. I read a magazine article a couple of months ago about a woman who had an accident the night before her wedding and had a traumatic brain injury. While she was unconscious she had this long-running, ultra-realistic dream about how she married the best man instead. Maybe this is something like that. Weirdly, I think I'd prefer to believe I'm just lying in a hospital bed rather than the alternatives: that I'm insane, dead or truly time travelling through my life.

I turn my attention back to my dinner companion. He's talking about wine and literature and the opera. And it's interesting. I'm enjoying his company, even if he's quite probably a figment of my own imagination.

I see Luke pull out his phone, possibly to text me, so I thrust my hand into my bag and push the button to put mine on silent. I don't want a loud 'bing-bing' to give me away when I'm only a handful of metres away from him.

He hovers near the bar in his stupid scarf tie for another fifteen minutes, looking like a lost puppy dog, and it's a relief when I see a smudge of red in my peripheral vision as Luke and his scarf exit the restaurant and stride back in the direction of London Bridge Underground station.

I turn back to my substitute blind date to find him looking at me, an amused twinkle in his eyes. 'You know, you're not quite what I thought you'd be.'

'I'm not?'

'I think I was expecting . . . I don't know, something more obvious.' He smiles again, and I take hope in the fact he doesn't seem fazed or even disappointed. 'But I did say I was prepared to be surprised, and I think I quite like the "secretly sexy librarian" approach. The red hair is a definite plus.'

What a weird thing to say. Is it a compliment? I think it is, but I honestly can't tell.

What does 'more obvious' mean? I'm puzzling over there 'secretly sexy librarian' bit. Do I look uptight? I know I can come off as a bit guarded sometimes, but that doesn't mean I don't know how to have fun. Maybe I'll just have to pick up the mood a bit, try and be a little more effervescent than I usually am.

When our starters are cleared away and the main courses are delivered, he stops asking me questions about myself and segues into a monologue about his work colleagues, especially his boss's boss, who is in town for some big event. It's obvious Brandon is desperate to impress him. And then just keeps droning on and on, for almost half an hour.

'You are paying attention, aren't you, Jessica?'

My eyes snap up to meet his. I'd been studying the dessert fork, thinking what a lovely shape it was. 'Huh?'

'You need to keep abreast of the names.'

'Oh, God . . . sorry.' He must have been able to tell I'd tuned out. How embarrassing.

He looks slightly peeved. 'You might have to try a bit harder, especially since we're going to be meeting up with them all later.'

'I am? I mean, we are?'

Is it just me? Or has this evening taken a diversion into Weirdsville? I mean, who invites their work friends to the tail end of a blind date?

'Yes.' He's getting more impatient now. 'At the awards ceremony. For Young Property Developer of the Year.'

I look at him blankly.

He throws his napkin down on the table. 'Oh, for God's sake. Didn't they fill you in on any of this? That's not okay at all.'

I stammer something about not knowing anything about an awards ceremony. I can't say why, can I? He'll think I'm a total loser if he knows I just pounced on him and hijacked his blind date.

He sighs. 'Well, I suppose it doesn't matter, does it? That's why I suggested dinner first. It gives us a chance to get to know each other a bit first before we rock up to the awards thing. I mean, we don't want people to think we're total strangers, do we?'

I laugh nervously. 'We don't?'

'No. I want them to think you're my girlfriend.'

I blink at him. I'm getting the feeling we're living in parallel universes.

'I suppose we could get to know each other a *whole lot* better if we went back to the hotel first.' He places a hand on my knee and runs it up my thigh. Thank goodness my dress is long enough that he's touching fabric and not my leg. 'I don't suppose anyone would mind if we were a few minutes late.'

I scoot back in my chair. 'I don't think so!'

He looks confused. 'But . . . but I booked you for the whole night. I don't know why you're so surprised about this. And the fee is a bit pricey if all you're going to do is be prim and have dinner with me.'

I stare back at him. I understand English, but somehow none of his words make sense. And then the penny drops. 'You think . . . you think I'm an *escort*?'

He sits back in his chair. 'Aren't you?'

'No!'

He lets out a small laugh. 'But at the bar . . . You knew I was looking for you.'

'I'm here for a blind date! Not to . . . to . . .' I break off to shudder. Urgh. I can't even say it. There is *no way* I'd ever sleep with this creep.

His face is a mask of shock. It would actually be quite funny if I wasn't so grossed out. 'Oh, my God . . . I'm . . . I'm so sorry!' He looks around frantically. 'But then where is the girl I'm supposed to be meeting?'

I throw up my hands. 'How should I know?'

The *woman* he's supposed to be meeting probably took one look at him and made a swift exit, having much better radar than I do for slimy idiots. I can't believe I thought he was charming at first.

'I'm going to go,' I say, but he's not paying attention. He's tapping away a message on his phone, swearing under his breath as he does it. I stand up, shake my head, and make for the exit.

I'm just emerging from the ladies when I notice a pair of slim lift doors to my right. The sign above boasts, 'Rooftop Bar'. I hit the button. So my 'avoid Luke' plan didn't go exactly as planned – maybe I'll take *myself* on a blind date and give up on men forever.

I'm standing on the roof terrace, a virgin mojito in my hand. The upstairs bar of *Rive Gauche* is very swish. It has an indoor area with folding glass doors that lead onto a large terrace that overlooks the cobbled roads surrounding Borough Market, Southwark cathedral availing itself as a backdrop. People down below flow in and out of various restaurants, kissing each other in greeting or parting, and I feel alone and completely separate from them, as if I'm untethered from reality.

'Jess?'

I freeze, my cocktail glass resting on my lip. I'd know that voice anywhere. Do I deny it, pretend I'm someone else, or do I turn?

I turn. Mainly because, after the day I've had, it's such a relief to see someone who belongs in my present-day life.

'Are you Priya's friend?'

I nod.

He presses a palm to his chest. 'I'm Luke. So sorry I was late! I thought I must have missed you. What luck to find you up here.'

What luck indeed.

He gestures to the space on the railing next to me. 'Do you mind . . . ? Or am I in the doghouse?'

I consider it for a moment. He definitely still is in the doghouse, but . . . I don't know . . . Maybe it's because everything has seemed strange and unfamiliar today but, even though he's twelve years younger than he was the last time I saw him, he doesn't. He just feels like Luke. Safe. Constant. Until he wasn't, of course.

But this Luke hasn't walked out the front door without looking back. This Luke hasn't told me he's had enough of being married to me. In this moment, I am enough for him, and I had no idea how much I needed that or how long that feeling has been missing from my life.

'It's fine,' I tell him. Because it is. For now.

He sighs with relief and smiles. 'Actually, I just got here.'

I raise my eyebrows.

He looks a bit sheepish. 'I spent the last hour barging through the doors of every restaurant and bar within a half-mile radius. Just in case I'd got the wrong restaurant.'

He looks so earnest, so heartfelt, that I want to take his face in my hands and kiss him, but I don't. This Luke and I are strangers. It strikes me that I always thought he went on this blind date because Ranvir pushed him into it, but if that was the case, he would have just heaved a sigh of relief and scurried off for the train home. However, this man scoured Borough looking for me, which is no mean feat, seeing as how this foodie heaven is cluttered with eateries and watering holes of all types.

I smile at him. 'I'm glad you did.'

After that, we fall into easy conversation, just as we did the first time around, talking about movies and books, work and, well, life. It's a relief for my overloaded brain to dive into a familiar dynamic. At the end of the night, he walks me to the station and kisses me softly on my cheek. Last time, I pulled on the lapels of his jacket and brought him closer, asking for more. This time, I let it stand.

CHAPTER ELEVEN

LUKE

Twelve Months Before the Anniversary Party

He stands in front of the tall shelves filled with ceramic items of all sizes and descriptions, from crockery and candlesticks to vases and salt and pepper shakers. In just over a week, he and Jess will have been married for nine years. He's always given her a traditional gift of the material associated with each anniversary, which means this year it's pottery.

He's not sure Jess gets particularly excited about pottery.

If he's honest, he's not sure *anyone* gets particularly excited about pottery.

Maybe he'll get her something else to go alongside it, but he wants to buy something ceramic too. It's become a bit of a tradition, something he doesn't want to break.

He sighs and wanders down the aisle a bit to stare at another banks of shelves, all similarly stacked. What would Jess like . . . ? An olive oil pourer, glazed in earthy colours? He pulls a face. Hardly romantic. It's the sort of present you might give your grandma, or a friend for a housewarming present. Not the supposed love of your life.

He picks up an egg cup, turns it over, then puts it down again. But maybe that's the problem. He and Jess have seemed more like roommates than soul mates recently. They don't argue. They still have sex, but . . . He doesn't know how to quantify it. It just seems as if something important is missing.

He's just about to pick up a small jug with hearts stamped on it when he hears an incredulous voice behind him. 'Luke?'

He spins around. 'Elena?'

She laughs. 'What are you doing here? Wandering round an artisan ceramics show is hardly the sort of place I'd expect to find you!'

'Looking for an anniversary present for Jess. It's nine years this year – pottery.'

She nods, smiling, but there's something in her eyes he can't quite identify.

'It's good to see you,' she says.

'Likewise,' he replies, and now he's got over his surprise, he pays a bit more attention. She looks good. Elena was always one to look effortlessly stylish, but today she looks especially good. The cream suit with striped shirt sits well on her.

They stand there, just looking at each other for a few seconds and then he says, 'Got any ideas for a suitable anniversary present? I'm struggling. I could do with your eye, if you've got a moment?'

At first he thinks she's going to make an excuse, but then she nods. 'Sure.'

They spend the next few minutes browsing the displays.

Every now and then she picks something up and offers it to him. Elena has always had great taste, even in their uni days when she'd been studying art. She'd been dating one of his flatmates and had formed part of their friend group for a while.

A few years later, at an unofficial uni reunion, he'd met up with his old flatmate again, and by that time Felix and Elena had been married. She was still making sculptures Luke didn't fully understand, but it wasn't bringing in the money, so she was dabbling in interior design, and he'd asked for her help. They'd *almost* ended up in business together, flipping houses. That hadn't panned out, but they'd kept in touch until four or five years ago, and then she and Felix had split up and she'd moved away. Since then, contact has been minimal.

'This has to be it,' she tells him, pointing to a white porcelain figurine on a table in front of them. It's about thirty centimetres tall and slightly abstract, but clearly the shape of a woman. Unlike some of the other pieces in the same range, this one isn't lying down, as if draping herself onto the shelf. This one looks strong, powerful, with her arm raised above her head in what looks like a punch of victory.

He picks it up and inspects it more closely. It reminds him of Jess a bit. She's strong and athletic without being bulky. But something about the pose seems a little off. Even so, he cradles it firmly against his chest as they continue to peruse the different displays. He's got to come away with something, right?

His phone vibrates in his pocket, and he puts the figurine down to check it. Probably his wife, but he's not in a position to reply right now, so he ignores it, intending to respond once he's back at the car.

When they finish going round the room full of pots and their wares, he's still holding the white porcelain statue. It seems his choice is made for him. There also isn't any more reason to delay his old friend. He pays for his wares, and she pays for the handful of bowls and vases she's picked up along the way to decorate her latest project with. They emerge from the barn into the gravel car park, blinking in the bright spring sunshine.

'It's been good to see you,' she tells him softly.

He nods. 'Yes.'

She regards him for a second and then gives him a slightly awkward hug. Her cheek rests against his shoulder for a moment before she pulls away again.

He's about to say, 'Bye, then . . . ' but she sighs and fixes her gaze on him. The sun picks out the warm honey highlights in her dark hair. She looks healthy. Vibrant. 'I've missed you,' she says, letting a sliver of the sadness he sensed earlier seep through her glossy facade.

He's not quite sure how to respond. He doesn't echo her words back together, but he wants to say something. 'It's been good to see you again.'

She nods, biting her lip slightly, and he can tell she's understood the almost invisible boundary he's set down. She smiles, waves, and heads back to her car and he watches her go. It's only when her BMW sports car has disappeared through the gate and away up the country lane that he admits to himself that he misses her too.

DIAMONDS

Gemstones that have been treasured since early history, which have the highest hardness and thermal conductivity of any natural material. Colourless in pure form, only a few types of impurity can contaminate them, often causing colour changes. One example, perhaps, where the presence of tiny defects makes an item both more beautiful and more desirable.

CHAPTER TWELVE

JESS

Waking up is like slowly floating to the surface from the bottom of a deep, deep ocean. I gradually become aware of my surroundings – the duvet, pleasingly heavy and squashy on top of me, the air cool on the arm that's flung above my head. Even through my eyelids, I can tell it's light outside. I exhale and stretch, my right arm reaching across the sheet, but I find the other side of the bed empty.

I frown, too sleepy to crack my eyelids open. And then I remember.

Luke.

Walking out the door.

Maybe walking out of our life together.

I squeeze my eyelids closed and curl into a ball. No. I am not awake. This is not real. I will slide back into unconsciousness, where it all hasn't happened. I try and will myself to fall back into the dream I was just having where we were only just beginning.

But . . . Oh, wow. The dream.

It was so weird. I don't think I've ever had one that vivid.

Feeling slightly paranoid, I reach out and investigate the

bed again. I'm relieved to find smooth cotton under my palm instead of hard plaster and wallpaper. I'm definitely not in a single bed. But the sheet beside me is cool, and I spiral back into feeling sick. It's not much of a choice is it? Heartbroken in the present day or confused and bewildered, reliving bittersweet memories from my past. I'm not sure which is worse.

But it doesn't matter. I'm awake now, so my choice has been made for me.

I stretch, roll over, and sleepily part my eyelids, staring at the white ceiling above me. I lie there for a few minutes, just breathing, trying to work out what to do, where to go.

Where will he be?

At a hotel? Crashing at a friend's? He might not have wanted to worry his parents about us just yet.

But do I actually want to find him? As much as watching him walk away took all the breath from my body, now the shock of that moment is waning, I'm not as angry with him as I was yesterday. Being reminded of who we were when we were first together has robbed me of that. Crap. It's much easier to be furious with him than feeling this crushing sense of rejection, the weight of sadness sitting on my chest like a boulder.

But at least I can still be cross about him inviting Mum to our anniversary party. How could he do that? How could he spring that on me?

I get a flash of my mother's face before I turned and stalked away. I'd been studiously trying to avoid looking her in the eye, but it seems I noticed anyway. She looked stricken. Not pathetic, as I'd often seen her when she was in an alcohol-induced haze but devastated. Broken. By me and my refusal to even acknowledge her.

But there are reasons for that too. And she knows that.

I'm not sure what to do about Luke, but I do know that I need a cup of tea. I throw back the duvet, plant my feet on the floor and stand up. But that's when the earth seems to shift on its axis once again. Where I'm expecting to see a framed print of a Picasso line drawing on the wall in front of me, there's a door. My old dressing gown is hanging on one of the hooks, along with a whole host of scarves I'd forgotten I owned.

Wait. What . . . ?

It's not . . . I'm not . . . I'm not back at home. I'm somewhere else.

Again.

And I recognize this place.

I reach out and gingerly touch one of the scarves. The soft cotton seems real enough beneath my fingertips. But how can this be? Am I still dreaming?

I grab the dressing gown and put it on, knotting the sash as I exit the bedroom and walk down the hallway, hardly noticing how cold the floor is beneath my bare feet. As I approach the kitchen, I become aware of the steamy roar of a kettle just about to boil. I arrive at the threshold just in time to see Hannah throwing a teabag into a mug. She looks up as I stand in the doorway, open-mouthed.

'Want one?'

I nod. And then, before she can pull another mug from the cabinet, I rush over to her and fling my arms around her.

She laughs. 'Oh . . . okay!' And then her arms come around me and she's warm and solid and just . . . Han. She has no idea how pleased I am to see her. This is how we became friends, when we rented rooms in a house in Catford for a couple of years.

I straighten my arms, keeping my grip on her, so I can look at her face. Yes, it's definitely Hannah. But younger. She's wearing the nose stud she abandoned after she got married, and her skin is smoother, especially around her eyes and on her forehead.

'So, are you dropping by the party this evening or not?' Hannah asks as she breaks away from me and continues making a cup of tea for us both. All I can do is stare at her, watch her move.

'Party?'

'Don't tell me you've forgotten!'

'Of course I haven't forgotten!' I retort, not knowing why I feel the need to keep a certain level of pretence going. I also have no idea what kind of party it is. But if I'm going to a party, then Hannah is too. Han loves a party. 'What are you wearing?' I ask her. Hopefully, her answer will give me some clues as to how I should dress myself.

She gives me a knowing look as she pours boiling water into each mug. 'You have *totally* forgotten. Just as well you have me as your back-up memory!'

She's right. I'm very grateful for what's inside her brain right now. I intend to mine it for as much information as possible.

'I'm not going,' she says.

'You're not?'

Her forehead crinkles as she squeezes a teabag against the edge of my mug with a spoon. 'Your family have only met me once. Why would they invite me?'

Oh. It's a *family* party. I rack my brains. Whose anniversary, birthday, or engagement could it be?

'I was only asking because you weren't sure if you could fit it in before you went out for your big romantic meal with Luke.'

Inside my skull, I have the sensation of things dropping into place, areas of thought and memory connecting themselves. At first I have no idea what these inklings are, but then they come more sharply into focus. 'What year is it?'

Her eyes narrow in confusion.

'Just . . . humour me.'

'Exactly the same year it was when you went to bed last night – twenty-fifteen.'

What feels like a blast of hot air passes through my body as I process her answer. 2015. I blink, unable to think of anything else but those numbers for a few seconds, but then I add, 'And what date?'

She shakes her head, bemused but not pissed off, as she heads to the fridge to fetch the milk.

'Han . . . ? What date?'

When her face appears from around the fridge door, she looks more worried than anything else. 'Seriously, Jess. How much did you have last night? I'm started to get a bit worried. It's not like you to drink like that.'

I know, I know . . . But I can't tell Hannah the truth, can I? Firstly, she wouldn't believe me and, secondly, I'm not sure if I know what the truth is myself. I must look fairly pathetic, because she relents and answers me. 'May the fourteenth.'

Staring straight ahead, I pull out one of the chairs by the small square dining table and my backside meets it with a thump. I knew she was going to say that, but I also didn't know she was going to say it at the same time. *May the fourteenth. Exactly one year after the day I lived yesterday.* How is that possible? What is happening to me?

But now I know exactly what party I'm supposed to be going to. The twins' birthday is on the eighteenth, so their celebrations often fall around that date. Hannah is watching me as she leans against the counter, sipping her tea. 'Are you okay? Did you and Luke have a fight?'

I stare ahead, feeling hollow inside. 'Something like that.' And the last thing I want to do is go out with Luke this evening. Not just because he's planned the most stupidly romantic dinner and it would just be too soul-gutting to sit opposite him after all that's happened, but because I remember exactly what Luke did on this night in 2015 – he asked me to marry him.

*

I go to work at Dobson's because I don't know what else to do, but I hardly get anything done, partly because I'm struggling to remember what used to be routine tasks, but also because I can't stop checking my phone. I'm waiting for a call I remember getting this afternoon, but I can't recall the exact timing.

At 2.45 p.m. my phone lights up with my stepmother's name. Finally! I snatch it up. 'Hi Lola!'

I know what she's going to ask, but I can't interrupt her to let her know that, so I'm going to have to wait for her to spit it out.

'Jess! Praise Jesus you picked up. I know you often let it go to voicemail when you are at work.'

I usually would. I did last time, if I remember rightly. 'I'm glad I picked up too,' I tell her, and I am. I regret not getting closer to Lola and the girls over the years, but I always felt like the fifth wheel when I rocked up to their house and stayed over. They seemed such a perfect family unit on their own. Why would they ever need me to intrude upon it?

And the secrets kept a wall between us too, I realize now. Not my secrets, but Mum's. Maybe I should have told them how hard it was, how alone I felt, but I think I'd just unconsciously adopted my mother's proclivity for sweeping everything under the rug. Deny, deny, deny.

'With God's grace, you said you may be able to attend the girls' birthday party this afternoon?' Lola says hopefully.

'Of course!' Even though I'd been a bit irritated Dad and Lola had scheduled it the same day as my one-year anniversary with Luke the first time around. You would have thought a Thursday night would be safe, but I remember something about a teacher training day, meaning their school will be closed tomorrow. 'Wouldn't miss it.' Last time I'd dropped in as a duty visit and fled as soon as possible so I could go and get ready for my big romantic night with Luke. But this is my chance. This is my get-out.

'We have eight girls for a sleepover – the twins and three friends each – and before that we have pizza and cake, a karaoke session and then a movie to, hopefully, get them all settled before bedtime. My sister was going to help me with it, but she has come down with a stomach bug that has been going round her school.'

Lola's sister is a teacher, so that makes sense.

'I wondered . . .' she pauses, and it makes me sad that she's hesitating to ask for my help '. . . if you could be here to help when we serve the food? I think it's going to be . . . What does your father say? I think it's going to be "mayhem".'

'Eight seven-year-olds sounds like *a lot*,' I tell her. 'Why don't I just stay all the way through?'

'Oh, I cannot ask you to do that!'

'Sure you can. And, anyway, you're not asking, I'm offering.'

'But are you not celebrating your anniversary with Luke this evening?'

I take a breath. Now's my opportunity. 'Yes . . . but we'll have been together a year whether we eat a meal together tonight or not. It won't take anything away from it if we postpone until tomorrow.'

'No . . . No, Jess . . . Honestly. I do not want you to change your plans. There may be someone from church I can ask . . . '

There is. Was. Whatever tense we're supposed to be in, it doesn't matter. One of the ladies from her Bible study stepped in last time and they all had a whale of a time, adults included. But it doesn't suit my purposes to let that happen tonight.

'I'm sure. And don't feel bad. I'd love to share this moment with my sisters, and besides . . . ' I smile to myself as I prepare to roll out one of my husband's favourite phrases ' . . . family is family.'

Despite Lola's protests, I assure her I'll be there to help wrangle the seven-year-olds later, and before I put my phone down, I shoot off a text to Luke. I don't risk calling him. Too many conflicting emotions I don't want to feel might be triggered if I do that.

I just want to get through this bizarre dream – or whatever it is – with as little fuss as possible. If I'm going to take a break from my disaster of a life for a few days, then I'm going to do it properly. I'm going to take myself out of the situation that's causing me all this distress as much as possible. How can I even begin to work out how to go forward unless I do that? Besides, I don't want to feel sad or angry or hopeless or rejected. I don't want to feel anything at all.

> So sorry, I type. Family emergency. I need to help with the twins' birthday party this evening. Can we do dinner tomorrow instead?

And then I press 'send' and let out a huge sigh of relief.

CHAPTER THIRTEEN

JESS

'Constance . . . ? Do you think you could . . . um . . . stop bouncing on the sofa?' I ask, standing in the doorway of the spacious living room in my father's house.

My half-sister is quickly joined by her twin and, within nanoseconds, all eight girls are jumping up and down on Lola's new corner sofa and cushions go flying this way and that.

I think of the table in the dining room, where slices of pizza lay haphazardly on plates, hardly eaten. It was probably a mistake giving them the orange fizzy stuff that came free with the pizza delivery but it's too late to do anything about that now. Rookie mistake, I bet. If Lola hadn't had to shoot off and leave me in charge for half an hour, there's no way this would be happening, but it was as if, the moment the front door slammed behind her, they all turned feral.

I check the time on my phone. She's only been gone ten minutes. It feels like at least an hour. And I've been instructed to make sure the girls eat a bit of salad too. Fat chance. I couldn't even get them to finish their slices of pizza before they started jumping up from their seats and running about the house like tiny demons.

'Constance!' I yell, as my other half-sister climbs on one of her friend's shoulders. I heard someone dare her – Jamilla, I think. Or possibly Evie – to dive from there onto one of the two large beanbags the twins like to sprawl across while watching TV.

Constance just shoots me a winning smile and launches herself from the other girl's shoulders, then lands bottom-first on one of the beanbags. There is a horrible ripping sound and tiny polystyrene balls shoot out over the floor.

The other girls squeal in delight and, before I can stop them, they're taking it in turns to jump from the sofa onto the beanbag, spraying the filling out until it's snowing in my father's living room.

I battle my way through them and manage to grab hold of the loop on top of the beanbag and pull it off the floor. Charity tries to pull the bag away from me, but I've got a good grip and my anger is building. Small white balls dribble from the gash in the side of the beanbag, which is now twice the size it was a minute ago.

My phone rings. I don't want to answer it because I feel that these little minxes will take any opportunity if I'm distracted to continue their chaos. There are moans of disappointment as I turn and stride from the living room, through the hallway and up the stairs. The only place I can think to secure the beanbag is in the old-fashioned wardrobe in the spare room. I throw it inside, lock the door, then slip the key into the back pocket of my jeans and pull out my phone.

I'm hoping it's Lola telling me she's on her way back from the supermarket. One of the girls is allergic to nuts, but it seems that message got lost somewhere along the way and Lola had to shove the gorgeous custom-made cake she'd ordered back into its box and go in search of a contaminant-free alternative so the girls can have cake before their karaoke session.

The good news? It *is* my stepmother. The bad news? The first supermarket she went to didn't have any nut-free cakes left. They do them, but those slots on the shelf are empty, and she's going to have to try Waitrose, which is another ten minutes away.

My heart sinks. That means at least another half an hour on my own with these children and I'm not sure the house will be standing if Lola gets stuck in traffic and doesn't come back within that time. However, I pick myself up and race back downstairs, the girls have just finished setting up the remaining beanbag as their alternative trampoline and Charity is priming herself to leap from the sofa. I snatch it up as my sister becomes airborne and she lands on the rug instead, executing a perfect roll to bring herself back up to standing. She plants her hands on her hips and narrows her eyes. 'Hey!'

I don't get a chance to reply, because there's a knock at the door. I point a finger at the twins, each in turn, letting them know I am not finished with them, and dart into the hallway. Thank God. Maybe Lola found an allergy-free cake at Tesco after all!

But when I yank the door open, I am not prepared for who I see standing there. 'L-Luke!'

He grins at me.

'What are you doing here?'

He frowns but doesn't answer my question. 'Why are you holding a beanbag?'

I glance down at my hand and realize that, in my desperation, I must have dragged it up the hallway with me. I hope I didn't take out any of Lola's treasured ornaments along the way. 'Long story,' I mutter.

'I thought maybe if you couldn't come out to celebrate, we could at least spend the evening together. Maybe we can go out once it's finished.'

'I really—' A crash from the back of the house stops me from telling him I don't have the time for this. I drop the beanbag and sprint back down the hall into the dining room, hoping I'm not going to be met by the sight of blood when I get there.

Eight pairs of wide childish eyes greet me. All of them are standing as far away from an upturned plant pot as possible.

'Don't any of you move!' I warn them, but it falls on deaf ears. The girls start nudging each other and bouncing. They all start whispering and pointing fingers at each other. 'It was you!'

'No, it was you!'

They begin jumping around the room, giggling and pulling faces at each other. I'm just about to lose my rag completely when an unearthly hush falls upon the room. I turn to see what they're staring at and find Luke towering in the doorway and taking in the aftermath of the polystyrene blizzard.

'Luke!' the twins yell in unison.

They're about to race towards him, but he holds up his hand and says, very calmly, 'Stop.' To my surprise, every small body in the room freezes. He looks at them seriously.

'I'll deal with the casualty,' I say, nodding at the plant on the floor, 'if you can deal with the entertainment.'

He instantly spots the karaoke machine Lola hired. 'Let's move this into the dining room so you can clean up in peace.' Then he picks up the machine and heads into the other room. 'Who knows how to get this thing going?' he asks the girls as they trail after him.

I vacuum the living room floor three times over to make sure

I get every last possible bit of beanbag and return the peace lily to its pot. By the time I've put the vacuum cleaner away in the understairs cupboard, the strains of 'Shake It Off' by Taylor Swift are blaring from the dining room. When I go to check on my charges, Charity and Constance are fighting over who's going to hold the microphone, and the other six girls are bouncing up and down trying to out-sing them.

I watch Luke as he deftly manages to avoid fights about who goes next and what songs they are going to sing. There's an easiness in his manner that I envy. But what I envy even more is the effortless sense of teamwork between this Luke and this Jess. It's as easy as breathing for them. No wonder that, eleven years in the future, the older versions of us are suffocating without it.

★

It's absolute chaos for the next hour. I get a couple of frantic texts from Lola, saying that she'll be back as soon as possible but traffic is bad around the one-way system. The girls get fed up with karaoke, so in my desperation, I suggest makeovers. I realize as soon as the words are out of my mouth that it's a bad idea. Lola's not too keen on the girls wearing make-up and has always vetoed the idea before, but now I've said it, I can't go back on it – they're all leaping around shouting out which colour nail varnish they want.

Thankfully, the guest bedroom here is also still unofficially my bedroom, and I have some a basic make-up kit stashed here for emergencies. I rush upstairs to fetch it while Luke turns a chair around from the dining table for our first willing victim – I mean, subject – to sit on.

'Right,' says Luke, as soon as I've returned with my cosmetics bag. 'Get in line!' He looks at me. 'I'll do hair; you can do make-up.'

Hair? I wasn't planning on doing hair as well! But now Luke has said it, it's going to be hard to come back from. Why didn't he ask me first? And then I sigh inwardly. Because I know exactly why Luke didn't ask me first. Being the oldest of five, and also the one his whole family seems to rely on for both practical and emotional support, he's used to making decisions fast and putting things into practice without much input from anyone else. I'm just as independent, but for different reasons, and it's a constant reason why we butt heads.

It's just like the situation with my mum on the night of our anniversary party. He just doesn't stop to think anyone else might have some useful input or, at times, a valid but alternative point of view. I'd let myself get all fired up about that again, but I don't have the luxury. We have eight fidgety girls to entertain.

'How are you going to do hair?' I ask him as he grabs another chair and puts it next to the first.

He grins and gives me a superior look. 'Used to do Cassie's hair all the time when I was younger. Piece of cake.'

Yeah. That's what he thinks. While Cassie, his oldest sibling and only girl in the family, can be a bit full on, I doubt she presented the same challenge as a gaggle of seven-year-olds hyped up on sugar. And then there's the fact that the twins have tight ringlets, a hair texture he has absolutely no experience with. He's in for a rude awakening.

'I think maybe *I* should do hair and you should do make-up,' I counter.

'Oh, ye of little faith . . . But I think we're better off doing it my way.' He nods at the make-up bag. 'I have absolutely zero experience with that stuff.'

An idea sneaks into my mind. I press my lips together to prevent myself from smirking and turn to the girls lined up beside the two chairs. 'Would you like to help Luke out?'

'How?' Charity says.

'Maybe . . . If Luke hasn't got much experience of wearing make-up, we should give *him* the makeover!'

The girls squeal their enthusiasm for this idea at such a pitch that I'm sure my ears are bleeding.

By the time Lola's key turns in the front door and she arrives panting, with a large supermarket carrier bag full of what I presume is a cake, Luke is colourful and sparkly and glorious. He's wearing a unicorn headband, and at least twenty glittery hair clips are jammed into his hair. Lola takes one look at his clown-like make-up, lets out a scream and drops one of her shopping bags.

'They got a bit bored,' I offer by way of explanation.

She picks up the bag at her feet. 'If beauty was a crime, you would be a free man,' she says with a glint in her eye.

Luke sighs. 'I'm guessing it would be a bad idea to look in the mirror?'

Lola chuckles and turns towards the kitchen. 'I will relieve you from your torture shortly. Please, give me a few moments to get this cake ready.'

Lola makes good on her word. Within five minutes she's flicking off the lights in the dining room and eight pairs of eyes grow wide as she walks towards them, cake resplendent with lit candles, and both her daughters rush to the table, getting ready to make their birthday wishes.

Once the cake is cut and the girls are busy demolishing their slices, she turns to Luke and me and makes a shooing motion. 'Go! Be free! I have it from here.'

I try to protest. I know just how difficult it is dealing with that lot single-handed, but Lola stops me. 'You have been a blessing to me today. And you . . . ' She pauses to smile indulgently at my boyfriend, and then gives him a kiss on the cheek, which makes him blush. 'You are an angel. Go celebrate your anniversary and let me deal with these children.'

We retreat to the far end of the kitchen. 'It's not late,' Luke says to me.

I check the time on the digital clock on the oven. It's only just past eight.

'Do you want to go out for a drink, grab a bite to eat?'

I shake my head. 'It's a lovely idea, but I'm just . . . ' I catch my reflection in the glossy black oven door. 'I look like the Wicked Witch of the West!' Although Luke looks as if he's been mauled by a pack of fairies, I'm not looking much better myself. My hair is a mess and I'm hot and sticky. Who knew chasing eight small girls around could be such an effective workout?

He steps towards me, brushes a strand of tangled hair out of my face and kisses the tip of my nose. 'You look beautiful.'

He's making it very hard to say no, but what I want more than anything is some elite snacks and a good book. 'Do you mind if we don't go out tonight?'

Instead of looking disappointed, Luke's smile brightens. 'I was hoping you'd say that.'

CHAPTER FOURTEEN

JESS

'I know you're the organized one in our relationship, but I have a Plan B all set up and ready to go.'

Luke opens the fridge door and pulls out a bottle of proper champagne, then also a series of trays and packets. A closer look tells me they're canapés and party bites, but more of the adult gourmet kind than the sugar and sprinkles kind in the dining room next door. I vaguely remember that he was carrying a bag when I answered the door to him, but I had no idea he'd stashed all of this in the fridge. He must have done it when I was busy getting ready to do the makeovers that never happened.

I don't know what it is, but I can't resist anything that comes in a bite-size morsel. I would eat just about anything if you presented it to me as a canapé. And the fact that Luke has remembered this and been resourceful enough to go out and buy some of my favourites — duck spring rolls, tempura prawns, tiny Yorkshire puddings with a sliver of roast beef and a smear of horseradish — is eroding my decision to keep my distance from him.

While our feast is heating up, he pours us each a glass of champagne and leads me out onto the large deck at the back of the house. We stand at the railing, overlooking the neatly tended garden. His hand goes up to his hair and he gently presses a clip so he can take it out. There is a muffled 'No!' from somewhere behind us and we both spin round to see at least five small faces pressed against the French doors.

'You can't take it out!' Constance mouths, looking almost desperate.

Luke shrugs and his hand drops to his side. The girls begin to cheer but then Lola catches them, shoos them away, and then with an apologetic smile, draws the curtains.

'I couldn't have done what you did back there,' I tell him.

He frowns. 'What? Put things in the oven?'

I laugh and punch him gently on the arm. 'No . . . I mean letting those monsters loose on me with lipstick and hair accessories.'

He chuckles softly. 'I know. You would have hated sitting there with them all touching you at once, not knowing what you looked like.'

'But it didn't bother you.'

'People are different.'

I study him carefully. 'Yes, we are.'

And I'm so used to seeing the differences between my husband and myself as frustrations that I've forgotten how marvellous they can be. I could never be that patient. But Luke . . . ? It didn't faze him. *Nothing* seems to faze him.

But then I have a memory of a door slamming, the look of dejection, anger and pain on his face before he walked out of the house on a day exactly eleven years from now, and I know that's not true. There's one thing that rattles Luke to the core. Me.

'But I like our differences,' he says, smiling softly. 'I think people are like jigsaw pieces . . . If we were all the same, if we were all squares instead of nobly asymmetrical shapes, life would be boring. And we wouldn't connect. Straight edges just slide past each other – nothing there to help them grip onto each other. It's the differences, the uneven edges, that not only make us interesting, but also lock us together.'

I don't think I've ever heard Luke say something so profound. The intensity in his eyes as he waits for a response makes me drop my gaze to my glass and shift uncomfortably.

He moves closer, places in arm around my waist and pulls me to him. Unsure of what emotion to feel, I shift my focus to his chest. 'A whole year since I first saw you standing on your own in that bar . . . ' he whispers in my ear.

He said 'bar' instead of 'restaurant', which gives me another clue as to how this strange universe I'm inhabiting works. It's clear what I did last year . . . yesterday . . . has become our history, rather than what I originally remember happening. I wonder what that means?

'Do you think about what the next year might hold for us?' he asks, and I detect a hint of nervousness in his tone.

I swallow. I don't know how to answer. Yes, if this was my normal life, I would be thinking about that. We clicked together so fast, so hard, it would be weird not to. But I don't want to think about that tonight. It's too sad.

Even though our past has changed, it seems our future is less easy to direct. I tried my hardest to avoid him today, but here we are, together on the anniversary of the day we first met. Just as we were on May the fourteenth one year ago. Fate has us locked in its grip, and it seems reluctant to let us go.

But I suppose I have changed one thing. Last time Luke

proposed to me, it was very romantic. He booked a table at *Rive Gauche* again. Or at least, I thought the table was in the restaurant, but when we arrived, Luke led me upstairs to the roof garden. Every table was empty bar one in the centre. It turned out he'd booked the whole rooftop out just for us, and then, just as dessert was being served, he got all nervous, and moments later, the words 'Marry me?' were spelled out in tiny fairy lights along the wall beside us and he got down on one knee. Tonight couldn't be more different.

Some of the tension eases out of my shoulders and neck. He's still wearing the wonky purple and blue eyeshadow the girls put on him and a smear of pale-pink lipstick that hasn't been rubbed off by sipping champagne beside his mouth. He'll save his big romantic gesture for a day when he's not covered in glitter and plastic hair clips. I feel a pang of sadness when I think of the rooftop bar, all booked out but standing empty, the fairy lights unlit, but I'm also relieved that, tonight, I'm safe.

We eat our canapé picnic undisturbed. Lola had planned a movie for the girls and it's not hard to guess they're all glued to *Frozen*, because the muffled voices singing along to 'Let It Go' are just about audible out here on the deck. I look at the drawn curtains over the French windows and sigh.

'What are you thinking about?' Luke asks me.

We've been chatting easily, probably because I've been able to relax more, knowing the rest of our future isn't going to be decided tonight. The champagne has also helped me let my guard down. My automatic response to this question – from anyone, not just Luke – is to bat it away and be vague, to say I was just daydreaming, but I find my actual thoughts spilling out of my mouth instead. 'They're so lucky.'

'Who? The girls?'

I nod, looking wistfully at the house. 'I always wanted a birthday party like this, but I never got one.'

'You didn't?'

Luke sounds so shocked that I turn to look at him. I can't believe I've never told him this detail about my childhood before, but maybe I haven't. I prefer not to talk about it. 'No.'

He frowns. 'But what in particular? The cake? The karaoke? The movie?'

'All of it.' He doesn't press, just waits. And I know it would be okay if I didn't say anything more. 'Dad is great with the twins, but he went AWOL for a while after he and Mum split up. I don't blame him, really. She was angry, devastated he'd left her for someone else, and she wasn't afraid to let him know it. But I don't blame her, either. She had every right to be hurt about what he did. But that's . . . ' I pause, not quite ready to say the words.

'That's . . . ?' Luke prompts softly.

I look down at the top of the beech garden table. 'That's when she started drinking too much.'

There. I've said it. Luke was the first person I admitted this too, although I didn't manage to spill the beans until our honeymoon last time. I kind of had to, after what happened at the wedding. But maybe because in my real life, he already knows all this and has done for years, it's easier to get over the mental barrier and reveal the truth.

I risk a quick glance at Luke. It's hard not to smile. His face is so serious, but I can't help noticing the glittery hair clips. 'I knew there was something going on between you and your mum,' he says. 'I just didn't know what.'

I nod. 'At the time, I just thought she didn't care enough. But the truth was that Mum couldn't cope. With anything, let alone arranging more than a card and a present for a birthday. At least she did that. But I was always getting invited to interesting activities or big parties that other parents threw for their kids. I loved going along, but there was always this ache in my heart behind my smile. So, yes, the girls are lucky – for having a mum and dad who put the effort in this way.'

'Are you angry your dad didn't do more for you after the divorce?'

I sigh. 'Strangely enough, no. Now, I can see he was going through some kind of mid-life crisis. Thankfully, Lola came along and straightened him out. Back then, even though he'd left, I kind of hero-worshipped him, probably because I was just desperate for any kind of attention he'd give me.'

It takes a moment, but I have a revelation about my relationship with my parents. 'I probably wasn't very fair to my mum during those years. I blamed her, even though I didn't know the details of what had gone on between them. That probably hasn't helped how our relationship ended up. I was already angry with her for being physically in the house but never truly emotionally present. I think I just heaped all that birthday disappointment onto her pile as well, instead of dishing it out evenly between my parents.'

'You know it wasn't anything to do with you, don't you?'

I try to speak but it feels as if my throat has swollen shut. My eyes blur.

Luke stands up, takes my hand and pulls me up to meet him. 'Jessica Boyd, you are worth celebrating. I just want you to know that.'

His words get me straight in my heart, like they always used to. And the reason I married him was because it wasn't just words; Luke always backed up his declarations with actions. At least, he used to.

He reaches up and bends one of the clips in his hair so it opens, then pulls it out. I hold my hand out so he can place it there, and then I help him remove the rest. I also take the pack of make-up wipes out of my back pocket and slowly wipe the blue and purple eyeshadow and the pale-pink lipstick off his lips. All the while he stares at me. Not in a creepy way, but in a Luke way. Like he's just enjoying looking at me, and it wouldn't matter what I looked like or what I was doing, he would always look at me that way.

When I finish, he takes the clips and wipes from me and puts them on the table, then says, 'That must have been hard to tell me – about your mum . . . her drinking.'

I swallow, and then my chin bobs up and down, just once.

He places a hand either side of my face and looks into my eyes. 'You don't know how much it means to me that you trusted me enough to tell me that.'

'Really?' My voice is strangely hoarse. I never saw this information as anything but a burden.

'Really. I know it's hard for you to open up.'

I feel a pressure behind my eyeballs as tears build.

Luke kisses my forehead and then my lips, so tenderly, as if I'm fragile . . . no, not fragile. Precious. 'I live for the moments that you let me glimpse what's behind all those shields,' he tells me. 'And I don't mind that it doesn't happen very often; as long as it happens sometimes, that I get to see the real you.'

My knees lose stability, as if someone has just tried to whack my legs from under me with a big stick. I'm not sure if I'm enchanted by his words or haunted by the knowledge that, after ten years of marriage, he's seen as much of the 'real' Jessica as he's likely to, and it turns out he doesn't like that woman very much.

I let out a shaky chuckle. 'Be careful what you wish for.'

He doesn't laugh along with me. Instead, I see sadness gather in his eyes. He sighs. 'I wish I could make you see yourself the way I see you, Jess. You don't see it, but when you let yourself, you shine.'

He falls silent. I try and process his words, but I can't. Shine. What does that mean? All I can think is that he sees me like a bare light bulb – functional and, yes, maybe not unattractive, but if you stare at it for too long, it'll hurt your eyes.

Luke looks as if he's trying to make up his mind about something, then he shakes his head, as if he can't quite believe what he's thinking. 'Stuff it . . . I had this whole thing planned, but I . . . I don't want to wait. I *can't* wait. And I always said today was our lucky day.'

'Luke . . .'

He's in full flow now, not listening to the warning tone of my voice. 'I want to see you shine more . . . every day. For the rest of our lives.' He reaches into his pocket and pulls out a ring box, quickly flipping the lid open as he drops to one knee. 'Jess . . . Will you marry me?'

My heart goes into free fall. I don't know what to say. I don't know where to look, so I focus on his great-great-grandmother's engagement ring.

Putting it on my finger, closing my eyes and wishing that somehow I could undo everything that had happened, was the last sensible thing I remember before I got catapulted out of my normal life and into this sideshow of an existence. I want to grab it out of its velvet cushion. Maybe I could get its magic to work again and it can take me back to where and when I'm supposed to be?

My fingers twitch, but I stop myself from reaching out and touching it.

'You can choose something else you like better if you want to,' he tells me, studying my face earnestly.

Last time I did just that. It's not that I didn't think it was beautiful, with its tiny emeralds entwined between the diamond leaves. But nobody had ever bought me an expensive piece of jewellery. Nobody ever went out shopping and thought about who I was, then chose something that represented me completely. I'd wanted that so badly. Not a ring that was picked for a woman generations ago that I didn't even know.

At the time, the ring seemed impersonal to me. Disconnected. But looking at it now, I realize I missed the true significance of what Luke had been trying to tell me by offering it to me.

Cringing as I think of it, I recall how I asked if we could get something different, and we'd ended up visiting a jeweller's the following weekend. I chose a square-cut diamond solitaire in white gold with tiny diamonds in the shoulders. At the time, I took Luke at his word, believed him when he said he didn't mind, but now I get the oddest feeling he was just telling me what I wanted to hear.

But I suppose I wasn't entirely honest with him either. Not long before Luke proposed, we went to Sunday lunch at his parents' house, and his dad mentioned the ring. Afterwards, I realized it probably wasn't a coincidence the subject had come up; Luke must have asked his parents for the ring if he knew he was going to propose.

Anyway, Ed told the story of how his mum and dad had a massive argument on their honeymoon because the ring had been a little too loose for his mum's fingers and when they'd gone swimming on a beach in Torquay, it had slipped off. They'd spent hours looking for it before the tide had come in and they'd had to go back to the guesthouse they were staying at empty-handed.

Grandpa Harris was angry she'd lost the ring and upset because it was a reminder of his mother, things had got heated and, by all accounts, he'd been talking about ending it all (although there are varying opinions within the family as to how serious he was about this or whether he was just having one of his much-reported tantrums).

Luke's gran had run from the hotel, crying, and sat on the beach until the sun started coming up. By that point, the tide had been retreating and she stopped to look in a rock pool and there, glinting atop a waving thatch of emerald seaweed, was the ring. It went straight back on her hand and she never took it off again. They were married for fifty-six years after that and she was utterly convinced it saved her marriage.

So, to be honest, when Luke pulled the ring out and proposed with it, I freaked out. All those stories of happy marriages and once-in-a-lifetime love stories . . . ? It seemed like an awful lot to live up to. While the Harrises might be good at those things, my family's track record was a little more . . . patchy.

Feeling panic rising inside of me, I'd reasoned that maybe it was better if the ring went to someone else, because it was very likely I'd be the first bride to wear it who would spoil the streak. I didn't want to curse our future together. I loved Luke so much that I didn't want to take that chance.

I place my palm on his chest. His heart is beating like a hummingbird's.

'I do love you, Luke, I really do . . . ' My voice is thick with tears. I'm telling the truth. As much as I hate him right now, I also love him. I've *always* loved him.

'Are you saying no?' he whispers.

I shake my head, moving my forehead gently against his. 'I'm not saying no.'

But I also don't know if I can bring myself to say yes. Even though I'm feeling all the things I felt the first time he asked me, there's also a new slice in my heart that just won't heal.

'The truth is, I don't know . . . We haven't been together that long. Are we rushing into things? Do you honestly think we're ready?'

He stares back at me, confusion etched all over his features. '*I* am.'

I know he's telling the truth. But I also know I have a unique advantage here. Two nights ago, this Luke was probably in the throes of planning his big romantic proposal. This Luke and Jess were besotted with each other and finding it painful to be apart. But two nights ago, I watched the man I love more than anything else in this universe give up on me. As honest and earnest as he's being right now, I can't let go of that.

'I'm not saying no, but I am saying "not right now". I'm sorry I can't give you another answer, I truly am.' And then I start to cry. For him. For me. For this whole stupid mess.

Luke puts his arms around my shoulders and waits a few seconds, silently asking me for permission, then pulls me close again. 'It's okay,' he says into my hair. But I can tell that he's quietly devastated by my answer and that only makes me cry harder. 'You're right. It's only been a year,' he adds, his voice having gained a rough edge. 'I know that I love you and you love me—' I nod against his chest as he says this '—and that's all that matters for now.'

He presses his lips to mine in a kiss that is rich with pain and emotion.

'It's okay,' he says, but I'm not sure which of us he's soothing. 'We'll just take it one day at a time.'

One day at a time. If only he knew.

I have no other choice at this moment.

CHAPTER FIFTEEN

LUKE

Ten Months Before the Anniversary Party

He stares at the notification on his phone. It's a short message and he can read most, if not all of it, without opening it up.

Hey. Just checking in.

It arrived a few minutes ago, an innocent message from a friend. There's no reason for the soft flush through his body as he hears someone walk up behind him and he turns his phone over so the notification is not visible.

'Sorry to disturb you,' Hannah says. 'What do you want to do about the Boston Road invoice? I've nudged them twice now and they're ghosting me.'

She's been working for Harris & Sons doing basic office admin for a while now, and he's glad that what was intended to be a lifeline for her when her ex left her high and dry with bills to pay has turned into something more permanent. Hannah is punctual and efficient and the clients love her.

He always feels a bit scruffy around her at work, though, unless he's off to an important meeting and has to wear a suit. She dresses as if she's at a high-flying firm in the City, all high heels and fitted dresses but, hey, each to their own. Not the most practical attire for a local building firm, nor he imagines, the most comfortable, but it's none of his business. Besides, it's great to see Hannah feeling good about herself after the mess of her divorce.

'Leave it with me,' he replies. 'I'll see if I can chase them down.'

She smiles, gives him a wink. 'My hero. Thanks!' she says, then turns to go back to her desk in the outer office.

'Does hero status get a bloke a cup of tea around this place?' he calls after her.

'Nice try!' she yells back and laughs as she disappears through the door.

He chuckles to himself, too. Well, it was worth a shot. And it's not as if he doesn't know how to operate a kettle.

He pulls the office phone towards him and punches in the number for the clients renovating the Boston Road house. Hannah is too nice sometimes. A call from the boss might be what's needed. While he's aware they were having cash flow issues, refusing to communicate is not an option.

Five minutes later, he's just finished working out a payment plan when a mug of tea arrives on the desk next to him. Hannah pushes it a little closer, careful not to spill any on the paperwork nearby.

'Thanks!' he mouths, as he listens to the promises pouring from the other end of the line. She gives him a one-shouldered shrug accompanied by a smile and disappears again. When he's finally ended the call, he yells, 'You're an angel!' through the open door.

'I know,' she yells back. 'Don't you forget that next time I'm due a pay rise!'

He laughs again, shaking his head and then his gaze lands on the mobile phone facedown on the desk. He could say all sorts of things in reply. *Hi! Nice to hear from you!* Or *Doing good. How about you?* All very friendly, non-committal responses that would be perfectly acceptable. So why is he hesitating? If anyone picked up his phone and looked through the thread, they would see it's completely harmless.

Which it is. Elena is a friend. He has nothing to feel guilty about. Nothing at all.

He picks up his phone and starts tapping. **Hey. How's things?**

GOLD

The most malleable of all metals, yet it can be drawn into a wire the width of a single atom and stretched considerably before it breaks.

CHAPTER SIXTEEN

JESS

I thought saying 'no' to Luke when he proposed might change the future, or at the very least delay things a bit, but, no, here I am, having woken up exactly 365 days later, standing in a wedding dress at the entrance to St Michael's church in Bromley.

This is cruel. Whatever is happening to me is cruel.

I know I can be tough on myself, that sometimes I beat myself up if I haven't been the perfect daughter or the perfect wife or work colleague, but if this is my brain playing tricks on me, it's taking it to new depths of self-hatred.

Luke's stupid 'lucky day'! Why, when he insisted we might as well not jinx it, that we should get married on May the fourteenth as well, did I not tell him to take a running jump?

I stare down at my left hand. I was hoping that maybe I'd have Great-Great-Grannie's ring, that I could borrow some of its luck, but my old diamond solitaire is sitting on my ring finger. Everything is exactly the same as it was last time. It seems there's no fighting it.

So, I put my wedding dress on this morning, allowed my hair and make-up to be done, and now I'm standing next to my dad, staring at a pair of closed doors that lead to the aisle of the local church. I glance behind me to see Hannah, my maid of honour, trying to keep my two overexcited half-sisters in check. They're all wearing gorgeous deep emerald dresses – Hannah in a floor-length bias-cut dress that makes the most of her slender figure and the twins are in dresses that stop just above their ankles with large bows at the back.

I turn around and take a deep breath. I don't know what to do.

I don't want to say 'yes' or 'I do' or whatever it is that will bind me to Luke for forever. I'm just not ready. But how do I stop this? My window for escaping this future is narrow and ever shrinking.

Music begins to play. The double doors open, and my father clenches his jaw and looks straight ahead. We begin to move under his impetus, his arm dragging slightly against mine.

I want to shout, 'Stop! Wait a minute!'. The urge to turn and run is so strong. I'm just about to unhitch my arm from my father's as Luke turns his head to watch me coming down the aisle.

Instantly, I'm in trouble. His expression holds both everything I want to see and everything I dread. Against my permission, my heart skips inside my ribcage and I flush with warmth. Even though a small muscle twitches in his jaw, I can see the love and hope in his eyes. He looks at me as if I am everything he needs. Nothing more, nothing less.

My throat thickens. He used to look at me that way all the time, but I realize that, back in my normal life, I haven't seen that look for months. Possibly longer.

A memory of Luke sitting across the kitchen table from me

comes into focus in my mind. We'd been discussing something, although I can't recall exactly what, and I realized I'd been doing all the talking for at least ten minutes. When I glanced at him, he was staring out the French doors into the garden. At the time, I'd got angry, thinking he wasn't listening to me, but now I feel a sudden pang as I realize there is another interpretation for that moment.

And I'd seen the same expression on his face a handful of times before our big argument on our tenth anniversary; I just hadn't registered there was a pattern.

It was me . . . I was the one who hadn't been paying attention.

Comparing how he looked then to how he looks today, I realize all the light had drained out of his eyes. Had all the love, too? I really don't know. All I know is that, in that moment, my husband looked . . . sad. As if he'd given up.

I'm only a handful of steps away from the front of the room and in a few short seconds, I'll be standing next to my groom. There's only one way to stop this now. I have to say, 'I don't' instead of 'I do'. I have to tell the minister I know a reason why we shouldn't be married when he asks.

My father and I come to a halt. He smiles at Luke and peels off to the left. Robotically, I turn and hand my bouquet to Hannah before she shepherds the twins onto the front pew and I catch a glimpse of the people crammed into the church – our families, our friends – all looking either happy or wistful or tearful, and then I turn back to face Luke.

If I pull the plug now, I do it in front of all of them.

A shiver reverberates through me. I meet Luke's gaze as the rest of the congregation sits down and the minister starts his speech about love and marriage.

How can I publicly humiliate him in front of all his friends and family? The simple answer is, I can't. I don't have it in me. So, when the minister asks me to say my vows, words of faith and love and devotion spill out of my mouth. When Luke is told he can kiss his bride, tears spill down my face.

The women in the room make sympathetic noises as I dab my eyes, because they think these are happy tears, but I know the truth. I also know this isn't the first difficult moment this day will hold.

★

I should be at the top table at my wedding reception, blissfully in love and cherishing every moment of my special day. Instead, I am in the ladies' loos of the Lubbock Hotel in Chislehurst trying to find my mother.

It doesn't take long, due to the loud watery sobs coming from the stall at the far end of the row. I knock on the door softly, find it unlocked, and nudge it open.

'Mum . . . ?'

She's sitting on the closed toilet lid, head buried in her hands, body juddering, and so caught up in her distress that I don't think she's even heard me. It's clear that she managed to snaffle quite a few of the introductory glasses of fizz at the welcome reception. Exactly like last time. Which is why I'm hunting her out rather than attempting to enjoy the meal. The first time I lived this day, it went steadily south as the day wore on, so I'm going to do my best to change that. Even though, as part of this strange experience I'm having, I can only seem to alter minor things about my life, *anything* has to be better than what happened last time.

I gently lay a hand on her shoulder, and she jumps. When she sees it's me, she leaps up and throws her arms around me and cries into my shoulder. I instinctively pull her close, as I have some many times before when she's been in this state, but I can't lie, I'm also a bit worried about her getting snot on my wedding dress.

'It's just s-so . . . hard!' she sobs into my shoulder. 'Seeing him . . . and with *her*.'

'I know,' I say calmly, because I don't know what else I can say. Mum always gets like this at family functions when she and Dad are going to be present. I don't understand it. They've been apart for sixteen years at this point, yet she can't seem to move on.

'H-he didn't even say hello to me,' she hiccups, lifting her head to look at me with bleary eyes. 'It's because of that bitch of a wife of his!'

'No, Mum . . . It really isn't.' Lola just hasn't got time for Mum's drama. She's always civil, if somewhat distant, with her predecessor. And I can't blame her.

'Don't you take her side!' she yells, letting go of me, then stepping back, stumbling because she's forgotten the toilet is in her way and steadying herself on the cubicle partition. 'You always do that! You always take your father's side! Never mine . . . ' And with that, she pushes past me and weaves her way out of the ladies, using the wall for support.

I stare after her, but I don't argue back. There's no point. She only remembers what she wants to remember, the things that line up with her feelings to justify them. And, of course, she doesn't recall all the times I've been there for her, helping her get into bed or making excuses for her to friends, family, even her boss. I shake my head.

It's always someone else's fault, isn't it? Never anything to do with the fact you create chaos wherever you go. That has nothing to do with why my father prefers not to interact with you unless strictly necessary.

Last time, I ran after her, comforted her. It didn't do me any good. So, this time I'm just going to leave her to it. Besides, I think I have a plan to stop her having her 'outburst' later, and it's probably a better idea to concentrate on that.

CHAPTER SEVENTEEN

JESS

I have to return to the top table to eat my main course, but I hardly taste anything, and once the last bite is finished, I make my excuses and weave my way through the function room, on my way 'borrowing' a floral arrangement from a table at the back of the room, populated mostly by kids and Luke's great-aunt Jane. She gives me a quizzical look as I remove the centrepiece, but I just smile brightly at her and disappear out the doors of the function room into the hallway. I hide myself away in an alcove near the hotel reception and stare at my ill-gotten gains.

Last time I got married to Luke, my mother caused a horrible scene, and it all started with the speeches, which are going to happen in less than half an hour. I'm hoping that if I can change what happens when Luke gives his speech, I can avoid the chain reaction of events that followed.

I should've thought about it the first time around, but I'd just been so happy in my bubble of bliss running up to my wedding day, that it hadn't even occurred to me that Mum might take offence at the gifts given out by Luke and me to people who had helped with our wedding.

Obviously, each of the bridesmaids got a gift. Luke's mum is an incredible baker and made the three-tier wedding cake for us, saving us a fortune, and Lola had made the twins' bridesmaids dresses herself after I couldn't find children's dresses to match the one Hannah had fallen in love with, so Luke and I arranged for flowers to be given to them both.

By that point in the day, Mum had been pretty drunk, even though I'd implored her to try and keep it under control, and she started making passive-aggressive comments about being invisible, because she must be, mustn't she, if she'd been overlooked?

I'd witnessed it all with the sinking feeling in my stomach. However, the truth was that Mum hadn't contributed anything in terms of finance or time in the planning of the wedding. I asked her if she wanted to go wedding dress shopping with me and Hannah, and she seemed excited at the time, but when the day came she'd had a raging hangover and cried off. There were a few other occasions I asked for her help, and she flaked out on me, so in the end I just stopped trying. I hadn't thought about getting her a gift because, honestly, there was nothing to thank her for but disappointment.

And even though it still seems unfair to me in this version of our wedding day, I'd rather be the bigger person and give her a gift, than endure the whole fiasco again. At first, I'd been relieved when she got up and stomped away from the top table, causing a bit of a stir, but about twenty minutes later, there was a commotion outside.

The Lubbock is a converted Georgian manor house with a wide paved terrace. I picked up the skirts of my wedding dress and hurried outside, followed by almost all of the wedding party, and a good number of the guests, to find my mother standing on the thick stone railing, facing the sloping gardens, rambling on about something. Somehow, she had yet another glass of champagne in her hand, even though I'd asked the waiters to cut her off.

As I drew closer, her slurred words became clearer.

'No one cares about me, anyway . . . ' she was saying to no one in particular, champagne sloshing out of her glass as she gestured to the night sky. 'Everyone would be happy if I just went away . . . disappeared. I might as well just . . . ' She made a motion, as if to launch herself off the railing into the darkness, and stumbled, causing the assembled crowd to gasp, before regaining her balance.

This was part of Mum's repertoire: play the victim, say the world would be better off without her. I realized years ago that she wasn't serious when she said things like this. It's all designed to make people feel sorry for her. However, there was a fifteen-foot drop to the lawn below and, while it might not kill her, she could end up with a few bruises, and possibly even broken bones.

Someone else at the reception had obviously been worried, because shortly afterwards there were sirens and blue flashing lights and two police cars sped up the driveway. She got down eventually when my dad stepped in and offered his hand, told her firmly but kindly it was time to go home. One of Luke's cousins drove her back and made sure she got into bed.

Everyone tried to get back to enjoying the party after that, but it all felt awkward and strained. I fixed a smile on my face but inside I was dying of shame. What must Luke's family have thought he was marrying into? And I knew that when people discussed the wedding in the coming weeks, it wasn't the lovely ceremony and reception we'd planned, or how happy Luke and I seemed together, that they'd been talking about.

Did you hear what the mother of the bride did? You'll never guess . . . ?

My plan is to make a similar floral arrangement to the ones I am giving the other mothers, so I've got one to give one to my mum as well. My floristry skills are limited but I'm going to do my best. I've been eying up the table centrepieces since we sat down to eat our meal, and I *think* I can use the one I nabbed from table eleven as a starting point. The flowers are similar colours, but it's a bit smaller than the ones I've got for Lola and Diane, so I need to find a way to pad it out.

I'd rope Luke into helping me because, being good with his hands, he's surprisingly good at flower arranging. I asked him about it once, and he said it was because when Diane was being treated for cancer when he was in his teens, he had to pick up doing some of the household tasks and looking after his younger siblings. Back in those days, hospitals were less fussy about flowers, and even if people didn't bring them to the hospital, they sometimes arrived at the house, and he didn't want his mum to have one more thing to do when she was so exhausted, so he taught himself how to do it.

However, I also think it's a hangover from those days that Luke can have very fixed ideas on how things should be done, and I suspect he would have a completely different plan to the one that's been forming in my brain, and I just haven't got the energy – or the time – to tussle with him about it right now. It's easier if I sort this out my way.

I sneak over to the doors to the function room and scan the tables. Can I steal another centrepiece, or is that going to look too suspicious? But then I spot the table in the corner with the wedding cake with the bouquets placed artfully around it. I don't want to decimate my one, as I'm doing a bouquet toss later, but maybe I could use one of the others?

It's just at that moment that I spot Hannah making her way through the tables to talk to a group of our friends and I intercept her path, slide my arm through hers and whisper desperately into her ear, 'I need your help!' She blinks, then nods and I steer her through the double doors and into the hallway.

'What's up? Are you doing a surprise for Luke?'

I shake my head. 'Would you mind . . . I mean, I don't know if you were intending to keep it or whatever, but could I please have your bridesmaids' bouquet?'

I go on to explain why. Obviously, I can't tell her the bits that haven't happened yet, like my mum's meltdown on the terrace, but I can explain she's going to get upset and that I've realized she's going to feel left out.

'I noticed she was a bit squiffy,' Hannah says, glancing in the direction of the function room, 'but I didn't realize she was that bad. Wait here a second . . . ' She slides through the doors, walks up to the wedding cake table, retrieves her bouquet, and nonchalantly strolls back out again. Nobody bats an eyelid. I let out of breath of relief.

Hannah takes the lead cannibalizing the bouquet and adding bits to the table arrangement. She helped me pick out the original floral gifts, so she knows what we're aiming for. We end up with something a bit more spectacular and a lot closer to the arrangements intended for the other mothers.

When the last stem is poked into the floral foam, I give her a big hug. 'You are the best friend ever! What would I do without you?'

Han gives me a wink. 'Partners in crime?'

'Forever,' I say firmly.

'You'd better believe it,' she says. 'Now give me those flowers before anyone realizes what we're up to.'

I make my way back to the top table while Hannah surreptitiously places the extra flowers with the others then has a whispered conversation with the best man about who to deliver the different presents to when the time comes. When she slips into her seat further down the top table and gives me a thumbs up, I breathe out a sigh of relief.

Mission accomplished. I think I may have just saved my own wedding day.

'Of course, we want to say a huge thanks, not only to the bridesmaids, but also to a few other people who've helped make our day special,' Luke says. He's standing up beside me, a microphone in his hand, and he has the whole room in the palm of his hand. His speech had not only me snivelling but seventy-five per cent of the guests too.

He waits while his best man and a couple of the ushers form an orderly queue, gifts in hand, and then he passes the mic to me. Crap. I forgot I insisted on doing the talking for this bit first time around. I stand up and clear my throat.

I thank Lola and Diane for the dresses and the cake and then I turn to my mum, who is scowling, as if she's already got it into her head that she's going to get offended. 'And I want to say thanks to my Mum too,' I say, smiling widely, 'for . . . ' I feel time slowing down, the way it does before a car crash or an accident of some kind. I don't know what to say! Quick, Jess . . . Make something up. Anything! 'For all the help she's been in preparing for this wedding, giving her opinion on . . .' Oh, Lord. There must be *something* she had some input on. 'On the colour of the bridesmaids' dresses . . .' (She suggested teal instead of green but it's close enough!) 'And for . . . for . . .' I can feel my face going red. It's starting at my collarbones and working its way up. I'm losing the power of cohesive thought.

'For giving birth to her in the first place!' Mum suddenly shouts from her seat, raising her half-drunk champagne for the toasts. Everyone laughs and Mum looks pleased with herself, so I smile nervously too, drop back down to my seat and give the mic back to Luke. He's going to have to handle the rest.

After the meal has finished and things are being set up for the evening reception, I ask the hotel if we could keep the doors to the terrace locked, leaving a side entrance into the formal garden as access to the outside for those wanting fresh air or a sneaky cigarette. No fifteen-foot drop, no problem, right?

And my plan works. Even though Mum says I wasn't as glowing in my thanks to her as I was to the other mothers, she's pleased with her flowers and chuffed everyone thought she was funny. When the music starts later on in the evening, she gets up on the dance floor and lets loose, having a grand old time, and I can't help hoping her love of Seventies and Eighties hits will keep her out of trouble for a bit.

But just after 9 p.m., right after I've finally let myself relax and enjoy the evening, I notice a group pointing and laughing at something outside the large windows. A few more people turn to look. The sinking feeling I get in my stomach is horribly familiar.

'What's going on over there?' Luke says beside me.

'Don't know,' I reply hoarsely.

He frowns and begins to walk in that direction. I trail after him, but when I reach the windows that look out over the garden, I see exactly what the cause of all the hilarity is. There, in the middle of the rose garden, is my mother . . . and she is not alone. She is most decidedly not alone, seeing how one arm is wrapped round the guy's waist and the other is cupping his left buttock.

And that's not the worst of it. The man my mother is snogging as if her life depends on it is not only fifteen years her junior, it's the minister who performed our wedding ceremony, and he seems just as much a willing participant as she is!

CHAPTER EIGHTEEN

JESS

I close the card and put it back in its envelope. Luke waited until we were alone to give me my wedding present – a beautiful pendant in white gold that echoes the style of my wedding band, and along with it, a card full of heartfelt promises. But then I think about the aftermath of what happened in the hotel garden and the glow his words put in my heart dims slightly.

Once Mum and Scott, the minister, realized they'd been spotted, they sprang apart with red faces – although I'm guessing Mum's complexion was more from the flush of the alcohol than embarrassment. The onlookers were distracted by the announcement that the evening buffet was ready and drifted back inside or away from the windows. To their credit, most of the guests tried to pretend it hadn't happened and carried on as normal.

Luke encouraged me to eat something, but I hadn't been able to face it. What a mess. In trying to avoid one disaster, I'd just created another. Different events but the same outcome: a cloud of shame hanging over my wedding day. *Thanks, Mum.*

I was exhausted, ready to check out emotionally and run away from it all. However, when I suggested to Luke that we depart early, he looked pensive. 'Don't you want to toss your bouquet? And there are friends and family we haven't had a chance to talk to yet. Yes, this is our day and, technically, we can do whatever we want, but it's also a day for the people we love to celebrate with us. I'd feel bad leaving earlier than planned.'

I nodded mutely. He was right. I knew he was right. Wanting to leave was selfish, but that didn't stop a part of me wishing he'd said, 'You want to leave now? Let's do it! Nobody else matters but you!' But I can hardly be cross with Luke for being the good son, good brother, good friend I've always known him to be. Isn't that why I married him in the first place?

It's after midnight, and I'm sitting on the bed of our room in a cute one-storey cottage at the edge of the Lubbock's grounds. Many of the guests are staying overnight in the hotel proper, but we opted for hiring out the gatehouse to give us a bit of privacy, and I'm very glad of that now.

Luke emerges from the en suite bathroom. A towel is slung round his waist and he's rubbing his wet hair with another. He takes one look at me, throws the towel he's holding onto a chair and comes to stand in front of me. 'You look sad. Why?'

I shrug. I really don't know how to define what I'm feeling at the moment.

He sits down beside me, slings an arm around me and pulls me against him so I can rest on his shoulder. 'Is it your mum?' He presses a kiss to my temple. 'I'm sorry that that happened. You did your best to hide it, but I know it took the shine off the rest of the day for you.'

I take a breath and hold it. The truth is, I don't want to talk about that now. It's too raw, too upsetting. I'm not ready to rip myself open and bear my soul to him. Not in the middle of this crazy nightmare of an experience, not while I'm jumping through the days of my life like that guy from *Quantum Leap*.

'How on earth did the pair of them end up like that anyway?' I ask as I pull away to look at him.

He shakes his head, a bemused smile on his face. 'I have no idea!'

'Is he . . . Is he going to get in trouble?' I have no idea about these things. Mum has never exactly been a churchgoer, which only makes the whole thing more surprising.

Luke ponders this for a moment. 'I shouldn't think so.'

The minister is a family friend of the Harrises. I'm aware they go to a local church that isn't part of a big denomination, although I'm not really sure what that means.

'I mean, he's single,' Luke adds, 'and all they did was kiss. I've known Scott since we used to be in the youth group together. He comes from quite a sheltered background and doesn't normally drink very much. I don't know . . . maybe it shows that ministers can be human too, that even they can be caught out by constant topping up of champagne glasses?'

That'll make sense, I suppose, but I just can't get my head round it. 'But of all the women there . . . My mum? He must be at least fifteen years younger than her!'

Luke's mouth pulls into something that's part-smile, part-grimace. 'To be fair, I'm guessing it's your mum who made the first move, but even if she hadn't, she's a good-looking woman. And, okay, he has a job that people have certain preconceptions about, but he's still a man. In the grand scheme of things, he got caught kissing someone in the garden. There's nothing horrendously evil about that. However, whether everyone feels proud of themselves in the morning will remain to be seen.'

I can't help but laugh at that. I relax against Luke and sigh. This feels nice. This was the time when Luke was my rock, my everything, and I need that right now.

Sometimes, I just feel so lonely. Even though I'm married to a man who is – or used to be – this kind and understanding, I've been feeling a gnawing sense of emptiness for a long time. And it's only become magnified since I've been having this weird, ongoing experience of déjà vu.

It's not as if I can tell anyone about what's happening to me. They'd think I was having a psychiatric episode, and maybe they wouldn't be wrong. On top of that, every day I'm reliving isn't a run-of-the-mill Thursday, where I go to work, come home, cook dinner, watch some TV . . . The last three days have been major milestones in my life, causing a rollercoaster of emotions. I'm exhausted.

So, when Luke runs his hand up my neck, pulls me to him and starts to kiss me, I don't resist. In fact, I kiss him back. Enthusiastically. I just want to stop thinking about it all. I don't want to think about anything, so I don't. I just feel. I let the sheer physical pleasure of my wedding night sweep it all away until I'm lying half-asleep in Luke's arms, my heartbeat steady and slow for the first time in days, and refusing to think about tomorrow.

CHAPTER NINETEEN

LUKE

Eight Months Before the Anniversary Party

Hey. I know you're probably very busy, but I wondered if I could ask a favour?

He reads the message and smiles. **Sure.**

I'm doing a house in Dulwich and I wondered if you remembered the name of that reclamation yard you got those amazing church pews from? My client is DESPERATE for some.

Sullivan's. That's the name of the reclamation yard. Near Paddock Wood in Kent. An absolute treasure trove of old doors, flooring, tiles and oddities. They nearly always had a church pew or ten in stock.

He taps the name of the place into the box and presses 'send'.

She responds with five thumbs-up emojis and a face with hearts for eyes, which makes him laugh. Elena is always so warm and enthusiastic, and it's nice to feel as if he's been helpful in some way. It's nice to feel useful. Wanted. He's about to add another message, reminding her that, because it's out in the back of beyond, the sat nav will try and take her down a dirt path with a gate at the end, but he's only typed two letters when he stops.

Stuff it. Who's got time for long-winded messages? It's probably just easier to call.

Seconds later, the phone is ringing and then a soft, warm voice says, '*Ola*?'

PAPER

How strange that a material made from a pulp derived from wood, rags, grass or even dung, can be a vehicle for great things. It's not the paper itself that is glorious, but the fact we can adorn it with our souls – art, music and words birthed in the secret places of our hearts.

CHAPTER TWENTY

JESS

The journey from asleep to awake is slow, warm, and deliciously fuzzy. My body is relaxed and satisfied, and the storm that has been whirling inside me for days is momentarily quelled. Warm skin touches my back, my thighs, my calves. A heavy arm drapes over my midriff and curls tightly around me. I fully breathe out, and it almost feels as if I've never done that properly before.

When I open my eyes, the room is dark, moonlight playing at the edges of the curtains. As my brain comes to life, I begin putting the puzzle pieces together – where I am, who I'm with . . .

I lie in Luke's arms, a strange sense of peace radiating from my core. I'd forgotten how happy we were in the days and weeks following our wedding. Life was perfect. I didn't care where we were or what we were doing as long as we were together. He was my safe harbour in the storm of life. He was my sun and I was happy to be the insignificant satellite that circled around him and bathed in his warmth.

But as I lie there, breathing, an ache begins to throb deep inside me.

Roommates? Best friends?

What have we done to ourselves?

Lying here with him is painful and glorious all at the same time. I feel raw, as if all my skin has been stripped away and every sensation is heightened. If he opens his eyes and looks at me the way he did the night he walked out the door, I don't think I can survive it.

I should go. I should slide out from underneath his warm arm, dress quietly, take the car and drive somewhere. Anywhere.

Luke stirs and I freeze. But then he exhales heavily, throws his arm back over his head, and his breathing becomes even again. The way is clear. I could edge out from beside him without waking him up.

I will. In a minute.

*

I can tell, even through the skin of my eyelids, that it's well after dawn. Stretching, I open my eyes and stare up at the ceiling. A white paper lampshade hangs from the ceiling above the bed. I instantly know exactly where I am – and that fills me in on *when* I am too.

This is the bedroom of the flat we rented after we got married, which means, as I guessed it might, that today is not the day following our wedding, but our first anniversary. I don't know if this is where I was when I woke in the night and plotted escape, but it's where I am now.

I check the clock on the bedside table, my eyes widen, and I elbow Luke softly in the back. 'Luke!'

'Mmpff . . . What?' he mumbles, rolling over to hide his head in the pillow.

'It's past nine,' I whisper, although I don't know why I'm keeping my voice down. There's no one else here. 'You'll be late for work!' I lost count of the number of times he slept through the alarm before he got his smart watch. And I still don't get how the annoying chiming of his phone did a worse job of rousing him than a soft buzz on the wrist, but he hardly ever needs me to elbow him out of slumber anymore.

The mattress bounces and he's halfway across the room towards his wardrobe when I hear him stop. A second later, the mattress dips again as he throws himself back down on it and scoots in to spoon behind me. 'Nice try,' he chuckles. 'It's Sunday.' And then he sighs. 'How many times am I going to fall for that one?'

Oh, of course it is! Even so, I smile to myself. I did love to tease him back in the day. The strange thing is, I didn't realize I'd stopped playing silly jokes on him back in our real life until now. It always feels as if it might hit wrong, and then he might get upset with me. But even though I've just woken my husband up, he doesn't seem to be irritated at all. In fact, quite the opposite.

His lips find the tingly spot behind my right ear. Heat floods me instantly. And the ache inside shifts lower, becomes greedy.

'Good morning, Mrs Harris,' he says, his voice rough in my ear.

I don't speak as I roll over to face him. We don't need words. I don't need to be in my head for this. All I need is for him to keep touching me the way he is right now, to make my brain stop and my body come alive and, just for a precious while, I can let whatever thoughts that are in my head evaporate and I can forget.

★

The next time I wake up, I'm second-guessing myself. I roll over to find the bed empty beside me. A radio is playing somewhere else in the flat, probably the kitchen. I flop over onto my back and cover my eyes with one hand. What am I doing?

As lovely as the last twelve hours or so have been. It's not real life. This isn't even the real us. Not anymore. It's just an echo. I can't let myself get swept up in it, can I? Because if things keep going the way they've been going for the last four days, I've got less than two weeks before I arrive back on our tenth anniversary and Luke works out I'm not what he wants anymore and he's gone. I need to start having some self-control. I need to start protecting myself a bit more, because—

My train of though is interrupted by the door opening. Luke comes in, backside first, as he obviously used it to bump the door open, holding a tray. Grinning, he circuits the bed and puts it proudly down in front of me. 'Blueberry and banana pancakes,' he says proudly.

I take in the misshapen offerings, some slightly singed, all bleeding purple juice from the plump blueberries dotted through them. A bowl of thick Greek yoghurt is on the side, as well as a bottle of maple syrup and a steaming cup of tea. And then I notice the card propped up against a small glass vase filled with blousy flowers – but not just any flowers, they look as if they've been exquisitely crafted from the pages of old books. 'Luke . . . ' I say, my voice thick, as I place a palm on my chest.

'It's our paper anniversary,' he explains.

'It is?'

He nods. 'Every year has a material attached to it. I looked it up. And I know we don't have a lot in the bank this year, and we promised each other we'd save fancy gifts for after we've got the deposit for a house, but I had to do something.'

I look at the flowers and then look at Luke. 'You *made* these?'

'Do you like them?'

I press my top lip onto my bottom one to stop it wobbling and nod in reply. I don't remember him doing this last time. I think the 'paper' bit of our anniversary was the card. Because how can I have forgotten something this sweet?

'You made me paper roses . . .' I mumble. 'And *pancakes*!' And then I begin to cry, which confuses the heck of my husband. It kinda confuses me as well, to be honest.

'Hey . . . hey . . .' Luke carefully lifts the tray off the bed, puts it on the floor then pulls me into his arms. 'What's all this about?'

I cry harder, then snuffle into his arm. 'I j-just l-love you.' I'm hit by the truth of my words as I say them. I do. I do love him. No matter what we will say and do in the future.

'I love you too,' he says softly, pulling back to look into my eyes.

I take his face in my hands. 'Do you? Do you really?'

He's smiling but his brow creases. 'Of course.'

A lump forms in my throat. 'Do you promise? Will you always love me? Will you always stick with me?'

Luke's smile disappears and he smooths one side of my hair flat against my head with a hand. 'Of course. That's what this day is all about, isn't it? Us. In it together. Forever.'

I suddenly remember those were the words he used when he proposed the very first time, and the ring that went with them. I feel it could come in handy now, a good luck charm that might help me navigate through the next nine days and reach a different destination.

'Thank you. For everything.' Lovely smells waft up from the plate sitting on my lap. I feel the need to lighten the atmosphere, because I don't know how to do 'mushy'. It starts off okay, but after a while I just end up feeling . . . naked. And not in a good way. 'But most of all for the pancakes.'

Luke waggles his eyebrows. 'I'm sure we can find a way for you to thank me properly later.'

I just smile back at him. I'm sure we can. And when he turns to leave, I can't help noticing how good his backside looks in his low-slung tracksuit bottoms and I reach out and cop a feel before he gets too far away.

'Hey!' he says, turning to look at me with mock outrage. 'Don't touch what you can't afford!'

I burst out laughing, and he gives me a backwards wave as he heads back to the kitchen. Shaking my head, I pick up my knife and fork and dig into my pancakes.

CHAPTER TWENTY-ONE

JESS

I'm rummaging through the kitchen drawers looking for serving spoons and chopsticks. I honestly can't remember where we used to keep them in this kitchen, which is so strange. However, when I think hard, I realize there are a lot of details I don't remember about this day. I recall the highlights with fondness, but the in-between bits are fuzzy. Maybe that's not surprising. The previous days I've lived through were possibly the most significant ones in our whole relationship. To be honest, I'm quite enjoying not remembering everything that happened before, because it means I don't have a script to follow.

I open the narrow drawer next to the hob and spot the chopsticks nestled under a few pairs of tongs. I'm just reaching for them when my phone, which is charging on the counter, rings. I change direction and pick it up. 'Hello?'

'Hey, gorgeous!' Hannah says. 'How's it going?'

'Good,' I say, reaching over and retrieving the chopsticks, then bumping the drawer closed with my hip. 'Luke's just out grabbing a Chinese takeaway.'

'A takeaway?' Hannah makes a soft snort. 'That doesn't sound very romantic!'

I bristle. I don't like the feeling that Hannah is judging us. 'Well, we're saving hard, as you know, both so we can put a deposit down on a house and so we've got a buffer when I start training as a physiotherapist. I like to think of it as if we're investing in our future together, which I think is *very* romantic.'

'Oh, God . . . You two make me sick,' Hannah says, but I can tell she's giving me an indulgent smile on the other end of the line. 'I can hardly believe it's been a whole year!'

Seriously, Hannah has no idea. 'Neither can I.'

'Is it everything you thought it would be?'

I take a moment to ponder my answer. 'It's . . . good. Amazing, actually.' The last day or so of my reality has blown me away, and with it, blown all the anger I felt towards Luke away, too. Of course I remember how happy we were in the early years of our marriage, but living parts of them again has brought those feelings back to life in all-singing, all-dancing Technicolor.

Hannah makes a soft gagging noise then laughs. 'No, seriously. I'm actually a bit jealous. I wish I could find someone like Luke.'

'You will, Han. You're amazing.'

He just might not be the first one she says 'I do' to, but I'm not going to tell her that now. I'm still holding out hope for that in the future, and back in our real lives, I've been getting a vibe that there's someone on the horizon, but she just hasn't been ready to spill the tea on him yet. 'How about I set you up with one of his brothers?'

'Isn't he the oldest? I don't want to go cradle-snatching!'

My phone beeps in my ear. 'Listen, Han . . . Can I call you back tomorrow? I've got another call coming in and I think it might be Luke asking if I want salt and chilli chicken or salt and chilli prawns. He always forgets which one I said.'

'Yes. Go. Go!'

'Salt and chilli *prawns*,' I say as I answer the call.

'Salt and chilli what?'

'Oh, sorry . . . Never mind. I thought you were Luke. Hi, Mum.'

There are a few seconds of silence before she responds, probably because, even to my own ears, I sounded less than enthusiastic. But that's hardly surprising. Her alcoholism goes in waves. She never truly dries out but sometimes it's definitely worse than others, and the past year has been choppy, despite her promises after our wedding to give up altogether.

'You don't have to say it like that!'

I rest my case. Mum sits at home, stewing over hurts, both real and imagined, and when she can no longer deal with a tornado she's whipped up inside herself, she dials my number. 'I didn't say it like anything,' I tell her. I'm lying, of course.

'I bet you don't talk that way when your father calls!'

'No—'

'Just what I thought!'

I was going to say that I didn't talk to Dad that way because he and I hardly ever talk on the phone, but she didn't let me get it out, and I can't be bothered to correct her now because she's on a roll. It won't matter what I say.

'I don't get it!' she says testily. 'Even though he abandoned us to go off with *that* woman, you still prefer him to me.'

'That's not true, Mum. I—'

'I don't understand why you worship that man so much, why you've always been so desperate for his approval.'

She may have a point there — about wanting his approval, anyway. However, that's hardly the point at the moment. I take a deep breath and attempt to respond calmly. 'I don't prefer him to you, Mum. I love you both.'

My mother makes a dismissive noise. Of course that's not good enough. Sometimes, I think she'd only be happy if I said I hated him as much as she does, but that wouldn't be true either. I don't think she hates him. I think she still loves him. I think she still pines for him and this is what fuels her frustration and anger.

'Well, I've hardly seen anything of you in the last year.'

'Mum, you know why that is.'

'Why?' she says, sounding genuinely bamboozled, and I roll my eyes. 'Oh . . . You mean the wedding reception. Well, yes . . . I know that was . . . unfortunate.' I didn't speak to her for four months after the wedding. She's lucky I've been in contact as much as I have. 'But you have to understand what a hard day it was for me, your father waltzing in with *that* woman . . . '

Sometimes, I think, when she's on one of her drunken rants, she forgets that Lola was nowhere in the picture when Dad left, and that she wasn't the one who had the affair with him.

'If there's anyone to blame for my state that day,' she continues, 'it was him. And you didn't help matters, did you?'

'What are you talking about?'

'You made me look stupid.'

'*I* made you look stupid?'

'Yes. You gave me those flowers after singing the praises of Luke's mum and . . . *her* . . . and made it obvious to everyone I hadn't done as much.'

My blood begins to lightly simmer. *Only because you got drunk and missed my dress fitting. Only because you'd rather spend your time and money on booze than doing anything to help Luke and me for our wedding.*

'It's no wonder I ended up doing something foolish . . . I was just trying to feel good about myself.'

What? She's making this my fault? My blood reaches a hard boil. 'You know what, Mum? You're right. I don't actually want to speak to you at the moment.' And I jab my thumb over the red 'end call' button, receiving a triumphant rush of endorphins as I do so, even though I'll probably regret it later.

Luke arrives back carrying a large paper bag full of Chinese food, a bag of prawn crackers and a bonus bottle of cola. He dumps all of them down on the counter as I scurry around getting plates and serving spoons. I'm just peeling the plastic lid of a tub of chow mein when he comes up behind me, puts his hands on my arms and kisses the side of my head. 'You okay? You look tense.'

I sigh. I could tell him all about the call I've just had but it's nothing new, and I'm not sure I can be bothered to drag it all up again. Besides, Luke is always full of advice about how I should handle my family but I don't want to get into a back and forth about why I don't think his suggestions would work, and I don't want to let a conversation about my unhinged mother ruin our evening. 'I'm fine. Just a bit tired.'

'You sure?'

I nod and start popping spoons in the different containers. 'Sure. Now why don't we eat this while it's hot, and decide what film we want to watch?'

CHAPTER TWENTY-TWO

JESS

We settle down with our takeaway and a cheap bottle of fizz to watch a film. It's a new release I hadn't heard of at the time called *Mrs Wonderful*. Since that night, it's become a bit of a comfort watch for us. It's a slightly quirky, retro-influenced mystery about a 1950s housewife called Jessica Martingale, whose best friend goes missing and she begins investigating her disappearance, all the while trying to keep her sleuthing a secret from her husband. He adores her but they're both trapped by the societal norms of the time – his role is breadwinner and hers is to look pretty, keep the house clean, and have his dinner ready on the table when he comes in from work at the end of the day. Of course, eventually she bites off more than she can chew, and her double life is revealed, causing all sorts of problems.

I glance across at Luke, shovelling noodles into his mouth as he's transfixed by the willowy brunette on screen in her full-skirted dress with the cinched-in waist, eyeliner and red lipstick. She's as delicious as the chocolate chip cookies she's pulling out of the oven to cool.

'You *so* have a crush on Anna Roberts,' I tease, knowing he always perks up when this particular actress is in something we watch. For years he denied it but one time I actually got him to admit it.

Luke keeps his eyes on his plate. 'She's okay.' But he's smiling, so I give him a playful punch on the arm.

'I bet you wouldn't mind it if your Jessica could make a lemon meringue pie without breaking a sweat.' I tried once and ended up in tears. Never doing it again. 'I mean, she's pretty much perfect in every way.'

Luke gives me a sideways look, still smiling. 'True.' I punch him a bit harder, so he puts his plate down, takes mine from me, then leans in and gives me a kiss. 'Just kidding. I'd much rather be having a takeaway picnic with the Jessica sitting right next to me. You're *my* Mrs Wonderful.'

'Right answer,' I tell him, and kiss him back, and the rest of the Chinese food goes cold while we find an alternative way to celebrate our anniversary, the film playing in the background. But that gives us an appetite, so with the help of the microwave and the rewind button on the TV remote, we have another go.

I wish what Luke said was true, but I know I am far from being wonderful. I know I sometimes infuriate him. I know I can be spiky and sarcastic, and I come out fighting if I feel backed into a corner. The real Mrs Wonderful would *never* do that. But it gets me thinking . . .

I can't seem to escape Luke while I'm having this bizarre experience. Even if I try to change history, it just warps and remoulds itself so we're back together again, and even though it's nine years away, I'm already feeling the spectre of our tenth anniversary casting a shadow over us.

If I can't run away from this, then I'm going to have to run towards it. If the last three days have taught me anything, it's that Luke is my person. I love him. I don't want to lose him. I've got to do better. I've got to become Luke's version of Mrs Wonderful. No matter what he says right now, while he's still drugged with newlywed bliss, I need to become who he needs to be nine years from now. Not with the lemon meringue pies and permanent high heels (as a physiotherapist, I would never), but I'm overtaken with the yearning to be the wife I should have been for him all along. I'm going to have to do better.

And maybe I can. I'm not going into this blind. I know things now that I had no inkling of the first time around. That has to help, doesn't it?

We're just getting to the bit of the movie where the other Jessica is tailing her suspect (bestie's seemingly perfect husband) and almost gets caught by him when my phone starts buzzing every couple of minutes. I don't have to look at it to know it's my mother, venting her frustration now she's had a chance to stew and refuel with a few more vodkas.

I must be giving some weird vibes off, because after about ten minutes Luke pauses the film and turns to me. 'Are you *sure* you're okay?'

I nod but undermine myself by blowing out a heavy breath.

'Jess . . . ?' There's gentle warning in his tone.

I pick up my phone and pull up the unread message thread with my mother. Just a quick glance confirms it goes from apologizing to blaming to self-pity and back again. I pass my phone to Luke. 'It's Mum . . . We had a rather heated phone call while you were out getting the food. I hung up on her.'

'That must have gone down well.'

'What was I supposed to do? Say "thank you very much" for blaming me for what she did at our wedding last year?'

Luke's eyebrows raise. 'She did that?'

I nod.

'Even so, it's a bit harsh to hang up on her, isn't it?'

Luke's family would never put the phone down on each other. They're all so nice and, well, normal. It makes it hard for him to understand the weird, dysfunctional dynamics I have with my parents. Sometimes I'm ranting about her, sometimes I'm defending her. And I don't even know why I do it.

'Maybe, but I'm so tired of it all. Just . . . over it. And when she said everything I did to make her feel special, to stop her acting out on *our* big day, was the reason she went and made a spectacle of herself, I just lost it. After she promised she'd stop drinking again, too! I mean, she did for a bit, but we all know that didn't last long. And she won't take responsibility for anything. She's toxic, Luke. She really is!'

He opens his mouth and I press a finger over his lips to stop him saying anything. I want to be able to feel how I'm feeling without any of his helpful 'advice' making me feel even more like crap. I expect him to try and talk anyway, but he just looks at me for a few seconds and then he kisses the tip of my finger.

I only have a vague memory of having a bust-up with Mum on this day, the first time I lived it, and it's quite possible I just swept it all under the rug, as I'd been intending to do this evening, but the older me on the inside of this younger Jess just doesn't have the capacity to do that anymore. So . . . So maybe I shouldn't.

I let my finger fall from Luke's lips and look him straight in the eyes. 'I can't keep going like this. I think it's time to go no-contact with her.'

'No-contact?' Luke says, as if he can't quite get his head around what I'm saying. 'Like . . . just never see her or speak to her again?'

'Not until she sorts her drinking out,' I reply, and I feel quite liberated as the words leave my mouth. Why didn't I do this earlier? Why didn't I do this right after the wedding?

'Wow.' Luke rubs his forehead with his fingertips. 'Are you sure this is a good idea?'

My jaw tenses and I reach for my glass of bubbles, take a sip and put it back down again. *Actually, yes, I do, Luke. It took another year of Mum's shenanigans first time around for me to cut her off completely, but why wait? I know exactly how this is going to go, and it's not going to get any better. What's the point in dragging it out?*

I fold my arms, scowling slightly, and look at my husband. I thought he was supposed to back me up on stuff like this, not make me doubt myself. 'Why *wouldn't* I do this? Give me one good reason.'

'Whoa . . . okay . . .'

I know I sounded a bit snippy, but it's his own fault. Sometimes, I wish he would just listen instead of jumping in and trying to fix everything. I stare back at him, waiting for him to give me his rationale as to why I shouldn't prevent my toxic mother from hurting me more than she already has.

'It's just . . .' He dips his head and gives me a knowing look. 'We know that your default response to conflict is to just run the other way.'

'This isn't the same.'

His eyebrows lift.

'It's not.'

He blinks.

I let out a frustrated sigh, because he's right. When it comes to fight or flight, I'm Usain Bolt not Tyson Fury. 'Okay, maybe a bit. But this isn't some little tiff with Mum. It's ongoing . . . draining.'

'But she's family.' The playfulness leaches from his expression. 'You might not like what I'm about to say, but I'm going to say it anyway. I wouldn't be honest if I didn't.'

I shift to turn square on to him, which has the added benefit of creating more space between us. I want to fold my arms, but I know it'll be a dead giveaway, so I plant my palms on my thighs and mentally glue them there. 'Go on.'

'You say you wish you had a family like mine, one you could be closer with, but the truth is, even if your parents created the situation you're all in now by their choices when you were younger, you join them in keeping the gulf in place.'

I look down at my hands. 'I know. Because . . . ' How much do I tell him? How can I say this without opening the floodgates and letting my whole soul pour out in a big mushy mess, never to be put back together again? 'Because it doesn't feel safe to let them closer.'

Luke leans forward and brushes my cheek with his fingers. When I meet his gaze, my eyes are stinging. 'I know your mum is — how shall we put it? — difficult to love, but your dad isn't who he was twenty years ago. I think you could be closer with him, and the rest of his new family, if you wanted to be.'

He's speaking the truth, but there's only one problem: I don't know how. 'But if I get closer with Dad, Mum will freak out and she'll be even worse,' I mumble.

'Yeah . . . I suppose you're right. I hadn't thought of that.'

That's because he didn't have to grow up second-guessing

everything he did, every word he said, in case he accidentally lit the touch paper that would make her explode.

Luke pulls me into a hug. We stay like that for a couple of minutes and then he pulls back enough to look at my face. 'You're right. I don't get it. I try to, but I don't fully. Not yet.' Warmth fills me at his words, and then he carries on, 'If you want to go no-contact with your mum, if you feel that's what you need to do, I'll support you. But I want you to be sure it's *really* what you want; you're not just reacting to the anger and emotion after the fight you had this evening. Take some time to think about it.'

'Okay.'

His eyes are such a lovely warm brown, with chestnut flecks. Despite the fact that, once again, he's trying to fix something I'm not sure can be fixed, and it's driving me crazy, I can see the love pouring out of them towards me, and I feel a stabbing sensation in my chest. He doesn't understand, but he's trusting me. Maybe it's time I did the same to him. I'll have to if I'm going to make this marriage work. I don't *have* to push back against every suggestion, do I?

'You're right. I know I run when I get scared, and maybe this is what I'm doing right now. I'll do it. I'll give her another chance, but if she calls and yells at me like that in the future, I'm going to put the phone down on her again.'

Luke's mouth curves into a smile. 'I think you should. Just because you're not cutting her off, it doesn't mean you have to put up with everything she does.'

Okay, then. That's settled. I feel we've reached an uneasy kind of compromise, but it's something I can work with. Running away from difficult situations didn't serve me well in the years following this one, did it? If I hadn't run out of our tenth anniversary party, maybe Luke and I would have had a more productive conversation and then he wouldn't have done the same to me.

And then I realize something: maybe, just maybe, if I don't cut my mother off completely, I can avoid that whole nightmare entirely. If she's still part of our lives, Luke can't invite her to the party behind my back, can he? And then I won't have anything to walk away from. It might be the key to solving everything.

And if it is, maybe I'll wake up in my own bed again tomorrow, nine years older and in my right time, and Luke will be next to me. The thought is so delicious, it makes my head swim.

I reach for the foil trays laid out on the carpet. 'Do you want that last spare rib? Because if you don't, it's got my name written all over it.'

CHAPTER TWENTY-THREE

LUKE

Six Months Before the Anniversary Party

He smiles at the picture message that has just arrived. It's of a beautiful dark-teal kitchen. It must be the house in Dulwich Village that Elena has been working on.

A text message arrives shortly after. **It's finally finished! What do you think?**

And then another picture arrives, this time some wrought-iron gates the owners of a house he'd been working on with his dad had been insistent on getting rid of, despite being over a hundred years old, and absolutely beautiful craftsmanship. Since he couldn't convince the owners to keep them, they'd been quite happy to sell them on and put the cash towards the brand-new, electronic gates with an intercom system they'd wanted instead.

Recognize these?

Sure do!, he types back.

'Hey, Jess!' The TV is blaring the latest Netflix series they are bingeing, and Jess is sitting on the edge of the sofa, hunched over her bullet journal, drawing lines and scribbling things down. It's the start of a new month and she always seems to have lots of scribbling to do around this time. 'Want to see those old gates I rescued restored to their former glory?'

Her head bobs up and she looks slightly confused. 'What?'

'The gates . . . from that house in Keston we worked on last month.'

He turns his phone around so she can see.

'Nice,' she says, but she glances away and goes back to her scribbling so quickly that he's not even sure she's had time to register the two gorgeous gates, which have now been turned into a focal point in the large garden. By next summer, Elena says they'll be covered in jasmine and honeysuckle.

It's absolutely stunning, he types into his phone. I can't believe they came up so beautifully. And the pews look great round that old refectory table. Wish I had a kitchen large enough to fit one of those in!

One day, Elena types back. And did you see the flagstones? We searched all around the country for those. Aren't they the most delicious colour?

Her enthusiasm is infectious. They spend the next couple of minutes chatting back and forth about the project, but he feels bad that he's totally lost the plot of the TV episode he and Jess are watching. He probably should try to be more present when they have a rare quiet evening in together.

Instead of firing off another reply, he puts his phone down on the sofa. 'It's a place Elena's been working on in Dulwich. Did

I tell you about that yet? I'd love to go and see it. Do you want to come too?'

He realizes that he hasn't mentioned to Jess he's back in contact with Elena. Not that he decided *not* to tell her. It's just that it started up again so slowly it hasn't seemed like a big thing to share, just something he'd get around to when he remembered. And now he's remembered, so . . .

'Jess?'

She doesn't even look up this time, just says 'Huh?' and carries on scribbling, and then she adds, 'What gates are you talking about again?'

At the same moment, another message arrives, making his phone screen go from dull and grey to full of life and colour. **So are you going to come and see it for yourself? The original wooden shutters in the dining room are to die for! The pictures don't do this place justice.**

He looks at his wife, who has stopped writing in her journal to stare at the telly. He doubts she even remembers she was waiting for him to answer her grunted question.

Sure, he types back. **Would love to.**

COTTON

A soft, fluffy fibre that grows in a boll around the seeds of the cotton plant. It is known for its breathability, absorbency and softness. While it may seem humble, adaptability and durability are its key strengths.

CHAPTER TWENTY-FOUR

JESS

I pick Mum up from her house in Orpington and drive a couple of miles to High Elms Country Park. The grounds near the car park are tended and mowed, but paths lead into sprawling woods that spread for a couple of miles. Down a short path is a wildlife conservation area that leads to a pond surrounded with reeds and buzzing mayflies with a cute café beside it.

I had no idea how things were going with Mum after the promise I made Luke last anniversary. I know I kept in touch with her the first time I lived these years, but it was very strained. I wasn't trying to mend things or be supportive; I was just trying to survive our relationship without too much further damage. However, I realized I have a secret weapon to help me navigate this new version of my life – my bullet journal.

I picked up the practice the year after Luke and I married after seeing a YouTube video. Not the artsy, decorative kind of bullet journalling you see a lot of on Instagram, but the method from the book: a pared-down system for focusing on what's important in my life and keeping track of daily tasks and events to accomplish those goals. Thankfully, I not only unearthed my very first bullet journal notebook, but also a double-paged spread of brainstorming on how to try and be a supportive influence on my mother. That's what Mrs Wonderful would do, isn't it?

The Jess who is here between the anniversaries I'm reliving is clearly quite committed to this plan, and she's put some steps in place that I honestly am envious I didn't think of first time around – like not inviting Mum to the house but going out when we get together. It gives us something to do/talk about and she's always clear in the head, if you know what I mean, at the beginning of the day.

I also learned from my bullet journal that I'd booked the day off work today, hoping Luke and I would be able to go off somewhere for our second anniversary, but life had other ideas and he has to work. I decided to take the time off anyway as I've got some plans for later on and I'd prefer not to have to rush things.

I buy us both coffees and we find a table overlooking the pond. It's such a glorious day. The sun is catching the reeds, making them glow almost neon green. Insects skate across the top of the water and butterflies dip and dive over the tops of the lily pads.

I reach into my handbag, pull out my purse, then push a few folded notes over the tabletop towards her. 'Will this be enough?'

She does a quick check. 'If you could throw another twenty in, that would be marvellous.'

I nod and add another note to the pile.

'Thanks,' Mum says, pocketing the money. 'I'll pay it back, obviously. It's just a bit tricky having gone down from full-time to part-time, and there was a bit of a gap between ending the old job and starting the new one.'

'Sure,' I reply, even though I am not sure at all. According to the log in the 'Mum' section of my bullet journal, she still hasn't paid back twenty pounds from the last hundred she borrowed, and the switch in jobs happened more than two months ago, so her paydays should have sorted themselves out by now. But I'm embracing Luke's motto of 'family is family', and doing my best to believe that Mum is trying.

I also don't mention that I suspect Mum's move from a full-time role at the solicitors to a part-time role with a charity is because she's finding it harder and harder to keep her drinking life separate from her work life. For so many years, she managed to compartmentalize, but I assume there may have been an 'incident' that prompted her recent career move.

I listen to Mum talk about the new office and why she doesn't like the manager who's there on Tuesdays and Thursdays, and then she goes on to the next-door neighbour's dog, who is always a source of irritation, and then on to plans for a trip away to a friend's caravan in Bognor Regis. She doesn't ask me about my life, but I'm used to that now, so when she pauses to take a sip of her cappuccino, I take the opportunity to speak up.

'I'll have to take you back in about half an hour,' I tell her. 'I need to pop to the big Tesco to get some supplies for this evening. I'm doing something special for Luke.' And this wasn't something I found planned out in the journal. This is something extra I decided on this morning, something to really make the effort for him from this version of me. I feel this is important.

Mum raises her eyebrows. 'Oh? Why is that?'

I look down and stir my coffee, even though I added no sugar to it, because looking her in the eye might seem like I'm making a point that she hasn't remembered or asked, and I'm not, but I do want her to take a bit of notice about what's going on in my life. 'It's our anniversary. Number two. Yay!' My cheer sounds pathetic even to my own ears.

'Oh, yes! Congratulations.'

'I'm making Luke a picnic.'

'A picnic?' She makes me think that somehow this idea has offended her.

'Yes.'

She shakes her head. 'Luke should be spoiling you, not the other way around!'

'We haven't got the cash to spoil each other, no matter who's doing it,' I explain. I don't point out the fact that the hundred and twenty pounds she's just pocketed would've covered dinner at a half-decent restaurant. 'Now Luke is working for his dad, we've had to tighten our belts a bit. The salary isn't quite what he was getting in his corporate job.'

A corporate job he hated. Despite studying business at university, Luke's dreams of being a titan of industry evaporated early. Maybe it was the firm he worked for. But he was finding the greyness of a City job, nine to five every day, draining. It didn't help that his last boss was a total cow.

And then, seven months ago, Luke's dad had a heart attack. He owns his own construction firm – just a small one, with a handful of guys and contractors working for him – but he was still on site a lot himself, and he had to take time off to recover. Luke worked alongside him as a Saturday job when he turned sixteen, and then Easter and summer holidays throughout university. It was either let the firm go under, or step up, so it wasn't really a choice. This is the way it went last time, and it has happened the same way this time. I have no issues with it.

I remember it being hard not having as much money, especially as we weren't overflowing with the stuff beforehand, and I had to put my budding idea of training to be a physiotherapist on ice for another year or so, but Luke had a spring in his step when he kissed me goodbye this morning, and that makes it worth it. There's something about creating things with bricks and mortar that fills his soul in a way typing into a computer and doing presentation decks never did.

'It's such a gorgeous day,' Mum says, 'You should've had a picnic here for lunch. Much better than in the evening when the grass will be damp, and it'll start getting chilly.'

'That was my first thought, but Luke just couldn't take the day off today.'

Mum frowns at me. 'I know Luke is very dedicated to his family, and that's all very commendable, but sometimes, Jess, you need to make sure he puts you first. It's just one day out of the year. Surely he could manage that?'

I fold my arms, slightly annoyed Mum is being negative about Luke. If it wasn't for him, I wouldn't be sitting here talking to her today; I'd have cut her out of my life completely. 'Although Ed has been directing from the office over the last couple of months, he had his heart bypass surgery on Friday. Luke's the only one holding the fort. Yes, it would have been nice to have the whole day together, but I totally understand.'

Even if it's going to make it harder for me to change the direction of my marriage if we've only got a few short hours together. But, if I remember rightly, on our 'first' second anniversary, I don't think we did much to celebrate. Luke's dad was in the hospital, and it just didn't seem the right time. We eventually ended up going out for dinner a couple of weeks later.

Mum seems slightly mollified, but she crosses her arms and sits back in her chair, looking steadily at me. 'Just make sure that you're not the only one putting the effort in, Jess. Don't let him get complacent. That was the mistake I made – I gave myself over completely to a man, only for him to walk away and tell me it wasn't enough. Maybe, if I'd made him work a bit harder from my love, he would've appreciated it more.'

'Noted,' I tell Mum. I can't explain to her here and now, but I'm not going to take her advice. I wasn't a good enough wife the first time around, but this time I'm going to be Mrs Fricking Wonderful.

CHAPTER TWENTY-FIVE

JESS

A large wicker basket is packed and ready on the kitchen table with a soft, checked blanket sitting on top. I hear Luke's key in the front door, and I jump up from where I'm sitting, eager to see him. We only had a scant, sleepy half hour together before he left for work this morning.

He strolls into the kitchen as usual, glances briefly at the basket, throws his keys on the counter and delivers a quick peck to my waiting lips. 'Just gonna dive into the shower and then I'm heading off to the hospital to see Dad.'

'Oh!'

He's already half turned to head upstairs when my exclamation stops him.

I didn't mean to say it. It just kind of popped out. I smile weakly and wave a hand in the direction of the basket. 'I . . . I kind of hoped we might have time to eat. I made a picnic. You know . . . ' I laugh nervously ' . . . a budget celebration?'

Luke stares at the basket and then back at me. I can see he's torn. 'Oh, God, Jess . . . That looks amazing, but . . . '

But . . .

There's always a *but* when it comes to his family.

' . . . Cassie and Zach are going to go for the second hour of visiting time, so we've got to fit it in before that.'

I cringe inwardly as I ask my next question. 'Do you . . . I mean, do you think . . . Do you have to go today?'

He went yesterday and the day before, and I'm sure he'll go tomorrow. The doctors are saying everything went fine, so there's no panic.

His shoulders droop. 'Dad was still groggy yesterday and not in the mood for talking much. And Mum says he's in much better spirits today. I haven't been able to have a proper conversation with him since the op.' He puts his phone down and comes over to me, puts his hands on my upper arms. 'Would you mind if we did this . . . '

'Later?' I finish for him and slip out of his grasp so I can go and put the stuff that needs to be kept cold back in the fridge.

He grimaces. 'I was going to say "tomorrow".'

I pause in unbuckling the leather straps of the old picnic basket I raced round to borrow from Han earlier this afternoon. I look back at him and try not the let the disappointment broadcast from me like a beacon. I tried so hard. And I've only got seven more days – seven more anniversaries – to salvage my marriage before I'm back at that party again. At this rate, this whole day will be a write-off, and I don't know if I can afford that. My efforts seem to be working, but are these tiny course adjustments on only one day a year going to be enough? I can't tell.

'I'm sorry, Jess, I truly am. I'm so touched you did this, but . . . '

'How about I come with you? We can go and visit your dad and then have the picnic afterwards?' I can't give up, and I have the sense Luke will only be ready to collapse onto the sofa and watch some mind-numbing true crime series when we get back home.

Luke looks unconvinced but he blinks slowly, looking wearier than I've seen him in a long time. 'Sure.'

★

It's cold outside the hospital. I'm sitting on a bench to the right of the front entrance, clutching the handle of the picnic basket on my lap. There are a couple of bits of broken wicker on the bottom that are digging into my legs through the flowery summer dress I'm wearing. I may have been overly optimistic about the temperature this evening.

I would have gone to visit Luke's dad with him, but there's a strict two-visitors-at-a-time limit. The sun was still above the surrounding houses when he went in, but now it's dipped behind the roofs and the temperature's nose-dived with it. I shiver and resist looking at my phone to check the time.

It's hard not to feel on the outside, both physically and metaphorically. It's not that Luke's family haven't been incredibly warm and welcoming to me. It's just somehow, even in the midst of all the hugs and talking and laughter, I always feel like the odd one out. The way they love each other makes my heart ache.

Luke finally emerges ten minutes' later.

'How's he doing?' I ask, standing up.

'Good,' he replies, rubbing his eyes. 'He was teasing the nurses, so he's definitely feeling more like his old self.'

I see the relief wash over my husband as he says this. He must have been more scared than he let on. I reach out and rub his shoulder. 'You must be starving. How about we wander round the corner to the "peace garden" and eat some of this before you drop where you stand?'

I can tell he's tempted to ask if we can take it back home, but he nods and smiles. 'Of course.'

A few minutes' later, the blanket is stretched out on the neatly clipped grass of the small garden full of benches with a fountain to one side, somewhere restful for patients or family members to sit in the midst of whatever crisis they're going through. I'm certainly praying it'll work its magic on us. I can do with all the help I can get.

We dig into the wraps I made and the little pots of deli items, finishing it off with a plastic flute full of cava. Only a small one for me, as I said I'd drive home, but we can polish the bottle off once we get there.

After we've finished discussing his dad's progress, Luke says, 'You'll never guess who I ran into last week. It's been so busy with Dad's op that I forgot to mention it.'

'Oh, really? Who?'

'Elena. Do you remember her? She was at our wedding. Her husband, Felix, was one of my college roommates. Well, he was her boyfriend at the time, but you know what I mean.'

Of course, I know Elena much better now than I did then, but I'd forgotten it was around this time they'd run into each other again. 'Yes. I remember her – and Felix.'

'Well, it seems they've moved to South East London because of Felix's new job in the City. She was all artsy back at uni, and still is, I suppose, but now she's doing interior design. I bumped into her at the tiling warehouse, where she was picking out flooring for a customer's kitchen.'

Elena is certainly not the sort of person you'd imagine frequents dusty, dirty tiling warehouses. In our future, I always thought she dressed like one of those women on *The Apprentice*, all tailored clothes and glossy, tumbling long hair. 'We should invite her and Felix round for dinner some time,' I say, pre-empting what I'm guessing will be Luke's next move. 'They're a nice couple.' For now, at least . . . 'And talking of people we've run into . . . Did I tell you I was going to meet Mum for coffee today?'

'You did?'

I nod and make a 'hope you don't mind' face. 'I, um . . . lent her a bit of money to tide her over.'

He finishes his mouthful of pitta bread dipped in hummus and asks, 'She's going to pay it back, isn't she?'

'Of course.'

Luke nods but I can tell he's got something on his mind.

'You said we should be supportive,' I remind him. 'And she needs the help.'

'I just wonder if it's the right thing to keep giving her little bits of money every now and then. We don't know what she spends it on.'

'Family is family, right? But that doesn't just apply to your family; it applies to my family too – no matter how dysfunctional we are. I mean, it's easy to be there for your family. They're all so lovely and it comes back the other way, too. My family are more . . . challenging.'

Luke sighs. 'I'm sorry. You're right. I just didn't think of it that way.'

'You wanted me not to run the other direction when things are uncomfortable, when things are emotionally difficult, and

I'm doing my best, Luke. And it's not like I didn't warn you what she was like.'

He leans over and kisses me. 'How did you get to be so wise and wonderful?'

It warms me that he chose that last word to describe me. Even so, heat creeps into my cheeks. 'I don't know about that.'

'Well, I do.' He lies down, putting his head on my lap, facing up to look at me and lets out a long, slow breath. 'Thank you, Jess. I must admit, I was so tired when I got in that I wasn't really in the mood for this, but now I realize it's exactly what I need. *You* are exactly what I need.'

I smile and kiss him on the top of his nose. *Mrs Wonderful* mode well and truly activated.

CHAPTER TWENTY-SIX

LUKE

Five Months Before the Anniversary Party

He can almost smell the money in the air as he arrives in Dulwich Village. It's hard to believe he's driven through rough areas and council estates on his way to this leafy and rather affluent suburb of South East London. The sort of people who live here can afford to send their boys to the exclusive private school nearby that has spawned politicians and literary greats for generations.

He pulls into the carriage driveway and up to the side of a large, white Georgian house. Stunning. He hasn't even stepped out of the car before Elena comes running out of the front door, a huge grin on her face. Also stunning. Her dark wavy hair is loose, flowing over her shoulders, and her eyes are shining.

'Gorgeous, isn't it?' she asks, with that slight twang of a Colombian accent that he hardly notices anymore.

He gets out of the car and closes the door behind him. 'Yes,' is all he says in reply. There are more words to describe this beautiful grand dame of a house, thousands probably, but none of them are within his reach right now; he's too caught up taking in her lines and proportions, her tall windows and long veranda with black-painted wrought-iron posts.

'Come,' Elena says, beckoning him. 'Come look inside!'

He catches a whiff of her perfume as she hugs him quickly, then she grabs his hand and practically drags him through the front door and into a hallway with smooth York flagstones and an elegant staircase with a carved mahogany handrail atop an ironwork banister. He steps closer to look at the details. The scotia moulding along the stringer run alone is enough to make his mouth water. And the gilded details on the metal uprights . . . chef's kiss.

'Is this original?' he asks.

'Some. A few sections were damaged, but the craftsmen did a good job patching her up, no?'

'No . . . I mean, yes. I can't even see the joins.'

Elena smiles at him. 'I knew you would appreciate this! I talk to my friends and tell them what I do, but no one else gets how satisfying something like this is.'

He smiles back, thinking to the half-second glance his wife gave his phone when he showed her the pictures of this place. 'No, they don't.'

He spends the next hour investigating every nook and cranny of the house, which is furnished and styled, ready for the new owners to move into. Elena has done one heck of a job with the design on this one.

They end up in the kitchen, which has three sets of French doors that lead onto the veranda. It's full of marble and clean lines, yet still feels homely. He spots the reclaimed church pews instantly. They look even better in the flesh – or the grain – however you are supposed to put it.

'Did you buy this one to flip it?' he asks, seriously impressed. The price tag on a house like this has to be upwards of three million.

'God, no,' Elena replies, laughing. 'This is beyond my budget. I did the design and also project-managed the restoration for the owners.' She wistfully runs her slim, elegant fingers along the marble worktop. 'I haven't flipped any houses in the last couple of years, but I'm thinking I'd like to get back into it.' She meets his gaze, a cheeky glint in her eye. 'Are you interested? You always said you might be one day. I could do with a partner.'

He looks around the light, airy space, despite the deep colour of the cabinets. What he wouldn't give to work on something like this. While even if they combined resources they wouldn't be able to stretch to this, maybe they could one day. It would certainly beat pouring the concrete foundation for yet another conservatory.

'I wish I could, but Dad is *finally* going to retire this year – or so he says – which means I won't have a lot of time on my hands for a side hustle.'

Elena pulls a face at his use of words but then laughs anyway. 'You make it sound like a dance,' she teases, doing a little salsa-like sidestep in demonstration, but when he doesn't laugh too, she stops and gives him a more serious look. 'Are you okay, Luke? I don't know . . . You don't seem like your usual self.'

He'd like to agree with her. On one level he does. He doesn't think he's always felt this way, with this vague sense of something heavy sitting on his chest, but he can't actually recall a time in recent years when he didn't. 'I'm good,' he says, pushing a smile onto his features. 'You know me . . . '

Elena nods but her smile is as half-hearted as his is. 'And Jess? How is she?'

'Good. She's good.'

She walks over to him and lays a hand on his arm. 'I'm glad. I want to see you happy.' Their eyes meet and they stare at each other for a few seconds, but then he breaks eye contact. She allows her hand to fall away and steps back. The brightness returns to her smile as she tips her head on one side and says, 'But if I can't convince you to go into business with me, can I at least take advantage of your knowledge? Consulting services, if you like. No one knows period properties, especially in this corner of London, like you do.'

LEATHER

A strong, flexible and durable material obtained from the tanning of animal hides. While wearing leather in the modern world suggests confidence, assertiveness and even rebellion, it has been used for thousands of years, most notably for armour and protection.

CHAPTER TWENTY-SEVEN

JESS

Luke brings the car to a halt in a residential street in Elmers End, a suburb a few miles away from where we live. I peer out the window at the tree-lined pavement and red-brick Victorian houses. 'This is it?'

Luke pulls the key out of the ignition. 'This is it.'

My fingers hover on the door latch for a second or two before I grab it firmly, pull it, and step out of the car. When Luke said he was taking the day off for our anniversary, this was not what I was expecting.

I follow him a short distance down the road to where a 'For Sale' sign stands, screwed into the gate post of a slightly raggedy-looking semi-detached. As far as I remember, our third anniversary was around the time we started looking seriously for the house we live in now, but this is definitely not our house. It's larger, and while ours needed a certain amount of work doing to it, this one looks as if it's more of a 'project'.

It's beautiful, though, with carved white masonry above the windows around the door and beautiful tall sash windows and a high gable roof. We can't afford this, can we? It looks almost twice the size of our terraced house in our other life.

When I glance at Luke, he's studying my expression carefully. 'What do you think?'

I swallow. 'I think . . . I think I want to see inside.'

I have so many questions, but I have a sense that my usual method of peppering him with enquiries might not be the right thing to do. I'm not sure why. Maybe it's because, when I don't always find the information I'm looking for, Luke starts to get a bit irritated. Sometimes, I think he thinks I'm being critical. I'm not. I just like information. I can't make a decision about things, fully process my thoughts, unless I have all the details, so sometimes I have to dig.

As we walk up to the front door, it opens, and a smart woman in a suit steps out and shakes Luke's hand, and then mine, vigorously. 'Great to see you! I'm glad you're interested in a second viewing.' She turns her attention on me. 'Want to take a look around?' I nod dumbly and follow her inside.

On the ground floor, there are two good-sized reception rooms and a narrow galley kitchen, pretty common with houses of this age that haven't been renovated by middle-class couples with a healthy budget. The wallpaper is ugly. The carpets are even uglier. But the house has good bones, and I'm hoping the plywood nailed to every door and under every staircase railing might be hiding beautiful original features. Perhaps there's even a cast-iron fireplace or two behind a more modern-looking surround.

When we've done the whole tour, the estate agent excuses herself, allowing us a moment to talk. Luke opens the door to the back garden, and we step out onto a tufted lawn that looks as if it was once cared for but hasn't been mown in a few good months.

I look up at him, my eyes wide. 'You want to buy this house?'

He nods. 'I know this isn't exactly what we talked about, but hear me out . . . okay?'

I turn around, shielding my eyes with a flat hand placed against my brow, and study the back of the house. French doors lead out onto a patio that would be a perfect spot for a kitchen extension. I don't even want to think how many years it would take us to save to do that, even if we could afford this place. 'Okay.'

'I know we've been looking for a place for ourselves, but I think this house could be a great opportunity to boost our deposit fund.'

I frown and look at him. 'You don't want us to live here?'

He laughs. 'No. I mean, yes . . . I would love to live here. I wish we could afford it, but remember that conversation we had last week?'

Damn. Of course I don't. But I can't tell him that, can I? Instead, I ask him to remind me of the details. It's been a long week. More than he knows!

'You know how frustrated I've been getting with Dad now he's back at work? How he absolutely refuses to do anything to pull his building firm into the twenty-first century? He won't even get a website, for goodness' sake! They're so much we could do to make Harris & Sons the premier building company in the borough. But he just won't listen.'

I dig around in my memory, and realize this rant seems familiar. Luke decided not to go back to his corporate job once his dad's health improved. It took him a while to admit it, but he'd never really enjoyed it. He loved working with family, building something that could be a legacy, possibly for our own children, but the generational differences when it came to running the company caused a lot of friction.

A snippet of a memory flickers across my mind. 'You want to buy this, do it up and flip it?'

'The only thing is . . . ' He pauses, purses his lips nervously.

'Is that you want to use our house savings to do it,' I finish for him. I remember having discussions about this around this time, although I have no memory of him bringing me to see the house, just that we talked about it. I'm pretty sure it never happened. I wonder what's changed to make him bring me this time? It can't be a bad thing, can it? He's sharing more with me, making me more of the decision-making process. That means my scheme to change the state of my marriage must be working somehow.

'Yes . . . ' He's perplexed I've hit the nail on the head. 'I know it'll put our plans to get a place of our own back, hopefully only by a year, but if this works out, we'll have even more to put down than we have now. We'll be able to afford something with a proper garden, possibly even a third bedroom.'

I stare at the house again. Some of those roof tiles don't look entirely sound. 'I know we've been saving hard, but how on earth are we going to afford something this big?' I know we don't have the budget for it. It was a scrape to put down the deposit on our much smaller house in a not-so-nice street.

He's saved from answering by the estate agent appearing out of the sliding patio doors. She's chatting to someone behind her, and when she steps out of the way, I realize I know exactly how Luke and I – or maybe just Luke – can afford to buy this house.

'Hey, you!' the woman says, smiling brightly at Luke, and then adds, just as brightly, 'Hi, Jess!'

'Elena!' I reply, smiling back.

'What do you think?' Elena asks, turning to take in the house. 'I think it could be a wonderful first project.'

I know. It would. But I also know the first time Luke brought this up, I wasn't ready to risk the money we'd been saving on something that might not work out. The thought of it still makes me nervous. 'I think it could be perfect,' I reply.

Both of them grin at me and then Elena turns to Luke. 'I had an idea about the area under the stairs,' she says, walking back in the direction of the kitchen. 'Let me show you what I'm thinking about.'

I trail back inside the house behind her and Luke, where she proposes putting a series of hidden drawers and cupboards to make the under-stairs storage much more workable. They bounce ideas of each other, and even the estate agent gets excited and chips in. I know as much about joinery as I do piloting spacecraft, so I stand in the corner of the hallway and try to look encouraging but end up wandering off to have another look at the front room when the discussion drags on. I want to check if the leaded lights in the top of the bay window are reproduction.

They turn out to be original, with brightly coloured Art Nouveau-inspired shapes, but two out of seven are missing, and the window frames are rotten as anything.

While I've got a moment, I pull out my phone and open my banking app. I quickly scroll through the list of pages and shoot twenty pounds off to my mother. Technically, after a couple of loans have remained unpaid for more than a year, we are not lending her any more money, but she phoned me up this morning in tears, really struggling. She didn't have any cash for groceries. I can't let her starve, can I, even if Luke says there are other kinds of support we can give her, that she ought to be standing on her own two feet?

As I head back towards the hallway, where the others are still talking, I hear the estate agent, Gillian, saying, 'Well, I think this is a great starter home for a young couple like yourselves, and you seem to be brimming with ideas on how to do it up!'

There's awkward laughter from Luke and Elena as I appear around the living room door. Luke slings an arm around my shoulder and kisses the side of my head. 'Actually, *this* is my wife.'

'Oh, God. I'm so sorry!' Gillian says, looking a little flustered. 'For some reason I . . . ' She smiles apologetically at me. 'I thought Luke said he was bringing his sister along to look.'

'Well, she does want to come and have a nose,' Luke says, laughing, 'but this isn't her.' He laces his fingers in mine, and I stand there, trying not to look bothered about what I just overheard.

Because I am. Bothered.

I can see why Gillian thought Elena and Luke were a couple. I can also see how easy a mistake it was to make. They make an incredible team.

CHAPTER TWENTY-EIGHT

JESS

'Wow, you look . . . fancy!' Luke says as I emerge from our bedroom. I know we're only going to a local Italian restaurant, but I've gone all out – heels, make-up, a little black dress. Mrs Wonderful would be proud of me. As much as I don't want to admit it, I kept replaying the moment the estate agent assumed Luke and Elena were husband and wife and I was demoted to annoying kid sister.

I kept seeing images of Elena as I got dressed, her effortless style, her beauty. Because Elena is beautiful. Not just pretty. Her hair is thick and glossy, her skin a gorgeous smooth golden brown. She has huge eyes, an expressive mouth, and more curves than I could ever hope to have.

I don't know if Luke notices, or cares, about the differences between me and Elena, but I notice them. And I don't like the fact that I do.

I walk over to him and kiss him softly on his cheek, taking a moment to linger before pulling back. 'You're worth the effort.'

He blinks and I see his pupils dilate as he looks me up and down.

'What time is our reservation?' I ask, a cheeky smile playing on my lips.

Luke doesn't even bother to check the time; he just scoops me up and heads for the bedroom.

I'm looking a little less, um, *polished*, when we emerge again, but I can't stop grinning. He's mine. Totally mine. In this moment, anyway. I just need to find a way to make sure things stay like this, so I'm quiet in the car on the way to the restaurant, trying to work out how I can up my game.

We get to the restaurant and begin our meal. I've hardly even put my knife into my Caprese salad when Luke asks me how I liked the house.

'I wasn't joking when I said it was amazing,' I reply. I may not have the skills and building knowledge Luke and Elena have but even I can see the potential. I put my knife and fork down. 'But it's a risk.'

'I know . . .' Luke pushes a bit of deep-fried squid around his plate. 'And I know it's asking a lot to put our savings into it. It's just . . . I really think it could work, Jess.' I can tell he's visualizing the finished property because his eyes light up. It reminds me of how he looked when he and Elena were discussing the under-stairs cupboard. 'And maybe this could be the start of something — something I can do on my own, outside of Dad's business if he won't let me do this kind of thing as part of it.'

It strikes me that maybe the best thing I can do for Luke is to trust him the way I was scared to the first time around. I can be brave. I can be adventurous. Just as his future business partner will be. That's probably one of the things I envy about Elena the most. Her confidence.

I look my husband in the eyes. 'I believe in you,' I tell him, and I see the flicker of gratitude at my words. Up until that moment, I didn't realize he had any doubts, but maybe he's not as sure as I sometimes think he is.

'I know you're not big on risks.'

'True.' I take another bite of my salad while I work out how to say what I want to say. 'But I don't always think being so risk averse serves me well. Sometimes, you've got to shoot your shot, right? I . . . ' I look down briefly, aware of how exposed I'm feeling. 'I think sometimes I hold you back by being scared about things. I hold on to things so tightly, but maybe I need to, I don't know . . . ' I meet his eyes ' . . . trust more?'

'You know you can always trust me.'

I nod, even though the sight of him slamming our front door behind him replays in my head for the millionth time. I can't bank on the fact it won't happen again, but maybe I need to not hold Luke so tightly because I'm scared of losing him. Maybe I need to let him fly, chase his dreams. Isn't that what Mrs Wonderful would do?

Looking back, I wonder if I've been a lead weight holding him down. No wonder he hasn't been happy. But if I let go of Luke, I will also have to let go of other things — our house, for instance. I know it's going to come on the market in about six months' time, and we'll put an offer in and by this time next year, we'll be homeowners. Only, if we use the deposit we've saved for this project instead of waiting until *after* we bought somewhere for Luke to spread his wings, that house will probably never be ours. I feel a stab of pain in my chest at the thought. I love our house. Our home.

But he's worth it.

'Let's do it,' I tell him. 'Buy the house. Do it up. Make us a great nest egg.'

Luke leaps up from where he's sitting, puts his hands either side of my face and kisses me as if I've just made all his dreams come true. I hear a flutter of reaction from the surrounding diners, but I don't care.

He can hardly stop grinning as we continue our meal, but when desserts are served, his expression becomes serious. He reaches into his pocket and pulls out a small square jewellery box and offers it to me. My eyes widen.

Is that it? Is that his great-great-grandmother's engagement ring?

Blushing a bit, I tentatively reach for the box and ease it open to find something glinting at me inside. Only, it's not one item but two – a pair of earrings – and that's when I realize the box isn't quite the same. It's dark green not dark blue and it has a little chain pattern printed in gold around the sides and no lettering on top.

'Oh, Luke . . . ' I say, trying not to let my voice wobble. Whether it's from disappointment or because I'm so incredibly touched, I can't tell. 'They're lovely. But how did you—'

'They're not diamonds, unfortunately,' he says. 'Just crystal, but the box is leather, which kind of counts, since it's our "leather" anniversary. But I don't know . . . Getting you a keyring or a purse or something didn't seem to be enough.'

I reach over and touch his face. 'I love them. Because *you* thought of it. Because *you* gave them to me.' I slide the hoops I'm wearing out of my ears, pop them in my handbag, then put my new earrings in.

But the more I think about it, the more I start to suspect

Luke's great-great-grandmother's ring might be the key to everything. While everyone else in the family makes fun of the fact Millicent believed the ring had magical powers, maybe she was right. I mean, I can't explain what's happening to me – going back in time, skipping through my anniversaries like they're a game of hopscotch – but if there's anything or anyone else in this weird corner of reality I'm living in that might have some of the same sort of supernatural power, I have to find it, don't I? I have to try to see if it will help get me back where and when I should be. It can't hurt to add an extra sprinkle of fairy dust to my ailing marriage, can it?

I check my phone for the time. It's almost ten. Maybe, if Luke is tired from the wine after we get home and falls asleep quickly, I can creep out of bed and have a bit of a hunt round our flat for the other jewellery box. It has to be there somewhere, doesn't it?

But even if I find it, I won't take the ring. I won't wear it. Not yet. Not until maybe I can signal to Luke I'd really like to have it after all. But just knowing it's there, waiting, will set my mind at rest. And if I can touch it, so much the better.

CHAPTER TWENTY-NINE

LUKE

Four Months Before the Anniversary Party

He stares at the empty seat on the other side of the battered wooden table. She only left a minute ago. He should probably leave too. Jess will be at home by now, probably thinking about throwing something in the oven for dinner. It's just . . . He needs time to think, and somehow that is getting harder and harder to do at home. Or anywhere, really. There's so much going on in his head all the time. But there's something about this small independent café, tucked away in the local parade of shops off the High Street, that is oddly calming.

He didn't hear much from Elena all over Christmas, mostly because she went home to Colombia to visit her family, but now she's back, and she sent him a message asking if he'd meet her for coffee. He thought she was going to bring some plans for him to look at or ask his advice on walls or ceilings or whatever, but she hadn't mentioned any of those things. She hadn't mentioned work at all.

They'd just chatted while they'd drunk their coffees, like

old friends, which they are, he supposes. However, anyone who glanced over could be forgiven for thinking they were on a date.

Which they weren't. So that's okay, isn't it?

She had asked for his help and support. A favour.

A secret.

He'd said yes, of course. She needed him. What else was he going to say?

But now he's wondering if he should have done. He won't be able to tell Jess about this, so it feels a bit . . . he's not sure how to put it. Not comfortable. Like he's crossing a line of some kind.

In the end, he gets fed up of staring at the empty chair and the brown frothy rings in his coffee cup and he goes home. When he opens the front door, he is greeted by the sound of banging from upstairs. A quick check of the kitchen reveals a cold oven and nothing on the hob. Just as well he stopped to grab some provisions on his way home. Jess must be busy.

He finds her in their spare bedroom, putting up a couple of shelves that he said he'd do three months ago, but hasn't quite gotten around to. She's making so much noise with the drill that she doesn't hear him until he's almost right on top of her. She jumps, pressing her hand to her chest and laughs, before leaning to kiss him on the cheek.

'Thought I'd get on with it,' she says by way of explanation. 'I know you said you were going to but, it has to be a bit of a busman's holiday doing DIY at home.' He must be scowling because she adds, 'You don't mind, do you?'

'No. Of course not.' If anything, it should be her who minds. She really shouldn't be doing the job he said he'd do, but he's glad she's not distant or irritated, as she sometimes is. At least there's that. It's such a relief, in fact, that he offers to take over, or at the very least help.

She smiles at him as she lines the drill up for the next hole. 'No worries. I've got this. I thought you were going to be home a couple of hours ago, but I guess things ran on at the site, yeah?'

He looks away. 'Something like that.'

'Why don't you make yourself a cup of tea and collapse in front of the TV. I'll be down in fifteen minutes or so – hopefully! And then I can rummage around in the fridge and see what I can rustle up for dinner.'

He waves in the general direction of downstairs, where he left his shopping. 'I picked some pizzas up at the Co-op, actually. I'll throw them in the oven.'

'Cool. Even better. See you in a bit.'

He backs out of the spare room, essentially dismissed. As he returns downstairs, he thinks that it would've been nice to put the shelves up together, even if he'd just handed her the screws, but of course Jess wouldn't think of that. She's so self-sufficient, so independent. It was one of the things that drew him to her in the early days. It was nice to be with someone who didn't always need something from him.

He makes himself a cup of tea and does as instructed, flicking through channels until he find something mindless about border security he can use as television wallpaper. As he sits there, he reminds himself that he should leave Elena a message, tell her that maybe he's not the best shoulder to cry on. However, by the time Jess is back downstairs, and the supermarket pizzas are in the oven, his phone has not made it out of his pocket.

SILK

A smooth, soft fibre produced by certain insect larvae to form cocoons which can be woven into a durable fabric with a characteristic sheen. While silk is one of the strongest natural fibres, it loses strength when wet and its elasticity is poor.

CHAPTER THIRTY

JESS

'Did you sleep in the spare room last night?'

My cutlery stops moving, and I glance up quickly from my eggs Benedict. 'No, why do you ask?'

'I woke up around five. You weren't there.'

This conversation has been brewing all morning, but I'm not sure I want to have it in the bougie new café in town where were having an anniversary brunch. 'No. I just got up early. Couldn't sleep.'

Mostly because I was too busy ransacking every drawer and cupboard in our flat for a small leather navy-blue ring box. Luke must have it stashed somewhere in the bedroom, because I couldn't find it anywhere else. I did, however, find this year's bullet journal, so that's a small win.

Aside from learning I'm good for a smear test for another three years, I was reminded that this is the year Hannah gets married to Connor and I will be planning the hen party, we've started house-hunting in earnest after the successful sale of Luke and Elena's first renovation project and, according to a log in the back of the book, I'm slipping money to my mother on a fairly regular basis and the total owing is always greater than the amount that has been paid back.

I'm sad about the house-hunting. After finding the journal, I hopped on Rightmove and discovered 'our' house is under offer – not to us. I'm heartbroken, but if this is what I need to do to save my marriage, so be it. If I don't succeed and Luke does want a divorce six years in the future, we'll have to sell it anyway, so it's a risk worth taking.

However, in all of the neatly bulleted task lists and journal entries, I find *nothing* to indicate why Luke and I must have argued last night. It's most frustrating. If I could work out what the issue was, we could talk it out and I could get on with the job of saving my marriage. I'm hardly going to make much of an impact the way things are now.

We're both being civil to each other, but the atmosphere lingers, the same way uneasiness does after a nightmare. Thank goodness I arranged to have the day off work. With so little time left to make a difference to our relationship, spending seven to eight hours away from Luke is just a waste of time.

'Spoken to your mum recently?' I ask, aiming for a subject that will hopefully ease the tension.

'Yeah. She rang yesterday,' Luke says as he concentrates on assembling the perfect forkful of a full English, complete with gooey yolk running down over the free-range Cumberland sausages. He frowns and looks up before he pops it in his mouth. 'She asked when we're doing something for my thirtieth, but I said we didn't have anything planned yet.'

Outwardly, I'm sporting a calm but slightly enquiring smile. Inwardly, I'm panicking. According to my bullet journal, I'm doing the same as last time and planning Luke a surprise party.

I'm sure I've told Diane it's all very hush-hush but I'm also sure she will be just as useless at keeping a secret and might end up accidentally blurting it all out to her son as she did last time. 'Do you have any ideas of what you'd like to do? Experience day? Meal up in London?'

Luke devours his forkful and thinks while he chews. 'I was thinking maybe we'd go away somewhere? I know we can't afford much because we don't want to eat into our house deposit, but how about renting a cottage for the weekend after my birthday?'

I keep smiling but it becomes even more rigid. 'That sounds great.'

'You don't sound that enthused.'

I'm not. That's the weekend of the party. According to the neatly ticked lists on a double page in my bullet journal, the function room is already booked, and invites have gone out.

I'm going to have to talk him out of this somehow. Last time, Luke loved this party, mentioned for years how much he appreciated me going to all that effort and how pleased he was that I knew that being with friends and family that day was the perfect way to celebrate. I'm worried that if it doesn't happen again this time around it'll put a big dent in any progress I'm making. I need the goodwill it will bring me in the coming years.

'You know I would love to get away, but things are a bit hectic at the moment, especially with the new renovation you're doing with Elena. What happens if you blow your budget for that? You're right – you don't want to dip into our savings to cover any extras. It might not be the best time to spend that extra money.'

'We're only going to be thirty once, Jess.'

Oh, if only he knew . . .

'We'll see,' I say, hoping I can fob him off a bit longer.

Luke's jaw tenses. 'In other words, you don't want to.'

'No,' I jump in quickly. 'It's not that. It's just . . . ' Urgh. How do I explain this?

'Never mind,' he says, stabbing at a bit of bacon with slightly more force than necessary. 'I should have known it was a bad time to bring it up.'

'What does that mean?'

He busies himself with his breakfast for a while but eventually says, 'When we argue, it's like everything I say is wrong. You have to push back on absolutely everything.'

'That's not true,' I say, maybe a tad too quickly.

It's not lost on my husband.

'I'm sorry, okay?'

He frowns. 'For what?'

'For . . . for last night. For all of it.' And I'm sure I would be if I knew what it was, but that doesn't mean I can't make a genuine apology. We probably bickered over who was supposed to unload the dishwasher or something.

'I know that, Jess. But we had an agreement. We're supposed to be a team, yet you continually leave me out of things I should be included in.'

'Like what?'

Luke gives me a steadying look. 'You know what. And if you don't, then I can't do anything to help you. Maybe you need to start paying a bit more attention to what's going on between us.'

Inside my head, I'm screaming. I can feel the day slipping away from me and I have no idea how to salvage it. All I can do is nod and pretend I know what he's talking about.

Luke pushes his unfinished breakfast away from him and

signals to the server for the bill. 'I need to get going. I'll see you later this afternoon.'

'You're going out? We're not . . . We're not spending the day together?'

He tips his head on one side and gives me a look that makes me wither a little inside. 'I've got to go to the flooring suppliers – I told you all this yesterday.' He shakes his head and pulls his phone out as the server comes over with the machine. 'Did you honestly not just hear what I said about paying attention?'

But that'll be hours lost and I can't afford that, not after the day has started so badly. 'I'm sorry, Luke, I really am. It's just I've got a lot going through my head at the moment. The house-hunting . . . Han's wedding . . . I know I'm messing up, but I want to make it up to you. Can I . . . Can I tag along?'

Some of the fire leaves his eyes. He sags a little. 'Sure. Knock yourself out.'

★

I shouldn't have come. I'm trailing around a flooring supply warehouse, trying to look interested, while Luke and Elena have intense conversations about the pros and cons of real wood versus Amtico, and I have nothing useful to contribute. I glance across at them as she laughs and places a hand on his forearm. He smiles back at her.

It was the fear that got me. Fear that I wasn't doing enough, that I wasn't being a good wife to Luke. I should've listened to my instincts. I know that he needs time to calm down after an argument, and I'm not giving him any space.

When my phone rings, and I see it's Hannah, I'm grateful

for a reason to exit into the sunshine and stand in the car park, even though the traffic from the bypass next to the retail park is hurtling nosily past. 'Hi. What's up?'

'Hey!' Hannah replies, and then she launches into a rant about how her soon-to-be mother-in-law is trying to convince her groom to wear a velvet suit to their wedding instead of the top hat and tails she and Connor had planned. I let her vent, making suitable outraged or sympathetic noises as needed. When she finally runs out of steam, she wishes me a happy anniversary. 'Did you get breakfast in bed and then just spend all morning in there?' she asks, laughing. 'Oh my God! Are you still in bed now? Want me to call back later?'

If only.

'No, you're all right,' I say with a sigh.

'I can't wait to be Mrs Rowbridge and have long, lazy anniversary lie-ins,' she says dreamily.

I feel a pang of sadness at her words, especially as, five years in the future, the end of her marriage comes after Connor has a series of long-lazy lie-ins with someone who isn't Hannah. 'You do realize that marriage is more than the bubble of love and confetti and rainbows it is at the beginning?' I ask her, hoping I can pierce the skin of that bubble with a shard of common sense. Maybe I can save her some of the pain that's coming a few years down the line. 'It's hard work. And both of you have to put the effort in.'

Hannah laughs. 'Of course. Everyone knows that!'

Or they think they do, I reply silently. I thought it myself until extremely recently, didn't I? I was so complacent.

'That's why we make sure we choose the person who's going to have our back, will still be in it with us when the going gets tough.'

Maybe I sound more serious than I intended to, because Hannah asks if I'm okay, and then she asks if I'm truly happy for her. My stomach nose-dives. The truth is, I'm not. I know what an arsehole Conner is and I so badly want to tell her, but she'll never believe me if I explain why and how I know.

'I just want what you and Luke have. That's not unrealistic, is it?'

'No,' I say quietly. It's what we all want when we say, 'I do'. I can't fault her for that. And I suspect even if I point out the red flags, she won't listen. All I'll do is alienate her, and she's going to need me in the months and years to come.

'Of course, I'm happy that you are deliriously in love. I've always wanted you to find your person, but . . . '

'But . . . ?'

How do I say this? 'I want you to know that I'm your person too. That I will always have your back. Just remember that, will you?'

'Aww, Jess . . . Now you've got me crying! I don't know what . . . Oh, God! His mum is calling me again! I'd better answer, otherwise I'm going to be getting married to a man who looks like he got his wedding suit inspiration from a second-hand sofa sale!'

We say our goodbyes quickly and she rings off. I stand in the car park, listening to the roar of the traffic and squinting against the sun. I'm sad. For my best friend, but also for myself. When I hear the love and hope in her voice, I remember that I was there, feeling exactly the same things, only four days ago, and yet – I glance back at the glass doors to the flooring warehouse – here we are. I don't remember arguing on this anniversary in the past, but we might have done.

As I lock my phone and shove it back in my jeans pocket, I turn and walk back inside. That's what this is, isn't it? A silly tiff. Looking back in my bullet journal, there's nothing big that Luke and I are struggling with at the moment, but feeling the seconds tick away, knowing our tenth anniversary is only a few days around the corner, I can't help but get paranoid.

I need to have faith – in Luke, but also in myself.

Luke and Elena are no longer where I left them, so as I wander up and down the aisles of laminate and carpet samples, I come to a decision. I'm going to stop reacting to every little thing as if it's a *Titanic*-level disaster and take a breath. I'll go home, take a bath, read a book, whatever . . . And when Luke gets back, hopefully we'll both be in a better frame of mind.

I finally spot Elena frowning at a rack full of luxury vinyl tile samples. 'Where's Luke?'

She nods towards a display with a miniature set of stairs, complete with runner and brass rods. Luke is standing nearby, deep in conversation with a man I think I recognize as having once worked for his father. It doesn't look as if he's going to be free any time soon.

'Actually, while I've got you on your own,' I say to Elena, 'I wanted to tell you about Luke's party.'

Elena frowns. 'He hasn't said anything.'

I dart a quick look at my husband. 'That's because it's a surprise.'

'Oh . . . I get it. That's why he was talking about . . . never mind.'

Luke's been talking to Elena about his birthday? Has he told her he's pissed off with me about not going away?

'Anyway, I think it is a great idea! What do you have planned?'

While we're waiting, I give Elena the rundown of the time and date. She even offers to create a distraction and bring him along to the party pretending it's a house viewing or something. I smile tightly at her. 'That's very kind, but I've got it covered.'

She just shrugs and does the cute pursed-lip smile that's her trademark.

'I'll send an invite for you and Felix,' I tell her.

'Sure.' For the first time since we've been chatting, her eyes lose a little of their sparkle. At first, Luke and I used to socialize with Elena and her husband a lot, going round to their house for dinner, grabbing cocktails on a Friday night, but it began to fizzle out. I got the feeling that everything was not rosy in paradise, and eventually I was proved right.

I check my phone for the time. How much longer is Luke going to be?

'You know what?' I say, looking again in my husband's direction. 'Could you tell him I've just realized there's something I need to do? If he texts or calls when he's finished, I'll shoot back in the car and pick him up.'

'Of course,' she says, smiling. 'But, you know, I could always give him a lift home when we're finished.'

'Would you? That would actually be helpful.' As Elena said those words, I realized I might have to forgo my long bath for another errand. There's something important to do with the party that I really need to make a decision on.

'My pleasure,' she says, and her smile is so warm and genuine that I actually feel a bit less intimidated by her. 'I've kind of got used to taking care of him,' she adds, laughing. 'It's not a bad thing, I think, no? For a man to have a wife at home and a "wife" at work?'

CHAPTER THIRTY-ONE

JESS

'Thanks for letting me drop in.' I slide into a stool at the breakfast bar on the kitchen island and warm my hands round the cup of tea that Lola has just made me.

She bustles around, opening cupboards, and returns with a tin lined with kitchen paper and filled with puff-puffs. I honestly can't resist the doughnutty little balls of fried batter, so I stuff one into my mouth and swallow it with a glug of hot tea.

'This is your home, too, Jessica. You know you are welcome at any time.'

I nod, even though, for most of my life, this has been a logical knowledge rather than a feeling that has lived inside of me. What I'm realizing now is that this has nothing to do with the hospitality of my stepmother and everything to do with my own reticence. Looking back in my journal, I can see I've been visiting my father and his family – no, *my* family – more often in the last twelve months, and I'm glad about that. Other Jess, the Jess who lives here in the in-between periods, might have left me in a mess because she got grouchy last night, but she's been doing some things right.

Lola rests against the stool next to me. 'You look as if you have something on your mind.'

'Well, you know I've been planning this party for Luke . . . '

'Yes?'

'I've been holding out sending the invitations because I just can't make a decision about something.'

'Is it the venue? Have you already paid a deposit? Because you can have it here if you want.'

I sigh heavily. 'It's less to do with the venue and more to do with the guest list. I was hoping to pick your brain about a tricky matter.'

Lola gives me a look that says, *Okay . . . Continue.*

'You see, the last time we had a big event, you know, hiring a venue and caterers, music and dancing, was our wedding. And you know how that went.'

I wait for a moment. The movement of Lola's eyes tells me she's sorting through a catalogue of memories from that day and then her eyes widen, and she nods. 'You are talking about your mother.'

'Yes. We've been trying to support her, you know. And I love her to bits, but I'm also worried she might do something to spoil the night. I know she doesn't mean to. I know she doesn't plan it, but honestly, I think she's in a worse place now than she was four years ago, and the potential for a repeat performance is high.'

There. I've said it.

Lola presses her lips together and nods, considering her reply. She pushes the tin of puff-puffs towards me and even grabs one herself. 'I'm very honoured that you wish to seek my advice, but I don't know if I am the best person to counsel you on this.'

I sigh again. I know this. But who else can I ask? I should be using my own mother as a sounding board, but unfortunately she's often the problem rather than the solution. 'I do know that, and I'm sorry if this puts you in a difficult position. I suppose I was just hoping for some family wisdom.'

Lola reaches out and touches my arm. 'I cannot give you specific advice about your mum — I think it would be wrong of me to do so — but wisdom is always free.' She thinks for a moment, then adds, 'The one thing you have to realize is that this is not about you.'

Oh. The smile falls from my face. She thinks I'm making it all about me? Am I being selfish? Narcissistic?

She catches my expression and quickly explains. 'I mean that your mum's drinking has nothing to do with you. You cannot stop her.'

Ain't that the truth! I've tried everything.

'But you also cannot *make* her drink. What I'm saying is that what you do or don't do will make no difference to how much she drinks or if she stops. Believe me, I know — my first husband's brother had these issues.'

I remember her saying something about that now, I realize, but it isn't a fact I would have recalled if not for this moment.

'I think I'd like to believe what you're saying, but I don't know if I do. She doesn't drink in a vacuum. What goes on in the world around her, including her relationships, has to have an impact, right?'

'To an extent. But the buck stops with her. She drinks because she chooses to, and she won't stop until she chooses to, and that won't happen until drinking becomes more painful than the things she uses it to escape from.'

'I don't think *she* sees it that way. She always said . . . ' I pause, unable to continue because my throat has swollen.

Lola gets up and puts her arms around me. 'Tell me?'

I rest my face against her shoulder and feel her solid warmth. 'She said she wouldn't have needed to drink if she hadn't been a single mum. When I was a teenager, she'd tell me I drove her to it because I was so difficult.'

My stepmother makes a dismissive noise. 'What nonsense! You forget I knew you during those years. When you came to visit us at the weekend, you were quiet as a mouse, always looking scared at me with those big eyes, always jumping up to try and help. Did you get moody sometimes? Of course! You were a teenager. But you were in no way a problem child, Jessica. Do not believe that of yourself.'

She pats me on the back, and I give her a little squeeze. When I pull back and blink my watery eyes, she smiles at me. 'I have been waiting for many years to have a chat like this with you, my daughter,' she tells me. 'I am glad you confided in me. As I say, I cannot give you counsel on what to do about Luke's party, but I will tell you this: listen to your own heart on this matter.'

'But—'

That's easier said than done with Luke's insistence that 'family is family'.

Lola holds a finger up. 'Ah! Do not argue with me. Be true to yourself, and do not cave in and do what you think everyone else wants you to do.'

CHAPTER THIRTY-TWO

JESS

Luke edges behind me in our narrow bathroom. He leaves a hand on my bare shoulder, reaching past me as I apply concealer and foundation, and grabs his aftershave from the shelf. He pauses for a moment, meeting my eyes in the mirror. We stare at each other for a full two seconds and then he kisses the top of my head. 'I don't want the whole of our day to be "off", if you know what I mean?'

I blink. 'I don't either.'

His muscular arms are heavy as he wraps them around my shoulders and brings his cheek next to mine. 'We'll work it out. It's not such a big thing that we should let it spoil us celebrating four years of being married.'

Relief surges through my whole body like a warm wind. *Oh, thank goodness.* 'I love you,' I say into the mirror. He kisses the hollow of my neck. All day I've been waiting for this, for this sense of togetherness rather than being opposing forces. But how do I keep it? How do I hang on to it?

Luke suddenly goes still and swears. 'I think I need to iron a shirt.' He untangles himself from me, gives himself a spritz of aftershave, and pops the bottle back on the shelf. I playfully swat his behind as he leaves the bathroom, smiling to myself as his usual retort of, 'don't touch what you can't afford!' echoes from the landing.

By the time my make-up is done and I'm ready to get dressed, Luke is in the living room manhandling the ironing board. A quick check of the clock by my bed tells me we're due at the restaurant in about half an hour. I'm still in my underwear when my phone rings. I grab for it and see 'Mum' on the screen. My stomach sinks.

'Hi,' I say breezily, hoping I can get this over and done with as quickly as possible.

'Jessica!' Mum says. She's not slurring. Yet. But I can hear the tell-tale softening of consonants that suggests it won't be long. 'Did you get a chance to drop that money in my account?'

I think back to the ledger in my bullet journal. I noticed the date on the last amount was yesterday, so I feel I'm fairly safe in confirming I did.

'Oh, thank you, sweetie! I promise I'll pay it back as soon as I can.'

I stare at my phone screen and shake my head. We both know that's not true. I think about doing what I'd usually do, saying the right thing to placate her, minimizing my own frustration at the never-ending cycle of lies and self-delusion, but then I'm brought back to a moment earlier as my stepmother looked me in the eye and told me the truth.

'Actually, Mum . . . there's something I need to talk to you about.'

'Yes?'

'I'm planning a surprise birthday party for Luke next month.'

'That sounds exciting!'

I pause for a moment, readying myself. I hardly ever talk to Mum about her drinking. I've been conditioned to leave that towering elephant in the room unacknowledged since I was barely out of primary school, but today I have to say something. 'I would very much like it if, when you come to the party, you promise you won't drink any alcohol – while you're there, and even before you come.'

I feel the silence frosting over down the phone line. 'I hope you haven't forgotten, Jess, that I am the mother, and you are the daughter, and it's not your place to tell me what to do.'

I close my eyes. I know what's coming. I hoped I could have a reasonable conversation with her, but deep down I knew it was impossible. She starts to rant, telling me how ungrateful I am, telling me how much she's done for me over my life, how I have no right to judge her, and when she gets no reaction out of me except a weary silence, she digs deeper into her arsenal.

'You know what you are, my darling daughter? You're unfeeling. Cold. You push away everyone who loves you, who tries to get close to you. Goodness knows I'm fed up with trying to make you love me back. And I don't know what I've done. In fact, I don't think anyone could be good enough for you, could give you enough. You better hope that beautiful man of yours doesn't work that out for himself, because if he does, he'll be out the door faster than a bullet out of a gun.'

Her oddly prophetic words slice into me, but at the same time, they do nothing.

'He's too good for you, but you always knew that, didn't you? But you won't be holding the moral high ground when he's left you for someone better. You'll just be the sad, discarded practice wife before he meets the real one, and *then* you'll understand how I feel.'

I stand there, motionless, as if I'm just listening to the weather report. So maybe she's right that I'm cold and uncaring. Maybe it is time to stop . . . to just *stop*.

'Actually, Mum, I've changed my mind. Drink as much as you like on that day.'

She makes a confused grunt.

'Because you won't be coming to the party. You're not invited. And I will make sure that two of Luke's bricklayer friends are standing at the door ready to throw you out if you even try to appear. Got that?'

For the first time in my life I wish I still had a wired phone like the one we had when I was a kid. It was so much more satisfying to slam the receiver into the base unit than jam my finger onto a glass screen to end the call.

My breath comes in short pants as I try and grasp what just happened. A muscle in my jaw ticks, warning me my teeth will start to chatter if it gets any worse.

I turn and run down the hall into our kitchen-diner, where Luke is standing over the desk tucked into an alcove that we use as a home office space. He turns when he hears me coming and I rush into his arms. 'I j-just . . . ' And then I realize I can't tell him I've uninvited her from the party, because he's not supposed to know about the party, and the words come out as a rough hiccup. 'I've just had it with Mum. I c-can't do it anymore. You should have heard the things she said to me, Luke! Things about our marriage! I . . . I really do want to go no-contact with her.'

It's then I realize that my husband is as stiff as the ironing board he must have just put away in the tall cupboard beside the desk. I pull back to look at him. 'Luke? What's the matter?'

'I honestly don't understand you,' he says, and he doesn't look confused; he looks pissed off.

'W-what do you mean?'

He reaches behind him and pulls a notebook off the desk. My bullet journal. 'On one hand you're crying about how mean your mum is and how you never want to see her again, but on the other . . .' he waves the book and it flaps open to where I'd carefully put a page marker ' . . . you're sending her money on a regular basis when I have a clear recollection of a conversation, ooh, maybe a year and a half ago, where we agreed we weren't going to fund her habit anymore. We agreed emotional support would have to be enough. Remember that?'

I swallow. 'I'm not . . . I don't give her money for drink. It's for bills. You know she's been having a tough time recently.'

Luke dips his head and gives me a steadying look. 'She *says* it's for bills, but you and I know where that money's probably going.'

I rub my lips one over the other to moisten them. 'I know what we said but . . . her drinking will get worse if she gets into debt, if she gets evicted, and you've helped your siblings out enough times when they've been in a hole.' The privilege of being the eldest brother with an overdeveloped sense of duty.

'That's not the same thing and you know it.'

I fold my arms and take a step back suddenly very aware I'm just wearing my bra and knickers. 'Why isn't it? As much as you say "family is family", why do I always feel as if I come second place to your family? And why does it always seem to be one rule for your family and another one for mine?'

'Because none of my siblings are addicts.'

Oof. Okay, he's got a good point there, but I'm not going to let that stop me fighting my corner. I'm fed up feeling as if I'm always in the wrong, no matter how hard I try to do the right thing. 'Oh, aren't you the lucky one.'

'Don't be like that, Jess.'

'Like what? Upset that you're chastising me like I'm a child caught with my hand in the cookie jar?'

Luke slaps the book back down on the desk, scattering a couple of bills. One floats gently off the desk and onto the floor. We both watch it until it lands.

'And why were you snooping around in my private journal anyway?' I ask, my spine straightening further. 'Don't you trust me?'

Luke very nearly rolls his eyes. 'One, it's not a private journal, like a *pour my secret thoughts out* journal. You've showed it to me before! It's full of lists and projects. And, two, you left it open on the page where you'd listed all your mum's "loans".' The fact he does air quotes when he says the last word infuriates me. 'I picked up a couple of pieces of paper on top looking for the note I made about the restaurant reservation this evening, so I wasn't *snooping*, as you call it. I just stumbled upon it accidentally.'

I haven't got much I can say to that, so I just stand and glower at him, desperately wishing I had something to cover myself up with. No one likes arguing in their underwear.

'And how exactly has this all got turned around on me, when you're the one who's been going behind my back?'

'It's not *wrong* to want to help my mum! You're the one who told me to, remember?'

'Yes, I remember. But that was three years ago now and

the situation has changed, and we've discussed it, put plans in place . . . boundaries . . . even though that's a foreign concept to her. But I do think you're wrong for not talking to me if you wanted to change what we'd agreed. We're supposed to be a team, Jess. That's what marriage means, doesn't it?'

Shame washes over me. He's right. 'I honestly don't think I can win here, Luke. I tried to do what you asked but I end up in the wrong. And if I do what *I* think is right, well, that's wrong too.'

'Well, I do think you're in the wrong,' Luke says. 'Earlier on you were all "we can't afford to go away for your birthday, Luke!" but now I discover you've spent at least that amount of money helping your mum out. Who's making who feel second-class compared to their family now, huh?'

I can't take any more of this. I turn and stomp from the room and head back to our bedroom.

'Jess!' Luke yells after me. 'Come back! We haven't finished talking!'

'I have,' I mutter under my breath.

But Luke doesn't give up that easily. 'Jess . . . For God's sake! Where are you going?'

I pause with one hand on the door frame.

'The Uber I ordered is going to be here in ten minutes,' I yell back. 'So, unless you want me to go out to dinner like this and get arrested, I'm going to need to put some clothes on!' *Argue with that*, I think, as I wrench the door open and stare unseeing into the back of my wardrobe.

CHAPTER THIRTY-THREE

LUKE

Eighteen Weeks Before the Anniversary Party

She sits in a large blue armchair, and he sits in a smaller one. The coffee on the small table between them isn't as good as the Colombian roast from the independent coffee house they met at last time, but it isn't bad. He's on his second cup.

He's here to listen. Elena needs him. Just talking, nothing else. They've agreed that's what this is, and there are reasons why she would prefer to keep her situation private at the moment. Good reasons. So why does he feel bad about telling Jess he was meeting up with a friend but conveniently skirting around giving her a name?

Elena sighs. 'You know what? I am sick of moaning about my life. Can we talk about something else?'

'Whatever you want. What do you want to talk about? The weather?'

She snorts softly. 'A very British pastime, but no, thank you. I am not yet ready to be that dull.'

He smiles at her. She's teasing him. He likes it when she teases him. It brings some of the vitality back to her eyes. Much better than the sadness that's been filling them lately. 'Football?'

That earns him a soft swat on the arm.

'Ow,' he says feigning pain, but then remembers himself. 'Read any good books lately?'

She presses her lips together while she thinks. 'I'm not sure if small talk is what I had in mind. We are past that, no, you and I?'

He supposes so. He's known her for well over a decade now, although they have floated in and out of each other's lives. But recently she's felt like an anchor for him. He's very grateful for her friendship. 'My next thought was films and TV, so I suppose that's out too. I'm not sure I'm very good at this.'

'You do okay,' she says, giving him a look he can't quite decipher. 'And you're here, which means a lot.' She sighs and looks out the large plate-glass window for a few moments, at the twinkling lights of the city.

'What do you need from me?'

Slowly, she turns her head to look at him again. 'I need to not feel so alone, as if I am the only one in the world who has troubles.'

He holds her gaze. He understands her words, but he's not sure what he can do about that. 'We could talk about the news, plenty of people in dire situations every day, but I'm not sure it's going to cheer you up much.'

She lets out a breath of laughter. It was a bad suggestion but she's indulging him.

'Maybe something closer to home. Tell me your news, Luke. What's up with you? Where are your struggles at the moment? Maybe they are not as large as mine but hearing about them – sharing with each other – may help.'

His eyes glaze over as he checks through his memory banks of the last week for something suitable. 'This sounds pathetic in comparison, but I accidentally bought the wrong paint colour for a job we're doing, and we'd done two rooms and a hallway before we realized. Going to have to reorder the paint and redecorate, and it was Farrow & Ball. Dad was not pleased when he found out.'

She blinks slowly and purses her mouth. 'You're right. That is pathetic. I meant tell me something about *you*, Mr Luke Harris. Or is your life as perfect on the inside as it always seems from the outside? In which case I will have to hate you, and you will be no use to me.'

He chuckles softly, even as a shiver shoots through him. His life isn't perfect. Nobody's is, but is it really that bad? Is 'not great' bad or is it just . . . not great?

'Come on, Luke. The night is still young.'

He looks more closely at her eyes as he considers his answer. She's wearing that slightly weary, slightly teasing expression, but behind it all he sees a plea. *Join me. I don't want to be alone in this.*

He takes a moment, digs deep. At first he thinks he's just going to unearth nothing, but then he hits something hard. Something painful. Something he'd rather not talk about, actually.

But he has to. For her.

He raises his chin slightly. 'I really want to be a father, but I'm not sure that's ever going to happen.'

She leans forward, her brow creasing. 'Why?'

He's not sure he wants to tell her. He doesn't want to expose himself – or Jess – but as he looks at Elena, he thinks about how much she's shared with him in recent weeks, how vulnerable she's been. It hasn't made him think any less of her. In fact, it's made him respect her all the more. Maybe he owes her the same?

'I don't know if my wife actually wants to have kids.'

Elena's eyebrows rise. 'You didn't discuss this before you were married? Or in the early years?'

'Oh, we did. I thought we were on the same page. She still says she wants to – or at least she did the last time I asked, which was probably more than a year ago now.' However, he's had an idea for an anniversary present for Jess, and it's got him thinking about it again. About family.

'But . . . ?'

He smiles slightly. She knows him so well, heard the unspoken word at the end of his sentence. 'But there's always something, always a reason why now's not a good time, why we need to put it off. I'm starting to wonder if she's just waiting for her biological clock to run down and then it'll be a done deal. Out of our hands.'

'You truly believe this?'

He gives a self-deprecating laugh. 'I don't know. Maybe I'm just being paranoid. Jess is a bit of a perfectionist. Maybe she's just waiting for the perfect time. Life has been a bit crazy in the last few years. You know how busy I am with the business now Dad has allowed me to add a few more strings to our bow.'

Elena seems to sense that he's said as much as he's able to, because she spends a while looking out the window, and then she closes her eyes. She's tired, he can tell, and he almost thinks she might have dozed off when she says in a whisper, 'I would like to have children too, some day. But, as you say, life gets in the way. I no longer have a husband, but I had my eggs frozen when I was ill four years ago.'

'You did?'

'Yes. But if I go down that path, I suppose I will need a . . . what do you call it?'

'A man?' he says, one side of his mouth hitching up.

She rolls her eyes. 'Not unless I can help it. I'm done with them, remember?'

'So I recall. But you will at least need some of his best swimmers.' The skin above her nose crinkles. She doesn't understand the idiom. Her English is so good he sometimes forgets it's not her first language. 'A donor,' he adds.

'Ah, yes! That is the word. A donor. Not now, of course. But maybe in a year or two, if I am lucky.' She looks at him with her large brown eyes, so wistful, but also so full of tentative hope. They hold eye contact as the seconds tick past but then he feels uncomfortable enough to look away.

God. What was that? Sometimes, when their eyes meet, it feels as if part of him is hooking on to part of her, but that time . . . Was she . . . ? Did she . . . ? Did that mean something? Is she saying she wants *him* to be the donor?

No. Of course not. Don't be so stupid.

'Let us not think of things that may never be,' she says matter-of-factly, and the moment is gone. Over.

He's always imagined what his kids would look like, wondered if they'd have white-blond hair like he did as a child, or whether a touch of Jess's red would be in there, turning it strawberry blond, but now another image scoots into his mind unbidden – a little boy, about eighteen months old, with golden skin, dark curls and ridiculously thick eyelashes. He shuts the thought down immediately, despite its appeal.

Not appropriate, Luke. Definitely not appropriate.

'Solving your problem should be a lot easier than solving mine,' she tells him. 'What do you think is going on with Jessica? Why has she changed her mind?'

He sighs. 'I wish I knew.'

'You need to talk to her, Luke.'

He nods. He knows. But he's scared of what she might say. Maybe she does want babies. Maybe she just doesn't want them with him.

WOOD

The structural tissue found in the roots and stems of trees and other plants, used for thousands of years as fuel, but also as a construction material, due to its stability and endurance. In many societies, wood symbolizes life, strength and growth.

CHAPTER THIRTY-FOUR

JESS

I wake up with a headache. Hardly surprising when Luke and I shared a frosty dinner at an overpriced Italian restaurant and then went to sleep on opposite sides of the bed.

I roll over and look at him. He's on his back, one arm thrown above his head. The hand resting on my thigh slides off as I change position. All the tension in his frame is gone. I breathe out. This is one time I'm grateful he's had a year's distance from our last anniversary, even if I've only had a reprieve of a few hours.

I twist my head to take in our surroundings and see cream wallpaper dotted with fleur-de-lys in gold leaf, gold damask curtains and upholstery, and beautiful polished mahogany furniture. *Oh, thank goodness. We're in Venice.* Just as we were last time. That argument over my mother didn't send things into a downward spiral so much that it changed our future significantly.

But then I think, *Oh, crap. We're in Venice!* And I know that last night was only a warm-up for the fight we had this year.

Luke doesn't look as if he's going to be waking up any time soon, so I slide gently from the bed, pad across the speckled marble floor and pull on some comfy clothes. I need some thinking space – and some coffee – if I don't want to repeat the disaster of our fifth anniversary.

Hotel Vincenzi is a renovated palazzo. I drink in the grand stone staircase with its carved columns and arches and deep red carpet as I descend, thinking once again how it makes me feel as if I'm in a period drama. A small breakfast room with a low ceiling painted in deep royal blue with gold plasterwork and shimmering crystal chandeliers sits opposite the reception desk. I grab a cappuccino and head through double doors with wrought-iron gates onto a small, paved terrace overlooking the Grand Canal and choose a table right next to the water.

I couldn't find my bullet journal in the hotel room, so the only thing I have to help me piece together what happened over the last twelve months is my phone. I scroll through the message thread between me and Luke. It all seems very normal. No major red flags there, thank goodness.

I also check my last text with my mother – eleven months and three weeks ago. There are further messages from her, asking why I'm not replying to hers and then a full-on, scroll-past-three-screens rant about what a horrible daughter I am; after that, nothing.

I let out a long, steady breath. This was what I wanted, and I know it's the right decision, but it doesn't make it any easier.

The early morning shadows slant across the canal, plunging the lone gondolier who operates a no-frills ferry service to foot passengers into shade and then brilliant sunlight as he crosses back and forth between the jetty next to the hotel and Campo San Samuele on the other side of the water.

I take a sip of my cappuccino and ruminate on how I can

change the course of this day. It *cannot* turn out the way it did last time. While we made up fairly swiftly, the wounds dealt by this conflict didn't fully heal for months afterwards.

If I'm remembering things correctly, we've been in Venice for two nights now and we're due to fly home the day after tomorrow. Last night, we got a phone call from Luke's mother, letting us know his sister has gone into labour three weeks early.

The fact that it's Cassandra, the next oldest Harris sibling, and Luke's partner-in-crime when he was younger, sent him into a tailspin of fraternal protectiveness, and he suggested cutting our anniversary trip short and flying home tonight – at the very time we should be having a fancy dinner in a restaurant we had to book three months in advance to make sure we got a table.

I (understandably, I think) was upset that he was ready to axe our celebrations at a moment's notice and disagreed but, Luke being Luke, he had very fixed ideas of exactly how the situation should be handled. The whole thing escalated until I accused him of always putting his family above me and he told me I was reading too much into things and I needed to stop being so defensive and insecure, which caused me to shut down completely. We spent the rest of the trip simmering away at the other's unreasonableness.

I do *not* want to live all of that again.

I watch a water taxi pull up to the stop near the hotel and see other holidaymakers dragging their cases onto the pontoon, looking hopeful and happy. *You only live once . . .* Well, I know that's not true. At least not for me. But I'm spending so much time panicking about getting things right that I'm not recognizing whatever's happening to me as the gift that it is.

Maybe it's because, inside, I'm actually five years older than

I look on the outside. Maybe it's the fact that I've been on fast-forward, getting snapshots of my life that add up to create a bigger picture, but as I look back over the last time I lived this day, I feel differently about what went on.

Luke was in full-on panic mode about his sister, and feeling he had to be the one to make it right for her. It wasn't anything to do with me. He just wasn't thinking.

But he should have been thinking about you as well, shouldn't he? Doesn't that just prove your point?

Shh, I tell the voice inside my head. I think he overreacted when he wanted to jump on a plane and head back home. Obviously, *I* know that baby Edie was born hearty and healthy, but we had no idea at the time, even though there was no hint we needed to be worried. But I overreacted too. Maybe, if I'd been more understanding rather than sulking, we could have ironed the situation out without ruining our trip. I can do more than just react this time. Just like the other days I've lived again; I can choose a different path. I can be the wife Luke needs me to be, but I can also choose what's best for me too. Those things needn't be mutually exclusive.

I finish my coffee and order room service before heading back upstairs to our room. When a soft knock comes at the door, I take the tray, carry it over to the coffee table and chairs just in front of the window, and then I touch Luke's shoulder softly. 'Hey, sleepyhead . . . Breakfast is served.'

He grumbles but opens his eyes and blinks at me. 'Breakfast?'

I stifle a smile. I knew that would get his attention. 'Mm-hmm. And I got *Ciambellone*, that cake you like.'

Luke frowns at me and then looks over at the tray laden with two cappuccinos and an assortment of pastries, bread and jam, and a selection of sliced meats and cheese. I can tell he's wondering where the normal Jess is, the one who would have backed right off until either one of us apologizes or enough time goes past that we become weary and fall back into our usual routine.

I sit in one of the chairs and load one of the small plates for myself and wait for Luke to join me, which he does a minute or so later. When he's had a sip of coffee and a couple of bites of cake, I say, 'I'm sorry about last night. About what I said.' While I don't remember the exact words, I know I can get spiky when I feel dismissed or overlooked. 'I do understand that you're worried about Cassie and the baby.'

He looks a bit taken aback. 'Thanks. I'm sorry too. I shouldn't have said you were being defensive and unreasonable.'

I sigh. 'I probably *was* being defensive, but I don't think I was being completely unreasonable. We've saved for this trip for almost a year, and it was meant to be a romantic getaway.'

'Wanting to book flights for today was possibly jumping the gun a bit.'

'Possibly?' I say with a twinkle in my eye.

'Possibly,' he confirms, a matching glint in his own.

'Look . . . ' I take a deep breath, knowing what I'm going to say next is stretching me to my very limit. 'Let's talk to your mum in a minute, get an update on Cassie and the baby, and we'll go from there, but—'

As if summoned, Luke's phone begins to ring. He answers it and stands so he can pace back and forth while he talks. I can tell it's his mum. I get the gist of the conversation just from listening to his end, but I can also fill in the gaps from my previous knowledge. However, I let Luke end the call and listen patiently as he explains to me that Cassie has had a gorgeous little girl and both mother and baby are doing fine, no issues at all, despite Edie surprising us all with her early arrival.

'Do you still want to go home?' I ask him. 'Because if you really want to, we'll do it, but I think we could also maybe FaceTime Cassie sometime today if she's up to it, and we'll be seeing our new niece within forty-eight hours anyway. But you can phone, text, whatever — as much as you need to — until that happens.'

Luke puts his phone down, comes over to my chair, takes me by the hands and pulls me up and hugs me. 'Thank you,' he whispers into my ear. 'Thank you for . . . I don't know. Just thank you. And you're right — we don't have to change our flights.' He reaches up and brushes my hair back from my face and then keeps his palms on the side of my face. 'I want to have that romantic getaway we planned.'

*

After a glass of Prosecco on the hotel terrace, feeling like movie stars as other tourists take pictures of the beautiful palazzo behind us from water taxis and tour boats, Luke and I head out on the twenty-minute walk to the restaurant we've booked for dinner. I can't wait.

It's been the most amazing day. After a lazy breakfast we made love and then spent the rest of the day visiting some of the famous sites: St Mark's Square, the Doge's Palace. We even climbed to the top of the Campanile di San Marco. The whole city was laid out before us, a higgledy-piggledy sea of terracotta roof tiles, grey-white stone, and church towers.

It's been *so* much better than last time. We did most of the same things, but instead of barely talking, we've walked hand-in-hand, stopping to kiss now and then like honeymooners. I felt so hurt last time. I tried to get past it, I really did, but it seemed impossible.

How strange that, while not easy, it was completely doable this time around. I'm actually feeling quite proud of myself. I haven't even minded that Luke's phone has been going off at regular intervals, and he had a long call with his mum while I had a siesta before our evening drinks.

'Do you have any baby pics yet?' I ask him, as we cross the Ponte dell'Accademia and pause to look at the lavender glow of the sky as the Grand Canal widens out into the lagoon just beyond a vast domed basilica whose name I can't remember.

'Not yet. Mum says she's going to send some later.'

'I can't wait,' I say. I want to see all the gorgeous wrinkliness and tiny fingers and toes.

'Do you think . . . ?'

I turn away from the sunset to look at him. 'Do I think what?'

'No, doesn't matter.'

Dinner is as delicious as I hoped it would be. We start with a local speciality of sautéed onions with raisins, herbs and anchovies, and then sea bass, before beef fillet. Each course is punctuated with a palate cleanser or an amuse-bouche of some kind. By the time I get my tiramisu I'm already full. Luke manages to clear his plate and, after answering yet another text from either his mum or his sister, declares he needs to use the bathroom and heads off towards the back of the restaurant.

He's only seven steps away when his phone, which is lying on the pristine linen tablecloth, buzzes again. I lean over to take a look, just in case it's the promised baby pics.

I'm lonely, the message reads.

I frown. That's a weird thing for Luke's mum to say — she's always surrounded by family, and today probably more than ever. And I can't imagine Cassie saying something like that either, after just having given birth to a bouncing bundle of joy. But then I look again, and I realize it's not from either of them.

It's from Elena.

Why is she messaging Luke when he's on holiday? And even if she did, surely it should be something to do with marble countertops or whether they can get the electricians to wire those wall lights in.

And then another message appears on the thread: **I wish you were here. I could really do with a hug x**

My stomach turns to ice. *What?*

I snatch Luke's phone up and stare at the message on the screen for a good five seconds, before swiping upwards, scrolling further back through the text chain.

And that's when I realize it's not his sister or his mum Luke has been messaging all day. It's Elena. His 'work wife'.

CHAPTER THIRTY-FIVE

JESS

We walk back from the restaurant through the streets of Venice, over narrow canals with gently arching bridges, the moonlight and streetlights glittering on the dark water. It's magical, but I feel sick to my stomach. When Luke tries to sling an arm over my shoulder, I shift so it slides off, making an excuse that it's too heavy. He doesn't seem to mind.

I didn't have long before Luke returned from the men's room, but I had enough time to see multiple messages between him and Elena every day, some of them work-related, yes, but many of them not. And if I thought Elena's message to Luke was bad, I hadn't factored in some of his messages to her.

You're strong, you're beautiful. You've got this! x

That one in particular sticks in my mind.

Elena might well be lonely. Her relationship with Felix fully fell apart in the last twelve months. It was around this time he disappeared completely from our lives, and then, last time, Elena followed, possibly a year or so later. But she wasn't in business with my husband in that version of our lives, seeing him at least two or three times a week. Did I inadvertently set the stage for this to happen by putting my trust in him? That seems too cruel.

I didn't have time to read the thread fully, dissecting each message and reply; it was more snapshots of different ones that jumped out to me. And yet . . . Nothing was *so* inappropriate it was completely incriminating. There was nothing steamy or sexual. Even so, it isn't right, is it? It isn't good.

I think about how Luke's phone buzzed when we went back to bed after breakfast. Did she message while we were . . . ? It doesn't bear thinking about.

I don't know what to do. I know I have to do *something*, but how do I even broach this subject? Part of me wants to bury my head in the sand and pretend I didn't see any of it.

When we get back to our hotel, Luke asks if I want a limoncello sitting on the terrace. I tell him I'm tired, that I'd much rather just go back to our room. When we've climbed the stairs and shut the door behind us, he turns to me. 'Jess, what's up? You've been quiet since dessert at the restaurant. Did something not agree with you?'

I shake my head and turn to the dressing table and start removing my earrings and other jewellery. 'No. I'm feeling fine.'

'But you hardly touched your tiramisu – and it was the bit you were most excited about.'

I carefully press the butterfly onto the back of my earring and place it in my jewellery case. 'I think I just wasn't hungry by that point.' Which is true. I couldn't have forced another mouthful down.

He comes to stand behind me, places his hands on either side of my shoulders. 'Jess . . . '

I go still. 'I'm fine. Honest.'

Luke sighs and his hands fall away. 'I think I'll have a shower.'

Moments later, I hear the water turn on and I let out a long breath. I know I just missed an opportunity. But I don't know how to say what I need to say. I don't know if I even want to.

Maybe I *should* just brush it under the carpet. There was nothing truly damning in those messages, even if it appears Luke and Elena are a lot closer than I thought they were. Maybe he's just being a good friend after Felix left?

God, I'm pathetic.

My gut is telling me there's more going on than I'm aware of and I'm ready to pretend it's not happening? But isn't that what Mrs Wonderful would do? She'd smile, keep her bright-red lipstick perfect, and woo him back with after-work martinis and divine pot roasts, all while looking like a Dior couture model.

Well, Mrs Wonderful can shove her martinis where the sun don't shine.

While Luke is in the shower, I run over to his jacket hung on the back of the door and pull his phone out. He did tell me his passcode, but I've never needed to use it before, so after five attempts I give up. I'm pretty sure I've got the numbers right; I just can't get them in the right order.

I'm just about to slide it back in his pocket when he comes out of the bathroom, one towel round his hips, rubbing his damp hair with another. He better not have used *my* bath towel for that, or I'll go nuts. Instead of replacing his phone, I walk towards him, holding it out. 'You want to know what's wrong? This is.'

He keeps rubbing his hair, but the top of his nose pinches in confusion as he takes it from me. 'My phone?'

'Your messages. With Elena.'

I don't miss the way his eyes widen slightly and then he turns away, obscuring his face for a moment with the towel. 'You went snooping in my phone?' He doesn't sound angry, just curious. Too calm for my liking.

'No. A couple popped up while you were in the bathroom at the restaurant.'

He nods, his lips pressing together slightly. 'They were probably about work,' he says, as he throws the towel onto one of the armchairs and reaches for one of the fluffy robes hanging in the wardrobe.

I blink. He just lied to me. Well, almost. He was very clever with his words. This is not the Luke I know and love.

'The messages I saw weren't about work.'

I'm surprised at how calm I am on the outside. Usually, in lieu of crying or getting sad about stuff, I just get angry. And it's there, burning away under the surface, but I'm able to hover above it. For now.

His frown deepens and he unlocks his phone and messes around on it for a few seconds – opening the messages app, I guess – and then he starts to scroll. A moment later, he freezes. 'Oh.'

'Yes, oh.'

His eyes meet mine. 'This isn't how it looks. You have to trust me on that.'

My eyebrows rise. 'I do, do I?'

Uh-oh. The zen-like hovering I'm doing above my rage is possibly about to undergo a crash landing.

'It looks very much to me as if the two of you are extremely close,' I add. 'Much closer than either of you has let on, actually. I think you better explain to me, in very clear terms, exactly what is going on between you, or I *will* think the worst.'

'You think . . . You think I'm having an *affair*? With Elena?'

If I wasn't so angry, his wounded tone might have been funny.

'You're so amazing, Elena . . . You're so strong and brave . . . ' I say, glaring at him. 'And she misses you. She wants to hug you!'

Luke looks as if I've slapped him in the face, which is rich. 'You read more than just those messages that arrived at dinner.'

'Wouldn't you? If you saw the ones I saw!' Just because I'm a bag of restless energy and I need to move, I stride across the room to stare out of the window.

'I think I'd be tempted, yes. But I would like to think I'd ask you about it before I jumped to conclusions.'

I spin around. 'I did ask you! You said they were about work!'

In Luke's eyes, I see the moment he slides off his high horse and meets me on even moral ground. 'Fair enough. But there's a reason for that—'

'Did you mean the things you said to her? About being brave and beautiful and strong?'

He doesn't flinch, doesn't look away. 'Yes.'

Inside, I fold up like a concertina. 'Of course you do,' I mumble heavily. 'She is all those things. Why *wouldn't* you feel that way?'

Oh, God. I've been kidding myself all this time, thinking I could be his Mrs Wonderful when, in reality, she is. It's always been her. Even other people see it, think she and Luke are perfect together.

'But just because I said those things to Elena, it doesn't mean I'm sleeping with her! It doesn't mean I don't love you!'

'And that's supposed to make me feel better? That you love us both? That you can't choose between us?'

Now Luke is the one striding around the room. It seems I'm annoying him as much as he is me. Good. 'That's not what I meant! I don't love Elena. Not like that!'

We're going round in circles, literally. I take a step sideways and collapse into one of the chairs next to the coffee table and put my head in my hands. 'Then make this make sense, Luke! Is it an emotional affair, is that what it is? Is prickly, sarcastic Jess not enough for you and you need someone warmer and more giving?'

His voice is low and rough when he answers. 'You know that's not true.'

I snap my head up to look at him. 'But that's the point! No, I don't! Not after what I saw this evening! Not after . . . '

'Not after what? What did I do?'

Not after you walked out on me saying you'd had enough five years from now, signalling very clearly that I can't give you what you need.

I shake my head wearily. 'It doesn't matter.' And it seems it really doesn't. No matter what I do, how hard I try to change myself, it's all going to end up the same way, isn't it? 'If it's her you want, go to her. Just end it now. I don't have it in me to drag this out anymore. I give up.' I plant my face back in my hands.

'You're giving up on me?' He has the nerve to sound pissed off.

I want to be childish. I want to say, *Yeah, well you did it first!* But I don't.

'What I'm trying to say is that I'm not going to make you stay if you don't want to stay.'

Luke comes over, kneels down in front of me until I have no choice but to look at him. 'Jess, you're my wife. You're the one I want to be with. It's not like that with Elena . . . It's . . . '

'Then what is it like?! Explain it to me, Luke! Before I lose my mind.'

He sighs heavily. 'Yes, I've been texting Elena a lot. Yes, I've been saying nice things to her to hype her up. But I'm doing it because she's ill, Jess. Elena has cancer.'

CHAPTER THIRTY-SIX

JESS

I feel as if I'm standing still and the world spins a full 180 degrees around me, so the sky is under my feet and the earth dangling above. '*What?*' While Luke's words are completely understandable, I can't compute the meaning.

'Elena has cancer. Breast cancer.'

'But . . . ? What . . . ?'

'So, yes, I've been texting her more than I normally would.'

I feel shame wash over me like a hot wave and I brace myself against it, stiffening my spine, ready to fight it off. 'Why on earth didn't you tell me?' I cry. Even more importantly, why didn't Elena tell me? I thought we were friends. Not besties, but friends all the same.

He shakes his head softly. 'She didn't want anyone to know.'

'But why?'

He shrugs. 'I don't get it either. I think she doesn't want anyone to see her as weak, as . . . less than, if you know what I mean? And her family is five thousand miles away in Bogotá, Felix is in the wind, so I've been trying to be encouraging, you know, be a good friend. I watched my mum go through this when I was sixteen and she still found it hard with the love and support of a big family around her. I can't imagine what it must be like to do it on your own.'

Of course he can't. And of course, he would step up and be the support system for someone struggling. This is Luke. I feel devastated for Elena, I can't even begin . . . but that doesn't mean I'm one hundred per cent happy that Luke has kept this from me. If he'd only been open about it, we might not be in this mess at the moment, but the truth is, Elena didn't trust me with this information, and neither did he.

'I wouldn't have told anyone. You know that.'

'Like I said, Elena wanted to keep it to herself.'

Somehow, I feel this is something to do with me, a flaw they both perceive that I didn't know I had. 'But you can see how those messages looked to me? You can see why I thought what I did? I mean, how was I supposed to know?'

'You could have just asked me about it.'

'I did!'

'Only after I had to pester you to tell me what was up because you were sulking.'

I push my chair back and stand, taking a few steps back. 'I was not sulking!'

Luke just looks at me.

Okay, so maybe I was.

'Anyone would have been blindsided seeing messages like that on their spouse's phone. What would you have done if you'd seen texts from a random man – say, Ahmed from the physio practice – saying he missed me and wanted to hug me? Are you telling me your alarm bells wouldn't have been ringing?'

Luke sits in one of the empty chairs around the coffee table, frowning. 'Okay, yes . . . I don't think I would have jumped right in and accused you of having an affair—'

'I didn't actually—'

'But I wouldn't have been happy, so you're right about that. But I don't know what else I could have done, Jess. I didn't want to betray Elena's trust, but I also haven't betrayed you in any way, you have to believe that.'

I rest my hands on the back of the chair I've just vacated. 'I do,' I reply, and some of the tension in my shoulders and jaw dissipates. 'I just wish you'd had a bit more faith in me, that we could have handled this as a team.'

Luke has been looking uncomfortable but amiable, but now his expression clouds over. 'Trust goes both ways. You went from a couple of ambiguous text messages to infidelity at light speed, not even stopping to ask if you were headed in the right direction. If anything, it's you who doesn't trust me, and that hurts, because never once have I given you reason to doubt me on that front.'

I stare back at him, unable to give him a good response.

'Why is that?'

'I don't know,' I answer quietly.

'Why was it so easy to believe that of me?'

'I don't know!' I'm feeling this horrible churning inside that's making my words come out louder and harder than I mean them to. How do I stop it? I don't like it. I don't like it at all. I feel the same way I do when someone calls unexpectedly and the house is untidy. I'm looking frantically at all the messy things I'm feeling, wondering where I can stuff them so they're out of sight, out of mind.

'Neither do I,' Luke says, turning his gaze to the flecks in the marble floor. He looks so hopeless, so crestfallen, that it brings tears to my eyes. I want to reach out to him, but I don't know if he'll want me to. When he meets my eyes again, he says, 'What have we got, Jess, if we don't have trust? Do you even love me if you think that badly of me?'

'I do love you!' I sob, even as my hands remain Velcroed to the chair back. If this weird nightmare has taught me anything, it's taught me that. 'And I . . . I don't want to lose you. Please, Luke. You have to believe me!'

He studies me for a moment. 'I do believe you love me, but . . .'

'But . . . ?'

'But what do we do if you don't trust me to stay, to be the husband I promised you I would be? It's going to eat away at our relationship and I can't see us making the next five years, let alone the next fifty, if that's the case.'

My throat closes at his eerily prophetic words, and I swallow.

'Do you even want that?'

I nod furiously, and Luke gets up and walks to the window to look out at the cobbled alley below. I stare at his back and try to work out what to do, what to say. I've been trying so hard for the last five days, but now I feel further away than ever from being the kind of wife I wanted to be for him. It's all amounted to nothing. I hear Mrs Wonderful's laughter in my head, mocking me for even thinking I could ever measure up to her.

Maybe I *should* leave him to Elena. She would certainly do a much better job than I have done. I wonder if I should go and stand behind him, wondering what words I can string together to make things right, but I have nothing, so I sit down heavily on the end of the bed and put my head in my hands. I've got nothing else. I give up.

'I'm so sorry, Luke. I do love you, I really do. And I know I don't always show it or say it, but I think . . . ' Words form in my head, but I have to push them out of my mouth. I despise myself for even half-thinking these thoughts in my darkest moments. These are things I've never wanted to admit to myself, let alone my husband. 'I think that I've always thought you'd leave me one day.'

Luke twists around sharply when I say this, his eyes narrowed.

'But that's nothing to do with you! It's to do with me, with how I don't think I'm enough for you. Why wouldn't you find someone better – someone like Elena – who isn't emotionally constipated, who doesn't back off and shut down when things get tough? You deserve someone like you, who can meet you as an equal. So, you're right, I don't have faith, but it's not you that I don't believe in. It's me.'

Luke rushes over to me and scoops me up into his arms. His voice is thick as he pulls me close and kisses my head, my face, my eyelids. 'Why would you think that? You're *everything* to me, don't you know that?'

I cry so hard that I lose my sense of time and space, of everything but the warmth of Luke's body pressed against mine. He holds me close as I let it all out, and when my sobbing gives way to sniffling, he pulls away, pushes my hair out of my face and holds it back with his hands so he can look at me.

'I believe in you,' he says seriously, looking deep into my eyes so I know he means it. 'And if you can't, I'll believe for the both of us. But can you believe in *us*, Jess? The fact that we're stronger together than we are apart? I need you. I know you may not believe that, but I do.'

I blink to release the tears welling up behind my lashes and nod. 'Yes,' I reply hoarsely. 'I can believe in us.'

Luke nods, as if he has decided something. 'Wait there,' he says, and goes to his bedside table and rummages around inside. When he returns, he holds up a now-familiar navy-blue leather ring box and carefully eases the lid open. 'I know I offered this to you once before, and it wasn't really what you wanted, but it occurred to me that something that didn't make a great engagement ring might well make a lovely fifth anniversary gift as an eternity ring. Do you want it? If not, we can get something different, although – due to current budget constraints – it might have to have fewer diamonds.'

I stare at the band, with its leaf-shaped diamonds and tiny, berry-like emeralds and my breath catches. It worked. It really worked. 'I love it,' I whisper, then meet his eyes with a smile. 'I would be honoured to wear it.'

Because now I know what it means to him. And to me.

Luke's expression of raw hopefulness breaks into a wide grin, and he takes the ring out of the box and slides it on my finger to nestle next to my engagement ring.

CHAPTER THIRTY-SEVEN

LUKE

Fifteen Weeks Before the Anniversary Party

Same time, same place, same not-quite-awful coffee. They've been sitting in companionable silence for a while, when Elena looks up from her high-backed blue chair. 'Did you talk to Jess about what we discussed last time we met?'

The evenings are slightly lighter now February has given way to March. Rather than complete darkness at six in the evening, the sky still holds the lavender hues of twilight. He stops looking out of the window and turns to Elena. 'I tried.'

'Tried how?'

'I was quite upfront about it, actually. I said I wanted to have a serious conversation with her about starting a family.'

'And she wouldn't talk about it? At all?'

He sighs heavily. 'Oh, she talked all right. First, she started going on about the training course she's doing, how it's really important, and she can't even think about something big until after that's over. But that's going to be months away. So, then I said maybe we could start trying before that. I mean, it could take a while before anything happens. But all she said was "we'll see". It's always "we'll see".'

'That's disappointing.'

He turns around, leans against the windowsill and looks at Elena, who is once again sitting in her high-back chair, a book on the table beside her, along with her phone and a puzzle book. He's sure his problems aren't as entertaining as the romcom paperback, but she seems to want to talk to him anyway. 'The more we talk about it – or don't – the more I think she doesn't actually want kids.'

'Then why doesn't she tell you that?'

He shakes his head. 'Jess isn't like you.' In fact, he can't think of two women who are more different. It makes their conversation easy. Refreshing. Lately, his communications with Jess seem more like wading through treacle. 'She doesn't open up easily.'

Once upon a time, she would. To him, anyway. It made him feel so special that he was the one person she trusted enough to do that. It was like owning a precious gem that no one else knew about. But now he seems to be on the outside, along with everybody else, and he has no idea how to get back in.

'Why wouldn't Jess want kids?' Elena muses.

He walks over to the empty chair near her and sits down heavily. 'I often wonder if it's her upbringing. It was . . . different.'

'How so?'

He goes on to tell Elena about Jess's mother – the drinking, the outbursts, the snippets of information his wife has let slip over the years, often unintentionally, that made him realize their view of family is very, very different. 'She no longer talks to her mother. Hasn't done for years.'

Elena looks horrified. 'I can't even imagine that.'

'Neither can I.' His mum is so warm and caring, his biggest cheerleader. 'And I worry about that. She once told me that I just don't get it, and maybe she's right. Maybe I don't. But I also don't understand how she can heal, how she can move on, if she won't engage with her mother.'

Elena rubs her temple thoughtfully. 'What about her father?'

'Their relationship is better . . . I think. He left when she was young and was out of the picture for a while, but he's been a fairly steady presence since she was in her mid-teens. He's married again and we see him and his wife and Jess's two sisters fairly frequently.'

'Every week?'

'Every month or so. And I don't get that, either. I would've thought, with one parent out of the picture, she would've made more of an effort with the other one, but it's like she holds back, keeps herself at a distance—oh!'

'Oh?'

He stands up again, needing to stretch his legs in order to help his brain think. 'I think I've hit the nail on the head. I get this sense that she's keeping a part of herself back. There's a particular vibe I start to pick up on when she does it with them. And I just realized I've been feeling that too lately. She's started doing it with me as well . . . ' He walks to the window and then sits back down in the chair, and where he can't have a proper conversation from six feet away. 'I don't know why I didn't see it before. It's so obvious.'

Did he hurt Jess? All he's ever wanted to do was to help her, to protect her. How can it have got to the place where he is the one who is making her clam up and shut down?

'I don't know what I did,' he repeats to Elena.

She reaches out and lays her hand on top of his. 'Only she can tell you.'

But that's the problem, he thinks. She won't. So where do they go from here? If she won't let him help, how can he?

'I don't know what to say,' Elena adds, 'but I know you are a good man, Luke, that you want the best for her. That's all you want for anyone, and if Jess can't see that, it's her loss. But I want you to know I appreciate all you've given me, all you are doing for me.'

He looks up at Elena. Her eyes are so warm and open. Why can't his wife be more like that?

IRON

A chemical element which is one of the most common on the planet, known for its strength, durability and resilience. However, if not treated properly, it is prone to corrosion and rust.

CHAPTER THIRTY-EIGHT

JESS

Without opening my eyes, I can tell it's morning. The sheet is warm beneath me but cool if I reach out. I am boneless, my soul at rest. I'm not in Venice anymore; I know that much, because I hear a car driving on the road outside.

I allow my lids to drift open and don't rush my eyes to focus right away. The ceiling is white. The walls are green. Not the flat, then. We've moved. We finally got our own house. I feel a pang of sadness for the one we lost, the one I lived in for five years but never had the opportunity to say goodbye to.

But then I let my gaze sharpen, wander around the top half of the room that I can see easily without turning my head. The light pendant hanging from the ceiling is familiar, practically the same as the one I chose for our other home. Most of the pictures on the walls are the same. One or two are different.

I roll over and face the windows. They're arranged in a square bay, just like our old house. In fact, the layout is almost identical. But that's not surprising, there must be hundreds of thousands, if not millions, of red-brick terraced houses like this all across

London, and while the design varies slightly from road to road, they're more similar than they are different.

I yawn, stretching my arms above my head, splaying my fingers, and that's when I catch a glimpse of a sparkle on my right ring finger. Great-Great-Grannie's engagement ring. I smile as I remember Luke giving it to me last night . . . last year. Its magic belongs to me now.

On one hand, I'm sad that finally owning it hasn't transported me instantly back to my real life but on the other . . . maybe it's better I ride this strange experience out. Luke and I are doing better in this reality. We couldn't have been doing worse in the other.

Luke isn't beside me, but the radio is on downstairs in the kitchen. I ease myself out of bed sleepily, pull my robe on, and open the bedroom door. When I see the landing, I stop, frozen in my tracks.

The landing is not just similar, but identical.

It can't be, can it? This can't be *our* house?

But as I make my way downstairs, I discover it must be, because the plaster moulding along the hallway ceiling is exactly the same size and shape as before. And there is the nick on the newel post near the bottom that someone damaged decades before we moved in, but we decided not to fill because it had character. History. We liked the idea that many families, hopefully happy, had lived here before us.

This *is* our house. It's like fate or the universe, or whatever it is that's playing this strange prank on me, is rewarding me, making up for the hell it's been putting me through. I'm so happy I could sing.

Luke doesn't hear me when I enter the kitchen – the fan is on above the cooker hood – and he's humming along to a Nineties hit on the radio. I'm tempted to surprise him by hugging him from behind, but it's probably not a good idea when there are flames and hot pans involved.

'Hey . . . ' I say softly, and he spins around, surprised. I can't help smiling. He's wearing the apron his gran bought me for Christmas three years ago over the top of his pyjama bottoms. Blossom and honeybees suit him, it seems.

'Morning, beautiful,' he says, dropping the spatula he's holding on to the worktop and turning to pull me into his arms. He kisses me softly and slowly at first, but then his hands begin to roam, and things get a little more urgent. It's only the acrid smell of something close by burning that makes us spring apart.

'Crap,' says Luke, looking at the frying pan.

'What was it?'

'Blueberry and banana pancakes,' he replies, taking the pan over to the bin, dumping the charred couple of doughy discs inside. 'But no worries. I've got plenty more mixture.'

While these were a firm feature of the early years of our marriage, I don't know if Luke ever made them for me once we moved to this house. Not last time around, anyway. That has to be a good sign, right? Something else to bolster this sense of buoyancy inside me, this feeling that something has shifted, that everything is going to be all right.

The day is sunny and warm, so we throw the French doors open and eat our pancakes at the bistro table in the garden. These are no misshapen dollops of good intention. These pancakes are perfect – golden and fluffy. The blueberries burst with a hint of sourness on my tongue. Luke keeps smiling at me as we eat, and I keep smiling back. Life is good. Life is really good.

Did you do this? I silently ask the circle of diamonds and emeralds on my finger. *Did you grant my wish?*

I don't know, and maybe I don't care, as long as it stays this way. I feel as if I can breathe out now, as if maybe I can enjoy the next few days rather than dread them.

I haven't had a chance to check my bullet journal yet, so I ask, 'What are the plans for today?', hoping it won't seem too out of place.

'I've got to finish removing that chimney breast in the house in Shortlands. Dirty work, but someone's got to do it.'

'Your dad couldn't put anyone else on it?'

'Maybe, but . . . I don't want to complain, you know. He was good letting me take time away from the business when the Sidcup house ran into issues, and I had to spend way more time there.'

I have no idea which house in Sidcup he's talking about, but I guess this must be another house flip with Elena. 'What's your next renovation project?' I ask, because I saw the look of wistfulness on his face as he talked about that house.

He sighs. 'I don't know. Everything was on hold while Elena was ill, and now she's visiting her parents, and she's not sure when she's coming back. I'm not even sure if she wants to continue, and it's not exactly the right time to badger her about it. I'll probably have to find a new partner if I want to carry on. Or just go solo.'

'But that's doable, right?'

His mouth twists into a rueful smile. 'Dad wants to retire in a few years. If he does, I'll have my hands full just keeping on top of Harris & Sons.'

I nod. This is what happened last time, but I never realized how stifled Luke felt keeping the family business going. Seeing how energized he gets when he's got a new renovation project on the go – even in these tiny snapshots of our life together I'm experiencing – is making me see things differently.

'Anyway,' Luke says, brushing the subject away with the pancake crumbs from the table onto the patio, 'we've still got dinner this evening to look forward to. That new Thai place on the High Street looks amazing.'

'It does,' I reply, but then I remember how I hugged the toilet in the middle of the night after our one and only visit there. 'But, I don't know, I'm not sure I'm feeling Thai this evening. Shall I see if I can get us a table at Arnaldo's instead?'

'Why not?' he says, but I'm not sure he actually wants Italian or whether he's just humouring me.

'We can do Thai if you fancy . . . ' There is another place a couple of streets over that's been around for a while and has a good reputation.

'No. It's okay.'

I stand up as I gather our plates and pause to kiss him on the nose before I take them back inside.

We wash up and tidy away together, and when the last spoon is put in the dishwasher, I reach for Luke and explore behind the apron front, full of taut muscle and soft bare skin. He pulls me in for a kiss, then holds me close. 'Have you thought any more about the conversation we had the other day? he adds and then gives me a cheeky grin. 'I thought maybe we could work on that after dinner.'

I raise my eyebrows. 'Conversation?'

Luke's smile fades, and I realize he thinks I'm not paying attention to things that are important to him, but I can hardly explain why I don't remember, can I?

'Oh, the one from the other night?'

He nods and presses the flat of his hand against my belly. 'I know it's a scary idea — becoming parents and all — but I'm ready if you are.'

I smile back at him while inside is a churning mass of contradicting emotions — yearning for a soft pink bundle of warmth to love and cuddle. Fear that I don't have very good role models when it comes to being an engaged and present parent. What if I can't do it? What if I mess it up? I would hate it if my child felt about me the same way I feel about my mother, or cried as hard as I did when I felt my father had moved on with hardly a backward glance. I want to give Luke that, but what if all it does is highlight my inadequacies in a whole new area of my life that we haven't even explored yet?

'We'll see,' I say, 'but it can't hurt to have fun trying.'

'I'm so lucky to have you,' he whispers into my hair as his hands move round to my back and he pulls me against him. 'I honestly don't know what I'd do without you.'

I melt against him, bathing in his words. 'I love you,' I respond simply, but with all of my heart.

'I love you, too.'

CHAPTER THIRTY-NINE

JESS

I'm just checking through my bullet journal for what might be on my agenda today when my phone rings.

'Hey, you . . . Fancy going out for a drink and some gossip this evening?'

'I'd love to, but I'm going out with Luke this evening – it's our anniversary.'

'Oh, God! Yes! What day is it today?'

'Saturday.'

Hannah sighs. 'For some reason it feels like a Sunday. I've been twenty-four hours ahead all day!'

I laugh. This is the most 'Hannah' things she could've said. 'How about sometime next week? Thursday?'

'Ugh . . . Connor is back on Thursday, so I'm probably going to want to spend time with him. Can you do Wednesday?'

I quickly pull up my calendar on my phone and check. 'I've got a late appointment – footballing knee injury at six – but I should be able to get away after that.'

'It's a date!'

'Where has he gone this time?'

'Dublin. I do miss him when he's away.'

'I'm sure.' I don't know what else to say. Future me knows that some of Connor's 'work trips' were less about hard graft and more about playing away. He's in sales for a luxury brand, so he always seems to be travelling. 'Do you speak much while he's away?'

'Not as much as I'd like. You know how it is. He's got meetings, client dinners . . . Sometimes it's hard to find a moment when we're both free. We text, though.'

Very convenient. I'm sure it would be much harder to FaceTime Hannah from his hotel bedroom if he had company. I can't tell her what's on my mind, but maybe I can point her in the right direction, help her see the red flags that are waving wildly. 'Do you ever . . . you know, worry about him while he's away?'

'Not really. He's a seasoned traveller and knows how to handle himself.'

'That's not quite what I meant. I meant . . . You know the kind of people he mixes with. And some of the women . . . They're very glamorous.'

'Oh.'

Yes, oh.

'You mean about him being faithful?'

I swallow. 'Yes,' I say carefully. I just realized I have no idea how I'm going to handle this if she says she has suspicions. What hole have I dug for myself now?

Hannah is silent for a few seconds. 'No,' she eventually says, sounding very certain. My heart sinks. It was such a blindside when she found out. I'd do anything to save her from even just a bit of that pain. 'He loves me. I'm sure of that.'

'I know.' I'm sure of it too. Connor does love Han in his own way. But that doesn't mean he's able to keep it in his trousers. He's all about the ambition, the upward motion. I don't think one woman will ever be enough for him, because there will always be lush green grass on the other side of the fence. Younger, prettier, richer — take your pick.

There's not much else I can say. I don't want to sour my friendship with Hannah on unfounded accusations. Connor hasn't actually done anything yet – that I know about.

'Anyway,' I say, changing the subject, 'where do you want to go on Wednesday? How about that new wine bar in Langley Park? It's not far from the physio practice I'm at that day, so I shouldn't delay the first tequila shot by too much.'

Hannah laughs. 'You know me so well. I'll see you then at, say, seven?'

'Better make it seven-thirty,' I reply. 'Rashid is a bit of a talker, and I hardly ever get out of his appointments on time.'

After speaking to Hannah, I check my journal for any other useful information. I've left myself the morning clear, but I have a few physio clients this afternoon. I flick back through the previous weeks and months, trying to glean details about my life since our Venice trip.

To my surprise, there are quite a few entries concerning Elena. I can see from the notes of events and to-do lists that I've been much more involved in her life than I was in the past. Luke and I have visited her multiple times. I've even run a few errands for her. When I pick up my phone and scroll through it, I see a friendly message thread between us, where I'm wishing her well and she's thanking me for my support. When I put my phone back down, I'm actually feeling quite proud of myself. I find it hard to open up to people, especially people that I feel might be secretly judging me or looking down on me. I think I always expected Elena to be doing that, not because of anything she said or did, but just because she is who she is and I am who I am. That was a bit immature, really.

I lean back in the office chair in front of the desk and stare at the wall. Did all of this with Elena – her illness, Luke supporting her – happen exactly the same way last time? At first, I want to believe this is something new, but as I think back over the years I already lived, I realize tiny clues are littered throughout my memories. I suspect she was ill last time, and I'm pretty sure Luke would have been a good friend to her; I just wasn't aware of it.

But why wasn't I?

On the night Luke walked out on me, he said I was oblivious. I was offended at the time, but now I'm starting to wonder if he was right.

I continue flicking through the journal, going right back to the front, and then also checking the back page, where I often scribble random things to myself or slapping a sticky note with a scrawled reminder that I will later add into my to-do list proper. There's a little paper pouch at the back of the book, and I notice a pale-blue piece of paper sticking out from it. I don't know what it is, but it must be important if I saved it there.

With a sense of foreboding, I pull the corner of the paper and release it from its hiding place. My stomach drops as I unfold it and see that it is not one sheet of paper but several, and all of them are covered with my mother's handwriting.

Dear Jess,

I know you probably don't want to read this letter. I probably wouldn't if I were you. I would have phoned or sent a message over social media, but I think you've blocked me on absolutely everything. I don't blame you for that, either. So this was the only way I could think of contacting you. Maybe I shouldn't have done, but when did I ever do the sensible thing?

Anyway, I wanted to tell you that you refusing to acknowledge me in any way was incredibly painful.

I bristle. Of course she would make it all about her. Of course she would talk about her pain first. Does she honestly not understand the concept of no-contact? I want to rip the letter up without reading the rest, but my curiosity — and maybe my hope — is insatiable.

But that was a good thing. At first, I was angry with you. So angry that I thought, 'I'll show her! If she thinks I'm an alcoholic, then I'll behave like an alcoholic!', so I went out and bought a large bottle of vodka and proved you right... all the way into a hospital bed, thanks to alcohol poisoning. I didn't kill myself, but I made a good start. Keep doing that on a regular basis and one day my body might not recover.

That scared me. I had no one to blame but myself.

I gasp at that last sentence. I don't think I've ever heard those words come out of my mother's mouth. I'm not sure I thought they even flitted through her head.

> *When I came home, I collected all the bottles I'd hidden around the house, including the ones on my dressing table that looked as if they were make-up remover but were actually gin, and I threw it all down the sink. Then I went online and found my nearest AA meeting. I went that night, and I've been going four to five times a week since, sometimes in person, sometimes online. That was just over eight months ago. I even got a chip for that last Tuesday.*
>
> *I wanted to thank you. That's why I'm writing this letter. You gave me a wake-up call. I want to do better, be better. But I know we've been here before, and you've heard this all from me before - well, some of it - but I wanted you to know it's different this time. I don't expect you to believe that, but it is. I suppose only time will tell which of us is right about this.*
>
> *And I suppose that brings me to the point of writing this letter. I've been going through the 'big book', doing the twelve steps, and I've got to the one where I need to say sorry, to make amends, and I would very much like to meet up with you, so I can do that face-to-face. If you feel you can, please give me a call or send me a text. I'm still at the same number. You know where I live.*
>
> *Lots of love,*
> *Mum x*

I don't know what to do. She's right: we've been here before. She's said a lot of this before. But it's the things that she's never said that give me a worrying glimmer of hope. It's easier not to hope, because it's exhausting to wait and believe, always wondering when the other shoe it going to drop. Part of the relief in going no-contact was that I'd ended that cycle. I told myself I didn't care anymore.

I could meet with her. She might say all the right things. But it's also highly likely she will not, that she will continue with her blaming and gaslighting, her complete lack of ability to take responsibility for anything, that she would attack me because she became painfully aware of the wounds she has caused me, blaming me for making her feel bad about them, and I just don't know if I can do that anymore.

I stare at the crumpled piece of blue paper I'm holding. It looks as if it has been folded and unfolded many times, and yet, as I scan back through my journal, I can find no hint I have ever acted on it, that I've contacted my mother since the day I blocked her on everything. I even go back through my journals for previous years and discover a note marking the day the letter arrived sixteen months ago.

Obviously, I didn't know about this letter on our last anniversary, because we were in Venice and my journal was tucked away safely back home, possibly even in this house, because I think we may have moved in fourteen months after we originally did. Glancing through the pages of my life held in these bullet journals, I get the impression that the sale to whoever else wanted it fell through and the house was put back on the market again just as we were ready for it.

We could've bought something bigger with the deposit Luke

got flipping houses, but I'm glad we didn't. Even if we let go of this house one day, I'm happy to be here now. One more change may be too much.

I fold the letter back up and tuck it in the pocket at the back of the journal, then place the journal back on the stack of notebooks at the side of the desk, ready for the next day. As I do so, I catch the sparkle of diamonds and emeralds of my new eternity ring. New to me, anyway. Not all change is bad. As I think back to my blueberry pancakes, I remind myself that some change is very, very good.

I trace over the tiny stones with the pad of my index finger, feeling the bumps and curving lines of the design. I don't need to decide anything about my mother right now. I stand with the Jess who's been living this life much more fully than I have, the one who made these notes. I'll let her make the call because I have something much more important to focus on.

This year is our iron anniversary. This year we are strong. We are unbreakable. And I'm going to enlist every ounce of the magic in this ring to keep it that way.

CHAPTER FORTY

LUKE

Twelve Weeks Before the Anniversary Party

'What do you think?' He pushes his iPad across the desk so she can see better.

She twists the case to avoid glare from the bright March afternoon sun coming through the office windows and concentrates on the image in the centre of the screen, then flicks through a few more.

'It's our tenth anniversary, and tin didn't seem very sexy, so I did a bit of rooting around on the internet and found this artist who does one-of-a-kind pieces in pewter. I was blown away, it's just . . . ' How does he say this without sounding disloyal or pathetic? It's a point of shame for him that he used to be so good at knowing what Jess wanted, what she'd like, but now he can't seem to get anything right. 'This is a bit out there. I suppose I just need a second opinion, and I thought you'd be the perfect person to give it.'

Hannah smiles at him. 'Luke . . . This is stunning! So different. I know I'd love to receive something like this.'

'But what about Jess? Do you think she'll like it?'

Hannah studies the images again. 'I . . . I think so. Like you say, it's hard to tell with her sometimes.'

He nods slowly. That's his problem. And it feels important that he gets this year's present right. He found last year's pottery figurine behind the weed killer in the understairs cupboard the other week.

For some reason, it feels as if he and Jess are about to reach a turning point. He doesn't know how and he doesn't know why, but there's been a steady gnawing in his gut that only intensifies as the date of their tenth anniversary grows closer.

'Hey,' she says, catching what must be a bleak expression on his face. She comes around the desk and rests a hand on his upper arm. 'What's up?'

He lets out a frustrated sigh and runs his hand through his hair, shaking his head. 'I don't know. Do you think . . . do you think I make her happy?'

Hannah pulls back, her hand dropping away. Her face a picture of shock, as if she couldn't imagine any other reality. 'Of course! Why *wouldn't* you make the person you're with happy, Luke?'

But she doesn't feel the gaping distance he feels even when he's in the same room as Jess. She doesn't know the feeling that Jess is in a boat floating away from him, and all he can do is stand helplessly on the bank and watch the current take her.

He clears his throat. 'Ten years is a long time . . . people grow apart.'

Hannah frowns. 'But not you and Jess, surely?'

He feels bad he's said something now. After all, this is Jess's best friend. But he's got used to opening up more during his chats with Elena, and now it seems it's happening with other people too, even if he doesn't plan on it.

He shakes his head and laughs. 'Ignore me . . . It's just been a busy year, what with my dad retiring from the business and me taking over the reins fully. And I suppose having a big anniversary coming up has got me thinking back over the years, how things used to be. But we don't stay the same, do we? We change. We mature.'

She slings her arm around him and gives him an one-sided, slightly awkward hug. 'You're being too tough on yourself, Luke. Honestly.'

He gives her a grateful smile. 'Thanks, but I suppose that's why I'm hesitating over this present.'

She moves back around to the other side of the counter and wakes the iPad up to look at the images of the sculpture a second time. 'Well, I think it's stunning, and if you're not a hundred per cent sure, since there seems to be an element of . . . personalization . . . needed, I can help, if you like. Then you can always blame those bits on me if Jess doesn't like it!'

'Would you? That would be amazing!'

She gives him a cheeky look. 'What's a Girl Friday for, if not for moments like this?'

'You're sure? I don't want to impose.'

'Of course. Actually, I have some things at home that might be perfect for ideas. Shall I bring them in for you to see?'

'Hmm. Best not. Jess drops in occasionally and, let's face it, I'm not the best at keeping my desk tidy, especially when it's busy. I don't want to give the game away before the big day.'

'Then pop in for a coffee some time; I'll show you what I've got, and we can have an in-depth planning session.'

'Okay, thanks. I'll order it later and then we can get to work.' He catches sight of the clock on the wall and switches gears. 'Okay, right . . . I need to be getting off now. I know it's a bit early but I've got a . . . meeting . . . to go to.'

He grabs his iPad and sticks it in his bag and grabs his phone and his wallet, while Hannah heads back outside to her own desk.

'Meeting . . . ?' she says, as he dashes past, one arm in his coat and trying to shrug the other on. 'I don't see anything in your diary.'

'I'll fill you in another time,' he yells over his shoulder, even though he knows he may never make good on that promise.

Half an hour later, he spots Elena, waiting for him. She's back in the blue armchair again, leaving Luke to his usual seat opposite her. She's taken up knitting and has brought some with her to while away the next couple of hours. He's not going to say anything, but whatever she's making . . . well, let's just say he hopes it isn't a present for him. He has enough monstrosities that his grandma makes him.

She looks tired. He slumps into the chair opposite her, definitely not feeling as weary as she does, but as if he's running on five per cent battery, and everything could flicker out at any moment.

'Life is crap, huh?' she says, but she's still smiling, despite everything.

He smiles back at her, genuinely lifted by her presence. 'Yeah. Life is crap. Sometimes.'

'Thanks for coming. I appreciate it.'

He shrugs. 'No problem. It's what friends do, isn't it? Help each other?'

'Yes,' she replies quietly. 'It is.'

WOOL

A textile fibre obtained from sheep and other mammals known for its excellent insulation and breathability. Wool symbolizes purity, warmth and protection and, in some cultures, sacrifice.

CHAPTER FORTY-ONE

JESS

When I wake up this morning the house is quiet. There are no smells of cooking pancakes wafting from the kitchen. Luke is beside me, sleeping so soundly that I have to watch his chest for a hint that he is actually breathing. I wonder if he is dreaming of something – possibly one of those strange ones where you're endlessly chasing something or running away from something – because even in his slumber he is frowning. I decide not to wake him. He looks as if he could do with the rest.

Maybe it's my turn to return the favour. I slip out of bed and go downstairs, then stare in the fridge for inspiration of what to make my husband for our anniversary breakfast. Luke is definitely more of a carnivore than I am, so maybe a fry-up? There's bacon and eggs, and I find some sausages in the freezer. A rummage through the cupboard reveals a small tin of beans. I gather all the ingredients together but hold off starting cooking. I don't want it to sit, congealing, while Luke is snoring. I'll start when I hear signs of life upstairs.

In the meantime, I hunt for my current bullet journal and leaf through it for clues. I find it under a mass of plans and paperwork on the desk, which means Luke must be in the middle of a renovation project that is requiring a lot of time and energy.

I have one cup of tea, and then another, and then another. Luke finally emerges just before noon, rubbing his face and yawning. He slumps into a chair at the kitchen table while I heat the grill and start assembling our breakfast.

He vows his undying love for me when I plonk his full English in front of him. My stomach is rumbling so I just grin, sit down and tuck in myself. We chat about nonsense, but I like it. It feels normal. It feels like *us*.

Luke has half an egg and a sausage left when his phone rings. 'Leave it,' I say, but he checks the caller ID and picks it up anyway.

'Hi, Dad. What's up?'

I can hear muffled talking as I stand to clear my own empty plate away. Luke listens for a minute or two, wearing the same frown he sported whilst fast asleep—

'Yes, I know . . . I don't think Warren realized—'

He begins to pace, nodding.

'Yes, but I had to nip over to the Shortlands house to . . . I know. I know. I'm sorry, Dad. I should have been there. I will next time, I promise. Listen . . . I've got to go. I'll call you tomorrow.' He listens some more. 'Yup, okay. Of course I'll help out. I'll give Matt a call later. Bye, Dad. Bye . . .'

He hangs up, places his phone on the counter and returns to his breakfast, but after another bite of egg he pushes his plate away.

'What's up with your dad?' I say as I pick it up, scrape it off and add it to the dishwasher. 'It sounded as if he was upset about something.'

Luke stares at the table and shakes his head. 'It's nothing much.'

I sit down opposite him. If anyone knows when someone is avoiding an issue, it's me. 'Luke?'

He sighs. 'There was an issue with the self-levelling compound for the kitchen extension we're doing at the moment. I left it to Warren because I needed to go and deal with a blip at the Shortlands place I'm doing up with Elena, and somehow he messed it up. It's got to be dug up and relaid – at our expense. Dad isn't pleased.'

'But Warren's been with your dad for years. He's easily experienced enough to handle it. And, anyway, why is it your fault?'

'It's not my fault exactly. But Dad prefers it when I'm there and the Shortlands house is really eating into my time at the moment. It's been causing a bit of . . . tension, shall we say, about how much time I spend with my own projects and how much I spend with those for Harris & Sons.'

'But you always make up the hours if you have to dash off to deal with a crisis,' I say, feeling indignation rise within me. 'It's not as if you're not pulling your weight.'

'I know that, and you know that, but somehow Dad feels my focus is split. This year was the year he was supposed to ease back and hand over the reins to me and I think it's just getting him stressed. To be honest, I think he'd prefer it if I gave up on the house flipping and just settled down with the family business.'

'But what do *you* want?'

He shrugs. 'You know I love taking an old house, stripping away all the stupid mistakes homeowners have made over the years and returning it to its former glory. I like creating homes, places where families can grow and make memories. Somehow, doing loft conversions and kitchen extensions isn't quite the same, but then again, I love working with Dad, creating a family legacy.'

I stand up, walk behind him and link my arms around his neck, pressing my cheek against his. 'Whatever you want to do – when you decide what it is you want to do – I'm right behind you. You know that, right?'

I feel and hear him exhale. 'Yeah, I know that.' He sounds pleased, but weary.

'Jess?'

I loosen my arms and step back, and he twists around to look at me. 'Yes?'

'Do you mind if we don't go up to London tonight? I'm knackered. Do you think we can just do a takeaway and a film like we did when we were first married?'

I'll gladly swap the noise and bustle of the city centre for a quiet night alone with my husband. It's not lost on me that I've only got two more anniversaries after this one before we hit number ten. Things are going well, I think, but I can't get complacent. 'Of course. And instead of getting takeaway, why don't I pop out and buy us some steaks? I could throw together a salad and do some of those rosemary and sea salt potatoes you like . . . '

'You're an angel,' he says, pulling me into his lap and kissing me. 'And while you're at the supermarket, I can nip out and help Matt with his bathroom.'

I probably should know why Luke's younger brother needs help with his bathroom, but I don't want to give myself away, so I just nod. 'Sounds like a plan.'

'We can always watch *Mrs Wonderful* if you like?' he says, brightening slightly.

Ugh. I don't think so. I'm beginning to hate that bitch.

'How about something different this year? Something with guns and explosions. I'm sure that's much more up your street.'

It's good to see him laugh. 'I love you,' he says and warmth creeps into his expression for the first time this morning.

'You'd better,' I say, smiling back.

*

I usually shop at Sainsbury's but for some reason I drive straight past it and head to the big Tesco in Orpington. And then I drive straight past that, make a few turns down side roads, and eventually pull the car to a stop on the other side of the street from a row of 1930s semi-detached houses. The one on the right, the one with the gardenia-painted render and rickety porch is my mother's.

I pull the handbrake and kill the ignition. It takes me a while before I turn my head to look at the house. I have no idea if someone is inside or not.

I've been thinking about the letter Mum wrote to me. It's still tucked into the pouch at the back of my bullet journal. I checked. I must've moved it from last year's book and put it into this year's but, even so, I could find no hint in the pages of either that I had contacted my mother. Other Jess has remained steadfast.

Is she right? Has she made the right choice? I feel my resolve slipping and that scares me. It hurt to shut the door on her, but it was way more painful while it was still open.

What if this is the time she pulls it all together, that she finally sticks to it? What then? I'd never know. I'd miss out. And I don't even know if I'm happy or sad about that. It's all so confusing.

My fingers are on the plastic of the key fob, ready to turn it, when the front door opens. I freeze, too shocked even to hunker down. I have no idea what I'm going to do if she sees me sitting here. All I know is, in this moment, I'm in no way prepared to talk to her.

But it seems I don't have to worry. The person who emerges is a grey-haired man in his fifties, not that tall, a little round around the middle. He's yelling back over his shoulder at someone inside the house. Has Mum sold it? Am I sitting outside some stranger's house, stalking them instead? I begin to think I'm right when a teenage boy, maybe seventeen or eighteen, follows him, laughing, then a third person joins them.

It's my mother. She's smiling. She's talking to the boy, and then to the man. They seem comfortable with each other. And she seems . . . normal. Not drunk. I mean, it's hard to tell from a distance but I'm pretty good at spotting the signs. It gives me hope. It also terrifies me.

They don't see me, so I watch them having a conversation about whatever they're having a conversation about, the man standing with one hand on the half-open gate. And then suddenly they're moving, walking down the road with purpose, as if they have somewhere to go, something fun to do. They look like a family.

It feels as if an icy javelin shoots through the top of the car, through the space between my shoulder and my collarbone, and right down through my torso. I suppose, if this is the man Luke told me about in the future, the man she ends up marrying, they *are* a family.

Another one that I am not part of.

I turn my gaze straight ahead, twist the key in the ignition, and take myself off to Tesco to buy some steak.

CHAPTER FORTY-TWO

JESS

Luke got me a beautiful anniversary gift. Seven years is wool apparently. Don't ask me why. As well as a lovely bracelet, he got me this beautiful sort-of cardigan, sort-of wrap thing from Etsy that you can wear in different ways, depending on how you put your arms in the sleeves. It looks like something Claire from *Outlander* would wear but in a soft pale green rather than a muddy brown or grey. I love it.

Luke is out longer than I expect. It turns out his brother needed help measuring his bathroom because he's going to do a refit. What puzzles me is that he has a partner who is quite capable of holding one end of a tape measure, so I have no idea why he needed Luke to go over there and do it. He probably didn't remember it was our anniversary, and Luke probably didn't remind him, not wanting him to feel bad.

Don't get me wrong, I love the fact that my husband is the guy that everyone can depend on, but then I remember the weariness in his expression this morning over breakfast. Matt is only three years younger than Luke. Surely, he could have worked it out by himself? But I think Luke's family have got used to him being in big-brother mode, charging in to the rescue, sorting out their problems for them, and I'm starting to wonder if they ask too much of him.

It gets me thinking about his professional life too, taking over the business from his dad. Is that what Luke wants, really? Or is it because it's what his father wants? As I wash the spinach for a bacon, mushroom and spinach salad, I mull over the situation. I know it wasn't exactly like this last time we lived these years, because Luke didn't have these side projects, he wasn't renovating houses, losing himself in original features and dreams of family homes, but does that mean he wasn't as frustrated with the day-to-day work of Harris & Sons? Is this something else I missed?

After we've eaten our steak dinner and tidied away as much as we can be bothered, Luke and I snuggle up on the sofa with a glass of red wine each and start watching one of their big action film hits of the previous summer. We've just got through the credits, when I reach for the remote control and hit the pause button.

I turn to Luke. 'Are you happy?'

He blinks and looks at me as if I just asked him if his leg fell off. 'Of course I am! What do you mean?'

'It's just . . . I was thinking about what we were talking about this morning over breakfast. I know you love working with your dad, and there have been plans for years for you to take over the business, but I don't see you get excited about that the way I can see you get excited about doing up your own houses, selling them on. Wouldn't you rather be doing that full-time than giving it up?'

Luke looks as if I've just punched him in the face. Talk about hitting the nail on the head. But he doesn't seem very pleased about it.

'I know your dad likes having you there because you're good – you keep an eye on things, you keep the standards high – but even if Warren isn't a great second in command, it doesn't mean you and your dad can't find someone who is. That would leave you free to do what you love.'

Hope flares in his eyes and then dies again just as quickly. 'It's fine. I don't mind stepping up for the family.'

Luke would never regret supporting his family, but I've had the benefit of seeing our life play out two different ways. 'Of course, I know that's true, but I've never seen you as happy at work as when you're trying to source the right age of fireplace for a property or when you come home and show me the pictures of the parquet floor you found underneath a carpet.'

'Jess . . . It's fine.' He's starting to sound a little irritated now. 'But—'

'But nothing. I'm going to take the business over from my dad when he retires and that's all there is to say.'

Can I please add 'pig-headed and stubborn' to the qualities of loyalty and dependability when it comes to describing my husband? 'Surely there's some way to find middle ground?'

'That's what I'm doing now, and it isn't working, is it? Or I wouldn't be getting calls like I had this morning.' He looks me dead in the eye. 'You just don't get it, Jess. How could you, when you decided to walk away from someone in your family? I just don't have it in me to do that.'

I stiffen. 'That's not fair! You know this is a different—' I catch myself. There was something in my tone just then that made me sound just like my mother. This is what she does . . . did . . .

whatever. Flare up and get defensive any time anyone says something negative about her, even if it's true. I take a breath and delete the sentence already composed in my brain and ready to come out of my mouth.

I cross my arms over my body and instantly feel the soft wool of the present Luke gave me under my fingertips. Wool . . . I've been thinking what a strange material it is to use to celebrate a wedding anniversary. Last year, iron made sense. It's strong, solid. In comparison, wool seems insubstantial, too light and fluffy to matter. But it's also warm, soft, comforting. Wool is what Luke needs from me right now, not iron. Not the hard-headed defensiveness I inherited from my mother.

I remember the anger I felt when Luke walked out the door on our tenth anniversary, how wounded and sorry for myself I was, but haven't I been doing the same to him the whole way through our marriage? Physically, I stayed, but emotionally I've been walking out the door on him for years, every time a conversation or a situation got too difficult.

If I want him to open up to me, then maybe I need to practise what I preach. 'Okay, that came off a bit harsh, but I do understand what you're saying.' I shift to get more comfortable. I don't think the action heroes on the TV screen are going to get unfrozen anytime soon.

'Sorry,' Luke mumbles. 'I didn't mean it to come out that way.'

'Thank you.' I reach out and touch his arm. 'But I'm not surprised you don't understand. There's a lot I haven't told you.'

I go on to tell him, in detail, of the nights I cried myself to sleep, of feeling so alone in our family unit of two that I might have been better off if it was just me in the house. I wouldn't have had to deal with the anger, the blame, the shouts of 'I wish

I'd never had you!'. That's something you shouldn't yell in a ten-year-old's face, isn't it? I tell him about the embarrassing things Mum did when she was drunk, filling him in on the 'falling down the stairs naked' story, and many others like it.

'The worst thing is,' I say swilling my wine round in my glass and then taking a sip, 'that she made me complicit. It was like being in a cult. I was conditioned to not say anything, even if teachers asked if I was okay, even if – in later years – my dad tried to check if everything was good at home. She made me keep her secrets, and then she hated me because I knew them. And I had to keep everything I felt about it all secret, too. I couldn't share it with anyone. I'm *still* not good at sharing things with anyone.'

I swallow, because the next bit is the bit I'm going to have to drag out of myself. 'And I think this is why I've been so vague when we discuss babies, why I joke but never actually get around to doing anything about it.' I look down at my lap. 'Because I'm worried that because I didn't have good role models, I'll be a bad mum.' I have to pause for a moment, because a lump forms in my throat and moisture fills my eyes.

Luke gently lifts my chin and makes me look at him. 'I don't believe that.' He waits until the truth of his words sinks into me. 'I think you're going to be an incredible mother.'

I lean my head against him and let the tears fall quietly, just for a minute or so, and then I take a deep breath and sit up again. 'Families are strange . . . We're part of them, but we're also our own people. But sometimes the lines get blurry, and that's why I did what I did with my mum when I cut her off. I had to make that dividing line hard – set a boundary – because I felt as if I'd lose myself if I didn't. I wanted to know for sure than I'm different from her.'

His expression is full of such love. And pain. I know he would absorb it all from me and bear it himself if he could. 'I think I actually understand that now.'

I nod, feeling oddly peaceful. 'Good. But maybe it's not a bad thing to find that balance with your family too.' I hold up a hand as he starts to speak. 'And, yes, I know they're not toxic and dysfunctional, but it's not wrong to want what you want, Luke, to do something for yourself. What do *you* want? Not your family, not your dad. You.'

'I can't let them down, Jess.'

'But finding a balance between what they need and what you need isn't letting them down. It could make all of you happier. Why do you find it hard to say no to your family?'

He sighs. 'You're right. I do love flipping houses, especially the hidden gems. But I also want to take up the legacy Dad wants to leave me. I don't want to hurt him.'

I smile gently at him. He *almost* said it. I know there's more. I know there are things he wants that maybe he's not even ready to admit to himself, let alone me. But . . . baby steps. After all, it took me a while to figure this out. I just need to show Luke the same patience he's shown me.

CHAPTER FORTY-THREE

LUKE

Nine Weeks Before the Anniversary Party

'What about this one?' He and Hannah are perched on stools at the breakfast bar in her kitchen. He points to one of the pile of photographs spread in front of them.

'Hmm . . . Not sure,' she replies. 'Let's keep looking.'

They sort through piles of different photos and look at even more Luke has collected on his tablet in a special folder hidden away where his wife hopefully won't find it. He'd hate to ruin the surprise.

He and Hannah chat about nothing – stupid things that have happened at work, mostly – but there's something that's been burning away at him that he needs another perspective on. He was going to ask Elena when he saw her for their regular date later that week, but maybe he's missing an opportunity here. 'I need a second opinion on something . . . '

Hannah looks up from the two photos she's holding up, side by side. 'I thought that's what we were doing here, that you needed another brain to help you with Jess's anniversary present.'

He shakes his head. 'It's something else. Something a little more . . . sensitive.'

She puts the photos down, sits up straighter and gives him her full attention.

He takes a deep breath and dives in. 'I may have done something stupid.'

Hannah's eyebrows rise.

'I've been in contact with Jess's mum, Alison.'

Her mouth drops open. Not a good sign. 'You've spoken to her?'

'Not yet. We've just texted a couple of times.'

Hannah's mouth purses and she chews the inside of her lip, something he sees her doing frequently at work when she's battling with a spreadsheet. 'Does Jess know?'

He shakes his head. This is where he's getting into 'stupid' territory. 'But now Alison is saying she wants to meet up and I don't know if I should.' He's not sure about anything at the moment. Should he confess all to Jess? Or should he just pull the plug and tell her mum it's all been a horrible mistake?

'Why now?' Hannah asks. 'What's caused her to reach out after all this time?'

How much does he admit? He was so convinced he was doing the right thing when he sent the first text to his mother-in-law but hearing the admission in his head makes him second-guess himself. Will Hannah think he's being disloyal?

'Actually, it was the other way around.'

'Oh . . . okay. Wow.'

He rubs his hand over his face. 'I know what you're thinking . . . but she's been sober for a while now. And I know, no matter how much Jess doesn't like to talk about it, that the absence of her mother leaves a huge hole in her life. I suppose I was just, um, testing the waters.'

'Why do you think she wants to see you face to face?'

He shrugs. 'Don't know. But if I was going to hazard a guess, it would be that she'd like to be a part of her daughter's life again. And that might not be such a bad thing, you know? If she's stable and sober. Maybe she and Jess could turn over a new leaf. But I won't know unless I talk to her. So what do you think? Should I go?'

She thinks for a moment. 'It's hard to call without knowing what she has to say, so maybe you should hear her out.'

That's what he'd been thinking. It's tough to make a decision on whether to bring Alison back into their lives based on a handful of text messages.

'Are you planning on telling Jess if you get to that point?'

'Of course.'

Hannah messes around with the photos laid out on the breakfast bar. 'I don't know what to tell you, Luke, except tread carefully.'

'You think it's a bad idea?'

'Possibly. Possibly not. Maybe you're right, and her mother holds the key. Just . . . tell Jess when you need to, okay?'

He nods and they go back to perusing the photos that will eventually become part of his anniversary present to Jess. A sculpture is nice, but if he could give his wife healing, closure, wouldn't that be even better?

He shuffles the pictures around and holds one up for Hannah's opinion.

'It's a great shot of Jess, but it's a bit blurry,' she says, her forehead crinkling in thought. 'Hang on . . . I think I may have some from your wedding day that will fit the bill. I can get one printed off at that place in the High Street if we need to.' She fetches a laptop and clicks and scrolls until she finds what she's looking for, then spins it around so he can see the screen. 'What do you think?'

It's a picture of Jess on their wedding day, joy sparking from her eyes, captured laughing as her veil blew around her face. 'It's perfect,' he says.

'And here's one of you looking very handsome from the same day,' she adds, clicking the mousepad a few more times. 'If you put yours on the left and hers on the right, it'll look as if you're smiling at each other.'

He grins at her. 'I never would have thought of that. See? This is why I shouldn't have attempted to do this alone. Honestly, Hannah, I can't thank you enough for giving up your precious free time to do this for me.'

She looks away and smiles. 'It's no problem, really. The least I can do after all you and Jess have done for me over the years.'

He gives her a gentle nudge with his elbow. 'Even if you're constantly calling me a tyrant at work?'

She chuckles. 'Even then.'

But then she sighs and stares out over the gloomy grey garden the other side of the bi-fold doors separating it from her kitchen. It's been drizzling all day. He cocks his head to one side and studies her. She looks sad, even though she was her usual, sunny Hannah self a few moments ago. He hardly ever sees her like this, although he knows she's been to hell and back in the last few years, and it brings to mind when Jess teases her best friend about her armour-plated fake grin.

'Everything okay?'

She inhales, nods and turns to him. The smile she gives him is the definition of bulletproof. 'I'm all right. It's just . . . ' She sighs again, shakes her head.

'Just . . . ?'

'It's so lovely, all you're doing for Jess.'

He frowns. 'And that's a bad thing?'

A small laugh escapes her lips but her eyes remain sad. 'No. Definitely not. But I see all the effort you're putting in to make her happy – trying to mend things with her family, creating this amazing, one-of-a-kind present, and I just realize that Connor never put half that effort in when it came to me.'

He raises one eyebrow. 'We have firmly established that Connor is an arsehole.'

That makes her laugh properly. But then her eyes go glassy. 'Yes, but now I'm on my own, and I don't know if I'll ever find someone who will do that for me.'

Oh, God. A bead of moisture escapes her lashes and rolls down the outside of her cheek. It's like kryptonite to him. He needs to do something. Now. To stop her feeling this way. He gets off his stool, spins hers round until she's facing him and wraps her in a brotherly hug. She pats his back in thanks, exhales and then sinks against him.

'You'll find someone,' he says softly. 'I know you will.'

After a few moments, he senses her collecting herself and she pulls away and dabs under her lower lashes with the tops of her fingers. 'You think?' she says with a shaky laugh. 'Because, if not, I can always go down to Foal Farm and rescue some cats. Twenty or so should do it.'

The smile is back. Bright. Tough. Sparkling. He admires her bravery, but he doesn't say so, sensing it will cause her carefully erected shield to waver. 'How about just starting with one? If you really want one, that is.'

She nods. 'Maybe I will. But in the meantime . . . ' She returns to her laptop and pulls up the photos of him and Jess she found earlier and positions them side by side. 'Perfect couple, yes or no?'

'Those are the ones,' he agrees.

But 'perfect couple' is still a work in progress.

BRONZE

A metal alloy primarily made of copper, with tin and other elements, known for its strength and ductility. Its real beauty lies in not only its sheen and warm tones, but in its ability to resist corrosion.

CHAPTER FORTY-FOUR

JESS

I hum to myself as I crack an egg into a bowl of flour and add a bit of milk. My eternity ring catches the light as I whisk, and my smile widens. I think we're getting there. And that's good. Because I only have two more of these 'days' before we're back at number ten. I can't drop the ball now.

Luke appears and comes up behind me while I'm flipping the first pancake, which means it ends up being even wonkier than a first pancake should be, but I just laugh and flop it onto the plate next to the hob. That's always my 'cook's treat', the not quite right one I nibble at while I make the rest of the batch.

Luke is making us both a cup of tea when his phone rings. Even though my back is to him, I can tell from the tone he adopts instantly that it's something work-related. He sounds tense. I keep half an ear on the conversation while I carry on pouring batter into the pan and flipping pancakes. There are lots of 'uh-huhs' and 'yeps', which sound fairly positive, but I still have a sinking feeling.

The pancakes are just about ready, and Luke is trying to round up his call when the doorbell goes. Crap. I turn the gas off under the frying pan, push it away from the hot ring, and jog to the front door. When I open it, Cassie is standing there with a three-year-old Edie in her arms.

'Thank goodness! I was so afraid you wouldn't be in.'

Well, it is eleven on a Tuesday morning, so I suppose it's not unreasonable to think we might both be out, even though my work schedule is a bit less regimented than a regular nine to five.

'What's up?' I stand back to let her pass, and she comes inside, shaking her head.

'It's a bit of a nightmare, actually.' Edie wiggles to be let down and, since she's a regular in our household, Cassie obliges. Edie runs through to the living room, where she knows a crate of toys is stacked under one of the coffee tables, and instantly sets to work.

We head into the kitchen, where Luke is still making 'I need to head off now' noises on his call.

Cassie keeps her voice low. 'My childcare has fallen through. I've got a good friend who moved to Scotland and she's visiting for a couple of days, and we arranged to meet for brunch. It's the first time I've seen her in two years! And then the mum from pre-school who was going to have Edie called me to say all four of her kids are crawling with lice and she doesn't think they should be around other children until they've been treated.'

'Urgh,' I say, shuddering.

'Exactly! There's no way I'm sending Edie round there. It makes me itch just thinking about it.'

I find I'm absentmindedly scratching my scalp. 'Me too!'

But then I have a horrible sinking feeling I know what's coming. I'm trying to work out how to politely say no, without coming off as a total bitch. My bullet journal confirms that Luke doesn't get many days off, and our time together is both limited and I really need this twenty-four hours to make sure my marriage stays on track. I love Cassie and my niece to bits, but I'm not sure I can risk losing precious hours today.

Edie appears from the living room, spots the plate of pancakes near the edge of the dining table and squeals with delight. Cassie picks her up, pops her on one of the chairs, pulls a pancake onto one of the waiting plates, slides the plate in front of her daughter, and then carries on talking as if she hasn't just hijacked the romantic breakfast I've planned for myself and my husband.

I'm so dumbfounded, I can't even find the words to pull her up on it. I mean, one of the things I like about Luke's family is that they don't stand on ceremony with each other, and usually I love the fact that she feels comfortable enough to come into my house, make a cup of tea and offer me one, but today is a little bit different. Luke gives Cassie a one-armed hug as he finishes his phone call and then pops his phone back into his pocket. 'Hi, sis.'

'Hey, big brother!' She kisses him on the cheek. 'I was just telling Jess my childcare has fallen through and I'm in a bit of a bind.'

Luke looks at me and I just give him a *I don't know how to say it* look. It will be much easier for him to say something to his sister.

'That was Warren,' he says, looking at first Cassie and then me. 'He's having a bit of a meltdown because the paving slabs he ordered haven't arrived on site and he can't get through to the suppliers. I'm just gonna have to make a couple of quick calls . . .'

He disappears off into the living room, away from the noise of two women and a three-year-old tucking into a blueberry and banana pancake.

Cassie glances at her phone. 'Oh, my God! We are supposed to be meeting at that new Lebanese place in Beckenham town centre. You know what the multistorey car park can be like at this time of day, so I thought I'd leave the car here and walk in, which means I'm going to have to dash.'

I try and formulate a friendly but firm refusal but come up empty. She kisses Edie on top of the head and gives me a big squeeze. 'I shouldn't be more than two hours,' she says over her shoulder as she jogs out of the kitchen. 'Thank you so much!' And then I hear the front door slam.

What . . . ? What the heck just happened?

I'm still standing there dumbstruck, when Luke returns, phone in hand, scowling. 'I swear, I'm going to give Warren his marching orders one of these days.'

'What's happened?'

'He sent the stuff to the wrong address! I'm going to have to go along with him in the van, pick it up, and take it to the right place.'

I glance at the rapidly cooling pancakes on the dining room table. 'Do you have to go right now?'

'The quicker I get this sorted, the quicker I get back.'

'But . . . but . . . '

He grabs his keys and his jacket and heads in the same direction his sister just did. Seconds later, the front door bangs again. I turn to look at Edie. She's a gorgeous kid, big blue eyes, cherubic blonde curls, and a nature to match – most of the time. She flutters her eyelashes at me as she reaches for a second pancake.

'Knock yourself out, kid,' I say.

My eternity ring better be ready to work its magic today.

★

A couple of hours Cassie said, but it's only just gone twelve and Edie is getting fractious. The box of toys and a bit of CBeebies kept her entertained for an hour or so but now she's bored and I'm running out of things to try. And Luke is going to be no help. He's sent a couple of messages saying Warren didn't even order the right stuff, his client is having a meltdown, and he's worried about potential negative reviews online if he doesn't sort this out quickly. He lives in fear of getting horrendous reviews online. In sheer desperation, I call Hannah's number.

'Hey, you!' she trills when she answers. 'What's up?'

'I'm stuck with a three-year-old and need back-up,' I blurt out. 'Are you off this afternoon?'

'Um . . . no.' She sounds confused, as if I should know this, which I probably should. I'm in such a tizz that I can't remember those sorts of things. 'Luke told me about Edie. I'm on the phone trying to help sort out this whole mess with the delivery so he can get back to you.'

Oh, wow. I've been leapfrogging through my anniversaries so quickly that it's completely skewed my perception of time. Since my 'yesterday', Connor cheated on Hannah, and she had to find herself a better paying job. Marge, who had done the admin for Harris & Sons retired this year, so Luke offered Hannah the job. She's amazing at it, modernizing the way it all flows in a way that seventy-year-old, technophobic Marge never could.

'Of course, of course . . . Thank you! I'd better let you get on with it,' I say, laughing on the outside and crying on the inside. 'Love you! Bye!'

I hang up and then wilt, before straightening and grabbing my handbag. 'Edie? Do you want to go out somewhere?'

'Yay!' Edie says, jumping up and down.

Well, that's sorted, then.

CHAPTER FORTY-FIVE

JESS

Twenty minutes later, I pull my car up outside my father's house. Thank goodness Cassie dumped Edie's booster seat in our hallway before doing a flit. I've tried texting Cassie again, as it's now half-past twelve and I didn't want her to arrive back at ours and wonder where the heck we are, but it's going straight to voicemail.

If I stop to admit it to myself, I'm livid. For myself, but also on Luke's behalf. His family ask too much of him sometimes. At least I think so; he never seems to complain. I can understand him wanting to be there for his mum and dad, who are now well into their sixties, but his siblings have got so much into the habit of relying on him for practical help, advice, and even money, that it doesn't occur to any of them that they could ask someone else or flipping well figure some things out themselves.

And then there's me. Living these days again has sharpened my perspective. I'm part of that equation too. Luke was always propping me up, making sure I was okay, and I was so wrapped up in myself that I didn't see that I didn't match his effort. I feel as if I must have been sleepwalking through my marriage first time around.

Lola greets us warmly when she answers the door. 'Praise Jesus you are here,' she says, glancing back inside the house. 'Your father still has not worked out what to do with himself now he has retired, and he is getting in my way when I have much to do. You are the perfect distraction.'

I bite back a smile. I remember this from last time. They eventually found their rhythm after Dad retired, but I heard my stepmother mutter 'Make haste to dismiss yourself from my presence!' more than a few times before they worked it all out.

Lola is working in her beloved garden and Edie is instantly captivated, asking if she can help grow flowers, so Lola gives her the smallest trowel she can find and says the first step is banishing the weeds, so the flowers have room. I slide into a chair at the garden table where my father is sitting with a coffee and the newspaper and smile as I watch them. Edie is full of wide-eyed adoration as Lola points out a weed and explains how to deal with it.

'She's so good with little kids,' I say to my dad. 'I remember her having such patience with the twins, even when they would cause a bit of a whirlwind.'

Dad nods. 'There is definitely something very steadying about her. I think that's what drew me to her, you know, after . . . ' He trails off, but I can finish the sentence pretty easily.

. . . after your mum.

It seems I was right, because after a couple of seconds, he asks, 'Have you heard anything from her lately?'

I shake my head. My regular check-in with my bullet journal this morning told me we've had no contact in the last twelve months. It also told me that I've been seeing a therapist. It's not hard to guess what some of the issues we talk about are, especially not when I also discovered a page full of links for articles about 'Adult Children of Alcoholics' in my notes app, and there's something else too.

'Actually, I've been going to a group at the old library in Bromley,' I tell him. 'Al Anon. It's for people who have family members who have issues with drink. I've been going for about six months.'

Dad is quiet for a bit. I know this is a subject he'd rather skirt around. 'Do you think it's helping?' he finally asks.

'I think so,' I reply. I don't know how this whole 'time travelling through my life' thing works, but I read a couple of the articles I'd saved links to and a lot of it resonated. I don't know if what happens in between the snapshots of my life I'm reliving has an impact on me, but I'm not as angry with her as I once was. Something is different, even if I'm not able to pinpoint it.

'Did you ever think of going before now?'

'No.'

'Why not?' He puts his newspaper down fully and leans in, waiting for my answer.

'I don't know,' I say, because I really don't know why I haven't thought of it. Possibly because it was hard to say the word 'alcoholic' out loud for so long. I still don't do it that much. Alcoholics are rage-filled men who beat their children, or the woman sleeping rough because she's lost her income and her home. That's what I always used to think, anyway. It seemed a bit of an extreme term for a woman who got a bit too sad occasionally, who held down a job and kept a roof over her head for decades.

But I realize now that might be because Mum minimized everything all the time. If ever I tried to bring her drinking up, she would tout out those facts as if they were proof of some kind. She would make it seem as if her alcohol consumption was only just a bit higher than normal, that it was no big deal.

'Maybe it's because I grew up with it,' I tell Dad. 'You learn not to ask questions, not to rock the boat. And I always felt I had to keep her secret. What would people say if they knew I went to Al Anon? She'd be upset and humiliated. So I didn't consider it. It was completely off my radar.'

Dad absorbs this information as he watches Lola quash Edie's efforts to pull a tulip up by its stem. She's firm but kind, and Edie seems eager to please her, practically glowing when Lola tells her how well she's doing. I sigh. What would it have been like if I'd had a mother like her rather than one who let so much stuff slide unnoticed and then blew up like a volcano at the tiniest thing if she wasn't in the right mood?

He keeps his focus on the work going on in the garden but says, 'When did it start?' When I raise an eyebrow, he adds, 'Her drinking.'

I don't think he's ever asked this question before. In fact, I don't think he's ever asked me much about what life with Mum was like after he left. 'I'm not exactly sure . . . I didn't know what the signs to look out for were at that age but, looking back, I'd say it started after you separated. It took a year or so before it escalated, though.'

Dad finally meets my eyes. 'I'm sorry. I didn't know. But I should have. I should have checked on you more, made sure things were all right.'

I shrug. 'It's okay. I probably would have lied, anyway.'

'But that made it even more important for me to have been paying attention,' he says. 'I'm so sorry.' His voice grows hoarse as he finishes his sentence and the sheen in his eyes makes my own moisten.

'It's okay,' I say again.

'No, Jess. No, it's not. I let you down.'

I appreciate his words more than he'll ever know. 'Thank you.'

He sighs. 'I can't change the past, even if I wish I could.'

I almost laugh out loud. Isn't that *exactly* what I'm trying to do, hopefully, so I can change my future?

'I love you, Dad,' I say and lean forward to give him a kiss, just as my phone buzzes on the table in front of me. He rubs my arm as I pick it up.

'Oh, my God, Jess! I totally lost track of the time! I'm so sorry I'm later than I said I'd be.'

'No worries,' I say through gritted teeth, then realize that, if I want things to change, I probably shouldn't mirror what Luke does and brush it all under the carpet. 'I'm at Dad and Lola's. Do you want me to send you the address or do you remember where it is?'

There's a sheepish silence on the other end of the line. 'Actually, could I pick Edie up from yours in about an hour or so? Nicole has a present for me, but she left it at her Airbnb. I was going to go back there with her and her husband is going to give me a lift back to yours. The apartment is only about five minutes away from you, and I don't want to put him out by making him drive all the way to West Wickham.'

I blink. Oh, so she doesn't want to put *him* out. Lovely. I'm tempted to throw my phone across the garden, but would hardly be setting a good example to my niece, now, would it? 'Fine. Whatever,' I say to Cassie then hang up before I say something I'm going to regret. 'Edie!' I call across the lawn. 'It's time to go!'

CHAPTER FORTY-SIX

JESS

It's three o'clock before Luke walks back through our front door, and still there's no sign of his sister. That's half the day gone!

'Ow!' he yells from somewhere in the hallway. A few seconds later, he appears in the doorway to the kitchen holding up a small plastic figure, which he brandishes at his niece, who is colouring at our kitchen table. Well, I say 'at' the kitchen table, but it's more like 'on' the kitchen table, as most of her efforts with the crayons are shooting right off the edge of the paper. 'Your work, I presume?'

Edie just giggles.

'Oops, sorry! Thought I'd found all the bits strewn around the ground floor.' I take it from him and give him a kiss on the lips.

He looks around. 'Where's Cassie?'

My smile fades. 'She said two hours when she left Edie here this morning, but it's been one delay after another and now it's been just over four.'

He shrugs one shoulder. 'Cassie never was great with time-keeping.'

He might be prepared to let this drop, but I'm not. For my

sake, and for his. Keeping an eye on Edie, I walk over to the kitchen area on the other side of the room, and motion for him to follow. 'She didn't even ask, Luke,' I say in a low voice. 'She just rocked up with Edie in tow, dumped her down and buggered off.'

He frowns. 'I'm sure I heard her ask, didn't I?'

'No, she just assumed. On our anniversary, too!'

'She probably forgot.'

I know he's not doing this on purpose, but I can feel my hackles rising. Old Jess would have reacted to this, but new, time-travelling Jess manages to keep a lid on her irritation. 'But if she'd asked,' I say, making sure my tone isn't getting strident, 'she would have known. I didn't even get a chance to tell her we weren't available.'

He leans across and flicks the switch on the kettle. 'You're right. She did kind of dump it on us.'

'And not only that, you knew you were about to head out of the house – I didn't, because we hadn't had a chance to have that conversation yet. So not only did Cassie foist babysitting duty on us as a couple, you then left me to it on my own.'

He comes over and puts his arms around me. 'Oh, God, I did, didn't I? I'm sorry, Jess. I just didn't think . . . '

I squeeze him back. 'That's because you're running around like a headless chicken most days, with hardly any time to do anything but react to stuff as it happens. You could do with slowing down a bit.'

'I know,' he says, sighing, but we're prevented from discussing it any further by a ring on the doorbell.

Cassie breezes in as if she hasn't been AWOL for most of the day. She's even an extra half an hour late from the time she gave me last time I spoke to her. She kisses Luke on the cheek but then bypasses me entirely when she spots Edie and goes to scoop her up, resulting in lots of kisses and giggles on both sides.

When she's finished, she pops Edie down and turns to Luke and me, smiling. 'So, sorry! You know what it's like when you finally get a day to yourself and get a chance to chat to grown-ups and feel like a human being again.'

'Chance would be a fine thing,' I mutter. A day to myself where I finally got a chance to chat to my grown-up husband was *exactly* what I had planned today.

Only, it seems my comment wasn't as quiet as I thought, because Cassie frowns. 'What was that? Is something wrong?'

I'm so tired, I'm tempted to do a Luke and sweep all of this under the rug to deal with another day. I mean, if I don't make the most of the next seven or eight hours before midnight rolls around, or whatever, and I jump forward another year, babysitting Edie in future years may not be a problem. For me, anyway. Not if Luke and I go our separate ways.

'No, it's—' I begin to say, but Luke starts speaking at the same time.

'Actually, Cass . . . You know we love you, but we'd rather you didn't just turn up with Edie in tow and make babysitting a *fait accompli*.'

She looks a little offended. 'I didn't "just turn up". I called you first.'

'About two minutes beforehand! You must have been sitting in the car outside.'

Cassie has the grace to flush. 'You always said you were happy to help.'

'We are!' I say, starting to feel uncomfortable now.

'We are,' Luke echoes, putting a hand on my arm to let me know he's got this. 'And of course we will help out when we can, even if it's at short notice, but you have to give us a bit more warning. Actually *asking* would be nice, rather than just assuming. We had plans today.'

I'm warmed to hear my words coming out of his mouth.

'You didn't say,' Cassie says, folding her arms, and pulling a face very much like her daughter does when she's about to have a sulk.

'We didn't really get a chance, did we? And, by the way, you haven't even a) thanked Jess for looking after Edie for most of the day or b) properly apologized for being so late. I'd like you to do that now.'

Wow. Okay. He really went there. Part of me is crawling with second-hand embarrassment at Cassie being made to say sorry to me, but another part is soaring. Luke drew a line in the sand with his family. For me. Boy, is he going to get lucky tonight.

'Well, of course I'm sorry I was late,' Cassie says, arms still folded, and not looking particularly repentant. 'And, yes, thank you, Jess.' And then she turns to her daughter. 'Come on, monster. Time to go.' Then she picks Edie up and bustles out the front door with hardly a backwards glance. Luke follows her to the door but returns only seconds after it bangs behind her.

'Well, that went well,' I say.

'It needed to be said. You're right – while we're happy to be supportive, it doesn't mean she should walk all over us. Well, you, today. Sorry about that.' He comes and puts his arms around me again and I lean into him, grateful for his solid warmth.

'Thank you for standing up for me,' I whisper into his chest.

'Always,' he mumbles into my hair. We stay that way for a few moments, but then he starts nuzzling into my neck as his hands scoot under my T-shirt.

I laugh softly. He's not as fresh as he could be after a day of rushing around hauling paving slabs. 'Why don't you have a shower, and then we'll revisit that thought. In the meantime, I'll make you a cup of tea and bring it up.'

'Cheeky minx,' he says and then sniffs his armpit. 'Oh, wow. See what you mean. I'd better go and . . . '

'Yes, you'd better!' I slap him playfully on the bum as he turns and heads out the door and before he can beat me to it, I add, 'And, yes, I know I shouldn't touch what I can't afford!'

★

After Luke is rested and showered, we decide to go out for a drink before grabbing a casual dinner. It's a lovely evening and warm enough to sit in the large garden of a pub within walking distance. I lean back in an oak garden chair, a glass of Pinot Grigio in my hand, and let the golden rays of the setting sun warm my face.

Luke's phone goes and he pulls it out of his pocket to check it. 'It's Cassie. She sent me an apology – for not being more thoughtful, but also because she realized it was our anniversary.'

'Well, that's good, isn't it?'

Luke sighs. 'I hope so. I just don't want things to be awkward.'

I sit up straighter and put my wine glass down on the table between us. 'Luke, we can't avoid saying what we need to because we don't want things to be awkward.' This makes me realize that what Cassie did today isn't the problem; it's just the symptom of a larger issue. 'Maybe it's time to set some boundaries with your family in general?'

'What do you mean?'

'I mean that they rely on you quite heavily for a lot of things.'

He takes a sip of his beer. 'That's the problem of being a builder, I reckon. It was the same with my dad.'

'Yes, but Zach and Nick are also in the trade and it's not as if Matthew is incompetent. Your dad made sure that all of you, including Cassie, can manage the basics. Anyway, it's not just DIY stuff, is it? Today's situation being a case in point.'

Luke goes quiet for a while. 'Why do I feel as if you're having a go at me for how I interact with my family?'

I reach over to touch him, just to make contact so he knows I'm on his side. 'I'm honestly not. I'm just trying to look out for you. I see how overloaded you are, and I get the feeling that . . . that maybe you don't enjoy working at Harris & Sons as much as you thought you would?'

Unfortunately, this does not make Luke look any happier. 'I've already told you the reasons I'm doing what I'm doing. I'm fine working with Dad. Absolutely fine.'

He stares out across the garden for a few seconds, drains his glass then picks up the menu from the table. 'I'll go and order the food at the bar, shall I?'

I slump back in my chair and watch him go. I feel like I'm banging my head against the wall, and he clearly doesn't want to talk about this. But there's an energy in the conversation I recognize. Defensiveness. Denial. However, in our past, the roles were usually reversed. It was me, defending my corner at all costs, him trying to break through the brittle walls I'd erected around myself. If Luke learned this tactic anywhere, he learned it from me. How he managed to put up with me digging my heels in for years on end is beyond me.

Only, he didn't, did he? That last night, he begged me to talk to him and I blew him off. I find I can't blame him any longer for walking out the door; I'm just surprised he didn't do it sooner.

And it's not about the babysitting or the putting up of shelves or the money lent. It actually wouldn't matter what the argument was about. It's the way I used to deal with it, as if everything was a personal attack. Probably because, at the time, it felt that way.

When he returns, I wait until I catch his eye and I say, 'I just want you to be happy.'

He hands me another glass of wine and puts a bottle of beer on the table for himself. 'I know that. It's just . . . I love my family.'

'That's one of the things I love most about you, how committed you are, how loyal, but sometimes I think your family take advantage of that, that's all I'm saying. I'm not saying you have to cut them off or anything like that.'

He nods. 'Okay.'

'I just don't want you to spend your whole life making them happy while forgetting about doing the same for yourself.'

The look he gives me lets me know my words have touched him, that he appreciates me looking out for him too, which gives me courage to raise my next point. I open my mouth, but Luke jumps in before I've got more than half a word out.

'I know what you're going to say, but I'm not going to jack it in and do property developing full-time. Dad has only just fully retired and it would break his heart if I sold the company.'

'Would you have to sell? Couldn't someone else be in charge of the day-to-day stuff?'

'Hiring a manager would eat into the profits, and the only other candidate is Warren. After today, even you can't suggest that would be a good idea!'

I laugh softly. I have to give him that. 'Okay, okay, I'll shut up about it.' For now. 'But that doesn't mean I'm going to stop trying to make you happy.'

He blinks at me, a slow lowering and opening of his eyelids, and somehow that one tiny gesture, combined with the gentle smile, is full of more love than a dozen bouquets of red roses or expensive jewellery. 'You're all right, you know?' he tells me.

'I know,' I say, smiling. 'You're not so bad yourself.'

I reach out and hold his hand across the table and the diamond and emerald eternity ring glints as the sun catches it. We are going to be happy, I promise both it and Luke, and then myself, too. We are.

CHAPTER FORTY-SEVEN

LUKE

Six Weeks Before the Anniversary Party

'I did it,' he tells her. 'I met up with Jess's mum.'

Elena twists in her high-backed blue armchair to look at him. 'How did it go?'

'Well, I think. She looks a decade younger the last time I saw her. It was almost like meeting a completely different woman. Not just from the way she behaved and looked, but also the words coming out of her mouth. She's been sober for four years now and is married again, happy. I don't think Jess and I ever believed this was going to happen, but it has.'

'That's amazing! And what does Jess think?'

He has the decency to look uncomfortable. It's not that he and Jess have been arguing, far from it. But it feels as if there's a wall of thick Perspex between them, and everything is just bouncing off of it. 'I haven't told her yet,' he admits slowly. 'I've been trying to find the right way to bring it up.'

She gives him a look that says, *coward*, but doesn't press the matter. 'Do you have any plans of when or where or how you might want to suggest a meeting between her and Jess?'

He takes a sip of his coffee. The woman who served him at the coffee outlet near downstairs forgot to give him one of those cardboard sleeves and it's burning his fingers. 'I'm not sure I know where to start. But I wondered about our anniversary party next month. It would be neutral ground and there will be lots of other people there. If Jess didn't want to say anything more than "Hi, nice to see you," she wouldn't have to. If she wants to have a more in-depth conversation with her mum after that, that will be up to her.'

Elena picks up the same knitting project she was working on last time he sat with her. It's a lot bigger, but he still can't tell what it is. 'Luke . . . ' she says, shaking her head. 'What am I going to do with you? I tell you not to get in contact with Jess's mum without telling her, but now you have done it anyway, and you still haven't told her?' She drops a stitch and swears in Spanish before looking him. 'Are you sure? Communication is important in a marriage, Luke. When I think back over the years I spent with Felix, how things were towards the end, I think that is what caused our marriage to fail. We stopped communicating well.'

The conversation drifts on to other things for a while but, eventually, they both fall silent. A nurse appears to adjust a few things then disappears again. He checks the clock. Another hour to go before she can be released, and he drives her home. He hates leaving her alone in her flat afterwards, all that medication flowing around in her system.

'What?' he says, when they have some relative privacy again. 'You don't think that's a good idea?'

She sighs. 'I don't know, Luke. Yes, on paper it seems like a good way to go, but you have to be careful. Your party is what? A month away?'

'Six weeks.'

She gives a shrug. 'That's a long time to keep a secret from someone you're living with; that's all I'm saying.'

POTTERY

The process of forming vessels and other objects from clay and other raw materials, and also the products made through this process. After firing at high temperatures, the once-soft clay takes on a much harder and durable form. Objects made are often useful ones, integral to everyday life, but this does not mean they do not carry their own inherent beauty.

CHAPTER FORTY-EIGHT

JESS

I lean over Luke's shoulder to see what he's scrolling through on his iPad. I'm surprised to see a page from Rightmove. It used to be his obsession, scrolling through countless property listings, trying to find the next gem he would like to restore, but I haven't seen him do it for years now.

I'm secretly pleased. Even though, in his timeline, it's a whole year since we had a conversation about this, it was yesterday to me. The seed I planted is starting to sprout. That gives me hope.

'Where's that house? It's gorgeous!'

He jumps, as if he didn't realize I was standing there. His finger hovers over the 'x' on the corner of the tab but then he moves it away. 'It's in Bickley. You know, one of those roads near the station that runs up towards the high school.'

I know the road he's talking about. Even the smallest houses on that quiet street would make a good-sized family home for a couple from the City. From the glimpse I got, it looked as if it hadn't been updated in decades. Luke's favourite thing.

'What made you to decide to look?' I ask, as if it doesn't matter what his answer is.

He takes a sip from the coffee mug on the breakfast bar and shifts on his stool. 'I didn't tell you this, but I ran into Elena a couple of weeks ago. She asked me if I wanted to do another project with her. I said no, of course, but it got me thinking.'

'You should've said. It would be nice to see her again.'

He gives me a sheepish smile. 'I bumped into her at that pottery place out beyond the M25 when I was looking for your anniversary present. I couldn't say anything because, you know, I didn't want to give the game away.'

Luke's present to me, an abstract figurine, is sitting on the mantelpiece in the living room. It's stylish and beautiful, possibly not what I would've chosen for myself. Last time, I wasn't sure about it, and it ended up in the cupboard under the stairs, but this time . . . I don't know. It's growing on me, but hearing that Elena had a hand in choosing it makes sense.

I decide not to press the issue of him flipping houses. It's enough that he's thinking about it. But I'm secretly hoping that by the time I wake up tomorrow morning, a whole year later, he might have made the jump and done something about it.

'What time do you think you'll get home from work?'

He drains his coffee cup. 'I may have to get everyone to stop early today, not just me. This weather . . . '

It's been unseasonably warm for May. We're having a bit of a heatwave in the UK, which is fine for the first twenty-four hours, with everyone stripping off their woollies and donning shorts and tank tops so they can blister in the sun, but we're five days into it now; everyone's wilting and moaning they can't sleep. You can't find a fan in the shops for love nor money.

'Take care of yourself,' I shout after Luke as he heads out the door. 'And remember to drink enough!' I swear, that man would be a shrivelled as a prune if I didn't remind him to hydrate.

Once he's gone, I continue my routine of scouring my bullet journal. Alongside a couple of things I want to set in motion today that will hopefully avoid the unintended fireworks that happened at our anniversary party in one year's time, I have a couple of clients later in the morning. Although neither Luke nor I booked the day off, I'm not as worried about it as I was in previous years. Things started off well for us this morning, very well, if you know what I mean, and the vibe I get is peace, happiness.

All I've got to do is keep this ticking over for another twenty-four hours. Something significant has to happen tomorrow. It's the day it all started. I'm hoping, if I get things right, that it will also be the day that everything stops, I'll be ejected back into my usual life and time will return to its mundane plodding through the days and weeks and months. Sounds like bliss.

★

'Jess! I'm so glad I caught you,' Hannah says at the other end of the phone. 'Is Luke there?'

I'm trying to shove a bowl of overnight oats down my neck before I head off to see my first client (elderly lady who just had a hip replacement). I'm eating at the counter, so I pop my bowl down. 'No. He just left.'

'Oh, good.'

'Good?' I assumed Hannah was already at the office and wanted to catch him for some reason.

'Yeah. Well, maybe . . . ' She doesn't sound like it's such a good thing. I wince, holding the expression as I wait for her to spit it out. 'I'm not quite sure how to say this, Jess, but I found something out that I think you need to know about.'

'Oh?'

'Yes. It kind of came out in conversation around the office — well, more like I overheard something.' She pauses to take a breath. 'Luke has been seeing Elena.'

A small tight knot had been forming in my stomach and now I breathe out and release it. 'Oh, yeah . . . He told me all about it.'

'He did?'

'Sure. They ran into each other when he was looking for my anniversary present. I think she might have helped him pick it out, actually.'

'Oh. Okay.' There's silence for a few seconds. I adore my best friend, but she does love to be the bearer of good gossip. I think I might have accidentally taken the wind from her sails by telling her I already knew. 'And you're fine with that?'

I decide I'm finished with my oats, so I move the bowl to the counter just above the dishwasher and turn my phone onto speaker so I can deal with the contents and load it properly. 'Yes.'

'Just be careful,' Hannah says. 'You always had a weird feeling about her, remember?'

'Yes, I know. But I think I was being a bit paranoid.'

Hannah makes a dismissive noise. 'You know my thoughts on the whole "girl best friend" scenario. That's how everything started with Connor and his side piece. I just don't want you to be complacent like I was, to be fobbed off with, "Oh, it's just platonic!"'

I completely understand why my best friend is fighting my corner on this. Connor told her for at least a year that the woman from the gym was just a friend. With benefits, it turned out. Lots and lots of benefits. He's now shacking up in her flat and Hannah is worried they're on the verge of announcing their engagement before the divorce is even finalized.

'Thank you,' I tell her, my voice full of warmth. 'I appreciate you looking out for me.'

'Just watch your back with that one. Do you remember how you told me she once called herself his "work wife"?' Hannah snorts, revealing exactly what she thinks about that. 'Well, she can fuck right off. That position has been filled. If anything, the way I keep this office running like clockwork, *I'm* Luke's work wife now, and you know I've got your back!'

I laugh at the thought of Hannah describing herself as Luke's work wife. They get on really well, but there is no way they would fit as a couple. He'd never be able to deal with all of Han's drama.

'And you're not worried at all about Elena?' she says again.

'Nope. Not worried at all. But I will bear what you said in mind.'

'Good. Oh, bloody hell, here he comes. I better get off the phone and look like I'm doing something useful.' Hannah hangs up before I can even say goodbye and I chuckle to myself.

No, I'm not worried. Four days ago, when we were in Venice, I chose to trust him, to put my faith in him. I'm not going back on that now. That's what Luke was saying, wasn't it, when we had that argument the night of our tenth anniversary party? He said I always thought the worst of him, and that meant I was always expecting him to disappoint me. No wonder he was upset. I'm not going to make that mistake a second time.

CHAPTER FORTY-NINE

JESS

I stand on the doorstep of my mother's house, my pulse pounding in my temples. It takes me a couple of seconds before I gather the courage to ring the doorbell. I know she's in, because I texted earlier today to ask if I could come and talk with her. That doesn't stop the hollow feeling in my stomach as I hear movement inside the house.

Mum opens the door, and tears instantly prickle in my eyes. She looks smaller. How can she look smaller?

'Hi, darling,' she says, only just holding on to her composure, and then she opens her arms halfway. 'Can I have a hug?'

I nod mutely then allow her to embrace me. Part of me wants to melt against her, but I stand there, stiff as a board, as she holds me softly for a few moments, rubbing my back, before pulling away again.

'It's good to see you.'

My voice is scratchy when I manage to speak. 'Yes.'

'Come inside.' I follow her into the kitchen, where the man I saw before is standing, barefoot, in a Pink Floyd T-shirt and jeans. Mum glances nervously at him. 'This is Jared.'

He smiles at me as he throws a teabag in the same mug I used to drink from as a teenager while I was doing my homework. 'Hi, Jess. Nice to finally meet you.' There's no judgement in his time, no blame for staying away, just friendliness. I unclench, just a little. 'Cup of tea?' he asks.

'No, thanks,' I say, flapping my hand near my face. 'Too hot.' What started off as an uncomfortably muggy morning has now bloomed into a scorching day.

'Something cold, then?'

I hesitate. I don't know if I can say what I want to say with an audience, as nice as he seems. Mum must guess what I'm thinking because she says, 'Why don't we take a walk and have something to drink later?'

I nod. 'That would be good.' I'm glad I lathered myself with sunscreen before leaving the house, and I reach inside my handbag to grab my sunglasses.

Once outside again, we turn right and stroll down the road, saying nothing at first. There's a park one street over, and I don't know how I know, but that's where we're heading.

Mum takes a deep breath and looks across at me. 'I meant everything I said in that letter,' she tells me. 'And I want to thank you – for going no-contact – it's what I needed. While I could blame you, and everybody else, for what was happening to me, I could fool myself that things weren't so bad, that I'd get a grip on it eventually but when, after being so very patient, you pulled the plug . . . It was the wake-up call I needed. I reached my rock bottom, Jess.'

'I'm sorry,' I mutter.

She shakes her ahead. 'No, don't be sorry. Like I said in the letter, after behaving ridiculously, I picked myself up, I started going to AA, and this time I really committed. I got a sponsor and I started to do the twelve steps. That was four years ago now.'

'That's great,' I say hesitantly. I sense the truth in her words, but I'm not sure I trust them. But if that's right, four years is way longer than she has ever stayed sober before. It's truly impressive.

We pass by the children's playground, unusually deserted, as everyone must have opted to stay home out of the sun, and pause our conversation briefly as we wait for a dog walker to shoo an inquisitive pair of cockapoos along the path.

'I've gained even more perspective since I wrote you that letter,' Mum says once we're past them. 'I probably don't get all of it, but I can see how unfair I was to you, even when you were still a child, and how hard the choices I made were on you. I know these might sound like empty promises, but my life is different now. *I'm* different now. I would like to be part of your life going forward, but I understand if you don't want that, or if you're not sure about that.'

I stop walking and look at her. We're standing just in front of a bench under the shade of a towering horse chestnut, and it seems natural for us both to sit down. For some reason it takes a while before I can form a sentence. 'Thank you. I want to believe what you're saying, but . . . '

Mum nods sadly. 'I know. If it's any help, it took me ages before I believed I could make it stick too. This is the start of a very long journey, I expect, for you and I.'

'Yes,' I reply quietly. 'I think it might be. But it's a path I would like to explore. That's as much as I can manage for now.'

I don't remember Mum smiling the way she is now when she and Dad were together and we were all living as a family, but she holds her joy in a bit, possibly because she's scared she might scare me off with it.

'I'm glad. How about we keep it casual, take things slowly. Would you and Luke like to come over for a barbecue on the bank holiday?'

I exhale. 'Yes. I think we'd like that.'

By the time I arrive home, I'm sticky, my dress clinging to my back, and utterly exhausted. I have a power nap and then a shower before Luke returns home from work. I want to think about what Mum said, try to unpick it, but my brain is steadfastly refusing. It's as if it's had enough to do today and is digging its heels in.

I tell Luke all about it when he gets home. I cry. Big ugly tears, the kind I never usually let him see. The kind I never usually let *anyone* see. Luke just holds me until I've let it all out.

And then he wipes my eyes. 'Are you sure you want to do this?'

I nod and snatch another tissue from the box on the coffee table. 'Yes. Like you said, I can't just keep running away from things.'

He takes my face in his hands. 'You weren't running away – I know I said that in the beginning, but I get it now – you were protecting yourself. You did the right thing going no-contact. But if she is where she is now, and you believe there's a way to move forward, I am one hundred per cent behind you.' He breaks off to give me a smacker in the middle of my forehead. 'And I am so fricking proud of you.'

That's all he needs to say. My heart melts. We spend the rest of the evening talking, eating, laughing. It reminds me of when we were first together, and we could easily stay up until the dawn chorus started tweeting.

However, even though we have an 'early night', we can't settle to sleep afterwards. It's too hot. The fan is on, our sash windows are open top and bottom, but it's still not enough. Just after midnight, I roll over and grunt. I'd like to cuddle up against Luke, but his body is like a furnace. The only contact we can manage without overheating further is allowing our little fingers to touch.

'I wish we had a pond,' I mutter.

'Huh?' Luke pushes himself up on one elbow and gives me a confused look.

'Just enough cool water, somewhere, where we could submerge ourselves and get some relief.'

Luke continues to look at me, but I can tell his mind is whirring.

'You're mentally working out how we could fit a pond into our garden and how big the hole would need to be, aren't you?' I ask him.

He laughs. 'Busted. Or at least, that's where I started off. Since then I've had another idea.'

'What? Fill up the bath and just lie in it?'

He jumps up off the mattress and holds out his hand. 'Better.' He picks up the thin, strappy cotton dress I was wearing earlier off the armchair in the bay window and hands it to me. 'Put this on.'

I scrabble my way to the edge of the bed and take it from him. 'What? Why?'

'My darling wife wants cool water? I'm going to give her cool water.'

CHAPTER FIFTY

JESS

'You're insane!' I tell Luke as he slows to drive down a narrow road between two low chalk cliffs, then pulls to a stop on a tarmacked promenade. A crescent of sand is spread before us, silvery in the moonlight. 'You drove us all the way to Dumpton Gap?' It's taken more than an hour to get here.

'You wanted cool water,' he says, mock-affronted. 'And I can't think of any place better than this. You've got the whole of the English Channel to cool your fevered brow here!'

'But we could have stopped at Whitstable or Herne Bay!'

He shakes his head. 'Stony beaches. Only the best for you, my sweet. Soft golden sand all the way. Come on . . . ' He opens the car door and gets out. Laughing softly, I do the same.

He jumps off the promenade onto the sand and waits for me. I kick my sandals off, and when I join him, he grabs me by the hand and starts running right down to where the frothy surf meets the sand. And then he doesn't stop running. The cold sea water is a shock to my system but a delicious one. However, Luke keeps going.

'Luke! My dress is getting soaked!' I scream, trying to pull him back onto dry land.

He resists at first, but then suddenly gives in. I'm pulling so hard that we both stumble back onto the wet sand and fall over. The next wave rushes in, crashing over my legs and drenching me up past my hips.

He just laughs. 'Then take it off . . . '

I scrabble out of the surf onto the hard, compacted sand, not sure if I'm choking on sea water or merely laughing. 'But we rushed out the house so fast I didn't even think to bring my cossie with me!'

He drags himself up the sand and starts peeling the spaghetti strap of my dress off one shoulder. 'And this is a problem . . . why?'

I gasp and smack his hand away. 'Oh, my God! This was your plan all along!'

His answering grin seals his guilt.

'But people will see us!'

He glances up at the headland. Although entrance of the beach is in a quiet residential area just north of Ramsgate, the low cliffs obscure the beach from most of the surrounding houses, except for a handful of buildings on the headland at one end of the small bay and what looks like a New England mansion on the other.

'Who's going to see?'

He's right. Not a light is twinkling in any of them, and the long rows of beach huts lining the promenade and the small café near the entrance road are in complete darkness.

I chuckle. 'So this is why you didn't turn off for Broadstairs? Too many buildings overlooking the beach there.'

'Exactly. Now, are you going to remove those things or am I going to have to do it for you?'

I lie back on the sand. 'I think you're going to have to do it for me.'

Luke gets serious then. Taking his time, he eases my arms from one dress strap and then the other, then peels it down my body and throws the half-sodden garment onto the sand above our heads. My bra is next, and he stops to kiss the skin he exposes, causing a dart of need to shoot right through me. The contrast of the cool water lapping at my legs and his warm hands on my flesh is heavenly. I grab for his open shirt and easily tear it from him and send it flying to meet my dress.

He eases my knickers down my legs, stopping to stroke and tease, until I close my eyes, throw my head back and dig my fingers into the gritty sand. And then it's my turn. I stand up to meet him, waves bubbling around our feet and remove his shorts to find he isn't wearing anything underneath them.

We stare at each other, smiling, and then he takes me by the hand and leads me into the waves. This time I don't resist; I just trust him, let him lead me deeper, and then the sand falls away beneath our feet and we're swimming. There's something about almost icy water flowing round my body that makes every nerve ending fizz.

We stay in the water for maybe ten minutes, hardly a word said between us because we don't need them. We seem to know when we want to lift our feet and swim, circling round each other, and when we want to pull each other close and touch, explore.

Luke plants his feet in the sand and I wrap my legs around

him, pull him close and start nibbling at his collarbone, just the way he likes it, when I hear a noise. I freeze. 'What was that?' I whisper into his ear and it sounds loud enough to carry all the way to France.

Luke also goes still. 'Dunno.'

We stay like that, locked together, only our heads and shoulders above the water, eyes wide, and then a swinging beam of light catches my eye. I prod Luke on the shoulder and point. He swears. 'Who bloody walks their dog on the beach at two-thirty in the morning?'

I shake my head and make a face. 'Insomniac with a really ugly mutt?'

Luke's shoulders begin to shake, and then I have to clamp my lips closed to stop myself from laughing too. 'What do we do now?' I whisper, when I'm able to do so without guffawing.

He shrugs his shoulders. 'Stay still and hope they don't notice us?'

We don't really have any other choice, so we cling onto each other, failing miserably to stop ourselves from snorting softly with laughter occasionally, and pretend we're invisible. Thankfully, while the dog runs a short way onto the sand, it comes nowhere near our clothes, and the owner keeps to the concrete promenade, which carries all the way round past the headland into the next bay.

We hold our breath for a few moments after the torch beam disappears from view and then let out the hilarity we've been holding back as quietly as possible. I smack Luke playfully on the shoulder, making a splash. 'You and your bright ideas! We could have ended up getting arrested!'

'But we didn't.' He leans in to continue kissing my neck, but I place my hands on his shoulders and push him backwards.

'I'm not risking getting caught a second time! Let's escape while we can.'

Dawn is close by the time we make it back home. We shower, together, and then finish what we started on the beach. Afterwards, Luke succumbs to sleep easily, but I lie with his arm heavy across my torso, staring at the ceiling. This was the perfect way to spend our anniversary. Doing something crazy and romantic and fun. I wish it could go on forever.

Tomorrow is the big one. Our tenth anniversary. If my life was a game of roulette, and the old version was black and this new one where Luke and I are happy, tonight, was red, I'd put it all on red. But that doesn't mean I'm not nervous.

But then something strikes me and my eyes widen. Technically, it's already tomorrow. And while I've stayed up past midnight on a few of our previous anniversaries, I've never been awake just as dawn is breaking, as it is now.

Could I beat it by staying awake? Could I keep myself in May the fifteenth instead of catapulting forward to our next anniversary? Oh, wow. And if I could, maybe I could stay here for the whole year. That would be three hundred and sixty-five days to build on what's happened today. I'd make that sacrifice, I'd live this whole year again, if I could be sure our next anniversary could be the polar opposite of the last.

Hope surges through me. I'm as close to being one hundred per cent sure I've succeeded in saving my marriage as I've ever come. It has to work; it has to.

I reach my thumb across the palm of my left hand to stroke my eternity ring, wanting the reassurance of its power to take me to the finishing line, but when the pad touches warm, smooth metal, I frown. And then I almost jump out of bed.

The ring is gone. Great-Great-Grannie Millicent's engagement ring is no longer on my finger!

Did I lose it at the beach? Please, no! I can't have. It has to be in the house somewhere. I took both it and my engagement ring off when I had my first shower of the day — after I got home from seeing Mum — but I honestly have no memory if I was wearing it or either of my rings when Luke and I took the second one.

I ease myself out of bed, grab my robe from the back of the door and then creep onto the landing, shutting the bedroom door softly behind me, and then I turn the house upside down.

I open every drawer in the kitchen, empty the bin, just in case, and then have to put all the gooey mess back in again. My muscles are heavy, and my eyes are drooping, but I can't stop now. I have to find this ring before I'm tempted to fall asleep. I try the desk, every available surface, nook and cranny, downstairs. I pull the cushions off the armchairs and sofa in the living room, ramming my fingers down the crevices but only find fluff and one of the old fifty-pence pieces.

After shoving the sofa cushions haphazardly back into place, I collapse down on top of them. It's 4 a.m. I've got at least a few hours, probably more, before Luke gets up. I'll find it before that, right? I make a mental list of all the places I haven't looked where it still could be. What about the car? Or could I have taken it off at the physio practice and not realized I'd left it there? In the version of reality I've been experiencing, I've only been wearing it for four days, hardly enough time for something to feel off if I forgot to put it on.

I suddenly realize my eyelids are closed. I force them open again.

Could it be in the dish in the hallway where we leave our keys? And I haven't had a chance to look around our bedroom yet, either. I'll go and check there next. I just need a few more seconds to gather a bit more energy . . .

But I never look there, because I slide into sleep sprawled out on the sofa, and I'm not even aware when it happens.

CHAPTER FIFTY-ONE

LUKE

Three Weeks Before the Engagement Party

'So, how are things going?' Elena asks as he meets her on the ground floor of the large, industrial-looking building, and they head upstairs to the room they've been chatting in on Wednesday evenings once every three weeks.

'Eh,' he says wearily. 'Not good.'

'How not good?' she asks, as they reach their destination. She slides into her usual spot and he into his.

'All we seem to do is bicker.'

She humphs. 'Isn't that what married couples do?'

'But it's over *everything*. Last night we argued about who accidentally sat on the remote so it changed channel. I wasn't anywhere near it, but Jess swore it wasn't her, and that made no sense to me, especially as she'd just sat down again after getting up to get a glass of water, and before you know it, we're both glowering at the fantasy boxset we're bingeing. And it's like that every night. We sit there, in the same room, watching the same thing, but we're not really together.'

Elena starts unpacking her bag of things that help her pass the time on these evenings. 'That doesn't sound good.'

He sighs. 'Sometimes I feel that even the way I breathe annoys her.'

Elena chuckles. 'I've been married myself, remember? It probably does. Sometimes . . .'

For some reason, he can't find it funny. 'I can't see a way out of it. That's why I'm more and more sure that getting her to sit down and talk with her mum will help.'

Elena picks up her knitting and her needles clack for a minute or two. He can tell that she's thinking something over. Eventually, she looks up at him. 'You know it's not your responsibility to fix her, don't you?'

He makes a face. 'That's not what I'm doing.'

'Isn't it?'

'No. I'm just trying to, you know . . . help her.'

'I understand that. That's who you are. And you know I appreciate your support, keeping me company while all this . . .' she indicates the pole, tubes, and machinery delivering the chemicals into her body '. . . is going on.'

'Good. That's why I'm here.'

'And I know you want to support Jess, which is wonderful, but nobody wants to feel like somebody else's project, let alone thinking their partner sees them as broken, needing to be repaired.'

Now he's starting to feel irritated with this woman too. 'I told you, that's not what this is.'

'Sure . . . Okay. But maybe ask yourself, what is it? What's fuelling this drive to bring Jess's mum into the picture, to heal things between them? Can you honestly say that's not part of your motive?'

'You and I have talked about that subject in depth over the last few months. I haven't held anything back.' And it's been so refreshing, he thinks. There's so much he holds back, mainly because Jess has so much to carry already. It would be cruel of him to ask her to carry his stuff too. 'You know that all I want to do is make her happy.'

Elena's needles start moving again. 'All you can do is work on how you show up in the relationship – not you solving everything else you think is a problem in her life.'

'Hey!' he says softly. 'You're supposed to be on my side.'

She rolls her eyes. 'I am on your side.' She ends with a Spanish word he doesn't understand but guesses means something along the lines of 'idiot'. 'But answer this question: is it that you want to make her happy, or that you *need* to make her happy?'

'Isn't that the same thing?'

'Not necessarily. When it becomes a need, it becomes more about you, about the role you assign yourself, rather than about her.'

She's talking nonsense. 'That's just semantics. What it boils down to is: if we can't make each other happy what's the point? We're supposed to be a team.'

'Which brings me back to what I have been saying for weeks. You need to talk to her.' She pauses while she does something tricky with her needles. 'But I think you're finding excuses to put it off.'

'Ouch.'

'You need to tell her what you are feeling, but also how you feel about her.' She turns her focus back to her knitting, smiling to herself, and lets the silence sit. He knows she's waiting for him to talk. This is a tactic of hers, something she does when she feels he needs to dig deeper. It's actually quite annoying.

'I suppose I don't know how to say it. I'm not good at big romantic declarations.'

'Felix was all about those – how did you say it? – big romantic declarations. It didn't help any. They're nice in the moment, but they don't matter if the day-to-day relationship doesn't live up to that, if it's full of tiny negatives that outweigh the big positive, if you know what I mean?'

He frowns. 'I *think* I do.'

'It's the small moments that count, Luke, being a team on the ground together rather than one of you being up on a pedestal. If I were ever to get married again . . . ' she glances up at him, meets his eyes, then returns to her knitting ' . . . I do not want a man who promises undying love and showers me with red roses, even though those things are nice. I would much rather have a man who told me I was his best friend. That's the foundation for everything. That's the kind of man, the kind of relationship, I want in the future.'

She meets his eyes and something passes between them.

'You will have to show her, Luke. Don't just tell her.'

He knows words are not enough. Every year, he tries to show her with his anniversary gift, trying to find something interesting and creative related to the symbol of their years together, to tell her that. She always smiles and looks pleased, always says how much she loves his gifts, but he's started to wonder if she's receiving the message he's trying to send her.

'I have a special present planned for this year. I couldn't make something of tin – it's too soft – but pewter is made of mostly tin, so I went with that.' He thinks about the hours he put into the thought and design, the extortionate amount he spent on the metal work and jewellery designer who helped him put it all together. The commission is something that hopefully will show Jess just how central she is to his life, that he would like her to be woven into every part of it. If only she'd let him.

And then there's the biggest surprise of all. Her mother. He's invited her to the party. And if those two things don't work together, he has no idea what he's going to do.

TIN

Tin is a malleable silvery-white metal that is most often alloyed. While it may borrow strength from the metals it is mixed with, tin will not tarnish or rust. It may seem lowly and unassuming compared to precious metals, but do not be fooled — there is nothing better for the purposes of storage and preservation. Some items made from this material may last a lifetime.

CHAPTER FIFTY-TWO

JESS

I wake up with a jolt. No! I can't have fallen asleep! I need to . . . I need to . . .

What the heck?

Last time I remember feeling sleepy I was on the sofa downstairs, but now I'm back in bed again. On my own, which must mean that I've slept in. How did I get here? I don't remember walking myself up the stairs!

Oh.

I'm too late.

My stomach swoops. This is it. Today's the day.

I bring my left hand out from under the duvet to where I can see it, but my ring finger still only has two rings on it instead of three. What am I going to do? And what is Luke going to say if he discovers I've misplaced a family heirloom? I'm going to have to try and find it, or at the very least prevent him from noticing its absence until this day is over.

Have I been without it for a whole year? That can't be good. When Luke's grandma lost it at the beach, it came back to her within twenty-four hours, but I skipped right over that day, and hundreds of other ones after it. What does it mean that it hasn't found its way back to me? Has it considered me somehow unworthy?

But there's not much I can do about that now. I'm just going to have to put my best foot forward, build on everything I've already tried to change, and hope I've done enough. I take a few deep breaths, flip the duvet back and get out of bed.

I find Luke downstairs, sitting at the kitchen table with a mug of tea, engrossed in his phone. 'Morning, gorgeous!' I say, cheerily. 'I think it's your turn to make the pancakes this year!'

He frowns at me. 'What pancakes?'

I put my hands on my hips. 'You know . . . the banana and blueberry pancakes. Our tradition.' Or it seems to have become that over the last few years.

Luke looks perplexed and he stands and goes over to the fridge. 'Do we even have any blueberries? Or eggs, for that matter?'

'Um . . . I don't know.'

He opens the fridge door and scans the interior. 'Eggs, no. Blueberries, yes. You can always have them with yoghurt.'

I blink. Yes, I can, I suppose. He stands back from the fridge door and allows me to gather what I need to make myself some breakfast. When he returns to the table and picks up his phone, I notice a plate with toast crumbs sitting next to his mug. He must have eaten without me.

As I dollop yoghurt into a bowl and start hunting through the kitchen cupboard for some almonds or pecans to sprinkle on top along with the blueberries, I start chattering away to him. 'When are you off work this afternoon?'

'Normal time,' he says without looking up from his phone.

'You're not finishing early because of the party?'

'You said you had it all covered. And we knew that was the downside of doing it on our actual anniversary rather than waiting for the weekend.'

'Oh, yes. I forgot.' I sit down opposite him with my breakfast, and he still doesn't look up from his screen. 'What have you got planned for today? Have you got any prospects on the go in terms of houses?'

'Houses?'

The only way I could think of to find out if he's finally made the break from Harris & Sons is by asking him outright. 'Yes. Anything on the horizon with Elena?'

That gets his attention. He finally lifts his head, looking more than a little flustered. 'Elena? Why would you mention Elena? I . . . I mean, *we* . . . haven't seen her in years.'

'But I thought—'

He stands up abruptly, jams his phone into the pocket of his trousers and starts whizzing around the kitchen, putting his stuff in the dishwasher, picking up his keys. I have the weird feeling that he's avoiding the subject for some reason. 'Right. That's me. I need to head off. I'll see you later.' He doesn't even meet my eyes as he gives me a perfunctory kiss on the cheek and leaves.

The sound of the front door slamming a second or two later makes me jump. I stand there in the kitchen, my arms hanging limply at my sides. 'Happy anniversary,' I mutter after him.

Feeling deflated, I go back upstairs, take a shower and get dressed. Is it me, or was Luke being strange? We had such an amazing time last night, our relationship seemed so strong in comparison to last time, that I thought at least I'd get a bit more affection from him. What's happened in the last twelve months? Have I jinxed it all by losing the ring?

I continue to ponder why things feel a bit off as I put my jewellery on. As I'm concentrating on inserting an earring, I let my gaze wander around our bedroom. Hang on . . . What's that print doing there?

I walk across the room to where a large vintage-style rail poster for the Lake District hangs above the chest of drawers. That shouldn't be here. It should be the black-and-white framed photograph of Venice we picked up there second time around, when we were happy and in the mood for gathering memories and souvenirs, rather than sulking with each other.

I shake my head. My memory is so scrambled at the moment. I must be mixing things up. What's really important right now is that I find that ring. Since the last place I checked was the living room, I might as well continue the search there before trying anywhere else.

I pull all the sofa cushions off again and have another rummage, to no avail, and it's as I'm putting them back again, that something catches my eye. The tiles in the fireplace. They're wrong. Because we bought the house a year later this time around, we couldn't find the same tiles. Instead of the cream ones with the red tulips we originally had, I ended up with large yellow flowers, but here are the tulips staring back at me.

No. It can't be.

I race into the kitchen diner, grab my bullet journal off the desk and leaf madly through it. When I can't find what I'm looking for, I pull the previous year's journal off the shelf and turn it to the fourteenth of May. My work commitments for the day are in there, but there is nothing to suggest I met with my mother that morning. I was sure I wrote that in there. I pick up another book and flick to the back. Where there should be a tally of all the money I lent my mother that year, that list that caused an argument six years ago, there is a creamy blank page.

I sit down heavily on the desk chair and stare across the room. No. This isn't fair.

It's not how this is supposed to go. I'm supposed to arrive on my tenth anniversary the same way as I arrived in all my others, building on the progress and course corrections made in previous years. I don't want to admit it to myself, but I have the horrible feeling that's not what has happened this time.

This house is *exactly* the same as the one I left the last time I lived my tenth anniversary. Luke didn't remember our new tradition about pancakes. And instead of being warm and affectionate this morning, at times, it felt as if he was looking right through me.

This isn't a new version of our tenth anniversary. This is the old one. The nightmare.

I glance down at the space on my ring finger where the eternity ring should be. Of course, I wouldn't be wearing it if I was reliving the first version of this day. Luke hasn't given it to me yet. Well, technically, he didn't ever give it to me. I just found it after he left.

That must be the reason. What else could it be? After all, the ring has been the key to everything so far – I don't know why I didn't put it together before now. I 'jumped' back in time after I found it the first time, and things weren't going well, no matter how hard I tried, before Luke gave it to me properly in Venice. After that, things got quickly better and stayed that way. And now the ring is lost, I'm back at square one.

That has to be it. It has to be.

A flash of memory, Luke shouting at me, the hopelessness in

his eyes, the front door banging behind him fills my mind. Oh, God. If I'm right, it's all going to happen again. And I've only got – I count silently in my head – twelve hours to change that.

I put my elbows on my knees and rest my head in my hands. What am I going to do? I can't live through that again. I let down every wall, every barrier. I gave it my all. If he leaves me again, I will just be a shell of a person, filled with longing and regret that will never leave me.

I will end up just like my mother. I won't have any other choice.

CHAPTER FIFTY-THREE

JESS

I spend the next couple of hours panicking, looking absolutely everywhere for the ring, but coming up empty. Eventually, after a third search under the bed reveals nothing, I give up and sit down cross-legged on the bedroom carpet.

Letting my emotions overrun me is not going to do me any favours. I need to think, come up with a plan. Even if I have somehow ended up back in the first version – well, the only version – of my tenth wedding anniversary, it doesn't mean it's hopeless. I might have lost all the progress I've made over the last twelve days, but it isn't over until the fat lady sings. Or, in this case, Luke walks out the door.

Just that thought makes my stomach wobble, but then I remind myself I'm not going into this blind. I've been here before. I know the key moments, the forks in the road, that led to Luke walking away. And I've learned a lot along the way. *I've* changed, even if the world around me hasn't. I still have a chance to change things around.

Like Luke, I have work to do today, but only until midafternoon. Like last time, I've given myself more than a few hours to get myself ready. But instead of taking a long, pampering bubble bath, I sit down with a notebook and pen and pick through my memories of my alternative life, trying to work out where the turning points were, how I managed to change things. I don't exactly have a plan when Luke comes home, in terms of what to do or what to say, but I do know that I need to keep my cool, resist the urge to erect my formidable defences and, well, just be nice to him instead of mildly pissed off the whole time.

My first test is the toilet roll incident. Once again, the holder is empty. But I reach into the cupboard and refill it before getting down to business. I'll still have to remind him later, but maybe, this time, I don't have to take the lack of loo roll as a personal attack.

The next hurdle is the unveiling of my anniversary present, which Luke brings home with him. He makes me go upstairs so he can put it where it needs to go, then comes to find me and brings me downstairs, instructing me to close my eyes once I reach the bottom step, then gently guides me into the living room and tells me I can open them.

The bare patch of wall in an awkward alcove in the dining room is bare no longer. A large metal sculpture now hangs there. I reach out and touch the silvery trunk of what looks to be a willow tree. 'It's made of pewter?'

Luke turns and looks at me. 'Yes. Good guess. Because tin is—'

'Too soft on its own,' I finish for him. 'It has to be mixed with other metals.'

He gives me a pleased but confused look. 'Yes.'

This is the point last time where I caught sight of the clock on the wall and panicked about not having started my make-up, but I think back to what Luke said in the taxi on the way to the party last time. Instead of focusing on my own disappointment, I turn my attention back to my gift while Luke rustles around with something on the dining-room table.

I didn't notice it before, but amidst the delicate leaves curling from the branches are little protrusions. I reach out and touch one. It looks like a hook . . . and they are grouped into clusters: twos and threes mostly, but there is a lone hook on the right-hand side of the tree and, on the left, a group of five together.

Luke pulls something from a series of boxes he has laid out on the table – two small metal shapes. It's only when he hangs them on the two hooks in the centre of the tree that I realize they are photo frames, made of the same beaten pewter, and they contain pictures of him and me on our wedding day. My mouth drops open. I had no idea . . .

Because you were too busy being in a bad mood, too ready to believe Luke didn't think you were worth something special, the voice inside my head reminds me.

He's chosen images that make it look as if we are turning to each other. He's smiling at me, his eyes full of adoration. I am half-enveloped in a cloud of white tulle (our wedding day was windy, and I could *not* control my veil) and I am smiling back at him. I know these photos aren't from our collection. Where did he get them?

He steps away and I hear rustling. A moment later he returns to stand behind me. 'And look . . . ' He reaches forward and hangs a smaller frame containing a picture of my dad on a branch shooting out above my photo on a tiny curling hook hidden amongst the silvery leaves. And then he adds Lola next to him and my sisters below and off to the side.

'It's a family tree,' I say softly.

'Now she gets it!'

A stab of regret hits me straight in my chest. This is stunning! This is . . . everything. And to think I was sulking about diamonds because, in my own myopic way, they were what signified that I was precious to Luke. I was blind. So, so blind. This is so much more. Because I know how much family means to Luke. It's his world. And there I am, right in the centre of it . . . with him.

'Where did you get this?'

'I found the artist online. She has some different versions, but they're all customizable, depending on your family.' He goes on to pull more tiny frames out of a tissue-paper-lined box and hang them on the branches on his side – his parents, Cassie and Greg with Edie hanging underneath, and then his younger brothers, Matt, Zach and Nick.

My gaze wanders back to my side of the tree. Yup. There it is. A tiny hook is hidden in the foliage on the other side of my father to my stepmother. Luke notices where I'm looking, and the tissue paper rustles again. I nod, and he adds an old photo of my mother to the branch. I've seen it before, and I would probably wonder where he got it from if I didn't already know he's been talking to my mother in secret to set up his 'surprise' later at the party.

A shiver runs through me. At least I won't be blindsided this time, but I can't say I'm not nervous. As much as Luke hinted Mum had made the same progress in this version of our lives too, is that true? Can I trust it?

'One last one,' he says, but when he holds the frame, it's empty. I give him a quizzical look and he puts it on a little silvery vine that shooting out from under our two pictures. His free arm comes around me and his palm splays flat against my lower abdomen. 'For the next generation.'

Hope slices through me like a knife, bringing joy but also leaving pain. I want this more than anything, but I also know what might happen later this evening, something that might crack this beautiful tree right down the middle.

I turn and kiss him on the cheek and then the lips. And then again and again. 'Thank you,' I whisper, when I finally let him gather his breath. 'I love it.' And I don't have to lie. I really do. The Jess who didn't even stop to look long enough to understand what this was seems so clueless, so critical now. No wonder things ended up where they did. He must have been able to sense that, even if I didn't say anything. I kiss him again, making sure he feels the truth of my gratitude, and then I pull away smiling. 'I'd better go and put my shoes on and touch up my lipstick. We don't want to be late for our own party!'

CHAPTER FIFTY-FOUR

JESS

This time, the ride to the party venue isn't fraught with tension. I place my hand over Luke's on the back seat of the cab, but not in apology this time, just because I want to. Out of the corner of my eye, I see his head turn. When I look at him, he's smiling, even if there is a slight crinkling of the skin between his eyebrows. I lean over and kiss him on the cheek, then rest my head against him as much as the seatbelt will allow.

Everything happens pretty much as it did before. We arrive, greet Luke's family and mine, and then I find Hannah. She rushes over, congratulates me then asks, 'What did you think about the present? Did you like it?'

'I really did,' I tell her. 'It was very thoughtful, very . . . Luke.'

She grins back at me. Maybe because I'm not low-key moaning about the gift this time, she adds, 'He was nervous you wouldn't like it, so he asked for my opinion, and I sort of ended up getting involved. Did you like the photos of you and Luke? They were ones I took on your wedding day!'

Oh, so *that's* why I didn't recognize them. 'Amazing,' I tell her, even though I wished she could have found an image of me where my smile looked less like a grimace, but maybe that was hard to do. I remember how tired my face muscles got from grinning so much.

I see the moment when the light behind Hannah's eyes dims. 'You're so lucky to have such a wonderful man beside you,' she tells me. 'I wish I could find me one of those!'

I hug her again. Hard. I know she doesn't know she's done all of this before, but I appreciate her helping me plan this party. 'I'm grateful for him, but also for you.'

I let her words, and mine, settle in my heart and mind. I *am* grateful for Luke. More than I ever was before. We're not perfect, but we have so much more potential than we've let ourselves realize. I feel as if I've matured hugely over the last twelve days. Last time, I was sulking at the absence of diamonds and roses and big romantic gestures, but love is more than that. It's trust. It's solidarity. It's having each other's backs, finding moments to connect in small ways every day.

Later, when Hannah taps the microphone and gives her speech, I take my turn once again. However, this time I thank not only our friends and family for coming, but I turn, make eye contact with my husband and thank him for all he is and all he's done for me. He looks surprised but pleased, and when Hannah instructs the DJ to play 'our' song, I can hardly wait to slide into his arms and feel his solid warmth against me. I wonder if they can play this song on repeat forever, because I'm not sure I'm ready to let go.

'I meant what I said,' I whisper into his ear as couples start to fill the dance floor around us. 'I love you, Luke.'

'Yeah, I love you too,' he mumbles back, but it feels as if he's checked out, just going through the motions, and I can hardly blame him for it because, last time, I was too.

I pull back so he can see my face. 'I mean really, *really* love you. I want this ten years to be the start of something, just the first chapter of the rest of our lives.'

He nods. 'Me too.' But there's a sadness in his eyes that worries me. I know he's telling me the truth – this is what he wants – I just suspect he's given up believing it's possible.

My thumb reaches again for the security of my wedding and engagement rings, and I can't help noticing the space where one is missing. I wish I had his great-great-grandmother's ring now, because what happens in the next half an hour is going to decide whether our marriage stands or falls.

Last time, I started a disastrous chain reaction when I flipped out after seeing my mother, one that ended with Luke walking out of my life. I can choose to handle the situation differently this time, and maybe that will be enough to stop him going. Yes, we have issues, big issues, to work on. It'll take time, but we can do it if one of us doesn't make a dramatic exit before we have a chance.

Just as he did last time, when the song ends, Luke looks at me and says, 'I think it's time to give you your final surprise of the day.'

I do my best to quell the quivering in my stomach. 'Really?'

'Yes. But I can't give it to you here. We need to go outside.'

I slide my hand down his arm and lock my fingers between his, then meet his eyes again. 'Then lead the way.'

A lone figure stands at the end of the terrace at the back of the hotel, hands on the stone balustrade, staring out into the evening. As our footsteps echo off the old manor house's walls, she turns, smile hesitant, eyes full of hope.

My stomach rolls, an echo of what I felt the first time I lived this moment.

'Hello, sweetheart.'

'Hello, Mum.'

We stand there, looking at each other.

'It's . . . It's good to see you,' she adds, her eyes darting to Luke and then back onto me. 'How are you?'

Having an out-of-body experience? That's what it feels like. The sense of déjà vu is so strong it's making me dizzy. 'I'm okay,' I finally manage.

I don't know what to think about the woman standing in front of me. I want to believe what Luke said about her is true, but I'm very aware that in this timeline, I received no letter from her. I even checked the back of all my bullet journals to be sure. Does that mean she's not going to AA, or doing the twelve steps? It's a possibility. And I'm not sure I have it in me to open the door wide to her again, not when she has such a capacity for friendly fire. I felt a genuine sense of hope for the Mum in my other life. This one I'm not so sure about.

'I tried to call you, contact you, over the years,' she says, 'but, you know . . . obviously, you blocked me, so we never . . . '

The hairs on my spine rise and I'm instantly on high alert. Did I just detect a hint of resentment, of blame, in 'you blocked me'? I don't know. I feel the old familiar flames starting to lick the soles of my feet, the anger I finally could not contain when she turned something around on me and made it my fault. Every cell in my body is telling me to turn, to walk away, but I stand my ground.

I'm still so angry with Luke that he did this. Even now. He's put me in an impossible situation.

I'm doing better, but I'm not fricking Superwoman. I need to get out of here before this control shakes apart. 'Listen, Mum. I think we need to talk, but I'm not sure this is the time or the place.'

Especially when there's an open bar thirty feet away.

'Oh.' Mum looks disappointed. 'Okay.'

But she doesn't yell or scream. Maybe there's still hope.

'I will get in touch next week and maybe we can meet up for a coffee and clear the air and, um, I'd really appreciate it if you didn't stay to the rest of the party, if that's okay.'

I can't be distracted, worrying if she's snuck a drink from somewhere and is about to embarrass us again. My sole focus needs to be on Luke and our marriage this evening.

A cloud passes across her features. 'Well . . . okay. In that case, I suppose I should get going.'

She leans in, gives me a brief kiss on the cheek, and then steps back.

'Why don't I walk you out front and get you a cab?' Luke says and turns to me. 'I'll be back in a couple of minutes.'

I nod and watch them go. I could go back inside, dance to ABBA with Hannah, but I end up mirroring my mother's pose, leaning on the stone balustrade and looking out over the lawn that eventually gives way to a golf-course sand trap. I'm still there when Luke returns.

He looks relieved. I wish I was.

'What did you think of your surprise?'

I let out a dry laugh. 'It was definitely a surprise.'

'It went okay, though, don't you think?'

I turn around and rest my bottom on the stone ledge. 'You and I need to talk.'

Luke looks confused. 'About what?'

'I appreciate that you tried to do something nice for me—'

'I *tried* to do something?'

'Yes.'

He shakes his head softly and looks away. 'And here's me, thinking you were about to thank me, say how grateful you were! I can't win, can I?'

The old me would have taken the bait, let the self-righteous anger fuel her, but I compose myself and ignore his comment. 'I wish you had talked to me before you invited her.'

Luke's head spins around and his eyes are slightly narrowed. He was preparing to batten down the hatches and weather out the 'Jess' storm. I've surprised him, I think. 'I did think about it,' he says warily. 'In fact, I mentioned it to— never mind. But it went okay, didn't it? You were pleased.'

'I know I didn't have a meltdown, Luke, but that doesn't mean I was pleased.'

'But you're . . . you're not *angry*, are you?'

I blink. 'Actually, I am. I'm furious.'

Luke's mouth drops open. 'Then why did you—?'

'Talk to her?' I finish for him.

He nods.

'Because I didn't want to make a scene. I didn't want to act like she does all the time.'

'But she's—'

'Sober. Yes, I know. Or so she says.'

He frowns. 'I don't remember her saying that while we were standing there.'

Oh, crap. He's right. I'm forgetting we haven't had the conversation yet where he tells me she's remarried, doing well. I'll just have to skip right over that and hope he doesn't notice.

'I've been extremely clear over the years about not wanting to see her. For the record, I did *not* want her at our party tonight, no matter what is going on in her life at the moment. It was wrong of you to invite her without asking me, for overriding my wishes because you thought you knew better.' My words come out calmly, but I'm aware I'm not pulling my punches. However, this isn't anger or hurt talking, it's just plain facts, ones Luke and I need to face if we're ever going to make it past this night as a couple.

'You have to admit that if you could find some peace about your mother, it might help things – it might help *you*.' He's angry I've pulled him up on this, which is slightly galling, but I can't get caught up on that. I know that, in his heart of hearts, he was trying to do a good thing, but that still doesn't mean he did the *right* thing.

'That's true. But it's not your job to fix that, Luke. It's mine. And my mother's.'

'But I—' He cuts himself off mid-sentence.

'But you what?'

He looks at me, holds his hands up, then lets them fall back down to his sides. 'Then I give up. I don't know what else to do!' He turns, but instead of heading back into the hotel, he jogs down the steps into a formal rose garden and heads off into the darkness.

Uh-oh. This is all feeling horribly familiar. It's like he's stuck in a groove he can't get out of, like he's reading our familiar script. My lines have changed but he's still sticking to his old ones. I pick up my skirts and run after him. There's a fountain in the middle of the rose garden, with a large fat, stone fish spitting water into a wide shallow bowl. He pauses there and I manage to catch up with him, but when he spots me, he starts striding again. 'Just give me a moment, will you?'

I step back. Um. Okay. A wave of nausea rolls through my stomach. In my head, I can see it all happening again, no matter what I try. Maybe he's right. Maybe we're doomed to this. I stand there, listening to the plops and splashes of the fountain, my breath quick and high in my chest.

No. Not again. I'm not giving up yet. I just need . . . I need . . .

I need help. Reinforcements.

Magic.

I need the ring.

CHAPTER FIFTY-FIVE

JESS

There's no point talking to Luke while he's like this. A walk around the grounds in the cool air will probably do him good. But when he returns, I'm going to be ready for him. I need all the magic his great-great-grannie's ring can give me. And, yes, it was lost in the other versions of our lives, but I'm not there anymore, am I? The ring can't be sloshing around with pebbles and empty shells somewhere just off the Kent coast, because in this reality or timeline or whatever it is, I didn't lose the ring! Luke hasn't even given it to me yet.

Oh, no. But that means it's probably back at home, like it was last time. And it'll take too long to Uber there and back again. I need to do something *now* to save my marriage.

But what if . . . ?

It's worth a try.

I run back into the function room and go to the table at the edge of the dance floor where Luke and I sat earlier. His jacket is slung over the back of one of the banqueting chairs and I delve into one pocket then the next.

A-ha! Got it!

Diane is sitting across the table and gives me a quizzical look. I can't open it here, can I? She'll recognize the ring and wonder why I didn't wait for Luke to give it to me. I smile brightly at her, and decide it's easier to take the whole jacket than risk her seeing what's inside the gift bag, so I turn, clutching it to me, and march myself out of the function room and back onto the terrace, where I throw Luke's jacket down and grab for the gift bag in the left-hand pocket and pull it out.

'What the hell are you doing?'

I jerk reflexively and the ring box jumps out of the tissue paper, bounces off the table and then lands on the floor. I turn around to face Luke, who's standing behind me with his hands on his hips. 'I—I was just . . . ' I trail off. There is no explanation he would accept or understand.

'You're spying on me? Going through my pockets?'

'No . . . Well, yes . . . But—'

He grabs his jacket from the table. 'I was on my way back inside to get this,' he says, then his gaze snags on the gift bag and he snatches that up too and shoves it back in his pocket. 'What is up with you this evening? You are behaving very, *very* weirdly. And why were you looking for this? How did you even know about it?'

'I . . . I don't know what to say.'

'An explanation would be nice!'

I give him a helpless shrug. That is honestly all I can tell him.

He runs his hand through his hair, and I see that same look in his eyes I saw earlier. Even though he doesn't move, I feel him stepping away emotionally. It won't be long before his body follows. I reach for him. 'Luke, please . . . ?'

This time he does step away, shaking his head. 'No. You tell me. What's going on, Jess? None of this makes sense at all. I've been feeling something has been off for weeks, months even. This is the evening – our tenth anniversary – when we should be so happy to have reached this milestone, when we should be celebrating, enjoying each other, but here we are, neither of us understanding what the other one is doing, let alone thinking. Is that what the next ten years are going to be like?' He shakes his head. 'If so, I'm not sure I can—'

'No! Don't say it!' I shout. 'Don't say it,' I repeat more quietly, and then I begin to cry.

Luke doesn't move. He's over it, I can tell.

He's over *me*.

I know I'm only seconds away from sobbing hysterically, but I gather every ounce of my energy, and I shove a lid on my panic, my grief, that this is all happening again – same conversation, different location. I feel as if someone has hollowed out my insides with a spoon. A memory slices through my brain: my mother, sobbing against the closed front door after my father left, her howls equal amounts of rage and despair.

I want to scream at him, tell him how hard I've tried, how he was already one foot half out the door when I arrived in this day, how it's his fault he didn't love me hard enough, make me feel worthy enough, but I let the words pass through my head and fly free. As much as I want to blame him, I know where that leads. I also know that where we are now is just as much my fault, but I don't know how to get out of this dead end I've driven myself into. I'm boxed in. Nowhere to go, except . . .

It's as if a door opens in my head and light shines through it.

There is a way. Just one. And it might be insanity to take that path. At the very least, it will require every scrap of courage and strength I've found within myself during the last thirteen days. I'm going to have to do the unthinkable.

'Okay,' I say. I walk over to the stone balustrade and rest against it, then gesture for him to join me. When he's settled, I clasp my hands in front of me, look him in the eye, and I start to tell him what happened on our tenth anniversary – not this time, the last time – and then I tell him what happened in all the days afterwards.

CHAPTER FIFTY-SIX

JESS

I finish speaking and Luke just stares at me, his jaw tight. 'Really?' he says, and the look of utter disgust on his features shreds my insides.

I try to speak but my throat is dry, and I have to cough before I can get a single word out: 'Really.'

He shakes his head and stands up. 'I thought things weren't great between us but I wasn't all the way there to thinking we were in a critical condition. I hadn't given up hope on you, Jess.'

'I—'

He holds a hand up. 'Let me speak, please. I gave you your turn – for what it was.'

I nod and swallow down my plea, even though it feels as if words want to explode from inside me.

'I thought we could find a way back to a good place. I thought we both wanted to make it work.'

'I do!'

He presses his lips together and shakes his head again. 'No, you don't. Because if you had *any* amount of respect for me, you would not have concocted a bullshit story like that. I never thought you were cruel, Jess. I never saw that in you. But I see it now. And I feel as if I don't even know you anymore.'

I begin to cry.

'It was bad enough feeling like you'd erected a glass wall between us, that I was always standing with my nose pressed up against the window begging to be let in, but this . . . ? This is worse. How did you even think it was a good idea to make something like that up?'

I didn't, I scream inside my head. *It's the most honest, the most open, I've been with you in all our years together. It's the most truthful I've ever been in the whole of my life.*

But it's not enough.

I'm not enough.

'Are . . . are you saying it's over?' I manage to stammer out.

He turns and paces round the room, rubbing his temple. 'I don't want to, but I can't see any other option. I deserve someone who isn't afraid to share the whole of themselves with me, Jess, who knows how to be authentic and honest. Someone I can trust. Someone who's my teammate.'

I nod as the tears roll silently down my cheeks. 'You do,' I reply hoarsely.

He suddenly lunges towards me, ending up down on one knee in front of me as I perch on the balustrade. If it wasn't some grotesque echo of the moment he asked me to spend the rest of my life with him, it might even be funny. 'Then *be* that person! Tell me the truth! Tell me what's really going on with you – and then we can start trying to rebuild, even if it takes counselling or therapy or whatever. I just need one sign you're in it as much as I am, Jess. One sign. Or you're right, there's no reason to stay.'

He stares deep into my eyes with such pain, such desperation. I know what I have to do to save my marriage.

I've got to lie. I've got to tell him I had a dissociative episode or something or just apologize for grasping at straws and making something up because I was so scared of losing him. He might not understand why I told that story, but he'll understand that I'm drawing a line in the sand, saying we're in it together. Forever.

But I can't do that. If I lie and tell him what he wants to hear right now, I'll be doing the exact opposite of what he's asking.

I wrap my skinny fingers around his much larger, calloused ones, and look into his eyes. 'I love you . . . so much. I will do anything for you. I know I haven't always shown that in the past, that I've been so wrapped up in myself and my own hurts that I was conveniently blind to yours . . .'

This earns me a lift of his eyebrows, a look of surprise and, yes, hope.

'But I can't lie to you, Luke. Not now. Not today. I can't change my story, as much as I wish I could, because if I do, even if we sweep all the mistakes we've made away, we'll be rebuilding our marriage on the bedrock of lies. Lies breed secrets, and secrets are a slow-acting poison to the trust we need to make our love last a lifetime. So, no, I can't tell you anything other than what I've already told you. I know it sounds crazy, but can you trust me, Luke? Can you trust me one more time?'

I feel as if I have just vomited up my soul and laid it at his feet. I have never in my whole thirty-five years on this planet felt so raw, so naked.

The seconds tick past as I wait for his reply, but Luke doesn't say anything. He just shakes my hands from his, rises, and walks away. I chase him, grab at his jacket, but he shrugs me off without looking at me. 'Leave it, Jess. I'm done.'

'Luke . . . !' I whisper as he jogs down the stairs into the rose garden, but he doesn't even break his stride. He makes his way down the path, through an arch at the far end of the garden and is swallowed by the night.

I try to run after him, but my leg muscles are jelly. I stumble forward, only stopping myself from falling down the stairs into the rose garden by grabbing on to the rough stone railing. I try to call after him as tears flow freely down my face, but no sound comes out of my open, howling mouth.

CHAPTER FIFTY-SEVEN

JESS

I don't know how long I stay slumped on the steps down to the rose garden. It's as if my brain just cuts out, unable to process anything else. After a while, it's as if I'm standing over myself, watching myself, only it's not me I'm watching but my mother.

That snaps me back to full consciousness pretty quickly. I stand up, brush myself down and walk shakily back up the steps and rest against the stone balustrade again, hands on knees, staring at the lines of cement between the paving slabs of the terrace, tracing the haphazard pattern with my eyes.

I have a choice in this moment. I can follow the pattern laid out for me by my mother. I can slip into the shoes she wore that have 'victim' written all over them in large dark letters, or I can take control. I can fight for my marriage.

What's the point? He'll just find another reason to leave.

The thought cuts into my brain with startling clarity. He walked out on me a second time, despite all my efforts to make things turn out a different way. Is this fate? Was it always going to happen this way, no matter what I did?

I chew on my bottom lip as I think that over. As much as

that feels a logical train of thought, I'm not sure it is. I don't know how or why I've had the experience I've had but in the back of my mind I felt it was the universe giving me a second chance. Why would that happen if the outcome was already predetermined? It would be cruel to dangle that carrot in front of me only to snatch it away again at the last moment. And I don't believe that whatever power runs this universe is that malevolent. I still believe in the goodness of things.

So, while things might not look very good at the moment, am I going to lie down and give up? I've relived thirteen days of my life together with Luke, including this one, and if there's one thing I've learned on this journey, it's that I need to have more faith. In life, in Luke. Even in myself.

Okay.

I stand up, even though I'm not sure exactly what I need to do next. I suppose, if I'm going to fight for my marriage, then I need find my husband. I need to try again. But that might be easier said than done.

Just like before, I send a series of texts that go unanswered. I leave voicemails. I even try calling Hannah to see if she's seen him, but my message goes unread. I'm just about to put my phone to sleep when I have a flash of inspiration. Why didn't I think of this last time? We use a location app. Well, when I say use, I'm not sure I've actually checked up on my husband's whereabouts before, but it's there on our phones, just in case there's an emergency.

I open it up, choose 'people' from the menu, and tap on Luke's name. It blinks for a while and then shows me that his smart watch is stationary and still within a hundred-metre radius. I hold my breath as I pinch the screen, zooming in. It looks . . .

it looks as if he's still in the hotel grounds, next to a lake I didn't even know existed.

Suddenly energized, I start moving but I catch a glimpse of something on the floor, just the other side of the table I stopped at earlier, a dark lump. It looks like a large pebble or . . .

Or a ring box.

In the heat of the argument I had with Luke, I totally forgot it fell on the floor, and he may not have noticed it fly out of the gift bag. I walk over, reach down and pick it up.

Is this fate too? Is this a good sign? I don't see why not. After all, the ring has been a part of this crazy journey I've been on. I should definitely take advantage of an extra bit of magic, shouldn't I? Very carefully, I prise the lid open. The tiny emeralds twinkle away, nestled between the leaf-shaped diamonds.

I'm so relieved to see it again, but when I touch it, it's cold and hard, just metal and stones. Very pretty metal and stones, but metal and stones all the same.

Is this what the success of my marriage hangs on? What good can it really do? But Great-Great-Grannie believed in its power, and it served her well. And Millicent's daughter after her, too. Why do I feel I need it?

I think back to the time when it truly became mine, in the second version of our Venice trip. What happens if there is no magic? What happens if I fight for our marriage, but I lose the battle? What then? What will I do if the worst happens, if Luke behaves just like my father and never comes back? I search deep inside myself for the answer.

I'll survive.

Although the thought of going forward in this life without Luke terrifies me, somehow, I know I'll survive. And if he's not going to fight for me the way I'm going to fight for him, maybe it's not that I'm not good enough for him, but that he truly doesn't deserve me. The thought is freeing.

But I'm not giving up yet. I *will* go down fighting.

I follow the curves and shapes in the ring with my index finger, watching it glitter as the light shifts, and then I close the lid of the ring box and put it back in its box – this is my task, and mine alone.

I walk down the steps into the rose garden and follow the path to the arch at its end. All that lies beyond is damp, tufty grass. I look down at my feet. I'll never make it to the lake in these shoes. I'll break an ankle. So, taking a deep breath, I kick my heels off, step out onto the chilly grass and start walking.

CHAPTER FIFTY-EIGHT

LUKE

A small narrow cloud slides across the crescent moon, plunging him into darkness. He's far enough away from the hotel and the surrounding streets that he can see no lights. It's just as well his eyes have had time to accustom themselves to the darkness and he can now make out the reeds at the water's edge.

His phone is in his hand. Jess has sent him a barrage of texts and voicemails and he's resisted picking up the calls she made. He's not ready to talk to her. It feels as if something inside him has snapped and is now forever changed.

There's a narrow gravel path running around the edge of the lake. He joins it and begins to walk. As he's about to put his phone away, another message arrives. He almost ignores it, but then he sees the name on his lock screen.

Hey. Everything okay?

No. It definitely isn't.

A few seconds later, another message arrives: I saw Jess leave the party and I couldn't see you anywhere either. Has something happened?

How does he even begin to explain what has just gone on between him and Jess? He has no words for it. Really, he doesn't.

Do you need to talk?

Jess will be mad if he talks to someone else about what's been going on with them. She's always been so private about their relationship. Well, about everything, really. He's the only one she allows to see her feeling less than her polished best, and those glimpses have become more and more rare in recent years. He's no longer her ally, her confidant. Tonight, it feels as if he's the enemy.

He rounds a bend in the path and comes upon a small folly standing at the edge of the water on a small promontory, where he pauses, considering his options, and before his brain actually makes a measured decision, his thumbs are moving across the keypad: **I could do with a listening ear.** If there's anyone who can help him make sense of what's going on, it's her.

Where are you?

He glances over the grass to where he can just about see lights behind a small copse of trees. The path must have taken him closer to the hotel without him realizing it, but he doesn't want to go back there. Mostly, because he's not ready to come face to face with his wife, but also because there will be too many people. No privacy.

Jess will definitely not be happy he's going to spill their secrets to one of their circle of friends, but you know what? Too bad. He's spent far too long playing their marriage by Jess's rules. Far too long trying to keep up to her standards in an attempt to stop her drifting away from him. But if she won't budge and inch for him, maybe he won't do the same for her.

Stuff it. He quickly types in a reply: **I'm down by the lake at the folly.**

I know where that is. Stay put. I won't be long.

The folly is a round structure, closed to the back, but open with pillars to the front. A curved bench fills most of the inside, probably giving a beautiful view of the lake on a sunny day. But sitting inside will hide him from anyone coming down the path, so he leans against one of the pillars and waits.

A few minutes later, he sees the glow from a mobile phone torch advancing down the path towards him. When she gets close enough, he smiles wearily, especially when she hands him a thick glass tumbler. He takes a sniff and then sips the dark liquid. Single malt. 'Lagavulin?' he asks.

'I know it's your favourite. You sounded as if you could do with one.'

He could. And of course she would guess that. She knows him so well. What surprises him is that she is holding an identical glass for herself.

'I didn't think you were a whisky drinker,' he says.

She brings the glass up to her nose and inhales softly. 'Not usually.'

He takes a sip, enjoying the earthy scorching at the back of his throat as it goes down. She follows his lead then splutters.

'This is one of the more powerful-tasting single malts,' he tells her. 'If you're not used to whisky, a smoother one would probably go down better.'

She laughs, looking away, clearly a little embarrassed, but she doesn't try to hide it, and without agreeing to, they both move over to the curving bench inside the folly and sit down. The silence around them is warm and inviting as they drink. He knows he won't be shut down if he opens his mouth and lets the words spill out.

'Jess and I had a huge fight,' he says, then goes on to tell her what happened that evening, away from the eyes of their guests, who probably still think they're the perfect couple. He doesn't leave anything out. He can't. He has to find some way to make sense of it.

She listens patiently. At one point, she lays her hand on his arm and leaves it there. When he finishes, her eyebrows lift in a sympathetic expression. 'I'm so sorry that happened.'

She doesn't need to apologize. It was nothing she did.

'Do you think there's any hope?'

He sighs heavily. He doesn't want to say 'no', but he can't see a way forward the way things stand. 'I don't know. Maybe.'

She puts her glass down and turns to face him. 'Luke, I don't mean to be nosy . . . or whatever you call it . . . but can I ask you something?'

He takes another mouthful of whisky, savouring the smoky, heathery notes, then rests his glass in his hands on his lap. 'Fire away.'

'I get that it's been a bad night for you – and for Jess – but what I don't understand is . . . ' She leans in a little, her eyes large. He gets a sudden whiff of her perfume and nods softly, letting her know it's okay to carry on. 'Why are you here . . . with me . . . instead of talking to her?'

That's a very good question. He's not even one hundred per

cent sure himself. He puts his glass on the bench, stands up and walks over to one of the pillars at the front of the folly. 'I needed a friend,' he offers. 'And you've always been a good friend – to both of us.'

And it's true. All the long conversations with Elena recently have helped focus his thoughts. He's got used to processing how he's feeling through conversation, and if there's any night he needed to do that it, it's this one. And she is the perfect person to give a perspective on his relationship with Jess.

Her lips curve slightly. She's pleased with his answer. She also stands, then walks toward him. 'It says something, then, that you chose to find me when you realized things had fallen completely apart with Jess.'

He frowns. 'I'm not—'

She rolls her eyes slightly. 'Come on, Luke. At some point you have to admit what this is. You can't protect your conscience with that lovely soft, padded wall of denial forever.'

Denial? He doesn't think he's in denial. Is she right? He's not sure. There's a flaw in her logic – she texted him, not the other way around. Would hers have been the first number he'd have pulled up if he'd been the one to reach out? He's not sure.

Or is he just kidding himself?

Has he been kidding himself about a lot of things? Until tonight, he wouldn't have said that his marriage had irreparable cracks. Sometimes, it takes a lightning bolt to receive clarity rather than a slow and steady awakening.

She's standing close, looking up at him with her big eyes, and as the silence lengthens, she places a hand softly on his bicep. It's a question. One he is scared to answer.

'I know we've always been good friends,' she says huskily,

'but there's a subtle hum beneath the surface, isn't there? The something "extra" we've never been brave enough to act upon.'

He opens his mouth to speak. This wasn't what he was expecting when he sent her the message telling her where he was. But she presses her index finger to his lips, almost seeming to enjoy his confusion. Looking at him from under her lashes, she closes the distance between them until their bodies are touching.

There are so many thoughts racing around his head – the party this evening, the way Jess seemed so different earlier on, as if she was a version of his wife that he didn't recognize – and it slows his reaction time.

While he's hesitating, she slides her arms around his neck, pulls him down until her lips are almost touching his. Her eyelids slide closed. 'You know it's me you want,' she whispers. 'Not her.'

CHAPTER FIFTY-NINE

JESS

It's hard going across the grass in my long dress. Halfway to the lake, I pause to catch my breath, but only for as long as I need to before I start jogging again. I can't waste a second. Thankfully, the clouds have cleared and the moon's light is helping me navigate my way to where the dot on my phone shows Luke's location to be. Eventually, I reach a path running around the side of a lake — well, large pond, really — fringed with weeping willows and bullrushes. Once on the path, which is thankfully not too rough on my bare feet, I slow to walking pace, my hand pressed against my breastbone, heaving a few much-needed breaths.

I check my phone again. He's just round the bend in the path now. It's not showing on the map, but I can see a small, round stone building facing the lake, where I *think* his dot is hovering. Thank goodness. We could do with some privacy for what comes next.

I pass a small sign that says 'The Folly' and search for a door or something in the smooth sandstone bricks, but as I get close enough to realize the structure is open to the air on one side, I hear voices — one male, one female.

'I know we've always been good friends,' the female voice says. I miss the rest as I stumble over a small shrub I hadn't noticed, and right myself again. As I round the edge of the folly, I catch a glimpse of two figures silhouetted in the moonlight by one of the pillars. They're standing very close. And then, to my horror, I see her loop her arms around Luke's neck and look up at him with unmistakable intent.

Her voice carries clearly on the night air. 'You know it's me you want . . . not her.'

No! I scream inside my head, but it's as if someone has pressed a pause button and I'm unable to move, even my mouth. I watch in horror as she lifts herself onto her toes and leans closer towards him. But then someone else says what I want to say.

'No.'

It's not a shout, but the declaration is firm, determined. Luke places his hands on her shoulders and gently but surely creates distance between them, then steps away entirely.

That's all I need. The pause button is released. I stride forward. '*Hannah?*' I yell as I barge my way into the folly. 'Get your fucking hands off my husband!'

CHAPTER SIXTY

JESS

'Jess!' Luke says, looking suitably horrified. 'This isn't . . . It isn't . . . '

'Oh, I think it's *exactly* what it looks like,' I tell him, then spin around and pin my gaze on my best friend. 'Don't you, Hannah?'

She blanches. 'Jess . . . I . . . I didn't mean to. This is all a horrible misunderstanding! I—'

I walk right up to her, much too close for comfort. 'Don't even try! I saw what you did! I heard you . . . "You know it's me you want".' I do a pretty good impression of her breathy last words to Luke before I disturbed them.

'Jess . . . ' Luke says from behind me. He knows I'm seriously close to losing control.

I hold up a hand, shoot a look back to him that says, *I'll deal with you later!* before turning my attention back to Hannah. She starts to cry but I feel no pity. If anything, it just makes me angrier. 'What did I ever do to you, huh? Was I that much of a crappy friend that you decided one day to just up and wreck my marriage?'

She has the nerve to look offended. 'That's not what happened! I didn't mean to—'

I throw my hands up in the air and step backwards. I have to get away from this woman or I'm not going to be responsible for what I do. I let out a harsh, dry laugh. 'Oh, well, that's okay then. You didn't mean it. That makes *everything* better.'

I walk away from them and stare at the inky ripples on the lake. *How did you miss this?* I ask myself. *On top of everything else. Were you blind to this too?*

I turn back around to face Hannah. My tone is calmer now, but no less harsh. 'Seriously, Hannah? I saw how it destroyed you when Connor was unfaithful to you. You know how much that hurts, and yet you were prepared to do it to me. My husband and my best friend? That's a double betrayal!'

She shakes her head. 'You don't understand!'

'Then explain it to me. I know I'm not perfect, Han, but I think I've been a really good friend to you, especially in the last couple of years.' I risk a glance at my husband. 'In fact, we've both been good friends to you: Luke gave you a job when you needed it. I was there for you any time of day or night while you were going through your divorce. Sometimes you were round our house so much it felt as if you lived there with us. And all the time were you just trying to steal my husband because you couldn't hang on to yours?'

It's a low blow, I know. Connor would've cheated no matter what Hannah did, but I want to hurt her like she's hurt me. I don't care if I'm being unfair.

But instead of putting her hands on her hips and scowling at me, Hannah steps forward, placing a gentle hand on my arm, her expression filled with pity. 'I'm so sorry, Jess . . . but we can't help how we feel. It's been brewing for months, years maybe, and I think your big anniversary just kind of put everything into perspective for Luke.'

I shake her arm off and shoot a worried look at my husband.

He meets my eyes. 'I swear . . . I have no idea what she's talking about.'

Now it's Hannah's turn to look confused. 'I know we've never really been brave enough to say it out loud, Luke, but now's the time . . . It's better for everyone — especially Jess — if we just rip the plaster off and tell it like it is. We love each other.'

'No,' Luke says firmly. 'I love Jess.'

'The Jess you just moaned to me about not ten minutes ago? The Jess who's oblivious to everything in your marriage and can't see how lonely you feel?' Hannah throws back. If I didn't know her as well as I do, I'd guess she was getting angry, but she's not. She's scared, desperate. Bizarrely, that causes hope to shoot through me like a lightning bolt.

'Yes,' Luke replies hoarsely. 'That Jess.' And then he turns to me, puts his hands on the outsides of my shoulders and looks me deep in the eye. 'I do. I do love you, even though all of what Hannah just said is true. I'm just not sure if you feel the—'

He's prevented from answering fully because I launch myself at him and wrap my arms tightly around his neck. 'I love you, too,' I whisper into his warm skin. 'More than you realize. More than *I* ever realized, too.'

His arms come around me, squeezing me to him, and then he pulls back, puts a hand either side of my face and then kisses me.

Somewhere behind us I hear Hannah let out a distressed hiccup. 'But . . . but . . . '

Luke and I pull away from each other and turn to face my supposed best friend.

'You *know* there's more to us!' she whispers, looking at him as if she's waiting for him to come and save her.

He just shakes his head.

'When you asked me to help with Jess's present, I knew it was because you wanted an excuse to spend time with me. You didn't need me to sort all of that out; you know you didn't! And we spent way longer texting and talking about it than we really needed to.'

Luke glances at me, then replies, 'Because I was uncertain about how Jess was feeling about our marriage, I was second-guessing myself horribly, and I knew I was going out on a limb choosing what I did. Getting your input saved me from losing my mind over that!'

Hannah's lip quivers. 'What about all the times you've been there for me, stayed late at work to talk to me? You're always hugging me, sharing secret jokes. You know there's something special there. I know you do!'

She looks so utterly desolate that if I wasn't a hairsbreadth away from clawing her face off with my blunt nails, I might feel sorry for her.

'I was being a good friend,' Luke says helplessly. 'That's all.' He turns to me again. 'That's all, I promise!'

Deep in my gut, I know this is the truth. I know Luke's need to make everything right for everyone can lead him into over-committing himself, to getting far too sucked into other people's drama that boundaries get blurred — something I realize we are going to need to talk about if we manage to hold on to each other after this night. I also know Hannah well enough to know how, after Connor, even a small drop of kindness from a decent man must have been intoxicating.

I understand it, but it doesn't mean I forgive it. Luke is at fault, maybe, for not seeing how vulnerable she was and how she might read more into things, but Hannah should have put the brakes on as soon as she knew she was starting to have feelings for him.

You're so lucky to have such a wonderful man beside you . . . I wish I could find me one of those.

Hannah's words from earlier that evening come back to me as a light bulb switches on inside my head. She hasn't been very good at hiding how she feels, even from me, and yet I was blind to all the red flags. Even when she got all territorial and was practically spitting with jealously over Elena.

Because I trusted her. As a best friend should. But I realize this is just a symptom of a wider problem: I've put my faith in all the wrong places.

I invested in my mother when she really wasn't ready for it and then couldn't bring myself to give her a chance when she was. The one person I should've trusted completely was Luke, but I let him down because I had no belief in myself. However, whatever errors I made trusting or not trusting, this current mess is all on Hannah.

'I think it's time you left,' I tell her. 'Luke and I have a lot to discuss.'

Hannah looks at Luke, who nods. When he reaches for my hand, she lets out a strangled sob, turns and runs down the path in the direction of the hotel.

Luke and I stare after her until she turns a corner and disappears from view, then turn back to look at each other, neither of us really sure what to say now our moment has arrived. It feels too big, as if so much is hanging on so few words.

Eventually, Luke clears his throat. 'Listen, Jess . . . I hope you realize there wasn't anything going on from my end back there.

I honestly wouldn't have gone round there if I'd had any idea she would—'

'No. It's okay. I saw you back off, even heard you say "no" to her. I'm not angry with you.'

He looks relieved but surprised, and rightly so. Probably. Old Jess might have got insecure and had a moment.

'But we do need to talk.' I'm hoping recent events might have shocked him out of his previous mood, that maybe I might be able to get through to him.

He nods. 'But not here.'

'No.'

We both look back at the white mansion that is just about visible through the smattering of trees near the lake's edge.

'I don't really want to bump into anyone,' I say, rubbing my arms, which have erupted into a million goosebumps. 'But my things are back inside.'

Luke catches my gesture and instantly peels his jacket off and puts it round my shoulders. I shoot him a grateful look. 'Thank you.'

He shrugs. I know he would have done the same thing for anyone, but I'm choosing to take it as a good sign. 'I'll sneak in and grab our stuff. What do you need and where is it?'

'My bag is at the table in the function room. That's it, really. Apart from my shoes – they're somewhere in the rose garden.'

'Your *shoes*?' Luke exclaims suddenly looking downwards, his eyes opening wide. 'Jess! Your feet must be freezing!'

'A little . . . ' I'm not looking forward to walking back across the damp, lumpy grass to retrieve them. On the journey out here, I was so powered by desperation, I hardly noticed it.

He looks at me and then down at my feet again, and before I

can even react, one arm comes around my back, the other under my knees, and he scoops me up. I instinctively cling on to him, looping my arms around his neck, and pressing my cheek into the warmth of his chest. 'Luke! You can't carry me all that way! I'm too heavy.'

He shifts me in his arms to get a better grip, sets his face in the direction of the main building, and starts walking. 'Watch me.'

★

Almost half an hour later, our Uber pulls up a short distance down the street from our house. We thank the driver and get out, then watch him drive away. Neither of us make a move towards our front door. I don't know what Luke's thinking but, to me, it seems as if all the old arguments and resentments are swirling around in the air waiting for us there. 'Do you think we can go somewhere else?' I ask. 'Neutral territory?'

He nods. 'Good idea.'

'But where?' It's after one and it's not like we're in the city centre, where we might find somewhere open until the wee hours. This is Beckenham, the heart of leafy, sleepy suburbia.

Luke tips his head to one side and looks at me. 'I think I might know a place.'

CHAPTER SIXTY-ONE

JESS

We arrive outside the iron railings of Kelsey Park. I close my fingers around one of the posts and try to open the gate. A chain on the other side rattles. 'It's locked.'

I hear a thud and when I look up Luke is steadying himself after landing on the path on the other side of the gate. 'I know.'

I look down at my dress. 'I'm never gonna get over there in this!'

'What do you mean?' Luke says a hint of dry humour in his tone. 'It's got a split.'

I stare back at him through the bars. 'You're delusional. Do you know that?'

He only smiles. 'Do you remember that night we snuck into the old open-air pool before it closed down so we could go skinny-dipping?'

A smile tugs the corner of my mouth, partly because of the memory of that night and partly because of another one that this Luke will never be party to, but is still fresh in my mind. 'We were a little crazy back then.'

He just stands there, waiting. I must be nuts too, because I hitch my skirt up to allow greater leg movement, then put one foot on the crossbar of the gate. It's easy enough to get to the top – thanks to my profession, I'm more flexible than most women my age – but it feels an awfully long way back down again once I'm up there. I look down at my husband. 'What do I do now?'

'Swing your leg over.'

I clutch harder on the railings on top of the gate. 'But I'll fall!'

'I'll catch you. Trust me.'

I haven't got much choice. He's on the other side, and we need to talk. But when I said I'd do anything to save my marriage, I'm pretty sure this wasn't what I had in mind.

I'm tempted to close my eyes, but I don't. Instead, I very gingerly swing my other leg over, place my heel back on the crossbar through the vertical struts and then . . . let go. A split second later, I meet Luke's solid torso.

'Oof!' he says, then gently lowers me to the ground. 'Okay?' I look after him, as he holds me steady, thinking how, earlier that evening, I wondered if I would ever get the chance to touch him again. I'm grateful for this small moment, when he's forgotten his anger, when he's looking down at me with that familiar protective expression.

'I'm good.'

He releases me and begins walking. I follow him. We walk for a few minutes without speaking, turning onto the main path that weaves through the park, past the waterfall, skirting the edge of the lake with its purpose-made island for ducks in the middle. I feel I need to be looking Luke in the eye when I say what I need to say, so I wait until we reach the playground and sit either side of a picnic table next to the locked-up kiosk that sells coffees and ice creams.

'So, what was all that rubbish earlier?' he asks me. 'If you wanted to address issues we have, that was a weird way to go about it.'

'I know that made you angry, and I'm sorry about that.'

'So, you're taking it all back?'

I take a deep breath. 'I can't, not if I'm going to be fully transparent with you, not if you want me to tell you the truth.'

A muscle in his jaw flexes and his shoes scuff on the tarmac. I know he's resisting the urge to get up and walk away, but I can't back down. All I would be doing is repeating the mistakes of the past.

'I have no idea what's going on with me,' I tell him. 'Maybe I'm ill, you know . . . ' I tap my temple ' . . . in here. Or maybe I just had a really vivid dream but, to me, what I told you feels real – as real as you and I sitting here right now.'

He's scowling, staring at the rough wood of the table. He's struggling to believe me.

'Look at me, Luke?' He obliges, his brows dipped low, eyes unsure. 'In all our years together, have you known me to lie – I mean, not just say "I'm fine" when I'm not, but make up huge, preposterous stories? If I lie, which I freely admit I have done in the past, it's nearly always by omission. I clam up. I hide things.'

He sighs. 'No. That's true.'

'I'm not asking you to believe everything I said, but can you at least give me the benefit of the doubt at the moment and allow that *I* believe it and listen to what else I have to say?'

'I suppose so.'

I rack my brains, trying to find something useful to start with. I tried the truth and it didn't work.

Or maybe I didn't.

I told Luke part of the truth, but I left out all the important bits. I think back to all the deep, honest conversations I had with the other Luke over the last five or six anniversaries, times when I dug into my soul, when I showed up as myself instead of who I wanted to be, or even who I pretended to be.

'I'm sorry,' I tell him. 'I've made a lot of mistakes along the way, although I didn't realize they were mistakes at the time.'

'You weren't the only one, believe me.'

I reach out and rest my fingers lightly on the back of his hand. He doesn't pull it away so I carry on. 'I realize I've been emotionally checked out for the last few years and that must have been very frustrating for you.'

His eyes narrow, as if he's unsure how I managed to hit the nail on the head. 'Yes. Why was that, Jess? Have you . . . have you fallen out of love with me?'

The pain in his eyes almost breaks me. 'No,' I whisper, because that's all the volume I can manage. 'I love you *so* much. Maybe that's the problem.'

'The problem?'

I start weaving together threads of heartfelt discussions I had with the other Luke, hoping I can form something he will understand. 'I was scared of losing you, of not being good enough for you.'

'That makes no sense. If you were scared, why didn't you just try harder instead of giving up?'

I sigh. 'That's what most normal people would do. That's what *you* would do, but it appears my subconscious had other ideas. I started pulling back, protecting myself. A punch won't hurt as much if you can't reach to get a really good hit in, will it?'

He gives me a look. 'I would never punch you.'

'You know what I mean. Deep down, I thought if I wasn't perfect, you'd leave me – and that's nothing to do with you!' I add quickly. 'I know you've always had my back. It's a "me" thing. I didn't think I was worthy, and I thought, one day, you'd realize that too, and it would all be over. So every time you brought up a very valid issue, it felt like criticism, as if you were just confirming everything I feared, and I panicked. But doing that for years on end is exhausting, so eventually, I put up walls to protect myself. I just didn't realize I was shutting you out at the same time.'

He turns his hand over and grips my fingers. His palm is warm and comforting. 'I've always known you were complicated, but I loved you because of that, not in spite of it.'

I smile weakly. 'Sometimes, I felt like a "fixer-upper" project you were being very patient with but might abandon eventually.'

Something glints in his eyes, and I know I've hit home with that. 'I'm sorry if I made you feel that way, but you have to know – I would never give up on you, Jess.'

I return the sceptical look he gave me a few minutes ago. 'That's not quite true, is it? You did. Earlier this evening.'

He exhales and grips my hand harder. 'That was me just getting frustrated, not seeing a way through. I wasn't one hundred per cent sure I was done, even though I said I was.'

'I understand why you said what you said. I just want you to know that I do love you, more than ever, and that I believe in you. I just didn't believe in myself very much.'

He lets go of my hand, lifts his backside off the seat and reaches over the table to hold my face, then delivers the softest, sweetest kiss. 'No worries. I'll believe in you for the both of us.' He lets go, untangles his legs from his side of the picnic table and I do the same and, suddenly, we're standing, wrapped around each other and our lips meet.

When we've finished kissing, I rest the side of my face against his shoulder, quivering on the inside as I ask, 'So, about the next ten years . . . yes or no?'

He pulls back to look in my eyes. 'I said "yes" ten years ago today, and I haven't changed my mind.'

We walk back through the park, my hand enclosed by Luke's larger one. 'Luke?'

'Uh-huh?'

'Around our fifth anniversary, you know, when we went to Venice, was Elena ill?'

Luke stops walking and looks at me sharply. 'How did you know that?'

Even though I felt sure of the things I'd experienced in my heart during the last two weeks, it gives me a jolt to know I'm right. 'You told me.'

'No, I didn't! She was adamant she didn't want anyone to know.'

'It was just something that happened, you know, while I was . . . doing my other thing.' I skip over using the words 'time travelling'. That sounds unhinged, even to me. 'But it's true? That definitely happened.'

'Yes.' Luke begins walking again. 'Actually, there's something I need to tell you too. It's back – Elena's cancer.'

My hand flies to my mouth. 'Oh, no! Oh, God! That's awful.'

He nods sadly.

'Like last time, she doesn't want it publicized. Even though she seems so confident on the surface, I think she hates the thought of anyone thinking of her as weak.'

I slide my arm around his back, pulling us closer together. 'I can understand that.'

'She's having chemo – well, just finished, actually – and I've been keeping her company during her sessions.'

My head swivels so I can look at him. He keeps walking, guiding us. 'You have?'

'Yes. I feel a bit ashamed I didn't tell you about it, now I think about it. You know I said I was helping at Matt's scout group on Wednesday evenings?'

I nod. I vaguely remember that happening back in what feels like the distant past but was actually only a fortnight ago.

'Well, some weeks I was with Elena instead.'

I absorb that information as we continue walking. 'It seems like there's a lot we've been holding back from each other.'

'Yup.'

'We probably ought to look at changing that.'

'Yup. Turns out I was doing exactly the same as I accused you of.' He sighs, stops and turns to me. 'I'm sorry, too. I thought I was saving you by not telling you how disconnected I've felt for months now, but I think it just made things worse. Elena kept telling me to talk to you, but I ignored her advice . . . mostly. I thought I was being noble but actually I was just being a wimp.'

'And how's she doing – Elena? Is it going okay?'

He nods. 'The doctors are hopeful. She's just waiting on the latest set of results.'

'Perhaps . . . perhaps we should have her round for dinner sometime soon. If she wants to come, I mean?'

'Yeah. I think she might like that.'

We smile at each other, and I feel a new warmth flowing between us. 'Did we just act like a team instead of boxers in opposite corners of the ring?'

'I think we did.'

I study the locked gate that is now only a short distance in front of us. 'I think we might need a bit more teamwork to get me over that gate, otherwise I'm going to flash my knickers to half of South East London.'

CHAPTER SIXTY-TWO

JESS

Luke's arm is wrapped tight around my waist, his chest and thighs warm against my naked skin. 'What time is it?' I mumble.

He yawns and moves his arm so he can look at his watch. 'Almost nine.'

I open my eyes. I'm in our bed, in our bedroom, exactly where I'm supposed to be. The million-dollar question is: am I *when* I'm supposed to be?

'What day is it?'

Luke wraps his arm back around me and nuzzles into my back. 'Friday.'

Yesterday was Thursday, which means . . . which means . . . I almost leap out of bed and do a victory lap around the bedroom, but then something stops me. Is it Friday 'the day after our anniversary' Friday, or could it be Friday because I've jumped forward another year and it's the fourteenth of May again, meaning it's our eleventh anniversary?

As much as I'm pleased that Luke and I are clearly doing better than we were before, I don't want to keep fast-forwarding through my life. If that happens, I could be dead in a few months!

I want the chance to live each hard-won day, to savour the love between us.

I swallow. 'No . . . I mean what date?'

Luke grumbles and checks his watch again, tapping it lightly then letting his arm fall heavily back over me. 'Fifteenth,' he mumbles into my back and then kisses my shoulder blade for good measure.

I almost cry with relief. It's the fifteenth of May. I finally did it. I finally woke up 'tomorrow'. My angels must be smiling over me, as Lola would say.

I yawn again, thankful that Luke and I booked this day off, thinking we'd need a rest after our party. We didn't fall into bed until almost three last night. 'What do you want to do today?' I ask Luke. The hours ahead seem full of possibilities.

He squeezes me tighter. 'Ask me *who* I'd like to do today and that's your answer.'

I laugh softly and shuffle around to face him. 'Happy anniversary, Mr Harris,' I whisper and then kiss him. Pretty soon, hands are wandering. Our lie-in lasts until almost lunchtime.

We decide to finally leave the bedroom when both our stomachs are growling. 'What do you want for breakfast?' he asks.

I grab his arm and pull it towards me so I can see his watch. 'It's noon. More like brunch, I'd say.'

'Whatever.'

'What are you hungry for? And don't say me! I need some calories before I can even think of round three.'

He looks thoughtful. 'Didn't you mention blueberry and banana pancakes yesterday?'

I smile. 'Yes, I did. And it's your turn to make them.'

'What do you mean it's my turn? How can there be "turns" when we haven't had them in years?'

'Trust me,' I tell him, flipping the duvet off him so the cold air will speed up the process of him getting out of bed and providing me with sustenance. 'It's your turn.'

Luke grumbles but obliges. 'We haven't got any eggs,' he says as he pulls on his shorts and T-shirt.

There is that. Sighing, I throw the duvet back from my side too. 'Okay, I'll pop round to the corner shop if you do the cooking.'

Teamwork. See?

'It's a deal.'

I watch Luke as he wanders out onto the landing, whistling to himself, and my smile grows wider. I'll get up and go shortly, but I just want to lie here bathing in this sense of . . . wholeness . . . for a moment. The barely conscious sense of panic every time I laid eyes on my husband is gone. It was there all the time, I realize, even when things were going well between us, all senses on high alert, just in case something went wrong. But now? Nothing.

Except peace, even though I know the challenges we'll face over the next decade and the next after that may not be easy.

I lift my right hand and look at the eternity ring sparkling on my ring finger. Luke gave it to me last night when we got home. I wasn't sure at first, but I decided to put it on my other hand. It felt like a declaration of some sort, a reminder that however pretty it is, it's just a symbol. The real power to make our marriage last a lifetime lies with me, and Luke.

We've still got a lot of work to do. Maybe we'll get couples counselling or something like that to help us on our way, but I think . . . I think we're going to be okay.

STEEL

An alloy, a joining of two different metals – iron and carbon – known for its high strength. Due to its unparalleled range of mechanical properties, it is extremely versatile. It is able to withstand pressure without fracturing and resists wear and tear, giving it excellent longevity.

EPILOGUE

JESS

One Year Later

I turn the page of the paperback I'm reading, let out a sigh of contentment and enjoy the feel of the Mediterranean sun on my bare legs. But then a spray of water droplets hit the skin between where my bikini top ends and my bikini bottoms start. 'Oi!' I say, as Luke, fresh out of the pool, collapses onto the sun lounger next to me.

He laughs and dabs half-heartedly at my stomach with his beach towel. 'There. Better?'

I look at him over the top of my book. 'Not really, but a mojito might console me.'

Luke rolls his eyes and heads off to the bar on the other side of the hotel swimming pool. I return to my romcom, smiling. This is our first time at an all-inclusive resort, and I'm making the most of it. Later, we'll venture onto the beach for a swim in the crystal-blue sea, eat dinner at one of the resort's four restaurants. Life honestly couldn't get any better.

Luke and I are finally paying attention to each other,

deliberately connecting every day, even if that's just sending some coded emojis while the other one is at work or somewhere else. Something to say 'I see you. I'm thinking of you'. I love him even more than I did on our wedding day. It's as if, now we've removed the walls and the filters, our marriage has gone from being black and white to being in colour. I never imagined it could be this good eleven years on.

Luke returns with a cocktail for me and a beer for himself, then stretches himself out on the sun lounger and we both devote ourselves to the bliss of doing absolutely nothing. That is, until my phone chimes and then Luke's does almost immediately afterwards. We sit up, look at each other, then snatch them up. An emergency?

'Cassie,' he says after checking his screen.

'Elena,' I reply.

Not an emergency, then. Merely a coincidence. I open up my message app and read.

Having a good time? How jealous should I be?

I smile and text back **'Very'** and then add a few cocktail glass emojis for good measure.

Bring me back a Greek god, she adds.

Sure thing, I reply. **If I can squeeze him in my carry-on.**

We've become friends – well, *better* friends – in the last year. I'm stunned I used to find her so intimidating, which I now realize was much more to do with me than anything Elena said or did. She truly is a marvellous, warm, loving person, and Luke and I were happy to give as much support as we could as she finished up her cancer treatment. She's doing okay now. Still not fully given the all-clear, but things are looking promising.

Gained a friend, lost a friend . . .

I haven't spoken to Hannah since the night I screamed at her in the folly. The next day, I blocked her on everything. It was awkward, of course, because she worked for Luke for a short while afterwards. Thankfully, she didn't fight it when he suggested it was for the best if she moved on from Harris & Sons. He even gave her a reference, which is more than she deserved, frankly.

How did I get it so wrong? The one person I should have trusted wholeheartedly – Luke – I couldn't stop being suspicious of, and the one person I never thought to doubt betrayed me completely. I don't care how messed up Connor made her. She crossed a line.

However, that's all behind me now. I turn to put my phone back down on the small table between us. 'What does Cassie want?'

'Not sure,' Luke replies. 'I saw "emergency" spelled out in capital letters at the top and decided not to read the rest. She put it in the family group chat, so I'm sure someone else will step in. Besides, there's not much I can do from Kos, is there?'

'Nope.'

I smile as I lie back down and close my eyes. Luke and I chatted about his family not long after our last anniversary. I also had a quiet word with his mum, just letting her know how sometimes the pressure of being oldest son and big brother weighed on him. Things have been a bit better since then. Of course, Luke still occasionally dashes off at a moment's notice, and he always will, but the load is shared more evenly across his siblings now.

Even better, he got up the nerve to talk to his dad about Harris & Sons. It turns out his youngest brother, Nick, is champing at the bit to do more for the family business but hadn't wanted to tread on his brother's turf. Luke has bought a house with Elena recently and they're going to flip it, with plans to do more in the future. Eventually, Luke hopes he can hand over the reins of the building company completely to Nick, although he'll always be involved in some capacity.

And things have got better with my family too. Well, on some fronts. We're spending much more time with Dad and Lola. The twins are about to head off to university in the autumn and I'm really enjoying interacting with them as adults, even if they've lost none of their cheekiness. I hope I can do a better job of being their big sister than I have previously, maybe lending a sympathetic ear if they have uni or boyfriend troubles they don't want to share with their mum.

'You've gone quiet,' Luke says.

'I was thinking about family,' I reply. 'How much has changed in the last twelve months.'

'Have you heard from your mum lately?'

I shake my head. 'No.'

'Are you worried about that?'

'Yes and no.' I met up with Mum a few times after our anniversary party. Only about once a month, as I wanted time to work out how to move forward without repeating the mistakes of the past. Going to Al Anon has helped. I'm more confident I can stand my ground and not enable her if things go sideways, and I've been very clear about my boundaries.

Maybe that's why she's gone quiet, something she used to do occasionally when she fell off the wagon — hiding away, feeling ashamed. Not wanting to reveal too much. I honestly don't know if she's drinking again, but my gut says she probably is, which makes me sad. However, there's nothing I can do about it.

But I have hope. My experience in my 'other life' has at least given me that. A different future is there for her to reach out and take. If she wants it. And in the meantime, I have two wonderful surrogate mothers — Diane and Lola — to fill that void.

Luke and I don't talk too much about what I told him about my time-hopping adventures the night of our tenth anniversary. We both have questions we don't know the answers to, but I think he prefers to believe it was just a horrendously vivid dream brought on by the stress of the argument we had. Sometimes, I almost believe that along with him. Other times, I'm not so sure. But there's no evidence of any of that time — I was the only eyewitness and even my memories of those thirteen days are becoming blurry and washed out.

After dinner, Luke and I go for our nightly stroll along the beach, hand in hand, and then back to our villa, where we pour ourselves a glass of wine.

'Fancy a dip in the plunge pool?' Luke asks.

I reach up and untie the halter neck of my sundress, so it slides onto the floor, and then I get to work on the tie of my bikini top. 'How about a *skinny*-dip?'

Luke's pupils dilate. 'Sounds perfect.' He makes quick work of his shorts then runs outside. I hear a splash and can't help laughing. Can't fault a man for being eager. I pick up our wine glasses and saunter slowly outside, enjoying the look on his face as I make him wait.

After placing our glasses near the edge of the pool, I slide into the water behind him, resting my backside on the ledge at the edge of the pool, curling my legs around him and locking my ankles at the front.

I lean forward and whisper in his ear. 'I love you.'

'Love you, too,' he says, picking up one of my hands and kissing it. We sit there for a while in silence, just enjoying the closeness.

'Luke?'

'Mm-hmm?'

'Know what?'

He pulls my arms more tightly around himself, giving me the feeling he'd like to erode the barrier our skin creates so we could climb inside each other and merge completely. 'What?'

I kiss his ear softly. 'You're my best friend.'

Acknowledgements

For a while, I didn't think this book was going to make it. Sometimes, life can get in the way of writing, and this was certainly the case when it came to *The Way I Loved You*. All I can say is that who knew that a 2mm crack in a water pipe could cause so much chaos, both personally and professionally! However, after eighteen months, one huge insurance claim, construction disasters galore, and a brand-new kitchen, the manuscript was finally delivered, albeit six months later than originally planned. I want to thank everyone who stood alongside me during the writing and publication process of this book for their patience, understanding and support to get it over the finish line.

Many thanks to my agent, Amanda Preston, who is always such an enthusiastic and wise voice in my ear. Huge thanks to Clare Gordon, my editor in the plotting and planning stages of the book, and to the amazing Kate Byrne, who took over in the writing and editing stages – thank you for your calm insight and fabulous ideas that helped me tease even more out of this story. I also want to voice my appreciation for everyone else at HQ who has worked on this book so far and will do in the future, especially the fabulous PR and Marketing teams. Additonally, I am very grateful for Anjolaoluwa Afolabi for her very thoughtful and helpful sensitivity read of the manuscript.

Last but not least, I want to thank the friends and family who kept me sane and cheered me on throughout the writing of this book, especially my long-suffering husband, Andy, and my two lovely daughters, Siân and Rose.

Discover *Always and Only You*, another unforgettable romance from Fiona Lucas . . .

Could the wrong man be the right one after all?

Erin is about to marry the love of her life. She and Simon have been together for eight years so it feels right that they're finally tying the knot. It's been stressful balancing the demands of friends and family – not to mention Simon's difficult best man, Gil – but Erin couldn't be happier.

Couldn't be happier, that is, until she walks down the aisle and finds the wrong man waiting for her. But is the universe playing a cruel trick on Erin, or could it be that her perfect life isn't quite what she imagined . . . ?

ONE PLACE. MANY STORIES

Bold, innovative and empowering publishing.

FOLLOW US ON:

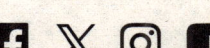

@HQStories